HALLOWED
BONES

Books by Carolyn Haines

Hallowed Bones
Crossed Bones
Splintered Bones
Buried Bones
Them Bones

———

Summer of the Redeemers
Touched

HALLOWED BONES

Carolyn Haines

DELACORTE PRESS

HALLOWED BONES
A Delacorte Book / April 2004

Published by Bantam Dell
A Division of Random House, Inc.
New York, New York

Delacorte Press is a registered trademark of Random
House, Inc., and the colophon is a trademark of
Random House, Inc.

Library of Congress Cataloging in Publication Data is on
file with the publisher

ISBN: 0-385-33778-7

Manufactured in the United States of America
Published simultaneously in Canada

BVG   10 9 8 7 6 5 4 3 2 1

For Larry Martin, my friend and guide

Acknowledgments

Books are never written in a vacuum, and it's a lucky writer who has such talented co-conspirators as the Deep South Writer's Salon. Many thanks to Aleta Boudreaux, Stephanie Chisholm, Muriel Donald, Renee Paul, and Susan Tanner. And to Steve Greene, whose input, help, and encouragement are invaluable.

This series wouldn't be possible without my agent, Marian Young. We've come a long way, baby!

A good book is only a reflection of a good editor, and to that end I thank Liz Scheier.

I'd also like to thank artist Jamie Youll. I didn't think you could outdo the cover for *Crossed Bones,* yet this one is the best.

HALLOWED BONES

1

WHEN THE BRISK WINDS OF OCTOBER SKIM OVER THE DRYING
bolls of cotton, I find myself caught in the web of time. In the rustle of the cotton leaves, in the clear light of autumn, and the grape smell of blooming kudzu, the past lurks like a siren, promising the pleasure of memory and delivering the pain of regret.

Sitting on the front porch at Dahlia House, sipping a third cup of coffee, I watch the sycamore leaves drift into the driveway. Dahlia House needs a coat of paint. I need so much more than that.

The leaves of the calendar seem to be shedding faster than the sycamores, and I'm caught in limbo. I went to bed last night thinking about Sheriff Coleman Peters and his pregnant wife, and I awoke this morning remembering the feel of Scott Hampton beside me. I sat up in bed, knowing that I let Scott walk away without a single word that might have encouraged him to stay. One word. Please. It might have been enough.

That I couldn't ask him to stay while I sorted through the secrets of my heart doesn't make it any easier to wake up alone, remembering a man's touch. October arouses terrible longings. The Delaney womb is sending a series of demanding and not-so-subtle messages.

"If I didn't know better, I'd say you were havin' a case of the low-down and dirties." The familiar voice came from behind me. "The blues, unless you're singin' 'em, are a total waste of time, Sarah Booth Delaney."

I sniffed the air, catching the tantalizing scent of a cigarette. I hadn't smoked in three years, but the craving was on me in a flash. Glancing over my shoulder, I was amazed to see Jitty, a circa 1850's ghost, reclining in a rocking chair, with one leg draped over the arm. A lazy drift of smoke curled from a cigarette holder in her right hand.

"What are you doing?" I was astounded at the cigarette and her outfit. Her dress was a short, tight tube of glittery mauve material layered with black fringe. A matching band of material circled her head, allowing some artfully arranged curls to escape. Clunky shoes with high heels were strapped across her feet, leading up to stockings with a seam.

"Close your mouth," she advised, clamping the cigarette holder between her teeth. "I ain't smokin', I'm just stylin'."

"What would it hurt if you were? You're a ghost," I pointed out. "You can smoke without any ill effects."

"Smoke won't kill you nearly as quickly as regrets," Jitty said matter-of-factly.

"What are you doing in that getup?" I asked, indicating her dress. "It's nine o'clock in the morning." Jitty, as the resident haint of Dahlia House, punched no mortal time clocks. She was on the job twenty-four/seven. "Not even ghosts have costume balls in the morning, and you're about a week early for Halloween."

"You are in a mood," she said. "Scott Hampton wasn't the man for you, Sarah Booth. He'da made one fine sperm donor, but he wasn't built for the long haul. Quit kickin' yourself and focus on the positive."

"Like what?" I asked, and then instantly regretted it. Asking Jitty such a question was a bit like inviting a vampire into your house.

"Do you know when women got the right to vote?" she asked.

I sighed. "No, I don't. And I don't care. My own personal history is troublesome enough without taking on the world. I know everything there is to know about me, and I still can't fix my life. Knowing all that history won't help anyone. It just makes a person run around in strange outfits."

"It was 1920. Up until your mother's generation, women couldn't even establish credit in their own name. Back then, a woman didn't have a man, she didn't stand a chance of survivin'. Leastways nowadays you can be an old maid and still keep your property."

I looked at my black coffee and wished for a good dollop of Jameson in it. To that end I got up and went inside. Instead of going to the parlor where the bar was, at the last minute I turned left and headed for my new office. I'd been up since five arranging the two new desks, two new chairs, filing cabinets, telephones, fax machine, and other office paraphernalia. I'd had a busy and productive morning. Until I'd started thinking about Scott.

Jitty followed me, lecturing as she went, but I wasn't about to encourage her by answering. The past haunted both of us, and I saw no good end in indulging in it.

The room I'd selected as the official digs for Delaney Detective Agency was a master bedroom suite in the east wing of the house. It was perfect because it had its own entrance and a small sitting room that would serve perfectly for a receptionist, should that day ever arrive when we could afford one. I'd kept the entire project a secret from Tinkie, but I was expecting her at any minute so I could spring the surprise. Her desk even had a nameplate. And the frosted glass exterior door said *Delaney Detective Agency.* The next lines were *Delaney and Richmond, Private Investigators.*

"What do you think, Jitty?" I couldn't resist asking her, though she had grave doubts about my ability to decorate.

"It would look a lot better if there were a few clients sitting around in it."

"I'll get another case," I said, wondering if that was true. Six weeks is a long time for a detective to lay fallow. "Maybe we should celebrate the new office with a Bloody Mary?"

"There was a time when a woman couldn't walk in a bar and order a drink." Jitty's chocolate eyes sparkled.

The part about bars got my attention fast. "When did that change?"

"Your mother's generation. At least, that's when it became publicly acceptable for women to drink in bars. 'Course, women have always drunk liquor, and I'm not talkin' about a dainty glass of sherry. The rule was that decent women didn't drink." She raised perfectly shaped eyebrows. "I guess a gal like you would've ended up in the hoosegow or scrubbin' floors in some mission."

Jitty's point was well taken. I was benefiting from many generations of work on the part of courageous women who demanded change in the way their gender was viewed and treated. I sat down at my desk and put my feet up. "Okay, so I've come a long way, baby. I concede that point. How about an exhibit of the Charleston?"

"Sit up straight and quit actin' like some kind of tart," Jitty said. "Our work's not finished. Not by a long shot. It ain't time to put your feet up yet."

My glow of feminism paled. Jitty had an agenda; I was going to suffer. This was one equation that never failed to prove true. "I need a new case, Jitty, not a social conscience."

"You need both of them. But even that won't fulfill your female destiny. What you need is a man. You're the generation that can have it all, remember?"

Leave it to Jitty to state the obvious when my friends weren't doing it.

"Thanks. I'll check the newspaper and see if they have any good sales going on men." But she had backed herself into a corner, and I was going to enjoy watching her try to squirm out of it. "Think about it, though, Jitty. If I'm going to be the spearhead for women's rights in Sunflower County, I think it would look a lot better if I were independent. You know, one of the I-don't-need-a-man-for-nothin' women. If I had a husband, it would make me look like a hypocrite, don't you think?"

"Ticktock, Sarah Booth. You gonna rationalize yourself right into barrenness."

"Go away and leave me alone." Jitty knew my hot buttons way too well.

"I'll be back," she said, and though it was spoken in a soft drawl, it had the definite ring of the Terminator. And then she was gone.

My attention was drawn to the green Caddy coming down the driveway, and I felt a little tingle of happiness to see my partner arriving.

The new office had windows facing the front and the side, so I'd have a good view of anyone driving up. This is a great advantage for an investigator, who should always present the illusion of never being caught by surprise. I smiled at the thought of Jitty and her new obsession. Some would say I was discussing illusions with a delusion.

I heard Tinkie's rap at the front door. "Come in," I hollered.

"I'm in the Peacock Suite." So called because of the huge vase of peacock feathers that stood in a corner of the room. I'd thought about removing them but decided Tinkie and I needed all the luck we could muster.

"What in the world are you doing on this side of the house? I was thinking when you called so early that you were probably making a batch of French toast. I just had my mouth set on—" She made it to the doorway and stopped.

Her gaze moved around the room, taking in every detail. At last it stopped at her desk and the nameplate. "Sarah Booth," she squealed in her best sorority sound of incommunicable happiness. She snatched up the nameplate. "It's wonderful!"

I was grinning big when Tinkie lowered Chablis to the floor and gave me a hug, her head tucked under my chin. The little Yorkie, delighted to be free, rushed toward the kitchen and my own dog, Sweetie Pie. The two were as unlikely a pair as Tinkie and I, but they were also great friends.

"I thought we needed a real office," I said.

"My name is on the door." There were tears in her eyes.

"You're half the agency."

"You're too much, Sarah Booth."

"And you're hungry. Let's go make some breakfast."

"French toast?"

"If that's what you'd like."

We were halfway to the kitchen when the red telephones began to ring. I'd stolen the red phone idea from Kinky Friedman, and I got a real thrill when they rang.

We rushed back to the office. I started to pick one up, but then I nodded at Tinkie.

"Delaney Detective Agency," she said, her eyes shining. "This is Tinkie Richmond speaking."

There was a long pause. "Yes, I see. Let me confer with my associate, and we'll call you right back." She picked up a pen and made a note of a phone number on a pad. When she hung up the phone her eyes were wide. "That was a nun from New Orleans. She wants to hire us to help a woman in Sunflower County Jail."

We needed a case. Or at least I did. Tinkie had a rich husband and a rich daddy. Financial needs weren't part of her landscape.

"A nun?" Sunflower County had a Catholic church, St. Lucy's. There was a priest, but the head count for nuns was zilch. "Did she say who the woman was or what she'd done?"

Tinkie nodded. "Her name is Doreen Mallory. She's charged with murdering her infant girl in New Orleans."

2

THE DITCHES WERE FILLED WITH THE NODDING HEADS OF BLACK-eyed Susans. Tinkie drove the big Caddy and talked excitedly about the upcoming interview with Doreen Mallory. I looked out the window and wondered what I would say to Coleman. I hadn't seen him since the August night that Spider and Ray-Ban had been arrested for the murder of Ivory Keys. That was the night his wife had caught us in an embrace and announced her pregnancy.

All in all, it was a low point of my life.

"I heard Connie's having a tough time with the pregnancy," Tinkie said.

"I'm sorry to hear that." But I wasn't. Connie had deliberately gotten pregnant because she knew she was losing her husband. I wished her morning, midday, afternoon, evening, and night sickness.

"I heard Coleman was taking her to Jackson for psychiatric help." Tinkie kept her eyes on the road.

"Probably a good thing." I felt a pang, but I wasn't certain if it was guilt or hope or revenge. I didn't want to examine it further.

"Did you ever talk to Coleman?" she asked point-blank.

I looked at her. "No. What was there to say? I'm ashamed of myself. And I'm embarrassed for him. He's married and his wife is having his baby. That's all there is to it."

Tinkie slowed the car. "I never thought you were dumb, Sarah Booth, but you're sure acting like blonde roots have snarled up your brain. You and Coleman have to talk about this and settle it once and for all. You can't leave things up in the air."

"Why not?"

"You're going to have to see him in just a few minutes. What are you going to do, pretend that you don't feel something for him?"

"That was my plan."

She rolled her eyes. "I never took you for a coward."

That stung, and my first reaction was an urge to lash out, but I didn't. Tinkie was never cruel. And this time she was right. Avoiding Coleman had been the easiest path. Now I was going to have to face him.

"I know I need to talk to him. I honestly don't know what to say. He's trapped. Nothing I say can change that. He can't abandon Connie now. The best thing we can do is avoid each other."

Tinkie sighed. "Do you ever hear anything from Bridge?"

Bridge Ladnier was a wealthy entrepreneur Tinkie had tried to set me up with. I'd mistakenly pegged him as a murderer in my last case. "He sent me my mother's earring that I dropped in his house. I thought he and Cece had sort of hit it off."

"He's a nice man," she said, picking up speed again. "He's developed a friendship with Cece. I know he was smitten by you, Sarah Booth."

Had Bridge come into my life at any other time, I might have fallen for him. "I made a mess of everything."

Tinkie pulled into a parking space at the courthouse square. "Not everything. You solved the case, freed Scott Hampton, salvaged Ivory's dream, and made Ida Mae a happy woman. That's not bad."

"With your help, Tinkie. But thanks, you always say the right thing." I reached over to touch her hand but she was already a blur of motion exiting her car.

"I'm going to the ladies' room," she said, dashing up the courthouse steps. It was only when she'd disappeared inside that I realized why she was in such a hurry. Coleman Peters was getting out of the car beside me. His gaze was locked on mine.

I slowly got out of the Caddy and stood with one hand on the door. He walked over, and for a moment I thought he was going to pull me into his arms. But he didn't. We stood staring at each other, and I realized that we didn't need to say much. I read everything on his face: futility, exhaustion, lost hope, a grim determination to do the right thing.

"How's Connie?" I finally asked, but there was no anger in it, no desire to wound.

"She's not well. I never thought pregnancy could kill a woman, but it looks like she may be the first. She can't sleep, can't eat. She's lost weight instead of gaining. She won't consider termination."

Coleman looked like hell. His blue eyes were still sharp, but they'd sunk into their sockets. Dark circles showed he wasn't sleeping either. "What does the doctor say?"

His laugh was bitter. "She refuses to see a doctor. She acts like this is some sort of punishment. For her and for me. She's going to endure it no matter what, with me suffering right by her side." He took a breath. "I'm afraid for her."

"I'd get her to a doctor."

"That's easier said than done."

Coleman could manhandle her, there was no doubt of that. But the resulting damage might be worse than waiting her out. He was stuck between a rock and a hard place.

"I wish things were different."

He didn't answer for a moment and I could see all the ways things might have been different flash in his eyes. "Yeah, me, too. Sarah Booth, I never should have touched you. I was out of line. I don't have anything to offer you and what I did by even letting you know my feelings for you was wrong."

He was telling me that he'd fulfill his duty to Connie. He wasn't even going to pretend that he wanted to "make his marriage work." But he would stay with his wife, and if he couldn't offer me a legitimate relationship, he wasn't going to offer me anything at all.

I both admired him and hated him. And I imitated him. "I knew the situation when I . . ." I faltered. "You never deceived me about who you are."

"Maybe I deceived us both."

We stood there, so many things unsaid. At last he asked what I was doing at the courthouse.

"Doreen Mallory," I answered.

His eyebrows arched. "How do you know her?"

"I don't. We got a call from a nun." I realized how strange that sounded. "Why would a nun in New Orleans call a detective to help this woman?"

Coleman considered a moment before answering. "I've talked with Ms. Mallory, and she was raised by nuns in New Orleans. She was an orphan. I've spoken with Sister Mary Magdalen myself, and I can tell you she sets quite a store by Doreen Mallory. She claims she's a miracle worker."

I watched Coleman's eyes carefully as he spoke. He was a man who'd learned to be extremely cynical from his work, but there wasn't a hint of mockery in his tone.

"A miracle worker?" I paused but he gave me nothing. "Like raising the dead and turning water into wine?" He still said nothing. "Or more like curing warts and reading tea leaves?"

"Talk to her yourself," he said, beginning to walk to the courthouse.

Coleman frequently left me to make my own conclusions, but he was never without an interest in which path I went down. "What aren't you telling me?"

"Let me tell you what I know about this woman," he said. "We found her in Pine Level Cemetery talking to her mother's grave. She's being held on a warrant from New Orleans that charges her with killing her own infant, a ten-week-old female child."

Doreen Mallory sounded more like a person with mental problems than a miracle worker. "How did the baby die?"

"Some type of sleeping pill, probably in her formula and fed to her. I don't have all the details."

We entered the courthouse, our footsteps echoing. "Is it possible she's just nuts? I mean, what motive would she have for killing her own baby?"

"The baby was ill. We're talking major birth defects."

"You're saying you think she killed her baby because she didn't want to take care of it?" It had happened before. It had happened with women who didn't want to take care of a healthy baby.

"That, on top of the fact that it looks mighty bad for a woman who claims to work miracles not to be able to help her own child." Coleman opened the door to the sheriff's office.

When we walked inside, I stopped dead in my tracks. Coleman should have warned me. Connie's best friend, Rinda Stonecypher, was sitting at the dispatcher's desk. Her brown eyes blazed with intense dislike as they focused on me. For a moment I felt a real pang of sympathy for Coleman. He was far more imprisoned than anyone in his jail. Connie was extracting a terribly high payment for his infraction with me.

"Rinda, you remember Sarah Booth," Coleman stated, setting the tone.

"Yes, I remember her," Rinda said. "Mrs. Richmond is in your office, waiting."

Coleman put his hand on my arm and led me into his private office, closing the door behind us. It was something he never used to do. Tinkie was seated in front of his desk. She scanned us with the intensity of a laser beam, looking for any signs of damage. Satisfied, she leaned back in her chair.

"So, it's your theory that Doreen Mallory killed her baby because it might interfere with her ambitions?" I asked him, taking the other chair that faced his desk.

"Not my theory. That comes from the NOPD. They're extraditing her for trial."

"Have you talked to her, Coleman?"

He hesitated. "Yes. I picked her up in the cemetery."

"And?" I saw something flicker in his eyes.

"She was cooperative. She denied hurting her child. In fact, she was shocked that she was being charged. The baby's death was originally ruled natural causes. There were a lot of physical complications, and the supposition was that she simply stopped breathing. Sudden Infant Death Syndrome seemed the most plausible explanation. Then the blood work came back and chemicals were found."

"I know you're impartial, Coleman, so what did you think about her?" Tinkie pressed. "This isn't your case. You can afford some thoughts."

I cast a sidelong glance at my partner. She was getting better and better. Finding out what Coleman thought would be a big asset in the long run. Normally, he was a "just the facts, ma'am" kind of guy, but as Tinkie so astutely pointed out, Coleman had no dog in this fight. He could afford an opinion.

"When I got the request from New Orleans to pick her up, I didn't think much about it at all. When I found out she was in the cemetery, I was curious. When I saw her, I was...stunned. And after I talked with her—" This time his pause was extended. "I'm not certain what I think, but I'm sure the two of you will form your own opinions."

"Now tell me again, exactly, what she was doing in Pine Level Cemetery. Talking to a grave?" I asked. Pine Level was one of the few cemeteries integrated since its inception. For many decades, the front of the cemetery was filled with the dead bodies of white folks. The back of the cemetery contained some of the oldest graves in the county. Slaves were buried there, many of the graves marked only with simple wooden posts.

"She was visiting her mother," Tinkie said. The excitement in her tone made me give her my full attention. "Her mother was Lillith Lucas. Rinda ungraciously gave me a few details."

I couldn't quite grasp the information. "Crazy Lillith?" I asked, a vivid picture of the flamboyant street-corner preacher coming to my mind. "Lillith never had children. She wasn't married. She had every one of us kids terrified of sex."

Coleman's soft chuckle accompanied the memory of a woman with long, stringy hair, raising a Bible over her head as she chased us along the streets of Zinnia, telling us that if we participated in the Devil's pleasure, our organs would wither and fall off.

"She didn't practice what she preached," Tinkie said, giving Coleman a wink.

"Are you sure about this?" I still couldn't believe it.

"Doreen says Lillith was her mother. She was given away in infancy or early childhood. Left at a convent in New Orleans, actually. Why would anyone claim Lillith for a mother if it wasn't true?" Coleman asked.

"A very good question," Tinkie said.

"And one we need to ask our client," I pointed out. "Can we see her?"

"Sure," Coleman said. "But she's headed to New Orleans."

"When?"

"As soon as they send someone to retrieve her."

We all stood up and walked into the main office. "Rinda, could I have the jail key?"

"Dewayne forgot to leave it," she said, not looking at any of us.

"I left my keys in my coat pocket," Coleman said, patting his hips. "I'll be right back."

As soon as the door closed, Rinda was out of her chair and churning toward me. She, too, had been a cheerleader, but she'd put on sixty pounds and lost her bounce.

"How dare you come in here?" she hissed at me. "You're determined to break up their marriage, aren't you?"

"Does Coleman know you're off your medication?" Tinkie asked sweetly.

"I'd watch my step, Mrs. Richmond," Rinda said. "She'll be after your husband next."

"I have no concerns about my husband's loyalties," Tinkie said, and her normally merry eyes were a chilly blue. "And you should be worried about your job, not other people's personal business. If Coleman had an inkling of this incident, you'd be fired."

"I doubt that," Rinda said with a smile. "Connie got me this job."

"Coleman will take only so much," Tinkie warned her.

She ignored Tinkie and pointed one red-tipped fingernail at me. Her figure had gone to hell, but her manicure was impeccable.

"I've got my eye on you. I know what kind of woman you are, and I can make you one promise: Keep chasing Coleman and everyone else in the Delta will know you for the slut you are."

"Has the elastic waistband of your pants shut off the oxygen supply to your brain?" Tinkie asked.

"You're a fine example that money can't buy brains," Rinda spat back at Tinkie.

I started to interject something, but Tinkie held up a hand to stop me. "Rinda, the only thing you ever had going for you was cute. I'd quit worrying about everyone else and start hunting for some of what you lost. If I hear one word of gossip about Sarah Booth, I promise you I'll be back to take it up with you. It won't be pretty."

Rinda was back at her desk before the door opened and Coleman reappeared. He assessed the room, probably catching just a whiff of verbally singed hair. "Everything okay?"

"Let's talk to Doreen," Tinkie said, her blue eyes clear and untroubled. "I can't wait to meet her."

3

IT WAS A RITA COOLIDGE ALBUM COVER THAT CAME TO MIND WHEN
I first saw Doreen Mallory. The long hair, the slender body, the
stance. "Bird on a Wire" played in my head. Doreen Mallory
lacked the Indian heritage of the singer; the freckles lightly scattered across Doreen's nose spoke of another gene pool. But her
black gypsy hair hung to her waist, and her hazel-green eyes
never flinched. She wore boots, jeans, and a loose white shirt that
only heightened her willowy elegance. There wasn't a single chro-
mosome of Lillith Lucas in Doreen's features that I could see.

Tinkie made the introductions, and I studied the haunted smile
that touched Doreen's lips. "I told Sister Mary Magdalen not to
waste her money on a private detective," she said in a voice both
cool and soothing.

"Why would she be wasting her money?" I asked, wondering

if Doreen was admitting to murdering her child. She certainly wasn't your typical grieving mother.

"Because I didn't do anything wrong," Doreen said. "I'm sure the police will sort it all out. I'm innocent. This is just a mistake." Her lips pressed together. "No one would hurt Rebekah. She was just a little baby."

"There were sleeping pills in her blood," I said, surprised at the harshness of my own tone. "That doesn't sound like a mistake. Someone put them in her baby bottle."

"The police must have mixed up the blood," Doreen said, undisturbed by my tone. "Rebekah wasn't drugged."

I was about to say something else when Tinkie stomped my foot so hard I thought her stiletto heel had gone through muscle, bone, and tendon. I stumbled back into the cell across the aisle, grasping the bars for support.

"What if this isn't a mistake?" Tinkie asked very gently. "What if someone did . . . something to Rebekah? Is there someone who might have wanted to hurt your baby? Or you?"

Doreen blinked. "No. No one would want to hurt either of us."

"What about the father?" I inserted.

"He has nothing to do with this. Nothing."

"We'll still need to talk to him," I said.

"No, I don't think so," Doreen answered with a hint of polished steel. "You'll have to take my word on it. He isn't involved."

"Tell us about your ministry," Tinkie said, giving me a "back-off" look. "I understand you're a preacher."

"Not a preacher," Doreen said. "More like a teacher. I try to show people how to live in peace and freedom. With themselves and others. The first step toward harmony is always made with ourselves."

"I understand you can work miracles?" I said, wary of Tinkie's right heel. She'd obviously taken a liking to Doreen Mallory and was ready to defend her.

Doreen's smile was amused. "Everyone can work miracles, Ms. Delaney. I'm no exception."

"But you have healed people?"

She considered it. "No, I can't really claim that I've healed people. On some occasions, I've shown people how to leave illness behind."

"Sort of like checking your coat at the door?" I asked, stepping away from Tinkie before she stomped me again.

"Yes, sort of like that," Doreen said, not the least offended by my flippancy. "If you believe the weather outside is warm, you don't need your coat. Illness is sort of like that. If you don't believe you need it, you can leave it behind."

"Science of mind?" I asked.

"Nothing that formal. This is very simple. It has to do with thought and energy," Doreen answered, and I got the feeling she was trying to explain herself to me in a way that I'd grasp. "May I ask you a question?"

"Me?" I was surprised, but nodded. "Sure."

"Why do you invest so much of your energy in the past, Ms. Delaney?"

When Doreen Mallory turned her green gaze on me, I felt totally naked. And exposed. "I'm not really the issue here," I said, deflecting the question. "What do you call yourself?"

"Doreen Mallory," she said, not bothering to hide her amusement at my discomfort. "As I'm sure you know, it isn't my birth name. There was an older nun at the convent who cared for me most of the time. Her name had been Mallory before she took her vows."

"I was asking what title you applied to yourself. Reverend, doctor, what?"

"I have no title and need none. Just Doreen is fine. Can you tell me about my mother?"

"What do you want to know?" I hedged. I didn't believe Doreen was a miracle worker, but I didn't see the need to tell her that her mother had been considered the town crazy.

Doreen's calm gaze never faltered. "I only found out a few weeks ago where I really came from. I thought perhaps my birth mother would have some answers about Robert's syndrome, which is a genetic condition. The nuns finally broke down and told me enough about how I came to live at Rosebriar that I was able to piece things together and find Lillith. It was too late, though; she was already dead."

It was the first hint of a chip in her perfect composure. Her daughter's many medical problems had sent her looking for answers into a past that, if Lillith Lucas was truly her mother, could hold only unpleasant surprises for her. But at least she'd made an attempt. That made me feel a little better about her.

"We didn't know Lillith well," Tinkie, ever the diplomat, answered. She didn't say that we were all terrified of Lillith because she had the fire of madness in her eyes and a tangle of gray hair that looked like Spanish moss. "The only thing we really knew about Lillith was that she was a religious woman. Some might say obsessed with religion."

"Everyone considered her crazy, didn't they?" Doreen asked.

Tinkie stepped closer to the bars and studied Doreen's face. "Yes. I'm sorry, but most folks in town thought she was a little mad. We kids were afraid of her. She waited for us on street corners, yelling Bible verses at us. We avoided her whenever possible. To be honest, I don't ever remember looking her in the face."

Doreen's hands went to the bars. Her slender fingers circled them. "Sheriff Peters told me a little about her. And that woman in his office said Lillith was insane. She told me she burned to death. And she said Lillith was nothing more than a whore who used religion to intimidate people out of their money."

"I wouldn't give you a plugged nickel for anything Rinda Stonecypher said." It aggravated me that Rinda could be so unnecessarily cruel.

"No one in town knew my mother had a child?" Doreen asked.

I shook my head. "None of us," Tinkie said. "Of course, grown-ups didn't talk about stuff like that in front of us kids, but we would have heard it somewhere. I'd have to say that somehow Lillith kept your birth a secret."

"She must have felt very alone and isolated," Doreen said.

"Lillith was obsessed with sex. That's mostly what she preached against. We never considered that she was having sex, much less that she'd had a baby."

Doreen smiled. "So often it's the demons we rail against in others who have us by the neck."

"Do you believe in demons? In possession?" I asked, wondering if she might have killed her baby in some attempt to cast out the evil demons of medical illness.

"No, not the kind you're thinking of. Rebekah wasn't possessed by Satan. To me, she was beautiful. I felt her spirit. She was truly a gift from God, even with all of her problems. She came to show me something wonderful, and then she returned to paradise."

For one split second, I caught the power of peace that Doreen Mallory offered. To honestly believe that your baby's death was part of a plan, part of something other than horrible bad luck and the normal grind of human suffering—that would be nothing short of miraculous.

But only a madwoman could really believe such a thing. As I stared into Doreen's calm green eyes, I wondered exactly who lived there.

"Coleman said you were at Pine Level Cemetery when he picked you up," Tinkie said.

Doreen nodded. "I went to visit my mother. I needed to talk to her."

"Doreen, you know she's dead." Tinkie was very gentle.

"Exactly what is death?" Doreen countered. "Her physical body has been shed, but that doesn't mean her spirit, her energy, is gone."

"Oh, so she's just hanging out at Pine Level?" I asked.

"It was the only place I knew to go. I don't have any idea where she lived in Sunflower County. I wanted to feel close to her. Sometimes the easiest way to do that is to go somewhere familiar to a spirit."

"Did you talk to her?" Tinkie asked.

"I was just beginning, when this older woman came up to put some flowers on a grave. I chatted with her instead. She told me a good bit about my mother. I think perhaps Lillith sent her to me."

Doreen had a neat way of turning events in her favor. She wanted to talk to her dead mother, but a live person showed up. Very convenient.

The door between the jail and the sheriff's office opened and Coleman ushered in a short woman in a flowing aqua habit. Coleman took in the scene before he closed the door, giving us our privacy.

The sister hurried toward us, worry etching a line between her eyebrows. "Michael is taking care of everything, but your followers are worried. The sisters have been praying nonstop. The sheriff says he can't set bond, that it's in the hands of the New Orleans justice system—as if there were such a thing!" The small woman almost hummed with angst and energy.

"Sister Mary Magdalen," Doreen said. "You shouldn't have come all this way. I'm fine."

Though we were standing only a few feet from her, Tinkie and I didn't register on the nun. She had eyes only for Doreen. "I look at you behind those bars and I feel an awful fear." Her eyes were large, her face pale.

"Fear isn't necessary," Doreen said. "As you can see, I'm perfectly fine. The sheriff was quite the gentleman."

"We hired a detective. We have to get you out of jail." The sister looked around with dismay. "I can't believe this is happening. I told you not to come here. The past holds no answers for you. There's only trouble here. I told Sister Mary Grace not to tell you about any of this. I—"

Doreen broke the riptide of the sister's words with an introduction of Tinkie and me.

"I'm sorry," Sister Mary Magdalen said breathlessly. She struggled to regain her composure. "It's just hard to see Doreen in a place like this. She wouldn't hurt a fly. Really. For them to say that she killed her baby is preposterous. She's a healer, not a killer." She flung a tear from her cheek with a gesture of frustration. "As if the loss of that dear child wasn't enough to bear. Now this!"

Doreen reached through the bars and lightly grasped the sister's shoulder. "I'm fine, Sister. It's a misunderstanding. Ms. Richmond and Ms. Delaney will straighten it all out for us. You can't get excited like this. It isn't good for you."

Sister Mary Magdalen took a deep breath, her gaze locked with Doreen's. Age lifted from her face. "Of course," she said. "Things will be just fine. I gave myself over to worry for a little bit there." She took another breath and smiled at us. "Okay, now what are we going to do to help Doreen?"

4

TINKIE AND I PONDERED A STRATEGY TO HELP DOREEN AS WE LEFT
the courthouse and drove to the health department to see if there
was an actual birth certificate for Lillith Lucas's daughter. It
wasn't particularly relevant to our case, but I just wanted some
confirmation that Lillith Lucas had indeed had a daughter.

It was a perfect fall day, the light clear and golden, with just a
bit of a nip. Tinkie snuggled deeper into her sweater since I refused to roll up the window of her car. For the four months of
summer my hair had been a ball of frizz. Now I gloried in the feel
of the wind lifting it off my neck. The fairy godmother of low hu-
midity had turned dross into silk.

"She didn't do it," Tinkie said as we parked in the shade of a
pecan tree. The nuts had begun to fall and several crackled beneath the tires. Three squirrels gave us murderous looks.

"How can you be so certain?" I was puzzled by Tinkie's defense of a woman she hardly knew. Tinkie wasn't a pushover. Most people had to earn her trust.

"I just know," she said. "Female intuition."

"Because *you* could never hurt an infant," I pointed out. "We always find it hard to believe someone could do something we wouldn't. But someone killed that baby."

"Maybe it *was* a mistake," she said, getting out of the car. She looked over the top at me, her face as serious as I'd ever seen it. "Mistakes happen. I mean, it's been three weeks since the baby died. There could have been a mix-up in the lab or something. The blood they tested might not even belong to Doreen's baby."

I didn't argue. Instead I took the five cement steps into the cinder-block–walled health department. At the door I was ambushed by a wave of memories. I'd come here as a child, a preschooler getting lined up for first grade. Vaccinations were mandatory, even though my mother had staged a first-class protest against the shots. She wasn't certain if the vaccinations were safe or even necessary, but she was damn positive that anything mandatory couldn't be a good thing. She protested and I ran. Nonetheless, they got me. Three employees had cornered me on the scuffed yellow linoleum and held me while the nurse pumped me full of immunities. It was a nightmare memory.

Walking into the smell of disinfectant and alcohol, I was glad Tinkie was beside me. I could tell that she was having a case of negative déjà vu as well. The reception desk was empty, so we walked down the silent corridor. In my memory, the clinic was always jammed with screaming, terrified children. Now there was no one around. Except the white-clad figure that stepped out to block our path.

Penny McAdams had not changed a whit in the twenty-something years since I'd been dragged into her office kicking and screaming. She wore the same white nurse's uniform and bat-wing hat. Her shoes were white and soundless on white-hosed feet and legs. She eyed me with a cold recognition.

"Sarah Booth Delaney," she said, nodding to herself. "I re-member you. You kicked me in the shins once. Your mama should have tanned your hide, but she didn't. She took your part in acting like a spoiled brat."

"That was a long time ago," I said, wondering if I should apol-ogize, but not feeling sincere about it.

"We keep impeccable records." The hint of a threat rode under her words.

I smiled. "That's exactly what I wanted to hear. We're on offi-cial business and we need a copy of the birth certificate for a child born to Lillith Lucas."

"Why don't you wait in my office?" she suggested. "I'll be right back."

We took a seat and Penny went to the front office and stayed there for over fifteen minutes. When she returned, she carried several file folders. She tossed one on the desk in front of me.

"You never came back for your diphtheria booster," she said, drilling me with her gaze. "Roll up your sleeve. My record on school vaccinations is perfect, except for you."

"Forget it," I said.

"I'd like your cooperation," Penny said with a smile. She was going to play hardball. To get what I wanted, I was going to have to give her what she wanted—a piece of my hide.

"Sarah Booth had the rest of her vaccinations at Bible camp in Jackson," Tinkie said with complete authority. "We can have them fax you the transcript."

I could have kissed Tinkie.

Penny pushed my folder aside and picked up another. "Tinkie Richmond," she mused. "You married well." She gave me an-other malevolent glare. My matrimonial failure was undoubtedly inked into my health department chart. I just wondered under what illness it would fall. Female disorders. Charm deficit. High levels of expectation. Absorbed in my own thoughts, I didn't hear what the nurse said, but I saw the reaction on Tinkie's face. She drew back in her chair. "What?" she asked. "What did you say?"

"Were you ever checked for worms?" Penny smiled.

"I've never had worms in my life. What would make you ask such a thing?"

"There's no test in your chart." Penny took on a concerned look. "Worms can be quite serious. It's a simple test. We could arrange—"

"I don't have worms and I'm not being tested for anything." Tinkie was completely taken aback. Normally Tinkie loved medical attention—from the proper physician, who would be male, handsome, solicitous, and comforting.

Penny was not to be deterred. "I've seen cases you wouldn't believe. Left untreated, worms can thread the digestive track and intestines, weakening the entire system until there's a blowout of the intestinal wall. This could happen at a formal dinner at The Club, or while you're shopping, or lunching with your friends."

"Tinkie doesn't have worms," I said, realizing that my earlier fear of the clinic was totally justified. Nurse McAdams was a sadist. "Do you have birth records for Lillith Lucas or not?" I asked in a no-nonsense voice. "Doc Sawyer sent us over here."

Doc was retired from private practice, but he was the emergency room physician and tended a few old-time patients. Some old gossip I'd retained in the back of my brain came into play. Penny McAdams had once had a crush on Doc. It was a trump card that produced amazing results.

"I can call Doc and check to make sure he sent you," she said, her eyes narrowing.

"Be my guest. He said to ask you 'pretty please' to help us."

She cleared her throat and reached for the stack of files. "Yes, well, there were three births registered to Lillith Lucas, though we had to send someone to the home and demand that she give us the information. All three babies were delivered by the mother, at home, without even the assistance of a midwife. It's remarkable that under those conditions only one of them died."

"Three?" Tinkie and I echoed each other.

Nurse McAdams assessed us. "Measles can sometimes cause deafness. I need to check your mothers' vaccination records and see about this."

"We can hear," I assured her, "we just didn't expect three births. We knew of only one."

"Even though you make it a point to poke into everyone's business, Ms. Delaney, you don't know everything." She muttered something under her breath that sounded like "Should have been immunized for nosiness."

"May we have the children's birth dates?" I asked, deciding that I'd rather be stuck in the butt with a needle than have to talk to this woman much longer.

She handed us the birth certificates with some reluctance. "If Doc hadn't sent you, I wouldn't show you these. I'm under no legal obligation to show you anything, you know."

I scanned the documents. The first was a baby boy born two years before I was. There was no name, no birth weight or height, no attending physician, no time of birth. No father's name. It was only listed as Baby Lucas, with just the gender and date of birth.

The second certificate was for a female. The age approximately matched Doreen's. Again, no father or other details. Another Baby Lucas.

The third was a boy born the next year. The certificate contained his birth day and the note that he'd died only hours after birth. He didn't live long enough to even be called Baby Lucas.

"Is there any way to tell why this baby died?" I asked the nurse.

"Sure, hire a psychic."

Tinkie, recovered from a momentary imaginary journey into the hellish possibility of worms, rose up to her full five-two height. "There's no need for such rudeness," she said. "We're not trying to hurt anyone and we're not asking you to do anything except your job. You can't jab us with a needle, so you're doing your best to make us suffer some other way. Well, it's not working. I'm marking the health department off the list of worthy projects from my civic clubs." Her eyes gleamed. "And I belong to every single one of them. You won't get another dime for renovation."

I zipped my lip. Tinkie had gotten Penny's attention.

"I remember the death of the baby clearly," Penny said. She wasn't friendlier, but she was more forthcoming. "It was a perfect baby in appearance, but it simply stopped breathing. That's according to Lillith."

"There wasn't an autopsy?" I asked.

"Hardly. Folks never considered that a mother could kill her own child back then. SIDS was a reality, of course, though we didn't call it that. Some babies just stopped breathing. It was a risk everyone knew about."

"The infant girl was left at a Catholic convent," I continued. "What happened to the first boy?"

Penny shrugged. "That, I couldn't tell you. Public health has no jurisdiction. Back then, not even the welfare department really jumped on that kind of case. I do remember that someone asked Lillith about the children, and she said they'd been given to good homes."

" 'She said'?" Tinkie didn't hide her incredulity. "Like, my dog had a litter of puppies and I found good homes for them."

Penny actually smiled. "Exactly like that. I don't know if you recall Lillith, but she was crazy. Today she'd be locked up. She wandered around town like an escapee from Bedlam, her hair in rattails, yelling and shaking a Bible at anyone who passed by her. Any home away from her had to be an improvement for a child. Folks like her should be sterilized by the state."

I stood up. We'd gotten everything she was going to give us. "Thanks for your time, Nurse McAdams."

"Tell Doc next time he needs my help, he should call me himself," she said.

"I'll be sure to deliver the message," I promised. With quick steps, Tinkie and I walked out into the October sunshine.

"That's incredible," Tinkie said with mounting indignation. "Those children could have been sold. Any kind of predator could have gotten hold of them."

"The past is over and done. There's nothing we can do. If the boy is still alive, he's older than either of us."

She leaned down to pick up a handful of pecans. Cracking them in her hand, she fished out the succulent meat and offered me a half. "Do you ever wonder why we ended up with the parents we got?" she asked.

I hadn't. Not until that moment. But it was a question that wasn't easily dismissed. Why had I gotten loving parents and Doreen was born to Lillith Lucas?

On the drive to Dahlia House, I slipped into a pensive mood. After Tinkie drove away with Chablis riding with her little paws on the steering wheel like she was driving, I walked across the sweep of front lawn.

When I was fifty yards away, I turned and looked at the old plantation house with fresh eyes. She was a beauty. Time had been kind to her—there was nothing wrong that a little paint wouldn't fix right up. My forefathers had built a house that endured. What role did I play in the Delaney line? It was a question I'd expect more from Jitty than myself.

I couldn't help but contrast Doreen with my memory of her mother. There was a sense of peace and serenity about Doreen that even I had to acknowledge. Lillith had been frightening. Integral to my case for Doreen would be the father of infant Rebekah. But I couldn't help but wonder who Doreen's father was and how he happened to get involved with Lillith, a woman whose sole religious ministry seemed to focus on the sins of sexual pleasure. What combination of genes had created a woman as physically lovely as Doreen from the raw material of Lillith?

Doreen Mallory had opened the door on a lot of questions that, in all likelihood, I would never know the answers to. But they were questions that also impacted me. How did it happen that I'd been born into the Delaney family? Was it just a random combination of chromosomes and molecular chemistry or was there something else at work?

Where Tinkie had found Doreen believable, I found her troubling. She'd accepted her baby's death with the serenity of the insane. And if she was crazy, she may have killed her own child and not even be aware of it.

Sweetie Pie, my wonderful red tic hound, greeted me from the porch, her tail beating a fast rhythm against the balustrade. We entered the house together, both of us thinking about food.

"*Is* she a baby killer?" Jitty asked from a corner of the parlor. She stood up, her hair tucked under a cloche hat and her body seemingly robbed of all its curves by a dress banded at her hips.

"I don't know." I couldn't help staring at Jitty. She frequently jumped decades, and she'd obviously found the stash of old *Harper's Bazaar*, *Vanity Fair*, and *Vogue* dress patterns from the 1920's.

"What do you mean you don't know? If you're gonna save her, you have to know that she didn't kill her own baby. Sarah Booth, you can't be runnin' around the county defending baby killers."

"Tinkie doesn't think she did it."

"Tinkie wants to build hair sculptures. Can you trust her judgment?"

"Can I trust my own?" I countered, passing through the parlor and dining room and into the kitchen. I went straight to the refrigerator and found some cold fried chicken in a deli take-out box from the Piggly Wiggly. I peeled the meat off the bone and gave it to Sweetie. She smacked it down and eyed the bone, which I carefully threw away.

"You'd better be able to trust your own judgment. Tinkie's got her a rich husband to fall back on if she screws up. You got a fat hound dog and a mortgage."

"Thanks for the reminder," I said sarcastically. In the back of the refrigerator I found some boiled eggs. An egg salad sandwich would be perfect.

"Is she a healer?" Jitty pressed.

"I don't know," I said, my voice echoing a little in the refrigerator as I searched for bread-and-butter pickles.

"I don't believe in magic. Sounds to me like it's some kind of New Or-leans hocus-pocus."

I looked over the door at Jitty. "Very interesting. A skeptical *ghost*. Most folks wouldn't believe in you, either."

"Most folks never get a chance to meet someone like me," Jitty sniffed. "I know things that would curl your toes."

"I get the impression that Doreen Mallory does, too. She says her baby wasn't murdered. And she's so calm and certain about it." I stared into Jitty's eyes, hoping for some insight. "Which means that if she really didn't do it, someone else did. I need to make her talk about the father of her child."

"The daddy would be the next logical choice," Jitty agreed, "especially if he didn't want to be no daddy." She frowned at the mess I was making on the table. I'd peeled the eggs, chopped them up with the pickles, and now I was adding mayo, salt, and pepper.

I paused in my culinary preparation. "Don't you think it's a little odd that no one has mentioned the father yet, and that he isn't here, trying to help Doreen?"

Jitty rolled her eyes at me. "Like sperm donation requires any future commitment from a man."

I was shocked. Jitty had become as cynical as I. It was a disturbing thought. Especially when it came to fatherhood, which was her one constant theme of harping at me. "Wait, so just any man won't make a good father?" I pressed, amazed that she'd given me such an advantage.

"The *duties* of fatherhood aren't for the faint of heart, missy. Not all daddies are like your daddy was. Some are no account. They got nothin' for the children that spring from their loins." She paced the kitchen, the short skirt of her dress swinging against her well-formed thighs.

"What's eating you?" I asked.

"Sometimes a baby is just a trap."

My heart squeezed painfully. Jitty hit where it hurt—and where it hurt was Coleman. "When a man dances the tune, shouldn't he pay the fiddler?" I asked.

"As long as he knows what tune he's dancing to," Jitty pointed out. "Sometimes a man is told he's dancing a waltz and it's really a bop."

It was at least fifty-fifty that Connie had lied to Coleman about pregnancy prevention, but that still didn't undo what had been done. "I don't want to think about this," I said. "But I do have a question for you, Jitty. Why do you think I was born to my parents?"

Her eyebrows lifted higher and higher. She reached out as if to touch my forehead, and I felt a feathery whisper of cool breeze. "You got a fever? You talkin' out of your head. You were born to them because they wanted you."

"They wanted me, specifically, or a baby?"

She nodded in understanding. "Girl, you're questioning the work of the Divine. All I know is that your mama often said that you were a special gift from heaven. I'm surprised you don't remember that. She said it just before she left, the night she was killed."

But I did remember. To my mother and father, it didn't matter what strange blend of biology or heavenly intervention had created me, I was the child they loved.

"Do you believe in some sort of divinely ordained plan for each person?" I asked Jitty.

Her eyes were liquid chocolate. "I may have an answer to that, but it won't do any good for me to tell you. That's something you have to figure out on your own, Sarah Booth."

5

SWEETIE AND I MOVED OUR LUNCH TO THE SIDE PORCH WHERE THE crisp October breeze blew even more memories over me. Long ago, I'd sat in this swing with my father while he sang old classics to me. Where my mother had a great love of the blues, my father had been more of a Cole Porter man.

Although it was a happy memory, I was left with a piercing sadness. Bittersweet was a word I was developing an intimate knowledge of.

"Let's go for a ride," I suggested to Sweetie Pie. Maybe a brisk canter around the cotton fields would clear the past from my brain. Living in Dahlia House I was always steeped in the history of my family, but it didn't often have the power to quick me as it had been doing lately.

I went inside and slipped into jeans and my riding boots. I was ready to go when the phone rang. Tinkie was on her way to her hair appointment. I thought there might be an edge to her voice, but the cell phone static made it impossible to determine.

"Sarah Booth, I was thinking what to do next. Do you suppose Coleman has any of the NOPD reports? We need to see them."

It was a good point. If Coleman had any reports, I felt certain he'd share with us. If he didn't, then I'd have to deal with the New Orleans Police Department, and that might take a lot longer. It was something that needed to be addressed before I escaped for my horseback ride.

"Good thinking, Tinkie. I'll take care of it right away."

"Sarah Booth, are you okay?" I heard Chablis' little bark in the background as if she echoed Tinkie's concern.

"Sure. I'm fine. Why do you ask?"

"You just seem...quiet. I don't know. Not really quiet, but sort of removed or unfocused. I mean, you're always the one who thinks of things like autopsy reports."

She had a point, but I wasn't going to give it to her. "Could it be, Tinkie, that you're just getting better and better as a PI?"

Her laughter sounded tinny and empty on the phone. "Well, I'll see you later, when I'm a glamorous Malibu blonde."

"You'd be glamorous if you were bald," I told her before I hung up.

I didn't want to think about the question Tinkie had asked me, so I called the sheriff's office. I needed official info and Coleman was the man who could give it to me. When Rinda answered the phone, I was determined not to let her get under my skin. I asked for Coleman.

"He's taken the afternoon off to be with his wife," she said. "Don't you get it, Sarah Booth? He's a married man, and he's *with* his *wife*. Why don't you give it a rest and call back Monday?"

"Tell him I need to talk with him about Doreen Mallory," I said, ignoring her insults.

"Doreen Mallory is the perfect client for you. If Dr. Frankenstein could blend the two of you together, he'd have the perfect Madonna-slash-whore complex. You, of course, being the whore." She laughed.

To be honest, I was more shocked than insulted. I'd never thought Rinda was smart enough to come up with a slam that combined horror, religion, and psychology.

"Rinda, remember when you used to do those handstands and cartwheels during halftime and everyone at the football game looked at you?"

There was a cautious pause. "Yes. I was the best cartwheeler on the cheerleading squad."

"Every time that little skirt went over your head, we could see the cellulite on the back of your thighs."

There was a gasp from her end. Smiling, I hung up.

I'd barely gotten the phone in the cradle before it rang. Millie, proprietress of Millie's Café on Main Street, was on the line.

"Arlin McLain is in the café," Millie said in a whisper. "You'd better get over here quick."

Arlin was a local lawyer and a man known for his calm and reason. He was a serious man who'd been the town's most eligible bachelor in his younger days. He'd never married, but he'd built a reputation as a fine lawyer and a man of ethics—a difficult balance. He wasn't the type to invoke a riot or require someone to whisper about his presence. "What's going on?" I asked Millie.

"He says he's been talking with your client. It would seem Doreen Mallory has come into some money." Millie rang up a sale on the cash register. I could hear her making change. "The best I can tell, Lillith Lucas left money in the bank when she died. Doreen's the heir."

"What is Arlin saying?" I asked, curious.

"Nothing to me. That's why I called you. He won't give me any details, but you know how this town is. He mentioned it to a couple of the courthouse crowd. It'll be all out of proportion and all over town in half an hour. Folks in here have been buzzing all day about Doreen killing her baby and how she should be sent to the gas chamber."

"I'm on the way," I said.

"Hurry up, he's about finished. I'll refill his coffee and try to hold him."

On the drive over, I called Tinkie just in case she wanted to meet me at the café. She was still at the salon, and her hair was pulled through a plastic cap so that her stylist could add those sun-gilded strands to her tawny mane. "I can't make it," she wailed. "Damn it. I hate this."

"This isn't exactly a matter of life or death," I assured her as I sped through the cotton fields. "I think I can handle this one."

"I never thought I'd have to choose between . . . vanity and career," she said.

"It's a choice no woman should have to make," I said with amusement. "I'll fill you in later."

I parked the car and walked into Millie's, caught, as always, by the aroma of fried chicken and other wondrous things. Arlin was seated at a corner table with several other lawyers. I took a seat at the counter.

Arlin was finishing the last bite of his apple pie and coffee, and I waited until he went to the cash register to pay.

"How are you doing today, Mr. McLain?" I asked.

"Why, Sarah Booth," he said, smiling, his eyes scanning my riding breeches and boots. "You look very fit and stylish. I hear you're going to help Doreen Mallory."

I nodded. "I hear you're involved, too." He'd been a friend of my parents and had often joined us for dinner.

Arlin took his change and settled onto a stool beside me. "I'd say your sources are much better than mine. I barely uttered

Doreen's name." He eyed Millie, sending her hustling into the kitchen.

"Are you representing Doreen on the murder charge?" I asked.

"No, I'm handling an inheritance matter for her. There's nothing I can do for her criminally," he said. "She's charged in New Orleans. She'll need someone with a Louisiana law license, and she'll need someone who knows the intricacies of criminal law in that state. It doesn't look good for her."

"She says it's all a mistake. She doesn't believe her baby was given anything."

"Yes, that's what she told me. And she's mighty calm about it all. If she did kill her own baby, I don't think she feels a whit of remorse over it."

Arlin was a man who weighed the guilt or innocence of his clients on a regular basis.

"She's an interesting woman," I said to volley the conversational ball back into his court.

"More than interesting. She's arrestingly beautiful. Stunning."

I sipped my coffee and let my gaze slide over to study him. Arlin was in his sixties, a gentleman, and still handsome.

"Do you really believe Doreen is Lillith Lucas's daughter?" I asked him.

"Without a doubt."

"Why?"

"When Lillith asked me to handle the money she'd set aside, she told me about her daughter. She said I'd know Doreen because of her birthmark. And I did."

I didn't recall that Doreen had a birthmark. At least not a noticeable one. "What type of birthmark?"

"She has a small red blotch on the inside of her wrist," Arlin said. "It has five sides. It's a most distinctive mark. I'm sure Doreen is Lillith's daughter."

"Did she tell you anything about her brother?" I asked.

Arlin couldn't hide his surprise. "A boy? There's another child?"

"Yes, an older boy."

He shifted his weight to his other leg. "Lillith never mentioned another child. Doreen is the sole heir. I don't believe she's aware there is a brother."

"Don't you find it strange that Lillith gave her children away and then left money in the bank for only one of them?" I needed to get the details on the inheritance.

Arlin shrugged. "There are no laws dictating inheritance."

"Where in the world did Lillith get enough money to set aside. She always looked as if she were half-starved."

He gave me a long and troubled look. "Lillith was a woman of intelligence and . . . charisma. If you ever looked into her eyes, you saw surprising things."

"Such as?" I was curious.

Arlin rose from his seat on the stool. "I knew Lillith when she was a teenager. She may have been the loveliest young woman I've ever seen. I had the sense that she hated her loveliness. That she sought to be viewed in a different way. And that quest took her to some very dark places within herself." He put a hand on my shoulder and his brown eyes were misted with the past. "Lillith was lovely, but your mother had heart. You look more like her every time I see you. If I closed my eyes and listened to you speak, I'd think she was talking to me. You have a nice day, Sarah Booth, and be careful with this one."

I watched him walk out of the café, leaving me with a truth I'd never had the insight to see. Arlin McLain had been in love with my mother.

REVELER WAS AS eager for a ride as I was. As I saddled my horse, Sweetie Pie spun circles around our legs. We set off to the south at a brisk trot, Reveler tossing his head and humping his back just to let me know he felt good.

When I hit a tractor trail beside an endless stretch of cotton, I let Reveler gallop. I was at last going fast enough to leave the past behind. The moment was all that mattered, my horse surging beneath me and my hound baying at my side.

I rode to Lunar Lake, so named because of its round shape and clear reflection of the nocturnal sky. There was also the fact that local high school kids parked there, often mooning each other. Oh, when the world was young enough that dropping your pants and bending over was considered cute and comical.

Lunar Lake contained bream, catfish, and a few small bass, but no one really fished there. During weekday afternoons, the lake was almost guaranteed to be abandoned. I enjoyed the solitude as I rode the trails around the lake, stopping at the edge to let Reveler and Sweetie drink.

I almost jumped out of my saddle when a male voice called my name. Reveler, who had far better nerves, merely lifted his head and looked at the bank where Coleman Peters leaned against a tallow tree.

"What are you doing here?" I asked, following it up with, "And where's Connie?"

"She's supposed to be at the doctor's office. I took off work to take her. I was determined to make her go, but she said she'd go if I stayed home."

There was something beneath his words, but I was afraid to probe. Coleman and his wife's medical arrangements could not be my concern.

"She's lying to me," he said matter-of-factly. "I went to every doctor in the county. Her car's not there. I stopped by Dahlia House and saw you'd taken the horse. I was hoping you'd come here."

"Maybe she went to someone in Jackson," I said, keeping the

focus where it should be—on Connie. "Maybe she decided to establish a medical link with a doctor there or in Memphis." The bigger cities had more state-of-the-art neonatal care.

"No," he said, "she isn't in Jackson. Or Memphis."

I held my teeth together so that my busy tongue would behave.

"Come up here and take a rest," he said.

I slowly walked Reveler out of the lake and up on the bank. Coleman had retreated to the shade of a white oak tree that rattled leaves down on us with the smallest gust of wind. The woods around the lake were beautiful. The South never saw the burst of color that marked the change of seasons for cooler climates, but the sumac, cypress, maple, and a few scattered sycamores shimmered in shades of red and gold. Instead of getting down, I remained on Reveler.

"Are you afraid of me?" Coleman teased.

I shook my head. "Not you. Me." I wasn't teasing. We'd come very close to crossing a line that would destroy us.

He walked up to Reveler and lifted me off the horse, gently setting my feet on the ground. My heart was hammering, and I didn't look at him.

"You're safe," he said. "You'll always be safe with me."

"You're breaking my heart," I answered, because it was true.

"I had decided to divorce Connie. I'd already talked to Arlin McLain about filing the papers."

I finally looked at him and put my fingers to his lips. "Don't say any more."

"She lied to me, Sarah Booth. She said she was on the pill."

"It doesn't matter. We can't change what's happened." When I started to turn my face away, he held my chin with his hand and forced me to look at him.

"I'm telling you this, not to seduce you or excuse myself. I'm telling you because I have to. For my own sanity. I can't go on torturing myself about what you may or may not know or what you may be thinking. I'm with Connie. You're off-limits. But never doubt that what I felt for you, what I feel for you, is real. I slept with Connie because she begged me to. It was pity that motivated me and fantasy that made it possible."

"I'm sorry," I said, my voice so low that Sweetie gave up digging for a gopher and came to check on me.

His hand moved from my chin to caress along my cheek, then dropped to his side. "We won't speak of this again. We're going to work together, and I'll be the friend you can count on for anything. Let me have at least that much." A smile touched his lips, and in that moment I'd never had more admiration for his courage. "Come sit with me," he said. "We'll talk about your client. Rinda paged me and said you were wanting reports on the case."

We settled against the trunk of the white oak, careful not to let our shoulders touch. Because I often stopped on my rides to read a book or daydream, I carried a halter and lead, and Reveler was grazing contentedly.

"I haven't seen any of the reports, but according to the detective in charge of the case, it's like I told you earlier. The ten-week-old infant was given a sleeping medication in her formula." Coleman looked out at the lake. "It's a sad case."

"Why would Doreen kill her own baby?" I honestly couldn't get a handle on the motive.

"The baby was born with problems. A lot of them."

I knew Rebekah had medical problems of a genetic nature, but I didn't know the details. "Exactly what kind of problems? What is Robert's syndrome?"

"Remember the thalidomide babies? It's something like that."

The term was vaguely familiar from a television news show, but I didn't remember the details. "Like brain damage?"

"The most obvious signs are the limbs. Sometimes they're nonexistent. The hands or feet are attached to the trunk. And there are other complications. Rebekah suffered from many medical problems."

I knew then what he was talking about. There had been a rash of babies born with these problems in the late fifties and early sixties. But those cases had been caused by a drug, which had since been pulled from the market. "Was Doreen taking something?"

He shook his head. "Not according to Detective LeMont. Rebekah's problems were genetic, as far as I know. It's a rare condition."

"So the NOPD is making a case for mercy killing?" I asked.

"No. They're saying Rebekah's birth has caused some of Doreen's followers to question her divinity."

The very idea of it made me furious. It was judgment of the cruelest sort, a condemnation of someone because of tragedy. "As in, why would God bestow such a baby on one of his chosen spokespersons?" I heard the heat in my words.

"Exactly."

"That is so ignorant. So Doreen killed her baby because Rebekah was an embarrassment?"

Coleman watched me. "That kind of baby can be very expensive, and not just monetarily. The care is almost superhuman. And there's no getting better."

"So is it greed, mercy killing, or just plain not wanting to be bothered? What are they saying *is* Doreen's motive?"

"I'm pretty sure they'll try to use all of the above," Coleman said. "And they've charged her with Murder One. I don't have to tell you that this case is going to generate a lot of press and a lot of high emotions. Your client doesn't present the most sympathetic picture. She hardly seems to grieve."

Coleman wasn't judging her, he was merely stating facts.

"When is she going back to New Orleans?"

"Sunday morning," he said.

"Can I get a copy of all of this?"

"Stop by the office early Sunday. I understand LeMont is coming personally to pick her up. It's a smart move on his part if she decides to spend the drive talking. Anyway, be at the office at eight. You can at least talk to LeMont. I've left word that you're to be allowed to see Doreen anytime you wish." He grinned. "I just love to make Rinda's butt pucker."

6

SUNDAY MORNING I WAS AT THE COURTHOUSE AS SOON AS IT opened. Coleman wasn't in yet, but to my surprise, Rinda was. She left me standing at the counter. Just to spite her, I lifted the countertop and walked into what she now considered her domain. I went straight to the coffeepot and poured the last cup, listening with glee to the shortness of her breathing.

The back door opened and Coleman stepped inside, followed by a handsome man in a navy suit. He was shorter and stockier than Coleman, and his dark gaze was quick, moving over the room and landing on me.

"Sarah Booth Delaney," Coleman said, "this is Detective Arnold LeMont. He's in charge of the case, and he's come to take Doreen to New Orleans." He turned to the detective. "Sarah Booth is a private investigator. She's been hired on Ms. Mallory's behalf."

LeMont rolled his eyes. "Everybody's got to earn a living, I suppose. Me, I got no real use for private investigators. Most of them are parasites."

"Sarah Booth is the worst kind of parasite. She latches on to another woman's—" Rinda started.

"Sarah Booth is a friend of mine," Coleman said, overriding Rinda and causing the detective to look at him with speculation.

"Yeah, I see," LeMont said, giving me a more thorough assessment.

The implication was unflattering to both me and Coleman, but Rinda was eating it with a spoon.

"As my friend, Sarah Booth will be treated with courtesy, won't she?" Coleman asked softly.

LeMont thought about it a moment. "No skin off my teeth."

"Rinda, make a fresh pot of coffee," Coleman said in a tone I'd never heard him use to speak to an employee. "Arnold, did you happen to bring your case file with you?"

LeMont was slow to answer. "As a matter of fact, I did. Why do you ask?"

"If it isn't too much trouble, Sarah Booth would like to look over your reports."

LeMont wasn't quick to jump into anything. He thought it through. "The defense will see them eventually, so I don't see what harm it would do for her to see them now. I left my briefcase in the car. But I got to be headed back to New Orleans soon."

"Rinda, would you go outside and get Detective LeMont's briefcase?" Coleman asked without looking at her. I had no doubt that next she'd be cleaning toilets. She had really pissed Coleman off.

He showed LeMont into his office and I followed. When Rinda brought the briefcase in, I took the files that LeMont handed me and sat down in a chair in the corner.

"Do you always help the local PIs?" LeMont asked Coleman. "Or is this one special?"

I listened with one ear, hearing Coleman explain that we'd gone to high school together and that I was a woman of integrity. I didn't look up. I didn't dare. And in a moment my attention was riveted to the papers I held in my hand.

The autopsy photos were graphic. Rebekah Mallory's abnormalities were gut-wrenching. The infant was better off dead. My judgment was instant and harsh, rendered on the basis of my own preferences. I tried to swallow the dryness in my mouth. Why had such a thing happened to an innocent child?

I thought of the woman in the jail cell. Doreen had not shown any grief for her baby. Nor had she shown horror or pity, though the birth defects were grotesque. I realized I understood nothing about the woman who was my client.

The autopsy report was clinical and clear. The cause of death was listed as barbiturate overdose. Traces of Seconal—a prescription drug I recognized from reading Jacqueline Susann's *Valley of the Dolls*—were found mixed in the undigested formula in the baby's stomach. There was no room for doubt. The coroner's ruling of homicide was factual and correct.

I put aside the autopsy and read the remaining reports, which included Doreen's statement. Doreen had told LeMont that she'd followed her routine schedule. She fed Rebekah and put her in her bassinet around nine o'clock. Doreen had remained awake for several hours after that, working on her sermon and drinking a single glass of wine. Rebekah was normally a sound sleeper, and Doreen checked and changed her again at midnight before she went to bed. Doreen arose at five A.M. and discovered that Rebekah wasn't breathing. She called 911 and an ambulance arrived. Rebekah was pronounced dead at the scene.

There was a sketch of the apartment, which showed that Rebekah's bassinet was in the first bedroom from the door. Doreen's bedroom was at the far end of the apartment, connected to the infant's room by a bathroom. I took note that Doreen's bedroom windows opened onto a balcony over Dumaine Street. From LeMont's notes I could tell Doreen's second-floor apartment was part of a large house that had been broken up. There was a central courtyard that gave access to the stairs.

LeMont had done an excellent job of detailing the scene. I couldn't help but wonder why—initially the baby's death had been ruled a natural death or SIDS—but I had the man in front of me and I asked him.

"The morning of the death we figured the baby was so sick that she just died in her sleep," LeMont said. "SIDS is always a questionable death, though, so we strive for a professional job at the scene, just in case something else shows up."

"Why was an autopsy ordered?" I asked.

"Police aren't coroners. The baby's death couldn't positively be determined by us. Autopsy is routine," LeMont said. "We went by the book, but we assumed the case was a natural death. It wasn't until the blood work got back from the coroner that we had any suspicions that the infant was murdered."

"Did you have any suspects other than Doreen?" I asked.

"In other words, did we rush to judgment?" LeMont asked.

I waited for his answer. LeMont wasn't going to be an easy man to work with. I lifted my eyebrows, inviting his response.

"At the scene we checked for forced entry; there was none. We asked Ms. Mallory if anyone else had a key to the apartment and she said only the maid. We also asked about the father, and she wouldn't even tell us who he was, much less where he was. Then we find out the baby died of an overdose of pills. When I go back to re-interview Ms. Mallory, I discover she's left town to come up here to talk to her mother's grave."

He put his coffee mug on the desk and stood. "Now I have to get back to New Orleans."

"Could I have a few moments with Doreen before you go?" I asked.

LeMont looked at his watch one more time. "Hurry it up."

COLEMAN CLOSED THE door to the jail behind me. I ignored the drunks and petty thieves as I walked back to Doreen's cell. She'd changed her blouse and now wore a red slipover that intensified her dark hair and fair skin. Arlin McLain was right. Doreen was stunning.

"They've come to extradite you," I said.

"Do you think they'd let me stop by the cemetery?"

I shook my head. "I seriously doubt it. The officer would have to assume too much personal risk. Besides that, he seems like he's in a big hurry to get home."

"Even if I make bail, they won't allow me to leave New Orleans," she said. "This may be my only chance to talk to Mama."

I shook my head. "Forget it, Doreen. But there are some questions I need to ask you before you go, and we don't have much time."

"Okay."

"Who is Rebekah's father?"

My question caught her totally by surprise. She started to say something, then stopped. "What difference does that make?" she asked.

"A lot. If it is proven that someone murdered your baby, the next logical choice after you is the father."

She was having trouble processing what I was saying. "That's ridiculous. Why would Rebekah's father want to hurt her?"

"For the same reasons the police think you hurt her. And possibly one more—to hide the fact of his paternity."

"This has no bearing on the case. I'm not going to tell you or anyone else. Rebekah's birth was a contract between me and the Divine. It had nothing to do with the father."

Patience had never been one of my virtues. "Don't be a fool," I snapped. "I'm not interested in your claims of divinity or immaculate conception. I need the father's name and I need to check on him now."

"No."

She was as stubborn as a mule. "This isn't optional, Doreen. If I'm going to help you, I need this information."

"It has no bearing. You have to trust me on this."

A terrible suspicion was forming in my brain. "Do you know who the father is?"

She looked straight into my eyes without the least bit of shame or remorse. "It could be one of several people."

I didn't care what Doreen's sexual habits were, but I could see that this wasn't going to make her very sympathetic to a jury. It was one more little indication that a baby with multiple birth defects would have a negative impact on her lifestyle. Doreen's habits were going to make her trial a public nightmare for her lawyer. "Give me the names," I said, pulling a small notebook from my pocket.

"No."

Her chin was up and out. I wondered for a moment if sexual behavior was hereditary. She hadn't known anything about her mother, yet she'd followed in her footsteps.

"Doreen, I saw the autopsy report. There's no doubt that someone killed your baby. Now, do you want that person to get away with it?"

Pain crossed her face. "You really believe someone killed Re-

bekah? Who would do such a thing? And why? She wasn't going
to live very long. Why would someone kill her?"

Here was the shock and grief and anger I'd expected to see
when I first met her. Perhaps Tinkie was right. Doreen had never
believed her baby was murdered.

"Tell me the names of the men you were sleeping with," I said.

She sighed. "None of them even thought they were the father. I
never wanted them to think about my baby as anything to do
with themselves, and they were glad not to. They all assumed the
baby belonged to someone else."

"The list," I said relentlessly. If stubborn defined her, tenacity
would be my prominent trait.

"These men have no idea they might be the father." She
gripped the bars. "They really aren't involved."

I held my pen over the pad and waited.

"What you're asking me to do is violate a type of confidence. I
was helping these men."

She had my attention. "Helping them?"

Her gaze never wavered. "Love is the most powerful of all the
weapons given a healer. Some men aren't capable of love. They
link sex and love together so tightly that the only way to reach
them is through sex."

My expression must have registered my incredulity, because
she shook her head and walked away, giving me her back.

"I know it sounds like I'm making excuses or rationalizing my
actions. That isn't the case. I was working with these men and
making progress. In order to love, you first have to believe that
you can be loved. Some men—and some women, too, but it's more
often men—have never experienced the true intimacy of love. Sex
is an access to intimacy. If I reveal the names of these men to the
police, I'll break the fragile bond of trust that I've been able to establish. I may do more damage than you can ever imagine."

I sighed. "Give me the list. I'll investigate them."

"And you won't share the names with the police?"

"Not at this time. Not unless there's some indication that one of the men is involved in murdering your child."

She nodded. "Thaddeus Clay."

I didn't even start to write. I looked at her. "*Senator* Thaddeus Clay? United States Senator Thaddeus Clay?"

"Yes. He lives in New Orleans."

I wasn't a maven of current events, but even I had heard of Thaddeus Clay, the head of the Senate Environmental Committee as well as cochair of Ways and Means. He was serving his fourth term. He was also married to a former New York model, Ellisea Boudet, known throughout the fashion world as El.

"I was also sleeping with Michael Anderson. He's in charge of the financial aspects of my ministry," Doreen said. "And Oren Weaver."

Once again the name stopped me. "The televangelist?"

She nodded.

Oren Weaver hailed from my neck of the woods. He'd come up hardscrabble, poor as dirt, but with a powerful ability to orate.

"Oren could be a great healer," Doreen said. "He hums with energy. Literally. But with all of this talent, he lacks the ability to love."

"He loves money," I pointed out. He'd been the subject of several television newsmagazine investigations. He'd made millions with his television ministry, rooking those desperate for healing and faith into sending in donations, promising that fifty-dollar prayer handkerchiefs could heal. Of course, when the prayer cloths didn't work, it was always because the buyer lacked faith.

"Yes, Oren loves money. But he has the *capacity* to truly love. And if that is ever unleashed in him, he could help thousands of people."

"And what is the senator's gift?" I asked. I could clearly see what an advantage it would be for Doreen to align herself with two such powerful men.

"If he were truly to love himself," she said softly, "it would influence our government, the policies that are made. He would look at the world, our natural world, as a place to cherish rather than rape."

"And Michael Anderson? What does he offer?"

"Michael offers hope. Beneath his mild manners, he's the angriest man I've ever met. He doesn't believe in love at all. He isn't a powerful or public man, but that isn't important. I don't select the men I help, the gods, or God if you prefer—it doesn't really matter what you call the Divine—put them in my path. I only know that given time, I can reach Michael. I can make a difference for him, and there is no telling the impact of one man who believes in the power of love."

I hadn't committed a single name to my notepad. I didn't need to write a list. The names were branded into my brain. "Is there anyone else?"

She smiled with a hint of a secret. "Not at this time. And you promised that you wouldn't reveal these names to the police, remember."

"At this time, I don't see a need. You're positive none of these men believed he was the father?" I could see motive a mile high with the senator and the minister. Both men would lose a lot if it became public knowledge they'd fathered a child by a woman who professed to use sex as a therapeutic tool. I'd have to dig a little deeper into Michael Anderson to find a motive for him, but I hadn't forgotten that he held the purse strings to Doreen's ministry. Baby Rebekah could certainly be bad for the faith-healing business if some of Doreen's followers ever began to ask why Doreen didn't heal her own child.

"Each of the men knew I had other . . . patients. That's an improper word, but the best one I can come up with. I led each one to understand that another was the father. And none of them knew the other men in my life."

"Were you in love with any of them?" I asked.

Again, the secret smile touched her lips. "All of them," she said. "Love is what I do. It is my special gift."

7

IT WAS NEARLY ELEVEN O'CLOCK WHEN I WALKED OUT OF THE courthouse and into the most gorgeous October morning that had ever been created. My mind was whirling with the angles of my new case, and for the first time in weeks, I felt as if my life was moving forward.

Doreen was on her way to New Orleans, and I was headed to the bakery to pick up some cheese Danish and coffee. Lucky for me my close personal friend, Cece Dee Falcon, society editor of the *Zinnia Dispatch,* was a workaholic with a looming deadline. I needed to talk to Cece, but I also needed access to the newspaper files. Sunday was the perfect time to look—without the scrutiny of the rest of the newspaper staff.

Bribe in hand, I went to Cece's office window and peeped in. The pale light of her computer screen highlighted her classic pro-

file and tawny hair. Her perfect nails were a blur on the key-
board.

Before Cece became society editor and long before she became
my source for historical Sunflower County facts, Cece was Cecil.
We'd gone to high school together. The weather put me in mind
of a few Friday night football games where we'd huddled beneath
the bleachers drinking Wild Turkey and Coca-Cola, talking
about our futures. I had wanted to be an actress, and Cecil had
wanted to be a girl. My trip to New York was daring, but Cecil's
trip to Sweden was the bravest single act I knew.

I tapped on the window and then walked around to the front
door as she unlocked it.

"Dahling," Cece said, reaching for the bakery bag. "These are
so fresh they're still warm." We walked back to her office.

I put a cup of coffee in front of her. Three creams, two sugars.
Just the way she liked it.

She took a bite of the pastry, revealing her strong white teeth,
and I had time to identify the Little Red Riding Hood nail polish
that was the hit of the season. She was dressed in a mocha turtleneck and brown suede pants that hugged her lean hips perfectly. I
frowned at her. "If you were a real woman, you'd have wider
hips."

She licked a bit of frosting off her perfect lips and smiled.
"Don't be a bitch, Sarah Booth, just because you have improper
distribution of fat deposits. That old 'more to love' crap is just
that—crap."

I laughed out loud. Cece was hard to best.

"What brings you to the newspaper on a beautiful Sunday?"
she asked. "Something about Doreen Mallory?"

"Tinkie and I are helping her."

"Did she kill her own baby?" Cece asked, suddenly still. She
was on the scent of a story.

"She says no." I was careful.

"And what do you believe, Sarah Booth?"

"I believe I have a lot of work to do to find out the truth." Incredible as it seemed, I was beginning to believe that the spiritual healer/sex therapist actually had not killed her own baby.

"And somehow I'm going to play a role in this truth-finding, right?" Cece was always willing to jump into the middle of a good case.

"Absolutely." I grinned. "I need to look up Lillith Lucas. See if there are any stories about her in the paper."

Cece lifted one eyebrow in a way that was strictly predatory. She licked her fingers. The Danish was gone. "I heard the rumor that Doreen is her daughter. I also heard that Lillith had over fifty thousand dollars in the bank when she died. Doreen is the sole heir."

Cece's sources were often as good as my own, but I had the scoop on her this time. "There's a brother," I said, watching her take it in. "He may or may not be alive."

"Boy, that Lillith. Talk about 'do as I say, not as I do.' Didn't she ever hear about 'practice what you preach'? Remember the night we left the junior prom early and stopped at the Revolving Root Beer? She was hiding in the bushes and jumped out at us. 'Sex is the Devil's highway.' That's exactly what she said."

"Then she said, 'And you're traveling down it at breakneck speed.'" It was a funny memory now. Back then she'd nearly scared us to death. I was caught between frenzied hormones, lack of real knowledge about sex, and total fear of a rogue sperm with superpowers.

"She looked totally insane," Cece recalled. "Her eyes were burning with that fervor that put me off religion once and for all."

"She was frightening."

"Remember what else she said?"

I did, but I'd rather have forgotten it.

"She said that God could smell sex on us. She said we reeked of it, and that we'd burn in hell."

"Now that's a series of images I'd rather not have in my head," I said. I had been kissing Roger Wayne Gillum that night and I went home and took six showers before I would allow Aunt LouLane near me. Lillith had truly scared me and most of my friends—but that was before we realized that Lillith was just a crazy old woman. I was thinking about the contrast between Doreen and Lillith. Doreen saw sex as the door to love. Lillith saw it as the threshold to hell.

I looked at Cece. "I wonder why no one ever locked her up?"

"Good question."

Cece eyed the Danish that I'd only taken two bites out of.

"Help yourself. Can we go to the records?"

"Of course, dahling. One should always take up activities that might make one blind just to help a friend."

Cece's fears were far overstated. I knew she wouldn't stay in the microfiche room and help me hunt. But she did get me started, and by noon, I'd found three references to Lillith Lucas. Two were notices of a tent revival where she was a featured preacher, and the third was a 1963 arrest for public drunkenness. That was it.

I left the newspaper a little disappointed, wondering what I'd hoped to find. None of this bore directly on Doreen, but somehow, I sensed a connection. Doreen had come to Sunflower County to search out her past—to talk to her dead mama. There was a link here, I just wasn't sure what it was.

I was tempted to stop in at Millie's for lunch, but I went home instead. I called Tinkie and filled her in on what had happened, and she filled me in on the fact that she'd arranged for rooms for us at the Monteleone Hotel in the historic French Quarter of New Orleans for the next several days. She explained that the bank kept several suites of rooms at the hotel for official bank business, but we could use them. Tinkie came through in the most unexpected ways.

"What's got you grinnin' like a 'coon in the chicken house?" Jitty asked from behind me.

I sat down at my desk and took in her latest outfit.

In contrast to my khakis and olive-green cotton pullover, Jitty wore a bejeweled gown that shimmered with iridescence when she walked. It was a sack design and it looked as if she'd somehow bound her chest to fit into the boyish silhouette. Nonetheless, she was stunning.

"I'm going to New Orleans for a few days. Remind me to call Lee and ask her if she'll feed Reveler and Sweetie Pie." Lee was a fellow horse-lover who adored her daughter Kip and all creatures with four legs.

"I love New Orleans," Jitty said. "That's the town that invented sin and then turned it into an art form. There's not a single vice, from eatin' to drinkin' to shoppin' to sexy late afternoons, that ain't been improved on in New Orleans. When do we leave?"

"We?" It had never occurred to me that Jitty would follow me to the Crescent City. Jitty was of Dahlia House. This was the only place I'd known her.

"I been to New Orleans. I went with Alice when she first married and Dahlia House was being built. We bought furniture and dishes, and they all had to be brought back up the Mississippi River and then carted overland in a wagon. I sat with all that china, cradling it in my arms like it was a sick baby."

I'd heard all the family stories of how Great-great-grandma Alice and the slave who'd been hired to be her nanny and who had become her best friend had seen to the design and décor of Dahlia House. Only a few years later, they'd watched as their home was nearly destroyed by a war that cost them both their husbands and the futures they'd dreamed of.

Jitty was a ghost with a mind of her own, but she wasn't going to New Orleans with me.

"Where we stayin'?" she asked.

"The Monteleone."

She nodded approval. "That's a hotel for nice women. They'll take care of you there. Knowin' you, I was afraid you'd stay in some fly-by-night flophouse. Tinkie musta found the rooms."

I gave her a sour frown. "Why don't you haunt Tinkie, since you think she's so much more refined?"

Jitty grinned. " 'Cause you the one who needs me. You're mine, Sarah Booth. Like it or not, you and I are bound together."

"Where are you headed?" I wanted to change the topic.

"A little speakeasy that just opened up." She grinned.

I never could tell when Jitty was pulling my leg or when she was serious. Her remarks and adventures were almost always thematic—aimed at telling me something I needed to know.

"You take so much for granted, Sarah Booth. You can pack to go to New Orleans without a husband or a father. There was a time that wasn't so for women."

"I know." Jitty had a point. I had inherited a lot of rights and privileges because someone else paid the price for me to have them.

"It'll do you good to get away from Zinnia. You keep seeing that sheriff every day, that fire you stomped out is gonna recombust."

I didn't bother to deny it. Seeing Coleman every day was like living in a candy store. The temptation was ever present and always hard to resist.

"Let me call Lee and make arrangements for the pets," I said, picking up the phone. It hadn't even rung yet, but there was someone on the other end. A very excited someone.

"Guess what, dahling?" Cece said, her drawl put to the test by her eagerness.

"What?"

"You're going to the famous Black and Orange Ball!"

We both squealed. Then I frowned. "What's the Black and Orange Ball?" I asked.

"Only the most fabulous Halloween ball in the entire world. It's held every year at the Bogata home in the Garden District. It is *the* ball of the year. And we're all going. Me, you, and Tinkie. Since you're going to be in New Orleans anyway, you simply have to say yes."

"How did you arrange this?" I asked. Cece must have pulled some mighty big strings.

"I simply said I couldn't attend because I had guests. The hostess graciously extended the invitation to you and Tinkie. And Oscar," she added without a lot of enthusiasm. "I wish it was just us girls."

"Oscar can dance with us," I said. He was a terrific dancer for a man who looked as stiff as cardboard.

"Now, you have to have a gown. It has to be black and orange only. Understand?"

"A new gown?" I was torn between economic pettiness and joy at the prospect of a ball gown.

"Black and orange. I've seen photos of some of the dresses and they are incredible. We only have a short time to pull this together. Tinkie is going to Memphis with me this afternoon to shop. Do you want to come along?"

I did, but I had a far better idea—and one I wasn't sharing. When it comes to having the best ball gown for a big society event, a girl can become quite competitive, even with her best friends.

"No, I have something I have to do. Then I have to pack. You girls have fun."

"What are you up to, Sarah Booth?"

Cece was nobody's fool. She knew I had an ace up my sleeve.

"Cece, I'm in the middle of a case," I said, trying to sound mildly injured. "I'm working."

"If you come up at the last minute with some excuse that you don't have a gown, Tinkie and I are going to wrap you in black garbage bags, tie an orange bow on you, and drag you to this ball anyway."

"I get the picture," I said, smiling. I had a far better plan than garbage bags.

MOLLIE JACKS WAS the finest seamstress in the state of Mississippi, or she had been until arthritis crippled her hands. But her husband, Bernard, had told me that Mollie still sewed for a few special people, and I didn't have to guess how much of a thrill she'd get out of designing a gown for a fancy New Orleans ball. My trip to Mollie's would also kill two birds with one stone. She lived right behind Pine Level Cemetery. I wanted to stop off at Lillith Lucas's grave. Call it gut instinct or total foolishness, I just couldn't let the Lillith thing go.

I headed out of town, the top down on the roadster, enjoying the golden breeze in my hair. October was my favorite month. In years past, my mother's birthday had always been a big occasion. My father would throw her a huge party, complete with PA system and a pulpit. It was her day to get on a soapbox about anything she wanted. Her friends came every year to hear the speech she worked on for weeks. No one could ever predict the topic. Mama always pulled the rug out from under folks.

My mind was in the past and I almost passed up the tree-shaded turn into the cemetery. I made a sharp right and pulled beneath the oaks. In the distance the old headstones were marbled with age. As a little girl, I'd loved to take rubbings from the stones. The sayings were wonderful. "She has risen into the light of heaven, our beloved mother." Or "The Lord has guided our best friend and husband into the land of plenty."

I parked and walked, wondering if I should have called a caretaker to try and figure out where Lillith might be buried. My gaze wandered over the monuments and stones, many of them ornate and lovely. I was drawn to a stone depicting a woman surrounded by flames. The cold marble seemed alive, the flames licking at her gown. Yet she looked up to heaven.

A jar of freshly picked lilies centered the grave.

Lillith Lucas
March 4, 1942–December 18, 1992

There was the standard quote from the Bible about God's rich and unfailing love, and then something more interesting. I read the words carved in the stone with a chill. "Born of fire, she perished in flame."

"Lillith," I whispered, "what secrets are you hiding?"

Movement at the back of the cemetery caught my eye and I saw Mollie slowly stand up. She'd been kneeling at a grave. Was it coincidence or synchronicity that had brought the woman I needed to see into the cemetery at the same time I was there?

"Mollie!" I called to her.

She turned and a smile lit her face. "Why, Sarah Booth, for just a minute there I thought your dear mama was calling me from heaven. You sound that much like her."

I took her arm and helped her walk under the shade of a big cedar at the back of the cemetery. It was a crisp October day, but the sun was still warm.

"What are you doing here?" I asked her.

"Same as you, visiting the dead," she said easily. "Did you see those pretty lilies I left at Lillith's grave? I met her daughter here."

"Yes, the flowers are beautiful." I was surprised. "You left them for Lillith?"

"More for that daughter of hers. I never much cared for Lillith. She was a woman tormented by her own hot blood. But I sure did take to her daughter. Doreen. She's got a gift."

"Where did you meet Doreen?" I was a little lost.

"I was here Thursday, putting some flowers on Bernard's mother's grave," Mollie continued. "Yesterday was her birthday and I always try to come and put out something bright for her. Anyway, I saw Doreen at the grave and we talked awhile. She had a lot of questions about her mama. Most of them I didn't answer, even when I could." She shook her head. "No point speaking ill of the dead, and Doreen seemed to have a lot to carry already. She lost her little girl."

"I know. It was a terrible thing." I didn't think Mollie knew that Doreen had been arrested for the murder of her child, and I wasn't going to tell her.

"What are you doing at Lillith's grave?" Mollie asked.

"Trying to sort out the past. How long has that gravestone been there?"

"Oh, about three years. Something like that. One day Bernard and I came out to visit our kin and the stone was there. Nobody knew a thing about where it came from or how it got put up. It was just there."

"Did you walk over here?" I asked, looking around for her car.

"I sure did. I got up this morning feeling fit as a fiddle." She smiled. "I'm going to drive into town and see about buying some material. I got the urge to sew again."

"Really?" I couldn't hide my excitement. "I was going to ask if you could make me a gown for the Black and Orange Ball in New Orleans Halloween night, but I wanted to make sure your hands were feeling okay."

"My hands are—" Mollie held them out, the fingers straight and lovely. She flexed them. "My fingers are just fine. Better than fine." She grasped my hands with hers. "Doreen held my hands, Sarah Booth. She held them tight and she prayed over them. When she let go, the arthritis was gone."

8

THROUGHOUT THE NIGHT, I'D DREAMED OF BALL GOWNS, PUMPKIN carriages, and a fairy godmother who looked exactly like Mollie. Anticipation woke me. By six o'clock Monday morning, I was dressed, packed, and eager for all the pleasures New Orleans promised.

Tinkie and I chose to drive south on Highway 61 and we rolled onto Louisiana soil not too far from Angola Penitentiary. The river formed the fourth boundary of the huge prison farm, and local lore had it that not a single inmate had ever been able to swim across to freedom. Those who tried had been sucked down by the powerful current.

We stopped in St. Francisville for breakfast, Tinkie still complaining that I made her leave her Cadillac and ride with me in the roadster.

"Oscar's coming down in a day or two. He can bring your car,"

I pointed out as I parked beneath the shade of a huge live oak laced with Spanish moss.

"I hate being without wheels." She got out of the car and stretched. An eighteen-wheeler that was passing the small café let out a blast on its air horn. The driver shrilled a wolf whistle at Tinkie. She was in a far better mood when we sat down at a small Formica table and placed our order for eggs and bacon.

I'd already filled her in on the case files I'd read and Doreen's unholy trinity of lovers, and over breakfast I told her about Mollie's hands. As amazing as the story seemed to be, I wasn't prepared for the slightly breathless, glazed look on Tinkie's face.

"Doreen is a healer," Tinkie said in a voice soft with wonder. "She really is. I sensed something about her."

"I don't know, Tinkie." I'd seen the evidence, but overnight I'd had plenty of time to think of other explanations.

"How can you not know, Sarah Booth? Mollie's hands were terrible. She had to give up sewing and she loved doing that. One doesn't give up the thing one loves because it hurts a little."

"You're beginning to sound like Cece with the royal 'ones.' "

"You have no faith, Sarah Booth." She was stricken by her own assessment. She put her fork down on her plate. "You don't believe in miracles at all."

"Guilty as charged." I tried another bite of egg, but my appetite was gone, too. "And I don't believe in Santa Claus or the Easter Bunny. So sue me."

But Tinkie wasn't in a litigating mood. She was, instead, sad. "Maybe that's why Doreen has come into your life," she said, "to teach you to have faith."

I picked up the ticket and pushed back my chair. I wasn't in the mood to be the recipient of someone else's charity, especially in the faith department. "I'm perfectly fine just as I am."

"I'll get the tip," Tinkie said, effectively ending the discussion in a way that made me suspicious. Tinkie never dropped a debate so easily. "What are we doing first when we get to New Orleans?"

"Checking in with the NOPD and seeing if Doreen has made bond. Then we need to interview the men she's been seeing. Do you have a preference?"

"Yes," Tinkie said sweetly. "You talk to all of them. I'll go through the financial records. Oscar said the baby was too young to have an insurance policy, so that's not a motive. But there might be a monetary reason someone wanted to frame Doreen and get her out of the way. Some kind of financial impropriety. Interview Michael Anderson last. Maybe by then I'll have something for you."

It was a brilliant offer, and one I snapped up. "You've got it," I said, wanting to hug Tinkie. More than televangelists, I hated math. But so did Tinkie. So why was she taking the grunt work and offering me the plum? I didn't intend to question this form of charity.

The entrance to New Orleans, from the south or east, crosses Lake Pontchartrain. As we drove over the huge lake, Tinkie talked about the Black and Orange Ball. I learned that it had been created as a mockery/salute to the Truman Capote Black and White Ball. Only at the Black and Orange, the guests were required to wear masks that could not be removed until midnight under penalty of being deleted from the guest list—forever.

Listening to Tinkie talk about past intrigues and romances that were Black and Orange legends, I felt a creeping excitement. Mollie had taken my measurements and assured me that my dress would rival anything there. I had ultimate faith in her. She'd have it ready in plenty of time, and it would be magnificent.

"We'll have to go to Dillon's Dominoes and get masks. Something with feathers!" Tinkie said, ticking off her list on her fingers. "And shoes! There's a terrific shop uptown. Walking into that store is an erotic experience. The beautiful design of the shoes, the smell of new leather." She sighed.

I was tempted to tease her that our visit to the jail would also be a visual and olfactory experience, but I didn't. Tinkie's pleasure was too pure to taint with an uglier whiff of reality.

We swung over the city, viewing the New Orleans business district of high-rises in the distance. We exited the interstate and looped down onto Canal, one of the boundary streets of the old French Quarter. Parking is always at a premium in New Orleans, and fortunately the hotel garage offered both convenience and security. We still had plenty of time for a leisurely lunch after we were registered and had been shown to our individual luxury rooms.

The saying is that there are no bad meals in New Orleans, and it's almost true. You have to hunt hard for bad food in New Orleans. We ate shrimp and oyster po'boys at a restaurant that had once been the site of slave auctions, then took a cab to the NOPD district that was handling the investigation of Rebekah's murder.

Detective LeMont was at his desk, his dark eyes cool as he recognized me. I introduced Tinkie as my partner.

"Arraignment is tomorrow morning," he said brusquely. "The DA is going to ask for a high bond."

"Why?" I asked, going into battle mode.

"She left town once. She has access to money." He leaned forward. "She's a nutcase. Her baby has been murdered, but it's okay, because 'death is just a transition.' She's just 'energy that will never be lost.'"

Oh, great. Doreen had really pissed this guy off. Tinkie stepped into the challenge with the sweetest of smiles. "It does sound a little unbelievable," she said, sucking her bottom lip into her mouth. She gave him a troubled look before the full, lush lip popped out. LeMont was mesmerized. "Doreen has to believe her baby is in a better place or else this would kill her. Maybe all of this talk is just a defense mechanism. But she isn't going to run away from this. Remember, she wasn't under arrest or even suspicion when she went to Sunflower County. And she didn't resist when the sheriff picked her up. She's willing to cooperate, because if someone did kill her baby, she wants that person to pay."

"There is no *if*. Rebekah Mallory was murdered." He stacked a pile of file folders, which slid back over as soon as he put them on his desk. "What can I do for you ladies?"

"We need to speak with Doreen."

"We're not running a hotel here. She's been with her lawyer all morning. Now the two of you are here. I should be her appointment secretary."

Perhaps it was just in LeMont's nature to grouse. Some men were like that. I gave him a smile. "We can't do our job if we can't talk to our client."

"And I can't do my job if you people keep interrupting me. There are other crimes to be solved, you know." He handed me a slip of paper. "They'll let one of you see her. Only one. Now I've got work to do."

We were dismissed, and we stepped out into the hallway. I looked at the paper, which bore the address of the city lockup. "I'll go talk to Doreen," I said, wanting to spare Tinkie what I knew was going to be a bad scene.

"No, I want to see her." Tinkie put a hand on my arm. She was dressed to the nines in a sienna silk pantsuit. Her suede heels were a perfect match.

"You aren't exactly dressed for the jail," I noted in a low voice. I'd opted for jeans and a blue sweater.

"Don't you worry about me." She took the paper from my hand. "I need to talk to her about her books. And I want her to tell me a little about Michael Anderson."

I nodded.

"I'll try to get her take on him." She grinned at me. "Other than the fact that he doesn't believe in love."

In truth, I was itching to talk to both the senator and the televangelist. I didn't care which one I got to first. Guilt made me stop in my tracks. "Are you sure, Tinkie?" I had a horrible picture of her walking down a line of cells while some pervert hurled bodily fluids at her, à la *The Silence of the Lambs*.

"I'm your partner, not your little girl. I can do this. No one's going to bite me."

Yikes. Tinkie was touchy this morning. Maybe she'd caught it from LeMont. "Okay," I agreed as we walked out onto the sidewalk. I waved down a taxi. Running the risk of her ire yet again, I held the door open for her and sent her on her way. Once she was gone, I pulled out my cell phone and began rounding up the numbers I'd need to get to both Oren Weaver and Thaddeus Clay. Michael Anderson would be last, per Tinkie's request.

STANDING ON THE shady front porch of the huge home, I listened to the somber tone of the doorbell. Senator Clay's residence showed all the traditional grace of the South. A maid opened the door and showed me in.

"Mrs. Clay will be with you in a moment," she said, indicating a formal parlor where I should wait.

"Excuse me, but my business is with the senator," I reminded her.

She gave me a sidelong look. "Mrs. Clay will be here momentarily." She was gone before I could raise another protest.

I took a seat and picked up one of the fashion magazines that featured the unmistakable image of El, the senator's wife.

She'd been a cover girl for *Vogue, Mademoiselle, Esquire, Modern Bride, Health & Fitness, Glamour, Paris,* and *Europe's*

Trends—every major magazine in the world. She was renowned on the runway and helped host the Cannes Film Festival each year. She was becoming a power to be reckoned with in the art world. And she ran the regional United Way fund drive. She was the perfect accoutrement for a U.S. senator with the ambition to be president. She'd taken Jackie O's attitude and put a spin on it that resonated with the culture of the new millennium—wealth, arrogance, and self-centeredness.

When she walked into the room, I almost stood. She commanded that kind of attention. I caught myself and waited for her to walk to me. Her gaze swept over me and one eyebrow lifted.

"Mrs. Clay," I said, extending my hand and giving her my name, though I knew she knew it. "I was hoping to talk to your husband."

"He's a very busy man. What's this about?"

"I'm sorry, I can't discuss this with you. I need to speak with him."

"His business is my business."

"I don't doubt that, but I have to talk to him." I saw the anger in her dark eyes. Her skin was flawless, her makeup perfection. She was very beautiful and very hard.

"I don't think he's available." She gave me a practiced smile that touched only the corners of her mouth.

"That's too bad. I was hoping to avoid taking this to the police." I rose.

"If this is blackmail, you can forget it. We don't pay ransom. I'll turn it over to my family. I'm sure you've heard of the Boudets." The smile was much bigger, revealing perfect white teeth.

"Oh, yes. Even over in Mississippi the Boudets are well known." I pulled a business card from my purse and handed it to her. "I assure you, your husband will wish he'd spoken with me. I know the way out."

I was at the front door when I heard someone behind me. The tread was heavier than the maid's.

"Ms. Delaney," a baritone voice called. "Please wait a minute."

I turned to see the very distinguished senator hurrying my way. "I apologize for Ellisea. She's just trying to protect me." He grasped my elbow. "What is it you'd like to speak to me about?"

Ellisea was probably lurking just around the doorframe. I had to use discretion. "It's a matter of religious principle," I said. "Separation of church and state. Ms. Mallory said I could count on you."

It was the use of Doreen's name that got him. He flushed and propelled me across the hallway into a book-lined study. He closed the double doors and turned the key. When he came around to stand in front of me, he'd composed himself. "What is this again, and forget the riddles: Just come out and say it."

"Doreen Mallory's been charged with the murder of her infant child."

He didn't register surprise, so someone else had told him. The skin beneath his sharp blue eyes was bruised-looking, and wrinkles were etched around his eyes and mouth. The senator had not been sleeping well.

"I hate to hear that. I enjoy Doreen's spirit. She believes very much in the things she teaches."

"So you don't deny knowing her?" I asked.

"Of course not. I've known her for over a year now. She's dedicated to teaching people. I've been one of her top projects."

"Do you deny sleeping with her?"

That stunned him. "She told you we were sexual partners?" he asked.

I took note of the fact that he didn't say they were lovers or were in a relationship. They were sexual partners. Doreen's gift of love hadn't grafted well. "Yes, in fact, she did." I got my notebook out of my purse. "You've been lovers since last summer. There is the possibility that you're the father of her child."

"No." He stepped away from me. "No, that's not true. I'm not the father. Rebekah isn't my child."

"How much did you know about the baby?" I asked. His reaction told me plenty.

"I knew she was born with a serious medical condition. I offered Doreen the best doctors in New Orleans, and she took Rebekah there. But there wasn't anything they could do. Rebekah was going to die, probably before her first birthday."

He had begun to recover his balance and he paced the room. "Doreen never said anything about me being the father. She never said a word. I'm positive it was someone else. Did she say it was me?"

I shook my head. "No." He was telling me so much more than he knew. "But she said you were a possibility."

"She had other lovers," he said, pacing once again.

"She told you that?" I kept my voice level.

"Doreen was forthright about her life. She felt no need to hide any aspect of it. And I am a cautious man."

I understood. "You had her followed."

He gave me a reproachful look. "I did."

"Who else was she sleeping with?" I had to be very careful here. I needed to know exactly what he knew.

"That's a question you should ask Doreen," he said.

My opinion of his intelligence notched up. "You had her followed but you never got a name?"

He walked to a crystal decanter on a sofa table and poured what looked like scotch into a glass. "Care for one?" he asked.

"No, thank you." It was bad form to drink with a suspect.

"I want you to do something for me," he said, coming to stand in front of me. "Doreen is a good woman. I don't know what's going on here, but tell her I'll help her any way I can, as long as she keeps my name out of this. I sent a lawyer to talk to her this morning. I'm picking up the tab for him and he's a good one. But she can't let my name get involved in this."

"What if you're the baby's father?" I asked.

"I'm not." There was iron in his words. "That poor, deformed infant was not my issue. As long as it stays this way, Doreen will have the help she needs from me. But if my name is so much as linked to hers—" He sipped his drink.

I tugged my sweater down my hips. I was ready to go. "Distancing yourself from that baby seems to be a very high priority, Senator Clay. I just wonder how far you're willing to go to keep that distance. As far as murder?"

This time no one stopped me at the door as I walked out into the October sunshine.

9

COMPOUND WAS THE PROPER TERM FOR REVEREND OREN WEAVER'S home. Chain-link fence with concertina wire secured the perimeter, enforced by armed guards who weren't the least bit discreet about the automatic weapons they carried.

Even though I'd called ahead and left my name, they made me get out of the car and stand in the bright sun. "What's the reverend afraid of? That hordes of the halt and lame will try to break in and get a free healing?" I asked.

The guards had no sense of humor. They held me at the gate for twenty minutes, but I didn't mind. I'd stopped by the hotel garage and gotten the convertible. Once they let me get back in my car, I pretended to take a nap in the warm October sun.

"Reverend Weaver says he doesn't have time to talk to you today," the guard said when he finally approached me.

"Tell him Doreen Mallory says otherwise. He can see me or he can see the police. And please tell him that I'll be sure and alert the media when the cops come calling." I closed my eyes and leaned back against the headrest.

It took another ten minutes and a pat down, but I was finally allowed to drive up to the "big house." Weaver's home, surrounded by smaller cottages, was classic Tara. I could only presume the hired help, or maybe the postulants, lived in the cottages. The grounds were immaculate, and I wondered how he kept the huge palm trees alive during the infrequent cold snaps that could strike the Gulf Coast.

He met me in the foyer and made it clear with his body language that I shouldn't expect to proceed farther into his home. His height surprised me. He was over six feet, with a body toned and lean. Dark hair was combed back in a pompadour, and he bore a slight resemblance to Elvis Presley. In other words, he was a fine-looking man.

I'd expected Weaver to be wearing a white suit with a Panama hat, but instead he wore somber navy with a red stockbroker tie—rather conservative. Then again, I'd heard he was a big contributor to political causes that ranged from oil-drilling in the Gulf and Alaska to war as a means of economic recovery.

"Make it fast. I have to give an interview in twenty minutes and I need to go over my notes," he said without bothering to introduce himself. He was on television at least eight hours a week, from his own religious service to talk shows about the Second Coming to Christian investment opportunities and world news with a Christian slant. In other words, wherever the Devil was doing his dirty work, which was mostly in the right ear of all liberals.

"Where were you on the night of October first?" I asked, deciding to oblige him and make it fast.

"What?" He frowned at me. "You said this was about a woman named Doreen Mallory."

"It is. And about October first. Where were you that night?"

"Right here. Where I am every night, except when I'm on a healing tour."

If he wasn't genuinely puzzled, he was a good actor, which of course he was. But the date of Rebekah's murder didn't seem to register with him.

"What's your relationship with Doreen?"

"I've been counseling her," he said smoothly. "Doreen has tremendous spiritual potential, but she's caught up on one of Satan's side paths. She believes she can heal folks, but she doesn't believe her gift comes from Jesus Christ. I've been talking with her about the power of Jesus and how all things come from him. She has to first admit the source of all miracles before she can become a true healer."

I was fascinated by the spin he was putting on the time he spent with Doreen, especially since I knew that the form of intercourse he'd been having with Doreen wasn't talk therapy. "What, exactly, does counseling consist of?" I asked innocently.

"Reading the Bible and praying."

"And do you lay hands on her?" It wasn't my most subtle remark, and he narrowed his eyes.

"What are you doing here and why did Doreen send you? Is it money?"

"You could only wish it was as simple as money," I said, smiling.

"What are you talking about?"

"Doreen's in jail."

"What?" He was genuinely shocked.

"I gather you don't watch much television news, except for the headlines you generate."

"I hate reporters. They snoop where they don't belong and twist everything. Why's Doreen in jail?"

Once again, Oren Weaver seemed to be honestly surprised. But he'd also seemed sincere when he was lying about his activities with Doreen. "She had a child, a baby girl, about ten weeks ago."

"Yes, Rebekah. She told me about her. It was a terrible thing, that little deformed baby. Doreen should take note—"

"The child was murdered," I cut in. "Doreen's been charged."

"That's preposterous. Doreen wouldn't hurt that baby. She was terribly excited about having a child. Even after Rebekah was born, she spoke of her only with joy."

"Did you ever see the baby?"

He shook his head. "No. Doreen was very clear that Rebekah was her special child. She didn't want me to see her."

"Do you know who the father was?"

"Ask Doreen."

"I did."

I let that hang out there while he thought it through. It took only a nanosecond for it to strike home. Fear washed over his face, but it was quickly replaced with concern.

"I don't know who Doreen was involved with," he said. "She's a strong-minded woman. I always suspected that she charted her own course in the physical world, if you know what I mean."

"Oh, I know what you mean to imply," I said calmly. "You mean to imply that Doreen slept around."

"You'd have to ask her."

"But did she sleep around with you?" I asked.

"That's preposterous."

"Reverend Weaver," I said slowly, "the police have blood samples from the infant. It's a rather simple DNA test to prove paternity. Now wouldn't it look terribly suspicious if you denied sleeping with Doreen and Rebekah's DNA matched yours. That would lead me, and the police, to believe that you are a liar."

"What do you want?" He didn't move at all, but he somehow seemed closer to me.

"I want the truth. Are you Rebekah's father?"

"I can't say. It was a moot issue. Rebekah was Doreen's child. Totally hers. Doreen would never allow me to lay claim to the baby in any way. In case you don't know Doreen well, she does what she wants, whenever she wants."

"What are you saying?" I wasn't going to make it easy for him.

"I suspected that Doreen had other lovers. She kept our relationship on a certain level. It's hard to describe. She's the most extraordinarily giving woman I've ever met, yet she also held me at arm's length." His eyebrows rose. "I always thought she was in love with someone else."

"You suspected, but you didn't know if she had other lovers?"

"Come into the den," he said. "Would you care for a beverage? Coffee or a soft drink? We don't have liquor here."

"No, thank you," I said as I followed him through a doorway. "Did Doreen ever talk to you about her lovers?"

"Why is this important, Ms. Delaney?"

"Because if Doreen didn't kill her child, then perhaps it was the father who did."

"Why would the father kill his baby?"

"Oh, maybe because he feared blackmail, because the baby's birth defects were so serious that medical care would be a big financial drain if he were legally pulled into the problem. Or maybe because he has a public image that would suffer greatly from being exposed as Doreen's lover."

He put one hand in the pocket of his trousers. "Wait a minute. I see where you're going with this and I don't like it."

"Rebekah was born with Robert's syndrome. Her arms didn't develop, and there were some structural problems with the palate and face. She also had respiratory and heart problems."

He looked at me. "What did Doreen tell you about me?"

"Enough. But I have to say, it's been even more fascinating listening to the line of bullshit you can shovel."

He didn't even bother to deny it. "Doreen promised me that

she'd never divulge our relationship. She said she only wanted to give to me." His lips twisted. "And I was just beginning to believe her."

"You should believe her," I said. "She didn't want to give me your name, but I told her it was either me or the police."

"The police!"

"Doreen is charged with murdering her own baby. Even if the police aren't concerned with who the father is right now, I'm sure a good defense attorney will be. Especially when the lawyer learns that the potential father has such a lot to lose by being exposed."

"I'm not the father! Doreen assured me that I wasn't!"

"Rebekah was born July fifteenth. You do the math." And he did. I saw him calculating the months. Doreen would have been only slightly pregnant when he was last with her. Not enough to show, but enough for the baby to belong to him.

"When *was* the last time you saw Doreen?" I asked.

"Last May. We met for lunch and a conversation. She was very pregnant and seemed very happy."

I was surprised that Weaver had continued to have contact with Doreen once the sexual liaison was over. He didn't strike me as the type who valued "good conversation" with a woman.

"Are you married?" I already knew the answer.

"Yes. My wife lives in Baton Rouge."

"You pay her to stay married to you. And to keep her mouth shut."

"Myra and I have our differences. She's content with our arrangement, as am I. And this is certainly none of your concern."

"Perhaps you're right. But October first is my concern. Where were you?"

He rang a small bell beside the chair where he stood. In a moment a young man so wet behind the ears that he was almost dripping came forward.

"Yes, sir?"

"Bring me my appointment book, please, Joseph."

Without another word, Joseph scurried to do his master's bidding.

An uneasy silence settled over us. I took in the room. It lacked the old-world grace of Senator Clay's home. This was all modern and angular. The sofa and chairs were white, the carpet white, the walls gray, and the throw pillows black. Monochromatic. Cece would have an absolute fit over it—for about half an hour. To me the design was slick, just like the owner.

Joseph returned with a large black book with slips of paper stuck all through it. Weaver flipped the pages until he stopped. "October first I was booked onto the *John and Sarah Good Time Hour.* It was a live broadcast." The appointment book slapped shut with a satisfied smack. "Does that get you off my back?"

"That show is broadcast from where?"

"In Slidell. At WCHT Studios." He pulled a piece of paper from the book and a pen from his shirt pocket. He wrote a number down and handed it to me. "Call them." He motioned to his telephone. "Call them from here. That way you can't accuse me later of getting them to lie for me."

In this incident, I believed he was telling the truth. It would be too easy to check out. "What time did the show air?"

"From nine until eleven," he said proudly.

"And it's about forty-five minutes to Slidell?"

"Depending on the traffic."

I nodded. "You still had plenty of time to get to the French Quarter and kill that baby."

"I might have had time to set an orphanage on fire!" Oren thundered. "Time isn't relevant because I didn't kill that baby. I had no reason to kill her, because she wasn't my child."

Oren could deny it until the cows came home, but I could see that his anger was a thin disguise for his fear.

———

I'D JUST LEFT Weaver's compound when my cell phone rang. Tinkie's voice had an urgency that made my foot press harder on the gas pedal.

"Meet me at the Café Du Monde," she ordered. "This is good. This is really good."

"Did you see Michael Anderson?" I asked.

"I can't talk now. Meet me in thirty minutes."

The line went dead and I concentrated on negotiating the heavy New Orleans traffic. I was right on time as I stepped beneath the green awning of the sidewalk café that served coffee and beignets.

"Sarah Booth!" Tinkie waved fingers covered in powdered sugar. She had a small white mustache and a lap full of crumbs. "There is nothing better than a hot beignet," she sighed, sipping her café au lait. "I ordered some for you, too. Lucky for me I was smart enough to find a ball gown made of spandex."

I groaned. Mollie had taken my measurements, but I might have to call and make some adjustments. I'd never hear the end of this from Jitty.

My order arrived and though I tried, I couldn't resist a beignet. It was worth an extra bulge or two.

"What did you find in the books?" I asked. "Did you see Michael Anderson?"

She bit her lip to hide her smile. "Both questions deserve an equal answer. I'll address the money first. I saw the books." She gave a low whistle. "Some books. Doreen gave me a note when I saw her in jail, which instructed her secretary to give me full access. I don't think even Doreen has a clue how much money she's making."

"And Anderson?" I pressed. "Was he around?"

"He came in. At first he was angry, but when I told him I was hired to help with Doreen's defense, he didn't say anything else."

"And?" There was an addendum to this comment. I saw it in her eyes.

"And he is one handsome man. He could be a cover model for some of those historical romance novels. And he's smart, too. I'd consider giving him my investment portfolio to manage."

I had to give Doreen the credit. She was three for three. Oren Weaver was handsome and charismatic. Clay was powerful and distinguished-looking. I was eager to see Michael.

"Did he seem upset you were looking at the books?"

"Not once he knew who I was. In fact, he was just the opposite. He found all the old records and told me to look as long as I wanted. I don't think I ever met a man with better manners."

I gave Tinkie the once-over. She was totally devoted to her husband, but there were moments when she could become infatuated with a good-looking man. She was a Daddy's Girl, but she was also human.

"So your first impression of Michael Anderson is—"

"He's not the father of that baby. He couldn't be. He's physically perfect. Or at least everything I saw. And Doreen is so beautiful. If they made a baby, it would be drop-dead gorgeous."

Tinkie knew as well as I that genetics couldn't be judged by the exterior. Leave it to her to be overwhelmed by a handsome man. "What about the books?"

"Doreen makes a lot of money. A lot." Tinkie ran her finger around the rim of her coffee cup. "I need to dig in this a little deeper. She has a lot of people with fingers in her pie, and some of them may be greedy. It's a possibility that someone wanted Doreen out of the way badly enough to set her up for murder." She looked up at me, her eyes wide. "She's on her way to becoming very wealthy. Michael's been smart. Risky, but smart."

"How does she make her money?" I asked.

"I had the books from 2000 until now. That's when she first incorporated. Doreen Mallory Ministries, Inc. That's when the money began to come in from her classes and her practice. She also started a small publishing company, Healing Words Press, which is becoming more and more lucrative. Sarah Booth, she's bringing in nearly half a million this year. Next year it looks like it could double."

My face must have registered my surprise.

"I know. Five years ago she was reading tarot cards in Jackson Square. Now she's renovating part of a building she bought on St. Peter for her healing center. She doesn't call it a church."

"I'm surprised she doesn't have her own television show."

"I found some offers, but she declined."

"I wonder why."

"You'll have to ask her that. I would have asked Michael, but he'd already left."

"Did he act nervous or anxious?"

She shook her head and gave a lopsided smile. "He said he had to go to Jackson Square to tell the people waiting for Doreen that she wasn't coming today. He said they line up every Monday and wait for her for hours."

"She still reads tarot cards?"

"Yes," Tinkie said, a strange calmness settling over her. "And sometimes she heals."

10

Tinkie was chomping at the bit to get back to work on the books. She'd developed a real interest in math—when it came to multiplication of dollar signs and nuptial possibilities. Tinkie's DG training had kicked in and I could see she was sizing Michael Anderson up as date potential for several friends who had missed the first boat of financially secure husbands.

It's an unwritten code among DGs that once one is properly married, she seeks suitable husbands for her friends. It's more than a code, it's a sacred vow. I dreaded the fact that I was among that number that Tinkie felt obligated to matchmake for, even though her efforts so far had proved dismal failures.

It wasn't that I failed to see Michael's many assets. He had the Midas touch, but I still had him on my list of potential murder suspects.

Since we were just across Rampart Street from Jackson Square,

I prevailed on her to walk over. I loved the Square, where artists rendered quick sketches in charcoal and tarot card readers dressed in everything from Scottish kilts to Viking horns read the future for twenty bucks a shot.

My first view of Michael Anderson literally stopped me in my tracks. For once in her life, Tinkie had been understated. Michael was tall and dark complected, with intense brown eyes.

He was standing beside a small table surrounded by fifty or sixty people. The crowd, judging by their clothes, was diverse. All economic backgrounds and ages.

"Doreen can't come today," he was saying. "Probably not for a while."

"Where is she?" someone asked.

"She's in jail," someone in the crowd answered before Michael could. Too bad. I was curious to see how he would have responded to the question.

He stepped away from the table and my gaze went from his broad shoulders to his trim waist and hips. The expensive suit covered him, but it didn't hide the body of a Greek god.

"Doreen *is* in jail and the charge is serious. As you all know, Doreen's infant daughter died in her sleep recently. Unfortunately, the police have begun to believe that Rebekah was murdered."

"Doreen wouldn't hurt that baby," an older woman spoke out. "The Lord just took her back. He never meant for her to stay here long at all."

A murmur of agreement swept through the crowd. "What can we do to help?" a young man with studs in his eyebrows, nose, and lips asked.

Michael shook his head. "Pray." He loosened the tie at his throat. "Doreen is okay. I spoke with her this morning and she's only sorry that she can't be here to talk to all of you."

"Will she be at the Center later?"

"I'll post a note on the fence when I find out the date she'll be back," Michael promised. "Just pray. Continue to ask for guidance and focus your prayers and energy for Doreen."

"My cousin is flying in from Portland," one woman said in a voice filled with stress. "She's coming just to see Doreen. She's got breast cancer and it's spreading all over her. She's gonna die. She's got to see Doreen."

Michael's handsome features hardened. "Doreen is in jail, charged with murder. Can't you look beyond your own needs for a split second?"

The woman paled and several of her friends huddled around her.

"I'm sorry," Michael said. "That was inexcusable. I'm worried sick about Doreen. I don't have to tell you what's at stake here. This is a capital murder charge."

"We're worried about Doreen, too," a thin, well-dressed man spoke out. "She's helped so many of us. Now we'll have to focus on helping her."

"Thank you," Michael said softly. "And as soon as she's able, she'll be here to talk with you and help you. But remember what she says: *You have the power to heal yourself.* Doreen has no magic. She only has belief. She's been teaching you how to think and explore. Go home and apply those things. Trust yourselves. That's what Doreen told me to tell you. Trust yourselves."

"That's exactly what she'd have said," a woman said with a teary smile. "Well, it's not doing any good to stand around here." She turned away and headed across the Square in front of the cathedral. Several others followed her.

The thin man remained, taking a seat opposite Michael at the small table. Tinkie and I walked forward. Michael had seen us out of the corner of his eye, and he introduced himself to me, and both of us to his companion, Alec Hathoway. Michael had obviously been told about me, either by Tinkie or someone else.

"Alec helps with the ministry," Michael said. "He runs the soup kitchen for us."

"We feed about a hundred people a day, mostly young kids," Alec said with a slow smile. "The Quarter has a lot of youngsters on the lam. Although we don't have the winters they do farther north, this can be a very cold city for a teenager with no money and no shelter."

Michael broke in. "Have you found anything that might help Doreen?"

If he had any reason to believe he was a potential suspect, he surely didn't show it.

"We have some interesting leads." I stepped out of the way of a gaggle of teenage girls who were laughing and pushing one another as they came out of Madeline's Bakery and Café.

"Doreen didn't do this," Michael said.

"No, it's impossible that she would do such a thing," Alec agreed. "Doreen loved her baby. Most people would have been devastated." He shook his head slowly. "I have to say, it hurt me to look at that child. How could so many things go wrong and the baby still live?"

"Doreen never saw any of the defects," Michael said. "She never grasped the reality of what Rebekah was."

"And what was that reality?" I asked.

"She was going to die." Michael stared into my eyes. "Doreen was going to suffer, no matter what she did."

"Is there anyone you can think of who might have wanted to hurt the baby?" I asked.

"Have you spoken with Pearline?" Alec asked. "She was always around Rebekah. Maybe she knows something."

"Pearline?" Tinkie and I asked in unison.

"Doreen's maid. She was more a nanny than a maid. She kept Rebekah when Doreen was working." Alec's frown was minimal, but present. "I would have thought she'd be one of the first people you'd talk to."

"She would have been if someone had told us about her," Tinkie said. She glanced at her watch. "Is she still employed?"

"She is, but she hasn't been in this week," Michael said easily. "When Doreen decided to travel to Zinnia, Mississippi, she gave Pearline the week off. And to be honest, there isn't much work for Pearline to do now that Rebekah is . . . gone."

"Do you have her address?" I asked Michael.

He wrote the street address and phone number on the back of a business card. "She has other clients, so call before you waste a trip."

"Thanks," I said, tucking the card into the back pocket of my jeans.

"Doreen's apartment isn't far from here," Tinkie said. "Would it be possible for us to take a look around?"

Michael nodded. "It would be, but I don't have a key. Doreen insisted that her private life be just that, private. I have keys to the Center, but not to her apartment."

"Would anyone have a key?" Tinkie pressed.

"I don't think so." Michael looked at Alec.

"Pearline had a key," Alec offered. "Even though you can't get in the apartment, you can look around the courtyard. I never went upstairs, but we sometimes sat on the patio and talked. Doreen was buying the entire building. It might be interesting to talk to the tenants. Maybe they saw something."

"We'll do that," Tinkie said, smiling. "I just want to get a feel of the layout. It could prove important in the case."

"Is there a convenient time when I can speak with you alone?" I asked Michael.

His intense eyes connected with mine. "I'm at your disposal, Ms. Delaney. Whatever I can do to help Doreen."

"This evening? Say, seven o'clock?"

"Why don't we meet at the Center on St. Peter? I can give you a tour. I'll also bring along some of the financial records that Ms. Richmond has asked to see."

"That would be perfect," I agreed.

Tinkie and I took our leave, walking along St. Ann to Dumaine, where we took a left. Tinkie stopped at a shopwindow that held an exquisite display of antique jewelry. "What did you think?" she asked.

She didn't have to say about what. "He's a handsome man," I agreed. "One of the handsomest men I've ever seen."

"And?" she pressed.

I tried to organize my feelings about Michael Anderson. He lacked the charisma of Oren Weaver and the power of Thaddeus Clay, but there was something there. An intensity that was compelling.

"I get the feeling that he's been badly hurt in the past." I stumbled over my words, trying to find the right ones. "Wounded," I said finally. "Somewhere along the way, Michael has lost a lot. I recognized that in him."

Tinkie lightly grasped my shoulder and turned me to face her. She was caught in a shaft of October light that seemed ancient, a hue haloed and muted by time. I was struck by the soft perfection of her skin and the real concern in her blue eyes.

"Are you okay, Sarah Booth?"

I thought about it. "Yes," I said.

"You haven't been yourself lately."

"I know." Lying to Tinkie was never smart, so I didn't try.

"Is it Coleman?"

"Partly," I admitted. "But it's other stuff, too. I think about the past a lot."

"I do, too," Tinkie said, rubbing my arm. We stepped closer to the storefront, to allow a cluster of tourists sporting cameras, hats, and varicose veins to pass by us. I was suddenly aware of the bustle of the street, the constant motion of the loud tourists holding Styrofoam cups filled with frozen liquor concoctions.

"I think about the future, too," she said. "This is a hard case for me. I want a child so much, and Oscar doesn't. He keeps saying he's not ready."

"Why does Oscar get to make this decision all by himself?" I asked.

"He doesn't. But he is an equal partner. If he says no, then it's no. I guess in this case the declining partner has a little more than fifty percent of the vote."

"Why?" I demanded, remembering my prior conversation with Jitty and her point that women had served for centuries at the bidding of men. "You could have a baby."

"I could, but how right would that be? I mean, put the shoe on the other foot. What if Oscar wanted a baby and I didn't? Would it be fair for him to trick me into getting pregnant or demand that I carry his child?"

Tinkie was not only becoming an excellent investigator, she was becoming an adult.

"Maybe he'll change his mind," I said, trying to find the best outcome.

"And maybe by the time he does, it'll be too late."

Her words sent a chill down my spine. It was as if Jitty had possessed Tinkie's body. "You have another ten years. At least."

She shook her head. "I'm not even talking biologically. The instinct to nurture and mother fades. It's the way God made us, so that we let go of our children and they can be independent and find their own lives. In another five years, I might not want to focus all my attention on a baby."

Tinkie had a valid point, and one that haunted me even when Jitty was far away at Dahlia House. "The future is out of our hands. Right now, all we can do is concentrate on our job. Let's check out Doreen's pad," I said, opting for the hip lingo of my mother's generation. It seemed to put a devil-may-care spin on things, even if it was only a superficial one.

Doreen's address wasn't hard to find. It was only a few blocks from Decatur and the French Market, in an area of big, historic houses that had been divided into street-front businesses and interior apartments. The stout, arched door was opened by a diminutive woman in a dance leotard.

"We're working for Doreen Mallory," I told the woman as Tinkie handed her one of our newly printed business cards.

She scanned it. "My name is Martha LaFoche. I've already spoken with Sister Mary Magdalen and she said to expect you. Come in," she said, opening the door wide. "The tenants have been talking together and we want to help."

"Did you see someone the night Rebekah was killed?" Tinkie asked eagerly.

"I didn't see anything. I was onstage. But some of the others may have ideas. I'll show you where everyone lives."

We followed her down a brick carriageway that gave a beautiful, arched view of a courtyard bursting with vegetation and a tinkling fountain. Stepping into the courtyard was like entering another world.

"That back apartment is Trina Zebrowski's," Martha said, pointing it out. "That one is rented by Starla Marston, and then Doreen is above that. To the right is my apartment, which is a two-story and the largest apartment other than Doreen's."

"Where is Starla?" Tinkie asked. She was hot on the trail of this interview.

"She's working. On the Square. She reads tarot cards."

"We'll find her on our way out," I said more to Tinkie than Martha. I walked to the center of the courtyard and turned around, taking in the physical reality of the place. LeMont had done a damn good job of drawing it, but he'd failed to capture the otherworldliness. "How old is this building?"

"It dates back to the late 1700s," Martha said. "Doreen knows all the details, but it's on the historic registry. It was once a home, and the back apartment was above the stables. The groom lived over the horses."

"It must be quite valuable property."

"Yes, it is. Even though the Quarter is gradually sinking, the real estate is prime." She gave a laugh that perfectly suited her tiny frame.

"Is it possible to climb to Doreen's windows from the street?" I asked, remembering the balcony that had overhung the arched doorway on Dumaine where we'd entered.

"A slender man or a woman, or of course a child, might be able to climb it. But the balcony is old. If you look closely you can see that the attachment to the old building is weak." She shrugged. "Do you think someone climbed in the window and killed Rebekah?"

"I don't think Doreen did it," Tinkie said stoutly.

"Neither do I," Martha said. "I saw her with the baby every morning. She'd come in the courtyard while Pearline went to Madeline's or the Café Du Monde for coffee and breakfast. Doreen would hold that infant in her lap and sing to her." She blinked, and I couldn't be certain if it was tears or not. "She acted like Rebekah was normal. She talked about her like she'd grow up. She asked me if I'd give her dance lessons."

"What about the maid, Pearline?" Tinkie asked.

Martha cocked her head. "She was totally devoted to that baby. Ever since Rebekah died, Pearline's been in a deep depression. Several times when she didn't show up for work, Doreen went to check on her. In some ways, it appeared that Pearline took Rebekah's death harder than Doreen."

I knew what she was talking about. Doreen's serenity sometimes made her seem to have less emotion.

"When was the last time you saw Pearline?" I asked.

"Oh, that would have been last week. She came to clean the
apartment." Martha glanced down at the ground, then back up
at me. "She was packing up the baby's things, to take them to
Goodwill. She was very upset."

"Is there any access into Doreen's apartment other than the
interior stairwell?" Tinkie asked. "I mean, it used to be one
house. Is there an adjoining door from your apartment?"

"The doors have all been sealed and plastered over," Martha
said. "Unless the killer climbed the balcony, he had to enter
through the stairwell."

"What about Trina?" I asked. "Do you know her well?"

"She's the newest tenant. She's also a mounted policewoman
and she manages all the repairs and maintenance of the whole
place for Doreen."

"Where was she the night Rebekah died?" Tinkie asked.

"She was with her boyfriend."

"Do you know his name?" I was pulling my pad from the
pocket of my jeans. Nothing like adding more leads.

Martha gave us a curious look. "It's Michael. Doreen's financial manager. Trina's seeing him." The sentiment "lucky dog"
was implied.

I looked at Tinkie. "Have they been seeing each other long?"
Tinkie asked.

"About three months. I mean, they knew each other long before that and were friendly. I always had the impression that
Michael was in love with someone else. He just never seemed to
notice when any of the young women made a pass at him, and
believe me, that's a lot of not noticing. I just began to think that
his heart already belonged to someone. And then all of a sudden,

Trina came home from work one day, changed into a dress, and said Michael had asked her to dinner."

"Are Doreen and Trina...close?" I asked.

"Very. Trina almost died before she met Doreen. She was ill. Trina doesn't talk about it a lot, but I think it had something to do with a tumor on her spine. Dismal prognosis."

"And now?" I asked.

Martha's laugh reminded me of Glinda the Good Witch when she was about to wave her magic wand. "She's perfectly fine. In fact, I've never met a healthier young woman. She passed the physical for the police academy and then followed her childhood dream and learned to ride a horse. She was given some kind of medal last year for her horsemanship in crowd control."

"What district does she work at?"

"The Eighth," Martha said.

Tinkie and I shared a glance. It was the same one where Detective LeMont was located. "Thanks, Martha. We'll be in touch," I said as we walked under the arched doorway and into the street.

11

As Tinkie and I retraced our steps to the Square, my friend was unusually quiet.

"Do you believe Doreen healed Trina's tumor?" she asked.

"I don't know," I said, because I really didn't believe it, but I didn't want to sound so cynical.

"I believe she did."

For that split second, Tinkie's belief was strong enough to touch me. I felt a waver of belief, but it flickered and disappeared. "Maybe," I said.

She glanced at me as we walked. "You don't believe, Sarah Booth. You're like Oscar."

I didn't take her comment as an insult. I knew how much she loved her husband. Still, I'd never in a million years thought I'd be compared in even the smallest way to a successful banker.

"Oscar believes in medicine. He believes in X rays and ultrasound and chemotherapy. He believes in surgery. If it looks suspicious or doesn't work perfectly, just cut it right out."

I noticed as we were walking that Tinkie's hand had strayed up. At first I thought she was fumbling with the button on her blouse, but then I realized what she was really doing. Her hand had moved up protectively over her breast.

"Tinkie?" She wouldn't look at me. I snatched at the hem of her shirt but she pulled free and kept walking.

"After the beauty salon, I went for a mammogram."

"Tinkie?"

"There's a lump," she said, still walking, her face turned to the windows we passed. "They're going to biopsy it when we get back from New Orleans. I don't want to talk about this again while we're here."

I wasn't able to share Tinkie's faith, but I felt her fear. "I'm sure it's nothing," I said, desperation cracking my voice. I got control of it. "Fibroid. Fatty tumor. It's just another way your body devised to get that good-looking surgeon to pay you some attention." I couldn't tell her that she couldn't be sick. Not really sick. Because I couldn't take another loss. So I lifted my chin. "You're a very clever woman."

Her smile was wan. "You knew I was pretending, some of those times when I had medical conditions."

It was a statement, not a question. I only smiled at her, successfully hiding my fear. "The doctor was cute. It didn't harm anyone."

"Now that I may be ill, I see how foolish I was. To pretend to be sick just for a chance to flirt is pretty dumb."

"No it isn't. It's creative. It was an opportunity to flirt without betraying Oscar." I put my arm around her shoulders and for a split second she stiffened. I knew then how afraid she really was. I held on until she relaxed.

"It's going to be fine, Tinkie. It's good to get it biopsied and seen to, but it isn't cancer."

"How can you be so sure of this when you don't believe Doreen healed Trina?"

It was a good question, but I had a good answer. "Because I know you. You aren't sick." I squeezed her hard. "You're healthy as a horse. I feel the health in you."

The smile that crossed her face was real. "You know what? I believe you, Sarah Booth. I trust you. I'm not going to worry about this anymore. Thank you." She stood on tiptoe and kissed my cheek. "Now, don't mention it again or I'll have to hurt you."

I felt the flutter of a butterfly on my skin and a chill to the bone inside. Like my faith, my words were hollow.

ALTHOUGH WE WALKED around the entire Square, we saw no one who looked like a Starla. When I mentioned dinner, Tinkie merely made the sign of the cross at me. By sheer will, she'd banished our previous conversation.

"Spandex will give only so much, Sarah Booth. I have to skip dinner tonight if I want to be able to go to Brennan's for breakfast tomorrow and still fit into my ball gown. And I do want that breakfast. I've booked us a table at seven o'clock."

"Fine," I agreed. I would have agreed to walk on nails for Tinkie at that moment.

Her blue eyes turned assessing. "You haven't mentioned your gown or even finding shoes for it. You are planning on attending, aren't you? Cece says she has a huge surprise for you."

"Oh, joy! I can't wait. Cece's last surprise was a book. *Thinking Your Sex Life Back to Life.* It had interesting tidbits such as 'Lie on your back in a dark room and visualize your phantom lover arriving. You are helpless to move and he begins to touch your thighs. You are begging for his touch.' I was mortified."

Tinkie laughed. "She meant well."

"I disagree. Cece meant to devil me, and that's exactly what she did. The book wasn't the worst of it. She kept making anonymous phone calls from my 'phantom lover.' "

Tinkie was laughing harder, and it made my heart lift. Tinkie had the best laugh in the world. "Anyway, I burned the book and threatened Cece with vocal-cord removal if she didn't quit calling."

"Cece can push a joke to the limit." Tinkie wiped her eyes. "So, did you get a gown?"

"I'm working on it," I assured her.

"I don't like the sound of that." She frowned. "You promised me you'd go to this ball and that you'd have a suitable gown."

"I'll bet you a hundred dollars that my gown will be stupendous." I tried not to gloat.

Tinkie's eyes tilted up at the corners. "My, oh, my. A hundred dollars. You must have something pretty spectacular up your sleeve, Sarah Booth. And you had to work quickly, too. I bought my dress at Isadora's Boutique in Memphis and paid them an extra two hundred to have my alterations done in time for the Black and Orange Ball. They're shipping the dress to me Thursday. But you haven't even been shopping, as far as I know."

A smirk tried to creep over my face, but I fought it. "I promise my gown will be extraordinary. Now will you accept the bet or not?"

"Who's going to be the judge of your gown?" she asked, her voice lilting with amusement.

"What about Oscar?"

"He's a terrible judge of style. No, he won't do at all."

"Cece?"

She shook her head. "Cece might be prejudiced."

"A panel of three strangers?"

Tinkie nodded slowly. "Now that's an idea. Can I pick the strangers?"

I knew she was loading the dice on me, but I didn't care. "Sure. You pick them."

She held out her hand and we shook, woman to woman, before she flagged down a cab. Her face was trusting and happy as she waved to me from the back of a taxi, bound for the financial reports that had so caught her fancy. I wondered if Oscar, the banker, was putting something in Tinkie's food to make her more financially responsible. If so, I wanted some of it.

I had an hour to kill before it was time to meet Michael. The sun was setting and I walked back through the Square, crossed the street, and climbed the steps to the levee that kept the Mississippi River from flooding the Quarter and a good portion of New Orleans.

Instead of eating, I decided to do a little power walking. The sun was setting and the air growing chill. It was perfect for some brisk exercise. From the top of the levee, I could see the entire river filled with boats, barges, and all types of craft. I paused for a moment, seeking something I couldn't find.

The character of the Mississippi changes as it meanders farther south. I felt no kinship with the broad, lazy stretch of water that seemed a highway for commerce without the romance of the river I knew.

Upstream, the Mississippi was a part of my heritage, the source of riches and heartache on a much more personal level. In New Orleans, she looked old and tired and dirty and tamed. It made me a little sad as I walked past teenagers drinking beer and homeless men looking for a place to settle for the night. To my astonishment, I realized I was homesick. I missed Dahlia House and Jitty.

There were other things I missed, too. Things I didn't dare dwell on. I increased my pace and walked behind the old Jax Brewery, now a tony shopping mall with cool stores and eateries. In the distance were the high-rise hotels and businesses of Canal Street. I turned and retraced my steps, fighting off the gluttonous desire for another beignet and more coffee.

Instead, I crossed Decatur and wandered around the Square. Darkness had sent the artists and tarot readers home, but the Square was a long way from empty. The teens had come out, complete with tattoos, nose and eyebrow rings, studs in their tongues, and hair long and multicolored. Instead of seeing them as the rebels they envisioned themselves to be, I felt a pang of deep sadness for them. They were lost children. But I reminded myself that every generation had lost children, and many of them found themselves a good life.

I began to slow my walking as I looked up at the numbers on the doors on St. Peter Street. A large cluster of street kids were standing at the door I wanted to enter.

"Hey, let her pass," one young man with a three-toned Mohawk said, elbowing some of his cohorts out of my way. "She's tryin' to get through, so push over!"

I was glad for his help, but didn't totally approve of his method, which was to clout anyone who didn't immediately move.

"Where's Doreen?" a teenager asked as she grabbed my arm. "Is she okay?"

I debated telling a fib, but didn't. "She's in jail. She's been charged with murder, and I'm a private investigator hired to help her."

"What'd she do?" the girl asked, stunned.

"She's accused of killing her baby."

An eerie silence fell on the kids. "Naw, not Doreen," one boy said, shaking lime-green dreadlocks. "Not her. She wouldn't hurt her kid. She wouldn't hurt anyone." He turned to a muscular teenager. "It's the cops. They do this shit all the time. They don't like Doreen 'cause she helps people like us, so now they're fuckin' with her."

Murder in the first degree was a very serious form of harassment, but I held my tongue.

"I shoulda known when that detective fella kept hangin'

around, that he was up to hurtin' Doreen. He kept askin' questions, wantin' to know who saw this or that."

"LeMont questioned you?" I hadn't seen that report. I obviously needed to see the entire case file.

"He talked to some of us."

"What kind of questions was he asking?"

"Wanted to know if we'd seen anyone hangin' around Doreen's apartment."

"And have you?" I asked.

Dreadlocks shook his head. "Naw. You gonna get Doreen out of this?"

"I'm working on it."

"We need to get some money together. If we get enough, they'll drop the charges. They just want a payoff. That's how it works around here."

"Is there anyone else who might want to harm Doreen?" I asked, focusing on the young girl who'd touched my arm.

"Doreen shocked people. She didn't believe what they believed. That upset some people, and they called her names." She blinked rapidly. "But no one would have hurt Rebekah. She was already so sick."

Michael's voice came from behind me. "Melissa."

At the sound of her name, the young girl turned. In a moment she was in Michael's arms, crying. "This is so terrible." The last word was a wail.

The kids around us had grown quiet. Michael handed me a key to open the gate, and we all filed inside. In a moment he had the kids organized into delivery teams. They headed to the soup kitchen that Alec Hathoway ran, to take hot plates of food around the neighborhood to the elderly and sick. Even Melissa had dried her tears and joined in the work.

Michael and I were left in the shell of a building that was in the process of a total renovation. Doreen was spending a lot of money on the Center.

"This is our meditation room, and here is where we're putting Doreen's offices and her consultation rooms."

I walked through the building, very aware of him. But strangely enough, he didn't seem to be aware of himself. At least not in a physical way. Not a hint of sexuality colored his posture or his speech. The intensity I'd first reacted to was still there, but it seemed genderless.

"Michael," I said once I'd seen the entire building. "I need to ask you some questions. Is there a place we can sit down?"

He led me to his private offices. During the day, the Center would be a busy place, employing at least twenty-five full-time people. He didn't bother closing the door. We were alone.

"What can I do for you?" he asked.

"Tell me about how you came to work for Doreen."

He nodded, his gaze on the top of his desk. "I was working for a C.P.A. firm on Canal. I got in the habit of buying a sandwich and eating it in the Square during lunchtime. That's when I saw Doreen reading cards and talking with people. I guess I was curious at first, in that nasty sort of way. You know, here was this woman suckering in a whole crowd of people. I wandered over to hear what line she was handing them."

His grin was charming. It could have graced the pages of any upscale men's magazine.

"But there was something about Doreen. I made it a point of listening to her every day. She'd read for a person and then talk a little about the power of their own bodies and what it meant to be truly alive and involved in living."

"You began to believe she was a healer?"

He held up a hand to slow my questions. "Doreen has never claimed to be a healer."

"But she does heal people. I heard about Trina Zebrowski."
I'd hoped to trip him up with Trina's name, but he only smiled.

"Trina will tell you that Doreen healed her, but Trina healed herself."

"Are you Rebekah's father?" I asked. Once again, my surprise
change of topic netted no results.

"No. Doreen and I were lovers, but Rebekah wasn't my baby.
She assured me of that."

"Whose baby was she?"

He stared at me. "That's a question you should ask Doreen."

"I did. She said you were a possible father."

"I never understood why Doreen wanted to have a baby," he
said. "When we were together, I assumed she was using some sort
of protection. I should have asked, but in this day and age..." he
shrugged, meaning that most experienced women took care of
the problem of birth control without discussion.

"Are you still intimate with Doreen?"

"She hasn't been intimate with anyone since Rebekah was
born. Actually, since a few months before that. She told me that
she was changing her life. She was caught up in the miracle of
motherhood."

"And how did that make you feel?"

His smile was charming. "The bedroom really isn't the place to
practice therapy."

"You knew?" I was surprised.

"I never let on to Doreen. She's so sincere with everything she
does. And she did help me a lot. Before Doreen, I had a terrible
time with intimacy. I had...scars from my early childhood."

As curious as I was about his early childhood scars, I wanted
to stay closer to the murder. "When did you become involved
with Trina?"

He gave me an appreciative glance before he spoke. "I'm glad
to see you're good at what you do, though it is a little disconcert-

ing to have it focused at me. I've been involved with Trina since last May."

"Where were you on the night of October first?" I asked.

"The night Rebekah was killed? I was with Trina." He paused only a few beats. "At my apartment."

"You're certain you were at your apartment?"

"Absolutely certain. Trina doesn't know that Doreen and I were lovers. It would have been mean-spirited to stay at Trina's. Why put that dynamic into action? Doreen and I were through, but Trina would never have understood what passed between us."

"I'm not sure that I understand it," I said.

"You'll have to ask her to explain it to you." He shrugged. "She wanted me to believe that I could be loved. That's what she said she wanted to give me."

"And what did you give her?" I pressed.

"Not a baby," he said, shaking his head. "What does it matter who the father is?"

Michael might be brilliant with money and investments, but he didn't have a clue when it came to motive. "There could be several reasons for someone to want to kill Rebekah. The father might want to hide his paternity. Or there could be financial gain," I said, watching the heat jump into his eyes.

"So that's why your partner is so interested in the books," he said.

"Partly. Money is always a good motive for murder."

"You won't find anything in those books. I'm good at my job and they are immaculate. Every penny is accounted for."

I nodded. "I'm only here to do a job, and part of that job is running down all leads that may give us the real killer."

"Good," he said. "Follow every lead to the end. That's exactly what we want. No matter where it leads." He stood up. "Is that all?"

"One more thing. Pearline isn't answering her phone. When was the last time you saw her?"

He thought a minute. "Last week, I believe."

"What kind of person would you say she is?"

"Reliable. Honest. Competent. She was devastated by Rebekah's medical problems at first, but when she got over the shock, she was totally devoted to that baby and to Doreen."

"So totally devoted that she might have viewed Rebekah's death as a form of euthanasia?" My first reaction to seeing the photos of Rebekah had bordered along this line.

Michael stared into my eyes as he thought. "No, I don't think so. Pearline would never have harmed Rebekah."

"What happens to the ministry if Doreen is convicted?"

"There is no ministry without Doreen."

"But there is a lot of money already accrued."

Michael kept his face impressively blank. "I can tell you that no action would be taken without consultation with Doreen, in jail or out."

"Thank you, Michael," I said as I started toward the door. "I'm sure we'll be talking a lot in the coming days. Do you know who Doreen has hired for her attorney?"

"Jake O'Banyon."

I turned to stare at him. Jake O'Banyon was the most high-profile criminal lawyer in the Southeast. "He's not a big gun, he's a cannon."

"Doreen has friends in high places."

I started to ask him exactly how much he knew about Doreen's relationship with Senator Thaddeus Clay, but I knew he would never tell me.

"O'Banyon's gotten the bail hearing set for the morning. He assures me Doreen will be out in time for coffee and beignets."

I nodded. "Michael, who do you think killed Rebekah?"

"I won't hazard a guess."

I gathered my purse. "I'm going to ask for a paternity test."

"Rebekah's already been cremated."

"The coroner will have enough material to run a DNA test."

"Tell Mrs. Richmond I had several boxes of records delivered to her hotel room as she requested."

"I'm sure she'll appreciate it."

"I've never known anyone like Doreen," he said, walking out with me. He touched my arm, and I was wrong to have thought him genderless. His fingers traced heat through my blouse. "She's a very powerful woman."

12

DAWN WAS JUST BREAKING ON TUESDAY MORNING AS I DROVE down the narrow street and stopped in front of the pink shotgun cottage where Pearline Brewer lived. It was a low-income neighborhood, but a neat one. The pink house was offset by blue shutters, and in the summer sun, it would be a bright and pleasant place. In the soft light, the house looked tired. The porch sagged a little as I walked to the door and knocked. An old Chevy in the driveway led me to believe that Pearline was home.

After two minutes, I knocked again, and louder.

The morning was brisk and I shifted from foot to foot as I waited. When there was still no answer, I resorted to pounding on the door.

A front porch light came on at the house next door, and a slender black woman in a purple robe stepped out.

"Whoever you are and whatever you want, you'd best be moving on before I call the police. Pearline's gone," she said. "Won't be back for a week at least. Her mama's ailin' over in Lafayette."

"Do you have a number where I can call her?" My voice showed my disappointment.

"No, she didn't leave a number," the woman said. "If she calls me, I'll tell her someone was looking for her."

I hurried down Pearline's steps and trotted over to the neighbor's house. Pulling one of my new cards from my pocket, I handed it to her.

"I'm working for Doreen Mallory," I said. "I need to talk with Pearline."

"I'll be sure and tell her," the neighbor said. She held the robe at her throat with one hand while she slipped my card into her pocket. Her gaze never left mine.

"Thanks." There was nothing left to do but meet Tinkie for the prearranged breakfast.

I drove slowly out of the neighborhood and cruised down the streets. Pearline's neighborhood was neat, but only four blocks west, the houses got bigger and were better kept. Gentrification would soon encroach on Pearline's street. The flip side of renovation was that an entire class of people got shoved out.

At six-fifty-nine, I parked the roadster and sprinted to the front door of the restaurant. Tinkie was already seated. I watched for a moment as every man who passed her slowed and looked. With her hair swept up in a soft cluster of curls, she looked like a movie star. The coral cashmere sweater she wore accentuated her assets. Her perfectly healthy-looking assets. Tinkie could not be sick. I examined her face as she studied the menu. I'd lost everyone I'd ever loved, and I realized that in the past year I'd come to love Tinkie with the most precious of bonds—friendship.

I took a deep breath, forced a smile on my face, and slid into the seat opposite her. "Find anything interesting in the books?"

She raised her gaze from the menu and studied me. "Where did you go? I rang your room at six."

"I went to Pearline's but she's gone to Lafayette to tend her sick mother."

"Right," Tinkie said, mirroring my own cynicism.

"I left a card. Maybe she'll call."

"Of course she will." Tinkie rolled her eyes. "In answer to your question, I did find one tiny little tidbit."

I leaned forward, unable to suppress my eagerness.

"Doreen wasn't paying Pearline's salary."

"Who was?"

"Now that's an excellent question," Tinkie said, her coral lips puckering. "I think it's a clue."

"I wonder if Michael knows?"

"I wonder if he'll tell," she said, arching an eyebrow. "But first I need sustenance. I'm having the Cajun sausage and green pepper omelet, biscuits, and coffee. What about you?"

"Tinkie, you have excellent taste. In partners, clothes, and breakfast. I'll have the same."

Ten pounds heavier and nearly in a coma of satisfaction, I stumbled out into the street with Tinkie. We'd decided that I would go to the bail hearing for Doreen and then stop by to talk with LeMont and, hopefully, Trina Zebrowski. Tinkie was going to the Square to talk to some of the other tarot card readers in an effort to track down Starla.

I dropped Tinkie off across the street from the Café Du Monde and headed down to the municipal court building for Doreen's bond hearing. It was set for nine. I'd be there right on the dot.

The hearing was a formality. I sat in the back of the courtroom and took note of Doreen. She sat perfectly still, her beautiful dark hair covering her like a cloak. The judge dispatched the case in less than five minutes, setting bond at two hundred thousand.

Jake O'Banyon didn't raise an objection. He nodded at a

young boy who sat behind him. The boy shot out of his seat and ran out of the courtroom like his pants were on fire. I figured him for the runner to the bondsman.

LeMont was on the prosecutor's side, and I watched him carefully as he started toward Doreen.

"My client has nothing to say to you," O'Banyon said, stepping in LeMont's path.

"I have some questions and she's going to answer them," LeMont said.

"I have a question for you, Detective. Why wasn't a juvenile detective assigned to this case? That's normal procedure. Why are you clinging to the case like dandruff to a black coat?" O'Banyon smiled like a shark.

"What are you implying?" LeMont said, his mouth so tight and thin I was surprised words could escape.

"I'm way too smart to *imply* anything," O'Banyon said, "but just let me point out that if anything funny's going on in this case, the stink's going to rub off on you."

O'Banyon took Doreen's arm and hustled her toward the front of the courtroom. They disappeared through a heavy oak door.

LeMont turned and when he saw me, he reddened. "What are you doing here?" he demanded.

"Watching the wheels of justice turn," I said, grinning. "Why *are* you handling the case, Detective?"

"There wasn't a juvenile officer available." He brushed past me.

"I talked to some kids at the Center last night. They said you questioned them. I'd like to see those reports. And any others you might have."

"People in hell want ice water," he said over his shoulder. He sped out of the courtroom without a backwards glance.

I ran after him, catching him at the front door of the building. "LeMont!" I grabbed his sleeve.

He started to shake free but stopped and faced me. "What?"

"The baby bottle with the barbiturate in it, did you have it processed for fingerprints?"

"At the time we thought we didn't have to. Ms. Mallory said she'd held the bottle. The only prints on it would have been hers. Remember, when we first investigated, we thought it was a death by natural causes."

Anger made my jaw tighten. "Things have changed since then. Doreen is charged with Murder One. I suggest you get that bottle printed."

LeMont gave me a disgusted look and pushed through the doors. He trotted down the steps and disappeared into the throng of pedestrians that now crowded the city.

I stood for a moment, torn between hunting Doreen down and going after Trina Zebrowski. I chose Doreen.

I didn't have to hunt long. Doreen appeared in the corridor while I was trying to decide where to look for her.

"Sarah Booth," she said, her smile soft. "I saw you in the courtroom. Thanks for coming."

"I gather you won't have a problem making the bail?"

She shook her head as we started walking. "It's covered. Michael is handling all of it."

We pushed through the doors and stepped onto the sidewalk.

"Where are you going?"

"To the Center, first. Then home." She stepped into the street, lifted her hand, and began waving at a cab five blocks away. "I'm glad to be out in the sunshine."

"Doreen, who was paying Pearline?"

She put her hand down and turned to face me. "I told Thad it wasn't a good idea."

"The senator was paying Pearline?"

She nodded. "Pearline works for him three days a week. He

sent her to me two days. She needed a full-time job, so he made these arrangements."

"And he paid for it?"

"Yes." She held my gaze.

"And Pearline was with Rebekah all that afternoon and most of the evening?"

"Yes." Her eyes held mine. "Pearline can't even step on a roach. There's no way she could've hurt Rebekah."

"Someone did."

"Not Pearline."

"Then who?" She'd given me so little to work with.

"Why would Pearline hurt Rebekah? What would she gain?"

"I don't have an answer to that question. Perhaps, though, she was acting for someone else?"

"You think Thad sent her to work for me like some kind of assassin?"

I'd wondered if Doreen could be rattled. Now I knew. She was spitting nails.

"If he thought the baby was his and he wanted to make sure you never filed a paternity claim, he could have."

"Thad isn't that kind of man."

"And you aren't that kind of woman, so who killed Rebekah?"

The taxi had pulled up to the curb and the driver shouted something out the window. Doreen ignored him. She stood motionless, looking into my eyes.

"I want you to find my brother," she said. "I want to give him half the money my mother left."

Doreen was a woman who operated on many levels simultaneously. I would be wise never to underestimate her. "That's two separate cases. I don't think I should splinter my time like that. He could be anywhere in the world."

"Just work on it when you have spare time. My baby is the main focus, but I would like to meet my brother. It's important that he gets half his inheritance. It's important that I have a chance to know him."

She opened the taxi door and got in. She leaned forward to give the driver instructions, and then she was gone. I stood on the curb for a moment, watching the cab blend into the packed traffic. I understood Doreen's need for a family, but I questioned her timing. A brother wouldn't do her much good if she was in prison.

My watch showed only nine-thirty, so I drove back to the Eighth District. LeMont needed another good prod, and I also wanted to talk to Michael Anderson's main squeeze, the mounted patrolwoman, Ms. Zebrowski.

LeMont growled an acknowledgment as I sat down beside his desk.

"I need your help," I said, deciding on my very best Daddy's Girl manipulation.

"Go away." He didn't even look up at me.

"Detective, an innocent woman may spend the rest of her life in prison."

He looked up at that. "Doreen Mallory killed her baby. That's what the facts tell me and that's what I believe."

"What facts?"

"She was alone with the infant. There's no sign of a forced entry. She admits to giving the baby the bottle." He sighed. "We've been over all this, Ms. Delaney. Not even Ms. Mallory can think of another single suspect."

"What if the barbiturate was put in the bottle during the day, when Doreen was at the Center. Someone could have prepared that bottle long before she gave it to Rebekah."

He put down the file he was holding. "No one else had a key to the apartment."

"Doreen had trysts with several men in the past year. They've all been in her apartment. They all had as much, or more, motive than Doreen."

"How so?"

"Paternity."

He actually flinched. "That's the most cockamamie thing I've heard in at least two weeks."

"The men are very powerful." I didn't want to tell him and violate Doreen's request, but I was prepared to lay it on the line.

"What, she's slept with the mayor and the police chief and who else, maybe the President? Now, four years ago, I might have believed that!" He barked a laugh. "Get out of here and quit wasting my time." He lifted the file. "I've got fifty more of these waiting for me."

"Doreen could well be innocent!" I stood slowly. He wasn't even interested enough in Rebekah's paternity to ask who Doreen was sleeping with.

He bent over the file, dismissing me.

"Have you questioned the maid, Pearline Brewer?"

He didn't look up.

"Detective LeMont, the maid had ample opportunity to mix the barbiturate in the formula. If you've talked to her, I'd like to see that report."

"Pearline Brewer has been out of town since the baby's death." He spoke to the top of his desk.

"You haven't talked to her?" I was shocked and didn't bother to hide it. "Maybe that should be the next item on your very busy agenda."

"Beat it," he said.

I stormed away from him and stopped at the front desk. It took only a moment to discover that Trina Zebrowski was riding a beat on Bourbon Street for a blues funeral.

13

THE FUNERAL PROCESSION MOVED SLOWLY DOWN BOURBON STREET,
led by the ancient black men who comprised the Excelsior Band.
They played a dirge as they drew abreast of me, then followed it up
with "When the Saints Go Marching In." By the time the procession was out of sight, the mourners, all holding colorful umbrellas
and wearing Mardi Gras beads, were dancing behind the hearse.
The cycle of life and death, New Orleans style.

Trina Zebrowski rode a heavy bay gelding. Horse and rider
seemed unflappable as they pushed back the tourists who didn't
realize that the funeral procession was real and not some the-
atrics provided for their entertainment. As she passed me, I made
eye contact. Her blue eyes seemed shadowed with grief.

I'd already checked the funeral route, and I was standing at
the gate of the cemetery when the procession arrived. Trina spot-

ted me instantly. When her duties were complete, she rode over to me.

"You want to talk with me?" she asked, a hint of the Midwest still discernible.

"I do. I'm working for Doreen Mallory."

The most amazing smile touched her face, and for a split second I could have sworn she was only a child. "Please help Doreen. I know she didn't kill Rebekah. She loved that baby."

"I know," I said. I was finding it difficult to crane my head up; the horse was a handsome seventeen hands. "Could we talk somewhere?"

She laughed softly and slid from the saddle to the ground. To my surprise, she was only a little over five feet tall. Mounted, she'd appeared much bigger.

"Let's walk," she said, pointing to a broad shell path that led through the mausoleums. "We have to bury the dead aboveground, you know. We're below sea level here."

I walked beside her and let her talk as she led her horse. We were well out of range of the burial when I stopped. "If Doreen didn't kill her baby, who do you think did?"

"I can't imagine," she said. "We all loved that baby."

"I understand you were with Michael that night."

"Yes, I spent the night with him." She was looking at the ground as she walked, but her smile was that of a woman in love.

"What happened?"

She looked up at me, and once again she looked like an innocent child. "We went to sleep. We didn't wake up until the morning, when Doreen called."

"How did Michael react to the news?"

"He was concerned for Doreen, supportive. He cares about her."

"And Doreen? How did she sound?"

"She's the most wonderful person in the world. Even when she called to say that Rebekah was dead and the police were there, she was so calm. She thought that God had just called Rebekah home."

"And what do you think?"

Trina frowned. "I don't know. Detective LeMont says Rebekah was murdered, but I know Doreen didn't do it." She hesitated. "Maybe this is a trial God has sent to Doreen, like the people in the Bible. God does that a lot, you know."

I started to say that I thought such a God was pretty awful, but she spoke again.

"God sent me a test. Doreen helped me pass it. She saved my life."

"Tell me about it."

"I grew up in Oklahoma, on a farm. I hated it. My parents were so...repressed. Anyway, about three years ago I moved here to New Orleans. I wanted to be a singer, but there are just so many musicians here. Anyway, I ended up really sick. I had a tumor on my spine."

"You had a medical doctor diagnose this?" I'd heard that Doreen had cured Trina's tumor, but I wanted proof that there had actually been one.

"Yes, at Oschner's Clinic. It was a fast-growing cancer. They told me I had maybe three months before I'd be paralyzed." She stopped talking and started walking faster. The horse, so well behaved, followed behind her on a loose rein.

I caught up with her. "So, what happened?"

"Doreen bought the building where I was living. At first I was totally disgusted with her. I'd go to the Square and watch her read for people and then touch them. I figured she was the biggest charlatan around."

"And?" I prompted.

"I saw her in the courtyard one day, planting some flowers. I was so angry. I could feel the tumor growing on my spine, pushing on the spinal cord. I knew I'd be in a wheelchair in a matter of days. And there she was, gardening, living the life I wanted. I just lit into her."

"You struck her?"

Trina shook her head. "No, but I started cursing her. I told her how unfair it was that I was dying and she was stealing money from people. I'd never done anything bad to anyone."

"What did she say?"

"She just stood up really slow and she asked me if I'd like some tea. She went inside her apartment, and she came down with two glasses of iced tea. When she handed me my glass, she touched me. And she looked right into my eyes, and she said, 'The tumor will begin to shrink now.' "

"Did it?"

"My next doctor's appointment, they were amazed. It was half the size. And the next visit, it was gone."

"How long ago was that?"

"About a year ago."

"And now?"

"I'm cancer-free."

I almost touched her. She seemed filled with a strange light. Her blue eyes held a sparkling translucence. "You believe Doreen healed you?"

Trina's smile made tears start in my eyes. "She says she didn't. She says I healed myself, with help from the Divine. The Divine can be God, or gods, or angels. It doesn't matter what you call it, because it's all love." Trina smiled at my skeptical look. "Doreen said I had a contract with the Divine. It was his choice to heal me, but I opened myself to the possibility. I'll tell you, I changed my life. I started taking riding lessons for police work. I'd ridden all my life on the farm, but I'm small. I never thought I could get a job with the police force. But Doreen thought of the mounted unit. Now I have my job, my horse, and Michael. Since that day when Doreen touched me, my life has steadily gotten better and better."

"Would you mind if I spoke with your doctors at Oschner's?"

Her laughter rang against the marble tombs. "Help yourself. In fact, when I get back to the District, I'll call Dr. Walsh and tell him to cooperate with you in every way."

"Thanks."

"Don't mention it." She circled around and we started back to the gate. The funeral procession was leaving. All of the joy that the band had created was gone. Women were softly weeping as they slowly walked through the tombs.

"Who died?"

"Able Macon. He was a fine trumpet player."

We reached the gate in silence. Instinctively I turned to offer Trina a leg up. She was short and the horse was big.

"I've got it," she said, hiking her left foot almost to her chin to put it in the stirrup. With a smooth motion she vaulted onto the saddle. "I have to be able to mount on my own. Police regulations!" Her smile slowly faded. "Can you help Doreen?"

"I hope so," I said. "Just out of curiosity, what time did you and Michael go to sleep?"

She thought a moment. "We had dinner at Port-O-Call, and we went back to his place."

"Where is Michael's place?" I asked.

"He's down on Barren Street, almost at the end."

I calculated the distance in my head. It could be walked in twenty minutes, jogged in ten.

"I guess we went to sleep around ten. I have to be at work at seven, so I'm not a night owl." She gave a soft chuckle. "Too many years of living on a farm, I guess."

"And you slept through the night."

"It was the best night's sleep I've had in months. Once I was out, I didn't wake until the alarm went off at six."

"And Michael?"

"He was right beside me."

"He's a sound sleeper, too, huh?"

"Like the dead. I'm normally the one who wakes up all through the night."

"So you would have awakened if he got up?"

"What are you saying?"

"I'm not saying anything, Trina. I just have to check out every angle."

"Why would Michael hurt Rebekah? He loved her. He loves Doreen. He'd never do anything to hurt either of them."

Trina wasn't privy to Michael's affair with Doreen, or the fact that he might be Rebekah's father. I wasn't about to tell her, either. I gave a crooked smile. "I'm only doing my job."

Her eyes narrowed, lightning flashing in the depths. "Maybe Doreen needs a local PI. Sister Mary Magdalen may not be the best person to pick out a detective."

"Trina, I'm only doing my job. Don't take it personally."

"I'll talk to Doreen myself," she said, closing her legs on the horse. She trotted out of the cemetery and down the street.

I'd hurt her, and from her point of view, it was without cause.

My cell phone rang and I dug it out of my purse with a sense of relief. Tinkie's timing was perfect.

"Tinkie!" I said.

"Miss Sarah Booth?"

The voice was older and confused. It took me a moment to recognize Mollie.

"It's me," I said. "Are you okay?"

"More than okay. But I need you back in Zinnia. I can't go any further on the dress until you try it on."

"You need me now?"

"Right this minute. The hem on this dress is a mile long and it's gonna take some fine hand-stitching."

I could hear Mollie's excitement. The dress was going to be a knockout!

"I'll try to get home this evening," I said. "I'll give you a call when I get to Zinnia."

"Hurry up, girl. This is gonna be the dress that gets you a husband." She hung up before I could argue with her.

I dialed Tinkie's number and counted five rings before she answered. "Meet me for lunch at Jonathan's," she said. "I have news."

I had news, too, but when Tinkie heard I was going to abandon her in New Orleans, she wasn't going to be happy.

I OPTED FOR a house salad with vinegar and a touch of oil. Tinkie had gumbo. We'd both come close to damaging ourselves at breakfast.

"I found Starla," Tinkie said as the waiter spread her napkin in her lap. "She heard someone in the courtyard the night Rebekah was killed."

This was good news. "Did she tell the police?"

Tinkie put her spoon down and slowly shook her head. "Because everyone thought Rebekah's death was accidental, the police never questioned Starla."

Detective LeMont's face jumped into my mind. He was so sure Doreen killed her baby. Why? "LeMont did a half-assed investigation."

"I know. And so does Doreen."

"Tinkie, I need to go back to Zinnia."

Her expression shifted to puzzlement. "Why?"

"I just have to."

"You're homesick, aren't you?"

I couldn't help but smile. "Just a little. I need to check on a few things."

"You aren't going to see Coleman, are you?"

I was surprised at the jolt of recognition. Tinkie knew me better than I knew myself. "I have something I need to see about."

"Sarah Booth, I wish I could change things for you."

"I know."

"Bring Cece back with you. She's all aflutter about the Black and Orange Ball. She swears she has a surprise for you that's going to make your panties hit the floor."

"Probably another guide to self-satisfaction," I said with a hint of fear.

Tinkie only laughed. "When will you be back?"

"Tomorrow, before lunch."

"Just drive safely."

"What are you going to do?" I felt as if I were abandoning Tinkie.

"Don't worry. I'm meeting Michael to talk about the books, and I need to talk to Doreen." A shadow crossed her face.

"Tinkie, don't put your faith—"

"It's my faith to put, Sarah Booth. Just because you don't believe, don't push that off on me."

"Tinkie, I believe Doreen's a good woman, but can—a lump isn't something to mess with."

Her face had paled at my near mention of the dreaded word. "I'll be fine, Sarah Booth," she said, her normally full mouth a thin, hard line. "I'll be just fine if you don't push it too hard."

She stood up, dropped her napkin on the table, and walked out of the restaurant.

14

PULLING INTO THE DRIVEWAY OF DAHLIA HOUSE, I WAS GREETED BY Reveler's welcoming whinny. Sweetie Pie, too, got in on the action. She flew down the steps with so much speed that she nearly knocked me off my feet when she slammed into me. Her drumming tail beat a welcome on my knees as she reared up to lick my face. Lee and Kip had done a good job caring for my pets, but I had been missed.

A drape in the parlor fluttered, and I ran up the steps to say hello to Jitty. I opened the front door, expecting a greeting, but the parlor was empty. The undulating sheers were the result of wind blowing through a crack in the window.

"Jitty!" I'd actually missed the haint.

"Sarah Booth."

I whirled to find her standing in the door. Lounging, actually. She held a cigarette in a long black holder, but it wasn't lit.

"I'm only home for the night," I explained. "I had to get my dress fitted."

"The Black and Orange Ball," Jitty said. "Sounds exciting." Her dress was short, the material threaded with gold.

"You look like you're getting ready to go to your own ball. You look beautiful." She was always elegant, but this dress was particularly flattering.

She lifted the cigarette holder. "You look sad."

I frowned. "I do have a lot on my mind. I don't know if I can help Doreen."

"And you don't believe that Doreen can help Tinkie."

"I wish I did." I slumped onto the horsehair sofa. "I feel like I'm failing Tinkie as a friend because I can't believe."

Jitty stepped, or slinked would be a more accurate description, to the sofa and sat on the arm. "If Tinkie truly believes, nothin' you do will shake her faith."

I sighed and flopped back so I was gazing at the ceiling. "I wish I could believe."

I felt a chill slip over my body. When Jitty didn't answer, I lifted my head. She was standing by the mantel, a painting of Great-great-grandfather Delaney hanging above her. He was Alice's husband. He went to war and never returned, leaving Jitty and Grandmother Alice to save the plantation. And they did.

"Faith is something each person comes to on her own," Jitty said. The cigarette holder was gone from her hand, and it seemed that even the gold threads in her dress had lost some of their glitter. In fact, Jitty was less substantial.

"I know that, Jitty. I just don't know how to get faith."

She shook her head. "Seek it."

"That sounds like a hocus-pocus answer." I was a little aggravated. I remembered Trina's face and the soft glow of belief that had made her seem youthful and innocent. How was it that everyone could find faith but me?

"The act of searching is a journey, Sarah Booth. It's individual. I wish I could help, but I can't."

"I don't even know where to look!" I stood up and went to the bar. I needed a stiff Jack Daniel's, not a lot of new-age foolishness.

"I wish your mama was here."

"I do, too." My tone was a little snappy, so I softened it. "Did Mama believe?"

"Not like the Baptists or the Methodists or the Catholics, but she believed." Jitty laughed softly. "She believed in herself, Sarah Booth. And she believed in her husband and in you."

"I can believe in people. That's not so hard," I said, realizing the moment the words left my lips that I was lying. It was very difficult to believe in another person.

"Do you believe in yourself?" Jitty asked.

"Sometimes."

She smiled, but her dark eyes were shadowed with sadness. "That's not good enough."

The ice bucket was empty so I poured a finger of Jack into a highball glass. I held it up, admiring the play of light in the amber liquor and the cut glass.

"You have to believe in yourself before you can believe in anyone else," Jitty said. She wasn't lecturing; she was trying to help.

"I don't know how to do that," I told her.

"Look into the eyes of your friends. See what reflection you see." She came back to the sofa and sat beside me.

Sweetie joined us, too. She sat on top of my feet, her soulful eyes gazing up at me.

"The day you were born," Jitty said, "your mama lifted you up right into a shaft of light that came through the window. Your mama said, 'This is my baby girl, a gift to me and the world.' That's what she thought of you."

My Aunt LouLane had told me that same story when my parents were killed. I hadn't thought of it in years.

"Your friends see you as a gift, Sarah Booth. That's how you've got to see yourself." She arched her handsome eyebrows. "But that doesn't mean you won't trip and wallow in the hog shit ever' now and then."

"Thank goodness you said something mean. I was beginning to thing you'd become some kind of fairy godmother while I was away." That would have really worried me.

"Don't go getting any ideas that fairy tales come true. Just remember, your foot's too big for any glass slipper. What size you wear? A ten?"

I took my first sip of the Jack and let out a sigh. I was home. It might be a sign of mental illness, but I'd missed Jitty's harangues and I'd missed my hound and my horse.

"Then again, it might take a fairy godmother to get you a man." Jitty stood up and began pacing in front of the sofa. "I bet you're home to call that lawman."

I shifted my weight.

"Quit squirmin'. That's a sure sign I've hit on the truth. You're back in Zinnia so you can tempt that sheriff."

"You like Coleman," I pointed out.

"He's married."

"Unhappily."

"Sarah Booth," Jitty said with a warning note in her voice, "don't go triflin' with another woman's man. That's white-trashy behavior."

"I have no intention of trifling with Coleman. Or anyone else."

Jitty's lips pursed as she studied me. "You might not do it, but you want to."

"What I want doesn't matter. Coleman is married, and his wife is pregnant."

"She may be terminally dumb, but at least she trapped a sperm."

"Jitty!" I'd had enough. "I'm going to get my dress fitted." I didn't give her a chance to dog me more. I hurried out the front door and headed to Mollie's.

Sweetie Pie met me at the car, and I motioned to her to jump in. I put on her black sunglasses and tied a scarf around her ears to keep the wind from blowing them. We blasted down the driveway, scattering sycamore leaves in our backwind.

I drove through town, noticing for the first time the Bradford pear trees changing color in front of the bank. The oaks on the courthouse square were bare of leaves, and the statue of Johnny Reb looked more worn and tarnished. I passed Deputy Dewayne Dattilo parking at Millie's, tooted my horn, and continued out County Road 42.

October had brought the first dry weather since last April, and I slowed the car to look at the cotton fields that stretched for miles on either side of the road. The cotton bolls had split wide, the huge white tufts exploding. Some of the fields had already been picked, and in the distance I could see one of the huge combines at work. It moved across the land, sucking the cotton off the plants and leaving behind black, empty stalks. The machine harvested seven rows at a time. It was a monster of efficiency.

With the dry spell, the cotton farmers were busy, as were the hay farmers over near Blue Eve. The October moon was the Hunter's Moon, but harvest was the true theme.

In the distance I saw the gray monuments that marked the cemetery where Lillith was buried. Even though I was pressed for time, I pulled into the cemetery and stopped. The angel in the blaze of fire was easy to spot. I walked over to her. It was the most artistically impressive monument I'd ever seen.

I read the troubling inscription once again. "Born of fire, she perished in flame."

The lilies that had been fresh a few days ago had wilted and died. I picked them up and carried them away with me.

Mollie's house was a short drive from the cemetery, and when I pulled up in the yard, she stepped out on the porch to greet me.

"Hurry up, Sarah Booth," she said. "I'm itching to hem this dress."

I almost sprinted up the steps and into the house, but in the doorway I stopped in my tracks. The dress was facing me on a dressmaker's dummy. Orange material swirled over the left breast and black over the right. A diamond-shaped placket of orange and black sequins joined the material just below the breasts. The skirt, tea length in front and floor length in back, was a flowing mixture of orange and black swags of chiffon.

"It's magnificent," I said, walking around to view the bare back. "Mollie, it's incredible."

"There's a lot of skirt there, Sarah Booth. Slip it on so I can start the hem."

I wasn't wearing the appropriate undergarments, but it didn't matter. The dress slipped on like a second skin.

"Here." Mollie handed me a mask, one side orange sequins and the other black. I slipped it on. "It's the best, Mollie." I hugged her tightly.

"I knew it would suit. I made a lot of clothes for your mama, Sarah Booth. This is a dress she would have loved."

I blinked back the tears and smiled. "I'm going to be the belle of the ball."

"You'd be that in a flour sack." Mollie led me to a small dais as she spoke. "Now stand up here so I can work on the hem. You've got some sexy shoes, right?"

"Some black heels," I said, going up on tiptoe. "They're wonderful. Nothing but straps."

"That's good. Now hold still." She knelt at my feet and started the tedious work of pinning up the hem.

"How's Bernard?"

"Fine. He's up at The Club. There's a party there tonight." There was the rustle of the pins. "Tammy was by here this morning. She's worried about you."

"Tammy?" I was surprised. Tammy Odom, known in town as Madame Tomeeka, was a longtime friend. "Why?"

"She had a dream about you."

"And?"

"She said you were in a white room with sheer white curtains dancing in the breeze. She said the room was bare, except for you and a black wolf and a lion."

"Great. I'm destined to be lunch."

Mollie wasn't going to be distracted from her story. "She said you held out a hand to each of the wild beasts. They both came up to you. You rested your hand on their heads. And then you had to choose. One or the other."

My stomach had knotted to the point that I thought I was going to be sick.

"It's only a dream." I forced the words out in a light tone.

"Tammy was crying." Mollie spoke softly. "She's worried about you. She said it wasn't a fair choice."

"A wolf or a lion." I visualized both animals. They were both powerful. Both predators.

"I'll give Tammy a call," I said as Mollie motioned me down from the dais. She'd worked quickly.

"Do that, Sarah Booth. And watch out for choices. Some of them are all bad."

I kissed her and slipped back into my clothes. My stomach was still knotted as I headed home.

Instead of going through Zinnia, I took a back road. I was only a mile from Dahlia House when I saw the blue lights in my mirror and heard the siren. I braked and pulled over. I hadn't been speeding or violating any traffic laws. I wasn't being apprehended for a traffic violation. It was much worse.

Coleman pulled the patrol car in behind me and got out. He was wearing sunglasses that concealed his eyes. I watched him approach in my rearview mirror. If my stomach was knotted before, now it was snarled.

"Sarah Booth," he said as he put his hands on the window. "And Sweetie Pie. A lovely duo out for a drive?"

"How are you, Coleman?" I reached up and removed the sunglasses.

"I've been better."

No kidding, I thought. He looked like he hadn't slept in five years.

"The case is a mess," I admitted. "I came home to get a dress fitted."

He laughed out loud, and I felt a smile tug at my mouth. It was good to hear him laugh, even if it was at me. "Appearances are very important to a private investigator. After all, who wants to hire someone who looks tacky?"

He laughed again and leaned down. "I've missed you."

"Don't—"

"I won't lie, Sarah Booth. I have missed you."

"I've missed you, too," I said. "Come by Dahlia House and have a drink. I'll tell you about the case."

15

I POURED US BOTH A DOUBLE JACK AND HANDED COLEMAN A glass. "Are you off duty?" I teased.

"I just clocked myself out," he answered. My fingers brushed his as he took the glass, and I felt a dangerous sensation race through me.

He took the wing chair, leaving me the sofa. I found that as I talked about Doreen and the case, I relaxed. Coleman and I had been friends long before we'd let stronger emotions flare between us. Friendship was the ground we had to rediscover.

"So you honestly believe Doreen is innocent?" He sipped his drink as he waited for my answer.

"Do you think I'm a sucker?"

He shook his head. "There's something about Doreen, a . . . a gentleness." He paused. "I did a little digging in the records, just to satisfy my own curiosity. Lillith was arrested in 1963 on a charge of public drunkenness. The arresting officer was Coot Henderson."

I remembered Coot. He was a good-looking man with a quick smile who, on occasion, turned his head when he saw an under-age teenager driving. "He's living out around Blue Eve, isn't he? He hasn't been a policeman for a long, long time."

"He started drinking. Bad. The county had to let him go." Coleman held up his glass to check the level. "Hell, even Marshal Dillon had a drink every now and again."

"Are you drinking too much?" His color didn't look good.

"Not nearly enough." He shook his head. "Let's talk about your case. I'm not a worthy subject."

I started to protest but felt the ice cracking around my heart. I retreated to my case. "Doreen loved that baby."

"But she couldn't heal her."

"That's not grounds for murder."

"Normally, no. But Doreen is a long way from normal." Coleman's gaze shifted out the window. The sun was setting and the sky was a glowing peach. It was a color that made me think of Tinkie.

"Do you think Doreen can heal people?"

Something in my voice must have given me away. Coleman's gaze zeroed in on me with sudden intensity. "Are you okay? You're not sick, are you?"

Tears gathered in my eyes, and though I tried to will them away, one slipped down my cheek.

"Sarah Booth," he said, sliding from the chair to his knees. He was beside me in a split second. "Are you sick?" His hand hovered over mine but didn't touch me. He knew the danger of the simplest of touches.

I shook my head. "I'm perfectly fine." But the tears, once started, wouldn't stop leaking.

"You don't look fine."

He was on his knees looking up at me, his hands lightly touching my arms. He was way too close. "I'm really okay."

He stood up. "I don't think so. I'm going to call Tinkie right now and ask her what's wrong." He started toward the telephone.

"Coleman, don't call Tinkie."

Something in my voice stopped him. He turned slowly. "It's Tinkie, isn't it? Something's wrong with her."

Coleman was a perceptive man. Now that he had the scent, he wouldn't give up until he knew the answer. "She has a lump."

"My God," Coleman said. "Is it cancer?"

I took a deep breath. "They don't know." Relief softened his face.

"It could be anything," he said. "Lot's of women get lumps and they aren't malignant."

"I know." I inhaled, belatedly remembering that crying made my eyes all red and swollen. Even worse, I needed a tissue. "But what if it's bad? Do you think Doreen can fix it?"

Coleman reached into his pocket and produced a clean white handkerchief. He handed it to me and managed not to watch while I blew my nose. "Don't go borrowing trouble, Sarah Booth."

"Where have I heard that before?" I asked, rolling my eyes.

He rocked back on his heels. "Tinkie's still in New Orleans?"

"She's on the case," I said with a large degree of pride. Tinkie was no quitter. I had excellent taste in partners.

"What does she think about Doreen?"

"She thinks Doreen can heal her."

That stopped Coleman. "Does she believe Doreen's innocent?"

"I guess we both believe it."

"So who killed the baby?"

"My bet is on one of the potential fathers." I filled him in on what I had learned, delighting in his shock and surprise at the names I listed. It was good to bounce my theories off Coleman. Unlike me, he was objective and trained.

"Do you have a favorite?" he asked.

"The senator has the most to lose, but Oren Weaver is running a close second. Michael Anderson could be the father, but so far Tinkie hasn't turned up any financial impropriety that would give him a motive. There's also the maid, Pearline Brewer. She has opportunity and she's been impossible to talk to."

"Keep me posted." Coleman stood up. He put his glass on the sideboard. "I have to get home."

"How is Connie?" I made it sound as sincere as I could.

"She's sick. She finally has a doctor in Jackson, but she won't let me go with her." He shrugged. "She has some prescriptions, and she's taking them." The light went out of his eyes as he talked.

"I'm sorry, Coleman."

He looked into my eyes. "Not nearly as sorry as I am." He picked up his keys from the sideboard and left. I walked to the window and watched as he got in his car, his back straight, his sunglasses hiding whatever he was thinking.

I felt a chill along my back and knew that Jitty was beside me.

"You did the right thing, Sarah Booth. You just took another step into the land of the grown-ups. You're right, I like Coleman. But he has nothing to offer you but empty hope. Heck, that ain't even as good as a delusion."

DAWN WAS JUST chasing the night away as I packed the car with clean clothes. I walked to the barn to bid Reveler a sad good-bye, when Kip Fuquar drove up. She was one helluva rider and she'd come to exercise my horse and love on Sweetie Pie, per her mother's promise.

I grinned big as she walked toward me. Sans the six pounds of makeup she'd once worn, she was a beautiful girl. "How's your mama?"

"Fine. She sends her love and said for you to come out and visit."

"I'll stop by later. I have to get back to New Orleans right away." It was Wednesday, and I felt time trickling away from me.

I put words to action and got in the roadster and headed to Zinnia. I had time for a cup of coffee at Millie's before I did anything rash like drive to New Orleans.

It wasn't even six and Millie's was already packed. I wedged myself up to the counter, sipped the coffee that Millie abstractedly poured, and waited. In less than ten minutes she came up behind the counter and let out a long breath. "It's hell during harvest. Every farmer in the county wants a hot breakfast."

I didn't blame them. If I weren't watching my figure, I'd have ordered French toast. "Have you heard anything?"

She shrugged. "Not many people care about a dead baby in New Orleans."

"Do you know much about Coot Henderson?"

"I know he's turned into a drunk. When his girlfriend burned to death in that fire, it changed Coot. He was always a little on the loose side. I mean, he'd drink on duty some, but not falling out drunk. But when—"

"You said his girlfriend?"

"Lillith Lucas." She leaned closer. "Back in the sixties it was a big secret. Lillith and Coot were quite a couple. When Lillith wasn't scaring the wits out of the teenagers about sex, she was doing the wild thing with Coot." She made her eyes big. "You can imagine the kinds of comments that were passed around over that one."

I put my empty coffee cup on the counter. "Thanks, Millie. That could prove to be very important information."

"You're welcome, Sarah Booth. How's the case coming?"

"Better and better," I said. I put a dollar on the counter and told her I had to get on the road.

The top was down and the air a little more than brisk as I headed south. It was going to be a much longer drive without Tinkie to keep me company.

I made the outskirts of Vicksburg before nine o'clock. It was safe to call Tinkie. I dialed the hotel room and held my breath through seven rings.

"Hello."

She sounded awake and chipper. "I'm headed back." I hated to use the cell phone in the roadster. The noise was awful.

"I was in the shower. Sarah Booth, instead of straight to New Orleans, zag over to Jackson and come down by the Mississippi coast."

"Why?" I liked the Mississippi coast, but I had no reason to visit.

"I found Doreen's brother. He lives in Pearl River County. You could swing by there on your way back to New Orleans."

"Sure," I said. I was curious to meet Doreen's sibling. What magical powers might he have?

"The family is J.J. and Janey Crenshaw on Alligator Road in McNeil. Number 2323. Her brother's name is Adam."

"Where'd you get this information?" I asked.

"Sister Magdalen. It seems the good sisters knew more about Doreen than they let on."

"I found out something interesting, too," I told her. "Coot Henderson, the deputy"—I gave her a second to connect the dots—"was romantically involved with Lillith. In 1963."

Although math wasn't my strong suit, I'd added up the time of Lillith's arrest and the birth of her children, and come up with a potential father for Doreen.

"Well, he was a good-looking man," Tinkie said. "I hear he's drinking heavy now."

"One of us should talk to him."

"Maybe Sunday," Tinkie said. "After the ball. And you'd better have a dress, Sarah Booth."

"You can count on me, Tinkie. So what are you doing today?"

"I'm going to talk to Doreen. I have some business with her."

My throat suddenly grew tight. "Okay. I'll take care of the Crenshaws. I'll call you when I finish."

THE CRENSHAW HOME was a modest brick house with a two-car garage. It was old enough to fit well in the large, tree-covered yard. There was a basketball goal, netless, on the garage door. It looked like a good place for a boy to grow up.

I rang the doorbell and was surprised when both J.J. and Janey Crenshaw answered it. They were in their sixties, but life hung hard on them. They wore thick glasses, and they looked at me with both sorrow and dread.

I explained who I was and asked if I could talk to them about Adam. Janey Crenshaw's mouth opened and a long wail of grief issued forth.

"Adam's dead," Mr. Crenshaw said as he put his arm around his wife. "Just come on in," he said as he led Janey to the kitchen. He installed her in a chair, where she leaned forward and wept against the polished oak table.

I stood in the doorway of the kitchen, too shocked to say or do anything. Mr. Crenshaw wet a paper towel under the tap and handed it to his wife. She blotted her face, swallowed a few more sobs, and then looked at me.

"I'm sorry," she said. "It's been four years since Adam died, but it hits me just like it was yesterday when somebody says his name."

"I'm so sorry," I said. They hadn't even asked me what I wanted with him.

"Adam's gone to live with Jesus," Janey said, new tears welling in her eyes. "I know he's in a better place. I just weep for myself. I miss him."

"How did he die?" I was still absorbing the shock. Adam would have been close to my age. That was pretty young to die.

"He drowned. It was a terrible accident," J.J. said. His voice roughened, as if he was fighting tears.

"Why are you looking for Adam?" Janey asked.

"I'm working for his sister. She asked me to find him." It was the truth, as far as it went. I decided against mentioning the inheritance until I spoke with Doreen.

"Adam had a sister?" Janey's eyes lit up. "If she's like him, she must be a wonderful woman. God-fearing, religious. Our Adam never missed a Sunday at the church. He was in the choir, and he spent every Saturday working for the Lord. Well, until he hooked up with Kiley. Why he married that girl I'll never know."

"He was married?" I don't know why I was so surprised. He was plenty old enough to be married.

"She's the one who killed him," Janey said, her mouth hardening. "She took him off to the river with all those worthless friends of hers. They got him to drinking. They got him out in the treacherous current. His death is on her."

J.J. put his hands on Janey's shoulders, a gesture that could have been comforting or restraining. I couldn't tell. "Tell us about his sister," J.J. said. "What's she like?"

"She has an interest in religion, too," I hedged. "She's very pretty."

J.J. nodded. "Adam was handsome, and he turned out to be a good boy. You can tell her that. We got him when he was a toddler. He musta had a hard life before us."

Janey sat up at the table. "The first word he ever spoke to us was the F-word. He just looked right at me and told me to F myself. I was so shocked I sat down and cried."

"But we knew God had sent us to help him," J.J. said. "When the welfare folks told us that he was in a really bad situation at his foster home, we didn't hesitate. We took him right in."

"It took a lot of work, but we got the Devil out of him." Janey sighed.

"The first few years, we had our doubts." J.J.'s voice was shaky. "We weren't sure we could reach him. When he got old enough to read, he took to the Bible. He'd read and study every night. We never really had to lead him there, he just went on his own."

"I got him a little suit with a vest for him to wear to church." Janey's face shone with love. "He was a handsome boy, and he enjoyed looking all cleaned up." Her face darkened. "I never understood what he saw in Kiley. He never seemed to care about the girls at all until she started wagging herself in front of him. She's just white trash."

"I'll be sure and tell his sister all about him." I felt sorry for them, trapped with all the "what might have beens" of a dead son.

"Wait just a minute." Janey got to her feet. "Come with me."

She led the way down a hall to a closed door. She opened it and snapped on a light. "Adam loved Jesus," Janey said, pointing at a poster that took up most of one wall. It was a graphic depiction of the crucifixion. One that made me take an involuntary step backwards. There was a well-worn Bible beside the bed and several other religious pictures on the walls. Other than that, the room was bare. "He understood that God sent his son to save us. We each and every one have a mission. Adam knew his, yet he walked away from it. It cost him his life."

"He had a mission?" I didn't understand.

"Adam was going to be a preacher," Janey said. "When he was ten, he started preaching at the church. He had a real gift. When he turned his back on it for that trashy girl, God called him home."

In the last few days, I'd learned that what people believed shaped their entire lives. The Crenshaws made me uneasy.

"Our Lord suffered mightily for us," Janey continued as she looked around her dead son's room. She didn't seem to notice that all of the pictures showed people in the midst of persecution. "The older Adam got, the more he studied the Bible. He loved the word of God. He could quote whole passages. That was before Kiley."

"And after Kiley?" I couldn't help asking.

"He got a job running wire for the power company. It paid good, but it wasn't what Adam was called for. He wasn't fulfilling his promise." Janey wiped a tear off her cheek. "He had a God-given talent to preach. Do you think it was a coincidence that his name was Adam?"

I looked around the room. "I don't know," I answered. I didn't know much except that I was more than ready to leave.

16

IT WAS OUT OF MY WAY, BUT I MADE A SWEEP BY PEARLINE'S HOUSE on my way back to the Quarter. It was a relief to be back in the city, but I hadn't completely left behind the sadness of the Crenshaws. Lillith Lucas had produced two children, both of them obsessed by religion. One was dead and the other was charged with murder. It was a tragic legacy.

When I saw the same old car parked in Pearline's drive, I stopped and walked to the house. I knocked on the front door with no results, so I tucked another business card in the screen.

Back in my car, I tried Tinkie's cell. A recorded message told me the phone wasn't in service. A chill swept over me. Tinkie never turned her cell phone off. Never.

The desk clerk at the Monteleone rang her room, and I left a voice mail for her to call me as soon as she got there. It wasn't like Tinkie to simply disappear.

Since I couldn't find her, I decided to pay a call on the senator. I had a question for him about Pearline's employment. I also wondered if the maid who'd answered the door on my first visit might not be the mysterious and elusive Pearline.

On the way, I telephoned Cece. She was supposed to be in New Orleans any day now, and I wondered if she'd talked to Tinkie.

"*Zinnia Dispatch,* Cece Dee Falcon speaking."

Cece's voice was rich and deep, with just a hint of boredom. I asked her about Tinkie and discovered her interest was already piqued.

"No, I haven't talked with her, but I ran into Oscar last night. He acted very strange."

"Oscar?" I was intrigued.

"He was at The Club, in the bar. I asked him about Tinkie and he started crying."

"Oscar?" I tried to sound puzzled, but it was fear I felt, not curiosity. I knew why Oscar was upset. The fact that he was crying made my stomach flip. Oscar didn't sweat the small stuff.

"What's going on?" Cece demanded. "One shouldn't hold out on one's friends."

More than anything, I wanted to tell Cece my worries about our friend, but it wasn't my place. "You can ask Tinkie yourself when you get down here. Which will be when?"

"Tomorrow. My dress is exquisite. And I have a date!"

She proclaimed the last with such satisfaction that I had to grin. "Good for you. Who is it?"

"It's a surprise, dahling. One that will knock you out of your shoes. Do you have a dress?"

"I will. I swear it."

"How's the case going?"

"I haven't stumbled on anything that will prove Doreen's innocence." I didn't bother to hide my disappointment.

"Well, dahling, I'd help you but I have my hands full right now. I'm plotting a coup!"

As worried as I was for Doreen and Tinkie, I couldn't help but smile. Cece had something special up her sleeve. "What kind of coup?"

"There's to be a very important society event after the Black and Orange Ball. A charity auction! All of us ladies who attend the ball will model our gowns at an auction. The proceeds will go to charity. And I was promised that I could be the emcee. But Ellisea Boudet Clay is trying to blackball me!"

Indignation rippled in Cece's voice. Surprise registered in mine. "Why would Ellisea blackball you?" Ellisea had been a big-time model in New York. She wasn't a provincial or a Baptist.

"When I interned for that summer at *Vogue,* I wrote an article about her."

"An unfavorable article?" This was like pulling teeth.

"It implied that her father's money bought her a runway job."

"Was it true?"

"In a word, yes. And she's never forgiven me."

"What are you going to do?" Whatever it was, I wanted to witness it. Cece and Ellisea going at it would be the catfight of the century.

"I have a friend at *People* magazine, and I asked him for a tiny little favor. He ran an auto-track for me."

"An auto-track?"

"It's a computer program used to gather background information. You know, neighbors, their phone numbers, addresses, that kind of info. Things have been slow around here, and I had some time. I learned some very interesting things about Ellisea Boudet Clay. If she screws with me, I'll blast her."

"Can I see what you got?" I hadn't told Tinkie anything about my suspicions about Senator Clay, but her instincts were killer.

"If you participate in the auction."

Cece loved nothing better than fashion and a runway. "You can have my gown, but I'm not modeling anything." Tripping on the runway was a definite possibility.

"If you want the info, you'll walk down the runway. And by the way, when I spoke to Ellisea yesterday, she asked a few questions about you and what you were doing in New Orleans. She put it together that we're from the same town. You've got her radar up."

"Give me a hint of what you found out," I begged.

"Dahling, the fact that her family is Crescent City Mafioso is old news. There's not an illegal activity that they aren't in up to their hairlines. The real dirt is that Ellisea has had laser treatments to remove the hair from her chin. Thick, black hair."

"Really," I said as I pulled into the senator's driveway. "Aside from unwanted hair growth, what else did you find out?"

"The Boudets have been rumored to make people disappear. Dahling, how do you think Clay got elected? It was the Boudet money and the Boudet muscle. People were afraid *not* to vote for him. Ellisea's neighbor, Mrs. Lorna Fitzpatrick, said she witnessed an altercation between Ellisea and a very upset woman who accused the Boudets of taking her husband to the swamp and killing him because he supported Clay's opponent."

"Anything ever come of it?"

"No charges were filed, but I did learn that Ellisea is a very despised woman. Mrs. Fitzpatrick referred to her as that 'ill-bred poseur.' I'll tell you the rest tomorrow at lunch. I can't wait to see you." There was a click and she was gone. It was just as well; I'd reached my destination.

I eased out of the car and started through the wrought-iron gate of the Clay home.

Someone had been decorating. Indian corn hung in clusters

around the porch. Unmolested pumpkins lined the steps. Jack-o'-lanterns were far too gauche for Ellisea. It was all very elegant, and oh, so dull. The madam of the house might have the final word in fashion, but it simply wasn't my style. My Halloween décor included cobwebs everywhere, spiders, grinning jack-o'-lanterns, and at least one ghost.

In answer to my persistent pressing on the bell, Ellisea opened the front door. Her beautiful mouth slanted down at the corners when she saw me.

"Thaddeus is busy." She started to close the door.

"I need to talk to him."

"You're a nuisance. If you don't leave, I'll call the police."

"Yes, I know what a wonderful relationship the Boudet family has with the police." I smiled sweetly.

"What do you want?"

"Tell Senator Clay I'm here. If he doesn't want to see me, I'll be glad to leave."

She hesitated, trying to decide if I was threat enough to bother with. She gave a noise of disgust. "Wait here." She slammed the door, leaving me no other option.

After ten minutes, I turned to leave. There was more than one way to skin a cat. I'd deal with the senator later; I felt a need to get back to the hotel to check on Tinkie. I was worried how her meeting with Doreen had gone.

Just as I made it down the steps, the front door opened and the senator stepped outside. Before he closed the door, I heard Ellisea.

"My brother can take care of her. And I just might call him. You're too spineless to step on a roach. You—" He slammed the door and took a deep breath.

"My wife believes abuse is what motivates a man to greatness." He looked me dead in the eye. "What do you want?"

"I want to know why you were providing a housecleaner and maid for Doreen."

He inhaled. "So you found out about Pearline."

"Yes. It's a little strange, don't you think?"

"Pearline is a good worker. She's also good with babies. She needed a full-time job, and Ellisea doesn't want her at the house five days a week." He shrugged. "I sent her to Doreen on Tuesdays and Thursdays. To help out."

"You cared about Doreen, didn't you?" Thaddeus was married to a viper. It was easy to see that someone as gentle and kind as Doreen might appeal to him.

"I did," he hesitated. "I do."

"Where is Pearline?"

"Lafayette, Louisiana. Her mother is ill. She's been there since Doreen was arrested."

At least I was getting the same story. Still, it was mighty convenient.

"I'll find her eventually. Do you have any idea why she might be hiding?"

The senator's eyebrows drew together. "She loved Rebekah. I know she stayed with her some nights when Doreen was preaching. She *volunteered* to stay." He stopped talking and looked down at his shoes. "Pearline told me one time that Rebekah was an angel."

I swallowed. Some might think that was a lovely sentiment. To me, it sounded ominous. "Do you think Pearline could have given Rebekah something to make her sleep?"

"Not with any malice. Maybe...No, I just don't see Pearline doing anything that would endanger that baby."

"If you hear from Pearline, tell her I'm looking for her."

"I will. And, Miss Delaney— Please don't come here again. It only upsets Ellisea."

We stared at each other a moment. I made no promises.

THE HOTEL DESK was busy, so I didn't wait to see if Tinkie might have left me a message. I went straight to her room. My knock went unanswered.

My room was next door, so I went there hoping to see the little red light on the telephone blinking a message from Tinkie. When I opened the door of my room, the wonderful fragrance of star-gazer lilies engulfed me. A huge bouquet was on the dresser.

I stepped into the room and stopped short at the reflection of an enormous bouquet of red roses on the bedside table. Another bouquet of gladiolus graced the desk.

Someone had delivered the flowers to the wrong place. There was no one in New Orleans who would send me flowers. Curious, I opened the card.

"I didn't know your favorite, so I sent a selection."

Wow. Someone had a real admirer. I searched the other bouquets but there was nothing else. I went to the telephone to call the desk. The light was blinking! I forgot about the flowers as I listened to the message from Tinkie.

She was fine and she was at Jackson Square. I was to join her if I got there before five.

I checked my watch. I had fifteen minutes to spare. I could either call about the flowers or find Tinkie. It wasn't even a choice.

I flagged a taxi in front of the hotel and made it to Jackson Square with ninety seconds to spare. Tinkie, lovely in a chocolate-colored suit, was sitting beside Doreen. A crowd of at least a hundred people was gathered around them. Among them were the teenagers I'd met the night before. And Michael Anderson.

None of them spotted me, so I took the opportunity to watch. The crowd was unnaturally quiet. Especially the teenagers. They were all looking at Doreen with rapt attention. As was Tinkie.

Michael stood a little apart, his focus on Doreen. When a middle-aged woman in the crowd stepped forward, Michael moved to intercept her. His job might be the books, but he was acting the role of watchdog.

Doreen stood and leaned across the small table in front of her. She reached out and put her hands on the woman's arms. To my utter amazement, the woman jolted, as if she were being shocked. A beatific smile touched her face. Doreen released her and the woman clutched at Doreen's hands.

Michael was there in a split second. He caught the woman's arms and gently tugged her free of Doreen. They disappeared in the crowd.

Doreen nodded at Tinkie, who jumped to her feet. Together, they started walking across the Square. I hustled to catch up with them.

"Sarah Booth," Doreen said, smiling, when she caught sight of me. I said hello, but my focus was on Tinkie. She smiled at me. It was the innocent smile of a child.

"Tinkie?"

"Sarah Booth," she said. "I've had the most wonderful day. And I've learned so much." She grasped my hand. "You can't begin to imagine the power you have inside you. We're all creatures of the Divine."

"Tinkie?" I considered shaking her to wipe the smile from her face.

"I'm going to be fine. I'm not going to have surgery, I'm going to will the lump away."

I cut a look at Doreen. "Everything's going to be fine," she said.

I thought of Sun Myung Moon and the Moonies. Just because Tinkie was wearing a Chanel suit and perfect makeup didn't mean she hadn't been brainwashed. If Doreen could make a breast lump disappear, it was fine. But if she couldn't, Tinkie was risking her life.

"When's Oscar getting here?" I asked. If I needed backup in the realm of practicality, Oscar was my man.

"Tomorrow. So's Cece. And her date!" Tinkie's face had lost the foggy look. "I can't wait. The Black and Orange Ball is going to be stupendous."

Relief made me smile. Tinkie might be gaga, but she still had her social priorities straight.

Doreen patted my arm. "Tinkie's fine," she said. "She always was. Did you find out anything about my brother?"

"Maybe we should sit down somewhere." I didn't want to deliver the news of Adam's death while we strolled by tourists and the circus life that made Jackson Square so interesting.

"Let's have a glass of wine," Doreen suggested. "You look done in, Sarah Booth."

I was tired. It had been a long and emotional day. And I'd been worried about Tinkie. I was still worried about her.

Doreen led the way to a small bar tucked into a courtyard. Obviously a hangout for locals, there was no sign outside.

Banana plants, huge and lush, were protected from the wind. Wrought-iron tables around the patio allowed some patrons to smoke, and I inhaled the scent of tobacco, thinking suddenly of Jitty and her latest fashion accoutrement. Illusion/delusion. Which was Doreen?

She took a seat and ordered white wine. Tinkie followed her lead, but I asked for Jack on the rocks. I watched Tinkie until the drinks arrived. It wasn't until she thanked the waiter for her drink that I could pinpoint what was different about her. She looked younger.

"Tell me about my brother," Doreen asked, her eyes expectant.

"His name was Adam Crenshaw—"

"'Was'?"

"I'm sorry, Doreen. Your brother is dead. He drowned four years ago."

"Oh." The expectation left her eyes.

"How did he drown?" Tinkie asked.

"I gather he was swimming in the river with his wife and some friends."

"Were his parents nice?" Doreen asked.

"They're very religious, but they seem to have loved him greatly. They are still torn up by his death." I hesitated. "There is a widow."

"Any children?"

"I assume no. I didn't ask."

"Could you find out?" Doreen asked.

"Sure," I said. Doreen was taking the news of her brother's death quite well. Then again, she'd never known him. "Adam was religious. Very religious."

"How so?" Doreen's brow furrowed.

"He was involved in the church and studied the Bible a lot." I tried to think of something she might find comforting, but there was little of comfort in the religion that Janey Crenshaw had shown me. "His parents are still very upset by his death."

"The Crenshaws shouldn't grieve," Doreen said. "He isn't gone. He's merely in a state of transition."

"Doreen, that's exactly the kind of remark that's going to hurt you with a jury," I snapped. I'd had it with the hocus-pocus talk. "It's normal to grieve when someone dies." I should know; I'd lost plenty.

"As long as you know the grief is for *your* loss," Doreen said.

"In other words, grief is selfish?" I was getting madder by the second.

"Yes," she said. "But that's not a bad thing. Grief is part of the healing process. It's only when you become stuck in grief that you give away your power. People who grieve too long end up trapped in the past. That's not a happy place to be."

It all sounded so damned practical, irritatingly practical. I started to say something, but Tinkie interrupted.

"Sarah Booth has lost a lot," she said with such tenderness that I felt tears sting my eyes. "She was so young, too."

"We all lose people we love," Doreen said. "But they aren't gone, Sarah Booth. They're with you right this second." She touched my hand, and a tingle shot up my arm. "Just like Rebekah is with me. If I didn't know that, I couldn't bear her death."

I wanted to believe. I wanted it badly.

"There are two things you have to accept as true," Doreen said, her fingers stroking my hand. "The first is, God is love. We are his creatures, and we share his divinity."

I felt as if I were falling into her green eyes. There was such peace there. Such comfort and joy.

"The second is, everything happens for a reason. Everything."

I thought of the night my parents were killed. I'd been sound asleep. There'd been a knock at the door. Aunt LouLane was staying over with me, and I heard her scream. When I ran downstairs, she was on the horsehair sofa, rocking back and forth, holding her stomach as if she'd die. There had been an accident. A car wreck on a straight stretch of road. My parents had been headed home. Something went wrong. The car went off the road, flipped, and caught fire. They were dead.

"My parents died for a reason?" I asked. The tingle was gone. I was suddenly cold.

"They did, Sarah Booth. You have to believe that."

I slowly pulled my hand free of hers. "No, I don't." The idea was beyond infuriating. I stood up and walked away, blinking back the hot tears that threatened to spill over.

17

MY HOTEL ROOM SMELLED LIKE A FUNERAL PARLOR. I CALLED THE desk to complain about the flowers. What had once been beautiful was now an aggravation. My mood was black, and it didn't improve when the front desk clerk insisted the flowers had been delivered to the correct room. He was so smug, I hung up on him.

I'd left Tinkie and Doreen at the bar, sipping their white wine. I paced the room, giving my anger at Doreen free rein. Her beliefs, as far as my losses went, were harmless. Tinkie was another matter. As soon as Oscar got to New Orleans, I was determined to have him intervene in Tinkie's relationship with Doreen.

The best thing to do would be to contact Sister Magdalen and quit. I owed Doreen nothing, not even a resignation. I sat down at the desk, whipped out the hotel stationery, and started to pen a letter to the nun. I'd only written a few words when I stopped.

If Jitty were with me, she'd be riding me hard. She'd be the first to point out that I wasn't angry with Doreen, I was angry with God. There was no reason for my parents to die. No good reason. I needed them. Even though years had passed, I still needed them. And they were gone, taken from me in one split second. To say that their deaths served any kind of purpose made me furious.

What good had come of it?

I sat down on the bed as I pondered that question. I couldn't think of a single thing. If this was God's way of showing love, I'd just as soon be ignored.

Quitting wasn't the answer, though. I owed Tinkie more than that. And I owed myself. Nothing Doreen said had been spoken in meanness. She just didn't understand how much death could hurt some people.

Loss weighed heavily on me as I clicked on the television. Wednesday night loomed long and lonely. I had a strong urge to get in the car and drive back to Dahlia House. At least I'd have Jitty and Sweetie Pie for company. And I could get up in the morning and ride Reveler in the crisp October sunshine.

Instead, I clicked through the TV channels, hunting for WWJD, the local religious channel. Oren Weaver had his own show. He had a terrific gimmick going, a huge circus tent that he moved from location to location, like an old-time revival. I'd taken the time to find out that he was currently set up on the old fairgrounds; I just needed to find out when his services began. I watched for a few minutes before I was rewarded. A handsome young man in a blue blazer was looking directly into the camera as he stood in front of a billowing blue-and-white tent.

"Reverend Weaver will perform a healing here tonight. Each and every one of you is invited to come and bask in God's healing light and let Reverend Weaver wash away your sins. Services start at eight o'clock."

I slipped my feet into my shoes, collected my car keys, and

headed out the door. I wasn't going to settle for watching Oren on television. I had a hankering to hear the great healer in person.

I rode with the top down, stopping once to ask directions when I thought I was lost. Oren Weaver had staged his show on the fairgrounds that were also the home of the Blues Festival.

The parking lot was filled to capacity. Once I finally parked, it was at least a good two miles back to the tent. I couldn't help but listen to the conversations of some of the people I passed, headed to the revival.

"He's got the power of God in his hands," one elderly woman said. "He's going to shrink my cancer until it goes away."

"We'll pray for you," her companion said. "Me and Bernice have been praying for you every day." Her voice held sorrow.

I passed them as quickly as possible. Sorrow was contagious, and I knew I wasn't immune. I came up behind an old man walking painfully to the tent. A young, handsome man was helping him.

"Take it easy, Grampa. Becky's saving you a seat."

"I want the front row. Revered Weaver might not see me in the back."

The back was exactly where I wanted to be. To see without being seen. People poured into the tent, desperation etched in their faces. Talk about the halt and the lame. My suspicions of Oren Weaver were turning into disgust. He was bilking these people, holding out a miracle with one hand while his other hand picked their pockets.

The choir, a cast of at least a hundred in scarlet satin robes, swayed from side to side as they sang "What a Friend We Have in Jesus." The tent filled fast. A young man in a dark suit stepped to the microphone and began to quiet the crowd with a gentle voice that spoke of God's love for his children. I hadn't been to church in years, but it was a familiar sermon. Impatiently, I checked my watch. Most of the audience was doing the same thing. They could get a sermon in their own churches. They'd come for a miracle.

"Now Reverend Oren Weaver," the young man said, backing away from center stage as Oren entered from stage right.

Oren was a commanding presence on the stage. The audience hushed. Everyone's attention was riveted where Oren stood, gilt-edged Bible in hand. He lifted the Bible, shook it once, and commanded, "Praise God!"

The audience responded with a roar.

"I say, praise God Almighty."

The din was deafening.

"We are all sinners here tonight. All of us, even me. But God's love washes all of our sins away. We come here tarnished and we'll leave clean. We come in despair and we'll leave in joy." He paused. "We come broken and we'll leave healed."

That drew another roar. An elderly woman next to me began to weep. Her hands were so knotted with arthritis that she could barely hold the tissue to her eyes.

The emotional charge in the tent was palpable. The crowd was alive with hope and expectation. It was all focused on Oren, and I wondered how addictive such rapt adulation could be.

"Reverend, help me!" A tall, thin man stood up and began to hobble toward the altar. "Please help me. I've been a sinner all my life, but I want to change. I want to walk in the light."

"You want to walk, brother, but I don't believe it's in the light. You want to walk back through that bar door to indulge in the spirit-killing alcohol!" Oren said. "God has no miracles for those who don't believe, and you, sir, are not a believer."

There it was again—the hitch to getting a miracle. All it took was belief. Of course, if the miracle didn't happen, then it had to be because the supplicant didn't have enough faith. It was sickening.

"Last night I had a vision," the man said, his voice pleading.

"God told me to come here. He said you could help me. I've changed, sir. I called my children this morning and told them I was sorry for the times I hit them. I sent a check for part of my back child support to my ex-wife. I shoulda done it long ago."

"God spoke to you?" Oren asked in a gentler voice.

"He did. I saw the man he wanted me to become, and I'm going to do it. Walking upright or hobbling, I'm going to do it."

Oren stepped down to the man. He put his Bible on the altar and clasped the man's head between his hands. It looked as if he were bending him backwards.

"Be he-aled!" Oren declared.

The man bucked like he'd been electrocuted. Two acolytes rushed forward and caught him as he fell to the ground. The crowd gasped as he twitched a time or two and lay still.

"Is he dead?" The question was whispered all around the tent. "Is he dead?"

"Rise up," Oren commanded the man. He lifted his own palm to heaven.

The man, with the assistance of the acolytes, stood. He seemed stunned and disoriented. He took a tentative step, his leg faltering. Then he took another step and another. He no longer hobbled. He walked upright, straight and sure.

"Praise God!" he shouted.

"Praise God!" Oren and the audience screamed together.

In front of me a well-dressed woman stood up, hands shaking in the air, and began speaking in tongues. She leaped on a pew and shimmied. Wild, unintelligible language rippled out of her mouth. As she spun on the bench, I could see her eyes rolled up in her head. Before I could move, she fell.

Two more acolytes were there to catch her.

"God is with us tonight!" Oren said.

"Amen!" the crowd replied.

"God is with us because we've come to seek him. He is there

for us, always. It's we who turn away from God. But now you're all here, back on the path of light. And God will shower you with his love. But it costs money to spread the word of God. It's expensive to travel and set up this tent and pay my helpers. So I'm going to ask you to help me continue spreading God's word. Just contribute what you can. My helpers will pass the collection plates while I take a moment to recover. God's work is mighty strenuous, my children." He slipped from the stage.

It was interesting that Oren was going to get his money up front. One little miracle and he was passing the hat. I took that as my cue to slip out the back of the tent. I had a little exploring to do. And I was curious about the man he'd healed.

The west side of the tent was where all the equipment trucks were parked. They'd make good cover. In the tent, Oren called for a series of hymns. I found an opening beside a sound truck and peeked inside, hoping for a little luck.

Several of Weaver's helpers, all dressed in dark suits and white shirts with red ties, were in a cluster talking. They looked like college boys from the fifties with their hair clipped above the ears and combed neatly back. Youth and passion gave them all good looks. I wondered what Oren truly taught them. I eased behind them.

Piles of what looked like amplifiers and other equipment were stacked behind the stage. I slipped around them and stopped when I heard voices.

"You were perfect, Bill," Oren said. He pulled something out of his pocket and gave it to the thin man who'd been healed.

"I have to say, my leg is feeling better." Bill jumped up and down.

"Now isn't the time for a medical report," Oren said tartly. "I think next time we should use the rodeo story. Folks like to think I'm helping a busted-up cowboy."

"Rodeo Bill, that's me." There was a laugh. "It makes all those Christian ladies feel real sorry for me. There *is* something about a cowboy."

"Get back out in the audience. Those people have paid to see a miracle. Show it to them. I'll heal Martha of her blindness after my break."

Bill wove through the equipment and disappeared. I wanted to follow him, but Oren was still fifteen feet away, standing by himself. Doreen berated me for my lack of faith, but look what faith wrought. It was just another tool to fleece people who did believe in a higher power with the ability to grant miracles.

There was the sound of something shifting. "What are you doing here?" Oren demanded.

I peeked around the equipment, but I could only catch a glimpse of a slender, dark woman. "I'm worried," the woman said.

"Hush your mouth right now. What have you got to be worried about?"

"I thought you could help her," the woman said. "But you didn't." Her voice broke. "God didn't help her."

"I tried." There was something in Oren's voice that made me risk another look. "I did the best I could."

The woman leaned into him, sobbing. He put his hand on her head and stroked her hair. I was fascinated by Oren's gentleness.

"I have to preach," he said. "They're on the next-to-last song before it's time for me to get back out there."

"I know." She straightened up and wiped at her eyes with her hands. "I'm sorry. I shouldn't have come here."

"No, you shouldn't have. Now, I'll show you how to get out of here without being seen."

They started away together but stopped when a big, well-built man in a black jacket and black T-shirt stepped in front of them.

"Samuel!" Oren actually sounded afraid.

"I think the little lady was leaving, right?" the big man said in a menacing tone.

"Yes, she was on her way out." Oren's voice softened as he turned back to her. "Go on home. This place is dangerous for you."

There was a lengthy silence and the sound of someone moving away. I was afraid to peep. Samuel was facing my hiding place.

"What is the meaning of this, Samuel?" Oren asked in a tone that tried to be haughty.

"That idiotic wife of yours has spouted off to a reporter about your little fling with that whore. I told you to break it off. Now here she is waving her fancy ass at a revival. I don't know what you're thinking with, but it isn't your brain."

"Myra can't prove a thing and you know it."

"She says she can." Samuel's tone was ominous. "I just got you out of a similar scrape. I'm not doing it again. If you can't keep your dick in your pants, maybe you'd better give up preaching."

Oren laughed. "If I don't preach, I don't make money. If I don't make money, you don't get paid. It's a simple equation, Samuel."

"You're getting careless, and I'm sick of picking up the pieces. Can you shut Myra up?"

"Maybe," Oren said. "She probably wants a new car or something."

"Well, give it to her. And pay off that whore and send her on her way."

"Thanks for the advice." Oren's voice was icy.

Samuel stormed toward me. I crouched among the equipment, expecting a huge hand to lift me up by my neck. The stack shuddered and several boxes toppled over. One struck my shoulder so solidly I almost cried out. Then there was silence. I waited at least ten minutes before I dared to move. When I did, the choir in the tent was belting out "Bringing in the Sheaves."

As much as I longed for a hot bath and a bed, I went back inside the tent to hunt for the miraculously healed Bill. I needed to talk to him. But he was in the middle of a large throng of excited people. There wasn't a sign of Oren Weaver's latest girlfriend.

TINKIE TAPPED ON my door, dragging me out of a sleep so sound I felt drugged. I'd made it back to the hotel room after the tent revival and crashed. Vague fragments of dreams clung to my brain, images of saints and sinners, angels and the damned.

The knocking at my door was persistent, and when I opened it, Tinkie stood in the hall with a tray containing coffee and hot croissants. She walked past me and put her burden on the small table near the window. She poured two cups of coffee and handed me one, black. "The Black and Orange Ball is less than sixty hours away, Sarah Booth. Are you getting excited?"

I had bigger fish to fry than dances. "Tinkie, I hope you aren't buying into this Doreen—"

"Sarah Booth, I love you, but we aren't going to discuss Doreen's beliefs. I know she upset you, and I'm sorry, but I won't choose between you. We're on a case. You were out last night. What did you find out?"

My first impulse was to lash out, but I couldn't do it. Tinkie had been too good a friend. "I found out some things about Oren Weaver. Let me just say that he's moved to the top of my suspect list."

Over coffee and a nibble of croissant I filled Tinkie in on what I'd witnessed, repeating Samuel's comment about cleaning up another of Oren's affairs.

"He's a charlatan. I wonder why Doreen thinks he's truly a healer?" Tinkie asked.

"Doreen may be a little naïve," I said as gently as possible.

"Maybe," Tinkie agreed, surprising me. "We need to get Doreen to demand that DNA test," she said. "She doesn't want to do it, but she's going to have to. I'll work on her."

If Tinkie had fallen under Doreen's spell, it certainly hadn't clouded her ability to see the case clearly.

"Can you make her understand?"

"I'll handle it. We'll get the order for the DNA by lunchtime. What are you doing today?"

"I'm meeting Cece for brunch."

"Sarah Booth, I want to see your dress for the Black and Orange Ball."

Spiritualism hadn't cured Tinkie of worrying about fashion.

"I don't have it here. I've got to pick it up."

"The ball is Saturday. That's two days. Where is the dress and when are you getting it?"

"The dress is in Zinnia," I said. "Mollie made it for me. And it's fabulous. I swear it. She's hemming it now."

"Mollie made it!" Tinkie squealed with pleasure. "You're going to look magnificent. I still have to go and get my mask." The prospect of shopping put a glow in Tinkie's eyes.

"Mollie's making mine," I said a little smugly.

"Sometimes, Sarah Booth, you do take the cake." She leaned over and kissed my cheek. "Would you mind if I joined you and Cece for brunch?"

"I'd love it."

COURT OF TWO Sisters was the place Cece had chosen. I went down the narrow hallway and was led to a seat in the courtyard. It was a beautiful place, if touristy. I ordered a Bloody Mary as I waited for Tinkie and Cece to join me.

Someone slipped warm hands over my eyes, and I heard Cece's voice at my ear. "Surprise, dahling."

"Take your paws off my face," I said a little grumpily, "you're smearing my mascara."

"Sarah Booth."

The voice was low and male and sexy. I put my hands up and felt the hands on my face. They were large hands, masculine hands. I whirled around and looked up to see Hamilton Garrett V smiling down at me.

"Hamilton?" I felt as if I'd fallen into a dream. He was the handsomest man I'd ever seen. With his dark hair and green eyes, he was better than a movie star. I felt a blush color my face as I remembered, in vivid detail, the hours of lovemaking we'd shared.

"You're blushing," he whispered in my ear. His lips brushed my cheek and sent shivers down me. "What are you thinking about?"

"Just remember, Sarah Booth, he's my date," Cece said, settling down at the table and signaling a waiter. "Sit down, Hamilton, every woman in this place is staring at you."

And they were. Especially me. I couldn't take my eyes off him. He'd been the subject of my first case, and for several weeks I'd believed he was a mother-killer. Of course, that hadn't kept me from falling into the sack with him. And my only regret had been that he'd returned to his home in Europe rather than stay in Zinnia and continue sinning with me.

"Did they deliver the flowers?" he asked, unfolding my napkin and putting it in my lap.

"The flowers! You sent them! To me! I thought they'd been delivered to the wrong room."

"Sarah Booth," Cece hissed, "you make it sound like you never get flowers. I've just been telling Hamilton how every single man in Zinnia has been courting you." I felt the pointed toe of her stylish boot bite into my shin.

"That's right. I get flowers all the time." I'd rather lie than let Cece kick me to death. "What are you doing in the States?" Turning the conversation to Hamilton was my only defense.

"I came to see you," he said. "I realized that I'd never drag you out of the cotton fields to visit me, so I came home."

"For how long?" My heart was beating fast.

"A week."

I wanted to ask, "And then?" but I didn't. Sometimes it's best not to know the future.

"I want to spend as much time with you as your case allows," he said, his gaze holding mine. "I'll take every spare moment you have."

"Hamilton is my date for the ball, but he can dance with you some," Cece said. She put in an order for two more Bloody Marys. "Make that three," I said. "Tinkie's—"

"Tinkie!" Hamilton said, rising. "How good to see you."

She sailed across the room and took a seat at the table. When she looked at me, her eyes were bright with happiness. "Sometimes God sends good things, Sarah Booth. You should never despair."

I was about to answer her when my cell phone rang. Everyone at the table was watching me as I answered it.

Coleman's voice was clear. "Sarah Booth, I've rounded up Coot and I think he'll talk to you. There's something you should hear. He thinks Lillith was murdered." There was a pause as he waited for me to respond. "Sarah Booth, when are you coming home?"

18

"TOMORROW MORNING," I SAID TO COLEMAN ON THE PHONE, NEVER breaking eye contact with Hamilton. I fought to keep my face blank.

"I'll be glad to see you," Coleman answered. "Call me when you get in."

He hung up and I held the cell phone to my ear another few seconds. I'd been reduced from delighted to conflicted. In Hamilton's absence, Coleman had entered my heart. But he was a married man. Now Hamilton was back, at least for a week. I wasn't certain what I felt.

"Sarah Booth, are you okay?" Tinkie was staring at me.

"I'm fine. Coleman got me an appointment with Coot. He believes Lillith Lucas was murdered."

"Murdered?" Cece and Hamilton echoed. I'd successfully thrown the two of them off the scent of my fluctuating heart, but

Tinkie wasn't so easily diverted. She stared at me with cool speculation.

"When's the appointment?" she asked.

"Tomorrow."

"Is Coleman going with you to talk to Coot?" She was as persistent as Sweetie Pie after a roast.

"I'll talk to him tomorrow when I go home," I said.

"I just remembered, I left my earrings at home. Since I have to go get them, I'll talk to Coot and save you a trip to Zinnia," Tinkie said quickly. "I'll pick up your dress, too. Tomorrow is Friday. Just one day to go before the ball."

I didn't want to argue. In fact, I didn't want to think about tomorrow. I had enough trouble with today. My fantasy, Hamilton, was sitting across the table from me, trying to figure out the currents that passed among the women.

"What do you have going now?" Hamilton asked me.

I looked at Tinkie and she nodded. "Relax awhile, Sarah Booth. Oscar won't be here until six. I'll check in with Doreen and then follow up on a few leads."

They were pushing me into Hamilton's arms, and though my womb said yes, yes, yes, my heart was a bit more reluctant. Hamilton had been a fantasy for so long, I didn't know if I wanted him to become real. There was too much danger of serious disappointment.

Instead of answering Hamilton's question, I diverted their attention by filling them in on everything I'd discovered at J.J. and Janey Crenshaw's home. I hadn't really gone into the details in front of Doreen.

"Sounds a little punitive," Tinkie said. "I don't know why some people want a religion that's founded on suffering."

"Tinkie, could you call the Crenshaws and check on Adam's widow, Kiley? Find out if there's an heir."

"Will do," Tinkie said. "On the condition that you and Hamilton enjoy the day. It's gorgeous. Maybe Doreen will read tarot cards for you. She's in the Square until six."

"Perfect," Hamilton said, though I wasn't as eager. I knew my past and I didn't want a glimpse of the future. I had too much potential for a major screwup.

"I have to go buy shoes," Cece said, rising. "I don't have a thing to wear to the ball."

She only had a thousand pairs.

"I'm off, too," Tinkie piped up.

They were gone before I could protest. I'd been set up. But when I looked across the table at Hamilton, I couldn't say I was upset about it. For the past year I'd trained myself not to think about him. He was the man who was out of reach—across the Atlantic Ocean. He'd been the first man in my life in a long time when I'd moved home. I'd never expected to see him again.

"Thanks for the flowers," I said, filling the silence, which was loaded with little pings of sexual desire. "They're lovely, and only a little extreme."

"What *is* your favorite flower?" he asked. While his lips spoke those words, his eyes asked a much different question.

"It's hard to say." My voice, at least, was composed. "Roses, lilies, gladiolus, I love them all. But I guess my favorite flower is the black-eyed Susan."

"The wildflowers that grow along the ditches?"

I smiled. "That's the one."

"No hothouse orchid for you, Sarah Booth."

"Too stifling." We didn't need a hothouse; we were creating global warming right where we sat. People at the tables around us were staring and whispering. And we hadn't even held hands.

When the waitress stopped by, he ordered another round of drinks. "I've thought about you so often, but you're even lovelier than I remembered."

"Thank you, Hamilton." I lowered my gaze, unable to look at

him for long. I still thought he might vanish or evaporate, as fantasies were wont to do. "How's Paris?"

"Beautiful. My work there is absorbing."

"What, exactly, is your work?" I knew he was in business, but I had no specifics except that it involved money.

"I find funding for an organization that searches for missing people."

"Runaways?"

"Political refugees."

"In war zones?" I didn't bother to hide my surprise. I was astounded. I'd always assumed he was a banker or a broker or something in a towering office building with lots of glass.

"Sometimes." A smile touched the corners of his mouth. "Don't make me into a glamorous adventurer. I'm the moneyman. I pull the funds together, nothing more."

"Does your organization ever hunt wealthy people?"

"Sometimes. When they've been taken by a political faction. Italy was a hot spot for that at one time. Now it's Central America. And to be honest, it's most often people so poor they don't have money for food."

My mother had joined the Peace Corps. She was a ruthless do-gooder who believed in action, agitation, and standing up for the underdog.

"Why are you smiling?" His finger teased the corner of my mouth. His touch thrilled me, but I had begun to see that Hamilton was a lot more than a fantasy.

"My mother would have liked you."

"My father talked about her on a regular basis. He admired her. He said she was a woman who spoke her mind with passion and intelligence." He gathered my hand and held it between his warm ones. "I've missed you. In fact, there were days when I thought I'd have to get on a plane and come home."

"Someone told me that there are telephones in Paris." I said it with wide-eyed innocence.

He laughed. "A call would only have made it worse. My life is very busy. I work long hours, sometimes without rest. When I would go home at night, exhausted, I would find myself lying awake in bed, thinking about you. If I'd heard your voice, it would have been much, much worse."

"Not for me." I squeezed his hand. "Why didn't you come home?"

He sighed. "My work is consuming. There's so much to be done, and money sources are drying up in this bad economy. If I can't find the funding, people die."

One didn't just hop on a plane for a lark and leave a prisoner to be tortured and killed. Damn. It would have been so much easier if Hamilton had been the banker I'd imagined. Oscar didn't have such conflicts of interest.

"But you're here now." Much to my conflicted delight.

"I'm working on a deal. There are a number of extremely wealthy exiled El Salvadoran families here. I came to personally tap into their pockets. I'm harder to resist in person."

That I had no doubt of.

"But I wanted to see you. I would have driven to Zinnia had you not been here for the ball."

"You called Cece instead of me. Why?"

"I wanted to see if you'd married or taken some strange vow of celibacy." He laughed. "Really, I didn't want to interfere if you had a relationship going."

"And Cece said . . . ?" She'd obviously kept her mouth shut about Coleman.

"That you were thriving in your business and head over heels in suitors, none of them serious. Would you care for another drink? Something to eat?" he asked.

"No, I'm not hungry." My stomach was so knotted with anticipation and shock that I couldn't have swallowed a peanut.

"Shall we go?"

"Where?" I asked.

"Wherever you'd like." He stepped around the table and smoothly pulled my chair out. "Just be warned, Sarah Booth, that I've come to take you back to Paris with me. I can't stay here, but I can't leave you. My intentions are on the table."

The flame of desire that had been tamped down by our serious conversation burst back to life.

We walked demurely out of the restaurant and into the street. Hamilton hailed a taxi and we both got in it as if we were going to church, but the cabbie eyed us in the rearview mirror and grinned. "Where to?"

I started to say the Monteleone, but Hamilton gave another address. It sounded closer, which was fine with me. We both managed the cab ride by staring straight ahead of us. I had no idea where we were when the cab stopped and we got out.

In a dream, I allowed Hamilton to escort me inside. I vaguely noticed the brass doorplates, the echo of our footsteps on the marble floor. Hamilton keyed the elevator, and we stepped inside, the heavy brass doors swishing shut.

I turned to him, and we looked into each other's eyes. There were questions I wanted to ask him, things I needed to tell him. But the overpowering desire to feel his arms around me was too strong to be stopped by mere words.

We stepped toward each other and I lifted my lips for his kiss. After that, it was only fire and electricity. I was half undressed by the time the elevator stopped on the fifth floor. I noticed nothing of the room that we stepped into, saw none of the elegantly appointed furnishings.

We finished undressing as we slowly made our way, pausing for long, deep kisses, to the bedroom. I did notice the huge brass bed covered with a tapestry spread. And then I was on the bed, and Hamilton was over me, kissing me, teasing me with his fingertips and tongue, transporting me away from everything except the power and the magic of his touch.

IT WASN'T UNTIL that afternoon that I came to realize we weren't in a hotel but in a private residence. It was a magnificent place, all dark mahogany, earth-toned colors, and polished brass. A loan from one of Hamilton's business associates, he said.

Around three, Hamilton called someone to deliver food. We were sated on sex but ravenous for food. We ate gumbo in Styrofoam containers and drank a light, crisp white wine that Hamilton pulled from the refrigerator and uncorked.

When he looked at me, I found nothing to say. I was back in eighth grade, terminally shy.

"Sarah Booth," he said, pulling the sheet up to keep the chill off my chest, "I've missed you. Not a day has gone by that I haven't thought of you."

I wanted to ask him if he'd been with other women, but I didn't want to answer the question in the reverse.

He fed me and talked about his life in Paris. As I listened, I couldn't stop the rush of my heartbeat whenever he sounded as if he might want to come home to Mississippi. And when he spoke as if he'd stay in Paris, I wondered if I could ever leave Dahlia House and all that I loved. I didn't know the answer to that.

Hamilton had been set aside in my mind. Never forgotten. Just moved to that place where other unreachable dreams were kept.

"You look far away," he whispered, a hint of sadness in his own face.

"No, I was just thinking about my life and how it twists and turns." I smiled to hide the shadow of my thoughts.

"Did you know that in France, they've invented a totally new way of making love?" His eyes were wicked, and his smile held the promise of fun.

"Right," I said, trying hard not to wonder who he'd learned his French tricks from.

"It's true. Would you like to try it?"

I wasn't certain I'd be able to walk. I couldn't believe he was recharged. "Are you sure?" I asked.

"Close your eyes," he said. "That's it, just lay perfectly still and keep your eyes closed."

I felt the sheet being slowly pulled down my body. Goose bumps, partly from the temperature of the room but mostly from anticipation, danced over my body. I felt something strange drop into my navel. Then another on my stomach, my torso, my chest. I started to peek, but Hamilton put a hand on my eyes.

"You can't cheat," he said, and he was about to laugh.

"What are you doing?"

"Do you like dark chocolate?" he asked.

"You know I do."

"And espresso?"

"Coffee in any form is a good thing."

"Then you'll appreciate how badly I want this. It's a chocolate-covered coffee bean. They're all over your body, and I intend to eat every one of them." His lips hovered teasingly over my navel, his tongue seeking what had been dropped there. I squealed with delight.

"The game begins," he said, grasping my wrists as he bent his head to find another treat.

AN HOUR LATER, we were showered, dressed, and walking in the Square. I hadn't pointed Doreen out, but Hamilton had noticed her. In fact, he was almost drawn to her. When we were catty-cornered from her, I touched his hand.

"That's Doreen," I said.

"My God, she's beautiful." His gaze never left her.

"Yes, she is." I started toward her and Hamilton followed. She was reading cards for a young woman and I didn't want to interrupt, but she caught sight of me, her gaze traveling to Hamilton and then back to me. She smiled.

I motioned that we'd hang around until she finished, and she resumed her reading. The young woman didn't look happy. In a few minutes she picked up her purse and left in a huff.

"Anything wrong?" I asked, watching the girl's back disappear in the crowd.

"People ask for the truth, and when they get it, they don't like it. That young woman needs to focus on her children, not her social life." She shrugged. "She has two children and not a single question was about them."

Doreen was beautiful, but she was also tired. I could see it under her eyes and in the paleness of her lips.

"Let me read for you," she said to Hamilton, after I'd introduced them.

I started to speak against it, but Hamilton wouldn't have heeded me. He was delighted. He took the seat in front of her and shuffled the tarot deck, his large hands easily handling the oversized cards.

"Do you have a question?" Doreen asked.

Hamilton considered. "Will I be alone much longer?"

"Cut the deck," Doreen told him.

Hamilton did that, and Doreen began to lay out the pattern.

"The pattern is the Celtic cross," she said, putting down more cards.

I studied the images. There was no Death or Hangman or Tower or Devil. It didn't look too bad.

Doreen studied the pattern, and then she looked at Hamilton. The saddest smile touched her face. "The first card"—she touched a Knight of Wands—"is you, Hamilton. You're an adventurer, a man of action and will. Therein lies your strength and your weakness."

Strengths I could deal with. Weaknesses were dangerous. To the people to whom they belonged, and others.

She studied the cards more, her hands hovering over them one by one. "You yearn for permanence." She smiled. "For the land and the vista of childhood, but adventure beckons you to other places. I see a house...no, an apartment, but it's rocking gently. It's a boat!"

"I live on a boat," Hamilton said. He was fascinated. "How did you know?"

"The present is easy," Doreen said.

Easy enough for Tinkie to have mentioned it, since it was obvious she was in on the big surprise of Hamilton's visit.

Doreen's eyes clouded, but she was looking at Hamilton, not the cards. "There's trouble in your fourth chakra. Or there will be." Her face was solemn. "News will come from a distance. Exciting news. You'll celebrate and then there will be sorrow."

My face must have reflected my reaction to her words. She reached out and touched my hand. "All of life is a balance, Sarah Booth. Celebration and grief, love and loss. It's the cycle of life."

"My experience has been more grief than celebration," I said.

She laughed. "I don't believe that. I look at you and I see joy."

"Thank you," Hamilton said, reaching into his pocket for his billfold.

"No charge," Doreen said. She gathered up her cards.

"One last question," I said. "Will Hamilton find true love?" I was unable to meet the amused glance he cast at me.

"Yes," Doreen said. "He will."

19

As much as I wanted to be with Hamilton, I needed to talk with Doreen. Tinkie was heavy on my mind, but I didn't want to discuss her personal business in front of Hamilton. When I told him I needed to work, he assured me that he had phone calls to return. He would wait for me at his place. I was invited to his private spend-the-night party.

Doreen and I walked through the falling dusk to the Center. Though we sauntered side by side, Doreen was far away. Several people smiled and spoke to her, but she didn't notice them.

When we got to the Center, I put a hand on her shoulder. I wasn't certain if we would have any privacy inside.

"I spoke with the sheriff of Sunflower County today. Doreen, this is hard." I took a breath. "Your mother was involved with a county police officer for several years. His name is Coot Henderson. I don't know how far into the past you want to go, but Coot thinks your mother may have been murdered."

Doreen seemed to look beyond me. I thought at first she hadn't understood what I'd said.

"Was my mother so hated that someone would kill her?" she finally asked.

"I wouldn't have thought so." I'd also asked myself who might have killed Lillith. And more to the point—why?

"Will you talk to this man for me?" she asked.

"Of course. Coleman's made an appointment. In fact, Tinkie's going to go to Zinnia tomorrow—"

"No, I'd like you to do it."

"Tinkie is perfectly capable of—"

"I don't doubt her skill. Tinkie doesn't need to be in Zinnia right now. She's focusing on something very important."

"The cancer," I said, wanting Doreen to know that Tinkie had trusted me with the knowledge of her illness. "And her *doctor* is in Zinnia."

"She needs to be here."

"She's supposed to have a biopsy, and I certainly hope you aren't discouraging her from that."

"The biopsy is November fifth," Doreen said, unruffled by my tone. "Until that time, Tinkie needs to be here."

"With her husband," I said forcefully.

"I'm eager to meet Oscar."

There seemed no way I could offend Doreen. We entered the Center and went to her office. Michael was there, his face lighting up when he saw Doreen.

"Don't forget your booking at the studio tomorrow," he said.

"Cancel it," Doreen said.

"What?" The joy evaporated from Michael's face. "We've waited four months for that booking. If you cancel, we won't be able to get that studio until after the first of the year."

"Cancel it."

"Doreen, this is the tape where you discuss the role of archetypes in illness. Your followers have been waiting for months already."

For a moment, Doreen looked at Michael. In three long strides she was beside him. She put her hands on either side of his face. "Michael, it doesn't matter." Her voice was very soft.

"It does matter, Doreen," he said. The edge was gone from his voice, but it was still strong. "You have commitments. You've made promises. I've spent the last four weeks setting this up. The CDs and tapes are due to ship out just before Christmas."

"And what will happen if the tapes are never made?"

"A lot of people will be disappointed. And we'll have to pay for the studio time anyway. That's a lot of money."

"Money isn't a consideration here, Michael."

"Of course it's not. Money doesn't matter to you because you never have to dirty your hands with it. I'm the one who takes care of all the financial problems. I'm the one who ultimately pays the bills for your decisions."

Michael's face was pale, his eyes angry.

"Michael, you're wonderful at your job. But it is my decision to make."

I saw the muscle in his jaw clench and then relax. He took a breath. "Yes, Doreen. It is your decision. But as your financial advisor, I have to tell you when I think you're making a mistake."

"You've told me," she said softly. "You've done your job. More than your job. As always."

"What about the people who're waiting for this tape?" he asked.

"I help all that I can. I refuse to accept that burden."

"I'm the one who initiated the campaign for these tapes. I'm the one who set the Christmas release date. And I'll look like a fool," Michael said bitterly.

"Not to me." She kissed his forehead. "Never to me."

Michael looked down at his desk. "You're the boss."

I couldn't read anything into his tone, but Doreen straightened up and nodded at me. "I'm going to Zinnia with you."

"Zinnia?" Michael asked. "Why?"

"Sarah Booth has discovered that my mother may have been murdered."

"Is that right?" Michael looked at me, his dark eyes troubled. "I'm so sorry, Doreen. I didn't realize why you were canceling the studio."

"Reschedule for after the first, and apologize for me."

"I'll go with you to Zinnia," Michael said. "If there's murder involved, you shouldn't be alone."

"I'll be with Sarah Booth," Doreen said with the hint of a smile. "We'll be fine."

"But what if the murderer is still around?"

"I doubt he's hanging around the scene of the crime now," Doreen said. "My mother's been dead a long time."

"Sheriff Peters will be with us," I said. "We'll be perfectly safe." We didn't need an entourage if we were going to talk about a potential murder.

"There's a small problem," Michael said, one corner of his handsome mouth turned down. "Doreen isn't allowed to leave the jurisdiction."

"I'll talk with LeMont," I volunteered. "Maybe he'll be able to get her permission to make a day trip."

THE BLACK KETTLE was a casual bar with a big business. The place was packed, and I stood on tiptoe trying to catch a glimpse of LeMont. I finally located him at the bar, where he was holding a stool for me by draping his leg over it.

His dark suit was rumpled and he finished one beer and ordered another. Judging from his posture, he was either tired or had just finished a discouraging day.

"Ms. Delaney," he said as he shifted his leg and offered me the stool. "What can I do for you?" There was a snap in his voice.

"Thank you for meeting me," I said. It would be best to get right to the point. "Doreen wants to go with me to Zinnia tomorrow. There's some indication that her mother may have been murdered. I'm going to talk to a possible witness to the murder." I was stretching things a bit.

"Her mother was murdered?"

"Possibly," I said, wondering at his sudden interest.

"And you think it would be a good idea to have Doreen with you when you talk to this witness?"

Put in that frame, I could see it wasn't such a good idea. "She wants to go."

He took a long swallow of his beer. "If that's what you want, I'll talk with the judge."

Now I was curious. Detective LeMont wasn't in the habit of tossing favors out. He'd obviously discovered something that worked in Doreen's favor. "Why are you doing this?"

He shrugged. "I don't view Ms. Mallory as a flight risk. But what I think doesn't matter. It's up to the judge and he's going to say no."

I wasn't buying that flip answer. I remembered the baby bottle. "What have you found out? Whose fingerprints are on the baby bottle?"

LeMont gave me a long, calculating look. "Doreen's and the maid's, as you'd expect. And Reverend Oren Weaver's. We had his prints on file from when his house was burgled a few years back." He paused, studying my reaction. And what a reaction it was. My mouth opened wide in the mouth-breather moment of shock that my Aunt LouLane would have slapped off my face.

"Oren Weaver? Why would he touch that bottle?"

"I was hoping you could tell me. What would the mighty tel-evangelist be doing holding a baby bottle for Rebekah Mallory?"

I shut my mouth and put a slightly more professional look on my face. "What does your investigation show?"

He grinned. "I'm just getting started. Now, I'll talk to the judge, if you'll tell me exactly what you know about the preacher man."

I was caught on the horns of a dilemma. I'd promised Doreen I wouldn't reveal her connection to Weaver, or the other men, un-less I had to. LeMont was sniffing on the trail, but he hadn't picked up the scent of possible paternity yet. By not telling him, though, I was thwarting an ally in proving Doreen's innocence. And Doreen had possibly lied to me. She'd assured me that none of the potential fathers had ever seen Rebekah.

"Sarah Booth, what's going on in that head of yours?" LeMont's eyes were flat and I had the sense that he needed to move or drown.

But my word had been given. "I can't help you," I said.

He rose from his stool, finished his beer, and smiled. "I got a call from that sheriff of yours. He's mighty fond of you."

And LeMont was pretty damn good at throwing curves. "What did Coleman say?"

"It wasn't so much what he said as how he said it." He arched his eyebrows. "None of my business, though. I got my hands full in New Orleans."

I leaned against the bar. "What about the judge?"

"You won't help me, but you still expect me to help you?" He furrowed his brow. "Okay. I'll talk to the judge because I know it won't do a bit of good. And you're gonna owe me." He pushed his glass back. "I'll find out how Weaver's involved in this any-way."

He walked out of the bar, never once turning around to look back at me. I ordered a vodka martini, dirty, and sat at the bar until it was gone. With just a hint of a buzz, I made my way to Hamilton's apartment and the comfort of his arms.

As the sun edged over the horizon, I drove across Lake Pontchartrain, my body sated and my thoughts on Arnold LeMont. True to his word, LeMont did call the judge. True to LeMont's prediction, the judge refused to let Doreen leave New Orleans. On this Friday morning, I was traveling alone, and glad for the solitude.

I'd spent the night in the arms of a fantasy. The movie theater of my mind had been given a whole new reel of images to play again and again. The last one was of Hamilton sleeping, a dark stubble on his handsome face, his hair rumpled on the pillow, and a smile on his lips.

Now I was heading back to Zinnia, back to my normal life. Or was it normal? In the past few days I'd slipped my mooring. I was drifting. Life in New Orleans bore no resemblance to life at Dahlia House. I was caught in a time warp, where memory was more real than anything else. But memory fades.

As I was heading back to Mississippi, the last few hours in Hamilton's bed seemed more like a dream than reality. Yet when I was spooned against Hamilton, it had felt so real, so perfect. I'd run my fingertips across the light sprinkling of dark hair on his arms, felt his fingers curl around mine, known the sensual delight of his leg pressed firmly against my own, sunk into solace with the rhythm of his breathing.

Now the highway stretched in front of me, a washed-out gray in a blur of pine trees and fallow fields. And this was my reality. I was hurtling through time and space at eighty miles an hour as the sun rose to my left, jewels of dew glittering all around me.

Behind me was Hamilton. In front of me was my home. And Coleman.

I drove in a turmoil of emotions, stopping twice for coffee and a bathroom. When I finally turned down the drive, Dahlia House awaited me through an alley of leafless sycamore trees.

Sweetie Pie greeted me with a chorus of barks, her tail whipping my legs as she whirled around me. In the back pasture, Reveler whinnied a welcome.

I rushed into the house.

"Hold up your hands," Jitty said in a gunslinger voice.

"Jitty?" She stood in the doorway of the parlor, her elegance as cold as her attitude.

"Hold them up. Let me see."

I slowly held up my hands, palms out. "What's wrong with you?"

"What's wrong with *you* is the better question." She stepped closer and I caught a fragrance that reminded me of my mother's mother, Grandma Baker.

"Evening in Paris?" It was a light, talcumy odor.

"Which would be Evening in a New Orleans Hotel Bed without Benefit of a Ring if you were wearing it."

It was instantly clear what was eating at Jitty. "I thought you'd be happy that Hamilton was back in the States."

"For how long? Long enough to put a ring on that finger and make you an honest woman?"

I took a deep breath. "I am an honest woman, Jitty."

"Liar."

She spoke with such certainty that I felt my temper rise. "I am not a liar."

"You the worse kind of liar. You lie to yourself. You go on about how you're satisfied with a few nights in Hamilton's arms. That ain't the truth. You want him here, in Zinnia. Full-time."

"I'm not so certain about that." Truth be told, I wasn't certain about anything. And Jitty was giving me a pounding headache.

"A full-time husband might interfere with your daydreams about that sheriff leavin' his wife and takin' up with you."

"I've never asked Coleman to leave his wife. Never."

"You haven't asked, but that don't mean you haven't thought about it."

I wasn't going to lie. I had thought about Coleman leaving Connie. He didn't have a real marriage. She'd tricked him back to her with the most low-down trick in the book. "I've never encouraged him to break his wedding vows. And he won't."

"No, he won't. And that leaves you standin' on the outside lookin' in. You know, eighty years ago, a woman didn't have the right to pop in and out of bed with men. Back then, she'da been run out of town on a rail. It wasn't fair, because men could do as they pleased and never suffer a bad reputation. But this today ain't good. A man won't buy the cow, Sarah Booth, when he's gettin' the milk free."

Jitty shimmered, as if a heat wave had rippled through her.

"Don't you dare disappear," I hissed. But it did no good. She was gone and I was left alone with her bitter words of wisdom.

20

I MET COLEMAN AT THE CROSSROADS BESIDE PLAYIN' THE BONES, A fine blues club run by Ida Mae Keys and her son Emanuel. The club looked great. There were new shells in the parking lot and a marquee announcing the latest blues act.

There was also a long, tall lawman. To my surprise, Coleman was in his pickup, and he wore jeans and a flannel shirt. The blue of the plaid colored his eyes a deeper shade. I watched him walk toward me with pleasure and sadness. Two men could not be more different than Coleman and Hamilton. Even if I had the chance to choose, could I?

"You look pensive," Coleman noted, getting into the passenger seat of the convertible. The top was down and the October sun flooded the interior of the car with golden warmth.

"Tired, maybe." Or was it guilt I was oozing? I'd been in bed with Hamilton only six hours before. Coleman wasn't a fool. "How do we get to Coot's?"

"Turn left here and head back toward Blue Eve. He's on Cotton Gin Road."

I drove with my eyes on the road ahead. Coleman watched me, drawing his own conclusions, and keeping them to himself.

Coot's house was a surprise. The man was an alcoholic. I'd expected a trailer with a mountain of beer cans in the backyard. Instead, the log cabin was neat and clean.

"Coot built it himself," Coleman said. "He cut the trees over by Oxford, had them milled, hauled them back here, and put it together himself."

"He must not drink as much as people say." I'd known a few alcoholics, among them family members. It was a road littered with unrealized dreams, broken promises, and half-truths. The cabin spoke of another kind of man.

Coot didn't wait for us to knock. He came out the front door and walked toward us. To my surprise, he was smiling. He was a man in his sixties, but he looked younger. Lean and freshly shaved, he smelled of Old Spice.

"I've been waiting for you," he said. "Ever since you called, Coleman, I've been waiting. I haven't had a drink in two days." When he held out his hand to shake mine, I saw the tremors.

We went inside and Coot served us strong coffee in hand-fired mugs. We settled around his small kitchen table.

"Tell me about Lillith's daughter," Coot said. "I hear she's beautiful."

"She is," I said. "Strikingly beautiful. And in a world of trouble."

"I know," he said. "I want to help her."

I wondered if he'd done the arithmetic, too, and figured out that Doreen might be his daughter.

"You never knew Doreen?" Coleman asked.

"Lillith was peculiar." Coot sipped his coffee. "She was private in a way that I see now was unbalanced. At the time, it was just convenient. I suspected she was pregnant, but she said she was going to see her mama for a few months. She was gone seven. When she came back there wasn't a sign of a baby. She left like that sometimes. Could be gone a week or several months. I didn't think much about it at the time. You know, I just didn't let it register. Lillith and I were together for the good times."

"Where did her mother live?" I asked.

"Natchez. I regret now I wasn't more attentive. If Doreen is my child, I want to try and make it up to her. I would have married Lillith. Ever since I heard about Doreen, I can't help but think about what life might have been like. We could have made a family."

Coot obviously wasn't aware that there had been three children. I didn't see where it was necessary to pour salt into his wound.

"Tell us about the night Lillith died," Coleman suggested.

"Well, it was a cold night. Musta been December or somewhere along there." He lowered his gaze. "My mind slips sometimes. I forget things. It makes me ashamed."

"It's okay, Coot," Coleman said. "We all forget. This happened a long time ago."

Coot looked up, his dark green eyes so intense that I was mesmerized. "It was a long time ago, but I dream it every night. I smell the smoke and I wake up choking. I see the flames between me and the bedroom, and I see Lillith standing in them, frozen, unable to move, the flames licking up to her waist. I see myself running out the front door. Running outside and saving myself. Saving myself and leaving her."

He got up and went to a cabinet to get a bottle of Wild Turkey. "I didn't want to be drunk when you got here, but I've got to have a shot right now."

"It's okay," Coleman said. "This isn't an interrogation, Coot. You're helping us." He paused. "And maybe helping yourself. There was nothing you could have done to save Lillith. The coroner said she died of smoke inhalation before the flames got to her."

"I saw her. She was standing in the flames."

Coleman got up and got two more glasses. He poured both of us a shot. "All these years you've been carrying a burden of guilt that wasn't necessary. Your mind played a trick on you. Lillith was dead." He reached into his back pocket and pulled out a coroner's report. "I made this copy for you."

Coot took it and read it slowly. "She was really dead? I just imagined I saw her?"

"She was really dead."

"I shoulda come forward and said I was there with her. But I couldn't. Folks didn't know Lillith like I did. They thought she was crazy and wild, consumed with that religion of hers. She was that, but she was kind and loving. Sometimes we'd go to the river for a picnic and I'd lie in the grass with my head in her lap. She'd stroke my hair and I'd forget everything that troubled me. She was a wonderful woman when she wasn't raving."

The woman he revealed fascinated me. I'd known Lillith only as a lunatic.

"Why was she the way she was?" That was an answer I might be able to take to Doreen.

"I can't say. She'd be taken in spells. They'd come on her and she'd say she had to preach. She said God was telling her to spread the Word."

"She didn't just preach. She terrorized us about sex. And yet she was sleeping with you." I needed to understand the paradox of her personality.

"When she got on one of her holy spells, she'd run me out, chasing me with pans of hot water or knives. She'd tell me I was

Beelzebub, come to tempt her. She'd say that I had taught her to like wallowing in wickedness and that we'd both burn in the fires of hell. Then she'd grab that Bible and go to town to preach."

"How could you endure that?" I asked.

"Most of the time she was a woman who enjoyed loving." He shook his head. "Heck, she could turn me inside out. Lillith didn't go no half-measures. She could wring a man out. Once I had a taste of her, I couldn't quit."

"But she believed it was wrong. Sinful."

He shrugged a shoulder. "We'd go along for weeks, then she'd have one of her holy fits. She'd run me off, but in a few days, she'd drive up to my house with homemade biscuits and sausage. She'd be back to normal, hungry for loving."

I wanted to ask him why he never got her psychiatric help, but I remembered the era when all this took place. People didn't pop into their therapist's office on their lunch hours. Mental illness was feared worse than venereal disease.

"Tell us everything that happened the night of the fire," Coleman said, pulling us back on track.

"Lillith and I had a fight. So I was sleeping on the sofa."

"What did you fight about?" I asked.

"We were both getting old. We'd been lovers for nearly thirty years. She wasn't troubled by her spells as much as she was by some bad dreams. I was still working and I wanted to marry, make sure she had insurance, get her some medical attention, that kind of thing. She didn't want to marry. She said she couldn't sanction a relationship that was born in sin. She said God would frown on two sinners asking for his blessing.

"I got in a huff and slept on the sofa. Like I said, it was a cold night. I stoked up the fireplace real good, put some big logs on, and then I went to sleep. The next thing I knew, the house was on fire."

"You don't recall hearing anything unusual?" Coleman asked.

Coot's brow furrowed. "Maybe, now that you mention it. Lillith was talking to herself. That wasn't normal. If she got a spell, she went straight to Main Street, no matter the time of day or night. She didn't waste time talking to herself."

"What did she say?" I asked, praying he'd remember.

"Spawn of Satan," Coot said without hesitation. "That's all I remember. I just went back to sleep. We'd both been drinking quite a bit."

"Coot, do you think Lillith could have been talking to someone else?" Coleman asked.

"I don't know. Maybe." I could see the thought troubled him.

"Was there anyone who hated Lillith?"

"She aggravated a lot of people, but I can't think of anyone who would hurt her. If she wasn't in one of her spells, she kept to herself. Lillith never did anyone a lick of harm."

"Who would she call a spawn of Satan?" I asked.

He shrugged. "Someone she thought of as a sinner, I guess. I never heard her say that before." He was frowning when he spoke again. "One of the volunteer firemen found a burned can. Like a gasoline can. They assumed it was used for the lawn mower. But I've been thinking on it. Lillith didn't have a lawn mower. I brought mine over to use to cut her grass. And I brought my own gas can, too. Someone else brought that gas can to her house."

COLEMAN AND I rode for a while in silence. We were both digesting Coot's story. Coleman had left a card with the number of a substance abuse counselor on Coot's table. Only time would tell if he would use it.

"What do you think?" I asked Coleman.

"I wish I could examine the fire scene."

"If we're exchanging wishes, I wish I could see into the future." But the minute the words were out of my mouth, I knew they weren't true. Doreen was right about one thing she'd said—the present was the place to be. The past and the future held only turmoil.

"Coot was a good deputy when he was on the force. His liaison with Lillith cost him a lot. Folks thought the worst of him because he never married, never seemed to care for anyone. Yet he stuck by Lillith until she died."

Coleman stared out at a particularly bleak cotton field that had been mauled by a combine. Once upon a time, we would have heard the voices of men and women singing in the rows. Now there was only the drone of machinery.

"Something else was strange," I said as I pulled into the parking lot of Playin' the Bones, where Coleman had left his truck. "Doreen's brother is dead. He drowned."

"There's a lot of death around that woman," Coleman said. "I'll check more on that fire. It does sound suspicious. The coroner's report showed she died of smoke inhalation. It could have been an accident or she could have been knocked unconscious before someone started the fire. That would make it murder." He leaned over and brushed his lips on my cheek. "You be careful, Sarah Booth."

He got out of the car and walked to his truck. I felt a loss so keen that I wanted to stop him. But I didn't. He was doing the right thing.

I couldn't face going home to Jitty's scrutiny. I knew there was something wrong with me, and I knew she'd point it out. I'd just left Hamilton's bed, yet I was grieving for the loss of Coleman.

I drove to Mollie's house. When she let me in the front door, I stopped dead in my tracks. The dress, fitted to the dressmaker's mannequin, stood in the front room. If Cinderella's fairy godmother had been standing there with her magic wand, I wouldn't have been surprised. Mollie had worked a miracle. Seeing the dress on another form allowed me to see how magnificent it was.

"It's finished," Mollie said. "You can take it with you."

"You must have hemmed all night long," I said.

"My hands feel wonderful. It was a pleasure to use my needle again." She held her hands out as if she were admiring a ring, but her fingers were ringless except for a plain gold wedding band. The deforming knots of arthritis were gone.

"What can I do to thank you, Mollie?"

"I'll send you a bill for the dress and material. What you can really do is save Doreen Mallory. That woman's been touched by God. She couldn't have killed her baby."

"I'll do my best," I said, helping her bag the dress, the mask, and the black-sequined wrap she'd concocted.

The dress was too beautiful to simply ignore, so I drove to Madame Tomeeka's to show her. Tammy would appreciate the ball gown, and I owed her a visit. I didn't want her to worry about me.

I carried the dress to her front door and knocked. She opened the door and pulled me inside.

"Put it on," she said, showing me to a bedroom. "I don't want to see it on a hanger. I want to see it on you." She closed the door.

I slipped out of my clothes and into the dress, feeling very much like a princess. The dress could make Humpty-Dumpty feel beautiful. I walked into her front room and did a twirl to her applause.

"Girl, you're going to make every man at the Black and Orange Ball swoon with desire."

"Hamilton'll be there," I said, grinning like a fool.

"I know." She didn't grin back.

"What's wrong?" I'd restored Hamilton's reputation when I solved the case. He hadn't killed his mother.

"Put your clothes on and come drink some coffee with me," Tammy said. She went to the kitchen while I pulled on my jeans. I found her there, the coffee and a storm cloud on her forehead brewing.

"I've been dreaming about you," she said.

"I know."

"Well, I know what the dream means now."

"The lion and the wolf?" I was curious but not disturbed.

"You were between them, petting both, caring for both. But it can't last. They're predators, and you must choose one or the other." She poured us both a cup of coffee.

I was confused. "They're dream creatures."

"Dream images represent real things," Tammy said. "I knew as soon as I heard that Hamilton was back in the States that he was the wolf. And the lion is—"

"Coleman." I understood.

"What I'm afraid of, Sarah Booth, is that once you choose, the other will destroy you."

"Neither of them is like that. They wouldn't hurt me."

"Not intentionally. But the longer you drag it out, the harder it's going to be. On you and on them."

She came to me and hugged me. "I had a dream about your parents, too."

"I could use a little good news."

"They were dancing in the parlor like they used to do. Your mother looked up at your father and he bent and kissed her lips. She said, 'I love you.' They were so happy. Then she turned and looked at me, and they vanished."

"And what wisdom am I supposed to take from that?"

"Love is eternal, Sarah Booth. Trust your heart."

"It would seem that my heart is a greedy organ."

Tammy gave my arm a squeeze. "I've known you for a long,

long time and I wouldn't agree with that." She checked her watch. "My client will be here any minute."

"And I need to get back on the road." I did. I knew Doreen would be waiting for me on pins and needles. "Thanks, Tammy."

"Be careful, Sarah Booth."

I didn't bother going back by Dahlia House. I headed south. I called Lee on my cell phone to make sure she and Kip could still tend to my critters. Once she agreed, I drove with a vengeance.

Getting the dress to my room without Tinkie seeing it was going to be a challenge, but I wanted it to be a surprise. I slunk through the lobby and tiptoed down the hallway to my room. When I opened the door, the aroma of the star-gazer lilies made me close my eyes and smile. The ball was going to be wonderful.

My message light was blinking, but I called Doreen before I did anything else. She answered the phone at her apartment on the first ring, and I wondered if she was haunted by the memories of her daughter like I was sometimes haunted by my parents.

"I didn't find anything conclusive, but there is a possibility that someone killed your mother."

"Who?"

"Coot Henderson said he thought she was talking to someone. Someone she called the spawn of Satan."

There was a long silence. "My whole family is dead," Doreen said. It was the first time I'd heard her sound even the tiniest bit defeated. "My mother and my daughter possibly murdered. One brother dead at childbirth and one drowned."

"I'm sorry, Doreen."

"How would my life be different if I'd known my parents and my brothers? If Rebekah had grown up to be a young woman?"

She was talking in the realm of the impossible, but I kept my lips zipped. Loss and grief were immune to rational thought. But she was right about the history of tragic violence that went core-deep in her family.

I had news for her that was either going to cheer her up or depress her more. "When I talked to LeMont last night, he'd had Rebekah's baby bottle fingerprinted."

"And my prints were on it." She sounded resigned.

"Yes, and Pearline's, and another set."

"Whose?"

"Oren Weaver's."

There was a pause. "That's impossible. Oren never saw my baby. He never once saw her. I made sure of that."

"Maybe he didn't just see her, Doreen. Maybe he murdered her."

21

AFTER I HUNG UP WITH AN AWAKENING DOREEN, I LISTENED TO MY messages. Tinkie had gone over the Center's books and was having dinner with Oscar. There were several investments she wanted to discuss with her husband. Cece was at Shimmy Chang's, a Chinese restaurant/floor show that specialized in the city's most beautiful transvestites who sang, performed, and embarrassed patrons half to death. I could only grin as I imagined the fun she was having.

There was a call from Hamilton. All he said was, "I miss you." But it was the way he said it. There was an invitation and a promise in those three little words. A delicious shiver went over me, and I sprinted out the door to his apartment.

On the way to Hamilton's I thought about Doreen. She had at long last begun to believe that one of her lovers might have killed her baby. I felt a little guilty at robbing her of her innocence, but now she'd begin to take the murder charge seriously. Once she believed someone had murdered her child, healer or not, she'd want vengeance.

I bolted through the door of Hamilton's building, earning an amused glance from the doorman. Where had he been the first night I'd come to this place? I'd been in a sexual trance. Smiling, I pressed the elevator button. My cell phone rang.

Tinkie was breathless with excitement. "Sarah Booth, you have to see this. It's big. Really big."

"Can you tell me on the phone?" I heard the elevator glide to a stop.

"No. You have to see it."

The door whispered open. I looked longingly at the elevator that could transport me to the penthouse and Hamilton. Damn! "Where are you, Tinkie?"

"At Luna Blue."

It was a small café on the river. I could walk there faster than a taxi could get me there. "I'm on the way," I said. I left the building with a lot less spunk than I'd entered. On the way I telephoned Hamilton and told him I had to work. I waited tensely for his reaction.

"I'll leave the door open for you when you finish. If you're too tired, I'll see you tomorrow."

He said it with such grace. "Thank you, Hamilton." I hung up and headed past the gaudy T-shirt shops, the frozen-daiquiri places, the gay bars, the Western bars, the leather shops, and antiques emporiums. I crossed Decatur and found the heavy oak door of Luna Blue.

Tinkie and Oscar were at the bar. Oscar came forward to greet me. The kiss on my cheek was a real surprise. Oscar wasn't demonstrative. In the quick glance I got into his eyes, I saw they were shadowed with worry.

"Look at this," Tinkie said, waving a document at me.

The light in the bar wasn't the best, but Oscar provided an intense penlight that made the numbers jump off the page. I could see them; I just couldn't understand them. "Please explain."

"Oscar found it. It's an investment line that's listed as Doreen's IRA."

"And?" The only thing wrong with that was that a tarot card reader in Jackson Square had an IRA. I didn't.

"It's the companies the money is invested in. One's a munitions manufacturer. Another is one of the biggest polluters on the face of the planet."

That was a little strange. Doreen was one with the universe. She didn't want to shoot it or pollute it. "Maybe Doreen doesn't know. I mean, a lot of people don't have a clue what the companies they invest in do."

"True," Oscar said, "but I looked over the books and I can't find out where the money came from. It's just there. I have no doubt Doreen earned the money, but it's just a little irregular. And guess who's listed as the beneficiary?"

"Michael?"

"On every single policy." Tinkie couldn't help but be smug. She'd done a fabulous job.

"The plot thickens," I said, telling her about Oren Weaver's fingerprints. "Now we have great motivation for each of them."

Tinkie's brow furrowed. "But who else would Doreen leave her things to? She hasn't any family. Perhaps it's all legitimate. Maybe she trusted Michael to continue with her work."

She had a point, but it would be interesting to hear Michael's answers and compare them to what Doreen said.

"Tinkie, you did an excellent job," I said, hugging her. I even got Oscar to unbend a little more when I gave him a hug and thanked him for his help.

I was about to make my exit and return to the arms of *amore* when my cell phone rang again. I hated the dratted thing.

"You'll never believe what that bitch Ellisea has gone and done." Cece had lost the veneer of sophistication she loved to convey. "Where are you?"

"Luna Blue."

"I'm right outside. Call Tinkie. We need a powwow."

"She's already here." Hamilton would have to wait a little longer. Sisterhood came first.

Cece breezed into the restaurant, bellied right up to the bar, and ordered a giant green goblin. "Not a word until I have something to drink," Cece ordered, waving us back from her.

I eyed the drink with some suspicion as the bartender mixed it and put it in front of her. She peeled a straw and proceeded to suck the entire concoction down. I was truly impressed.

When the last drop had been hoovered into her mouth, she turned on her bar stool and addressed us with her famous poise. "Dahlings, I've had the most traumatic evening."

The drink had revived Cece's decorum and a bit of her color.

"What happened?" Tinkie didn't beat around the bush.

"I was at Shimmy Chang's." She rolled her eyes. "Those gals are too much. I have to say even I was a little shocked."

"Go on," Oscar put in impatiently.

"Well, who should show up but Ellisea Boudet Clay. At Chang's! And she was outraged that I was there."

"How did she know you were there?" I asked, realizing there was more to this story than Cece was volunteering.

"Because I confronted her about that charity auction. I walked right over to her, and I told her that I knew what she was doing and why."

Cece was a woman now, but the vestiges of the balls she'd once had came through. I gave her arm a squeeze.

"What did she say?" Tinkie asked.

"She gave me this cold stare, like I was dog poo on her shoe.

Then her lip curled"—Cece demonstrated, showing perfect teeth—"and she told me to get lost or I'd be sorry."

"That's it?" I was disappointed.

"No, because I refused to go. I asked her why she'd tried to blackball me. I wanted to hear her say it. She denied she'd done it, and then this man came up to the table and she flipped out. She called me the most vulgar name. I retaliated by saying the name of her electrolysis clinic. That's when she lunged across the table."

We were all leaning forward in our chairs, even Oscar. "And?" he urged.

"And that man caught her by the arms and restrained her. She was spitting and hissing at him and telling him that he'd pay for touching her. That he was just a 'backwater dick' that her father had 'pulled from the slime.'

"He told her that her father would be furious if she created a public scene. He said she had a lot to lose."

"He was a private investigator?" I was intrigued.

"No, he's a cop. His name's LeMont. She called him by name." She grinned.

"Arnold LeMont?" Tinkie asked.

Cece shrugged. "She only used his last name. About six feet, dark hair and eyes. Maybe forty. Could be attractive, but something predatory in the eyes."

It was a perfect description of the police detective handling Doreen's case. And now he was dining with one of my suspect's wife—and obviously sharing a long history, if Cece had heard accurately, which she always did.

"What was Ellisea doing in Chang's?" I wondered aloud.

"I think she went there to meet that cop, because she knew no one on the social calendar would be caught dead in a restaurant full of transvestites," Cece said. "She thought she was safe there."

I gave Cece a power hug. She might never make the social register of Daddy's Girls or their New Orleans counterpart, but she was the real thing, through and through.

I was about to make my withdrawal from the group once more when the evil little gadget in my purse rang again. Desperate to get to Hamilton, I checked the number. It was from a local pay phone. With a sigh, I answered.

"I need to talk to you," the male voice said. "Right now. O'Flaherty's on Toulouse."

The line went dead. I looked at my partner and my friends. "Speak of the Devil," I said. "LeMont wants to meet me."

The detective's connections to the powerful Clay family were well worth looking into. The senator was a prime suspect, and Ellisea had the temperament of a cold-blooded assassin. Would she kill a baby to protect her position and power? I didn't have a doubt she'd eat her young if they got in the way of her ambition.

LeMont's investigation had been sketchy at best. He'd fingered Doreen and looked no further. Perhaps it was a simple rush to judgment, or it could be something much darker—a frame. If LeMont was owned by the Boudet family, there was no telling what he'd do to protect the senator or his wife.

Add to that the fact that LeMont had stayed on the case instead of turning it over to a juvenile officer, the normal procedure. The detective had claimed a juvenile detective wasn't available.

I hadn't told LeMont that I suspected Thaddeus Clay, but if he was owned by Ellisea, I didn't have to tell him. She would have. Which complicated everything.

Despite the protestations of my chums, I went to the bar alone. Since it wasn't far, I walked. My thoughts turned to my casual turn of phrase. "Speak of the Devil." "Spawn of Satan." Remarks with religious overtones were embedded in our language. But who could Lillith have been referring to? My gut told me that the answer to that would reveal some important facts. The trouble was, I didn't have a way to find that answer. The physical evidence of the fire had long been destroyed.

The only thing that remained of Lillith was her tomb. I stopped and a throng of Japanese tourists piled into my back. I apologized and stepped into a doorway to think.

The gravestone depicted Lillith surrounded by flames, just as Coot had described her standing in the bedroom. But Lillith had died of smoke inhalation. So she had never stood in the flames. Had Coot, in a moment of guilty remorse, paid for the tombstone? It was a question that needed an answer.

I whipped out my evil cell phone and dialed the Sunflower County Sheriff's Office. It was late and Rinda Stonecypher had long gone home, so I wasn't surprised when Coleman answered. I got the impression he went home as little as possible. That thought was a barb in my heart.

"Did Coot pay for Lillith's stone?" I asked.

"I don't know."

"Will you ask him?"

"I'd do almost anything for you, Sarah Booth."

LeMont was in a far corner of the bar, the long work week showing in his posture. Not twenty feet from him a dart game was going on, to raucous cheers. Across an alley, Irish music wafted out of a second bar. A golden voice sang a sad ballad.

I stopped at the bar and got a double Jack on the rocks before I went to the corner. LeMont didn't bother to stand when I got to his table. I took a seat and waited for him to talk first.

"Your clever little friend is going to regret upsetting Ellisea."

"My clever little friend, as you call her, thrives on upsetting people like Ellisea. I'm sure she can handle anything Mrs. Clay chooses to dish out. In fact, it will make fascinating material for Cece's newspaper column."

Ah, the pen was mightier than the sword.

"That's assuming she has a chance to write a column." LeMont grinned, and a cold chill touched my soul. "But let's not exchange threats. Ellisea was upset. She'd rather apologize than have this go further."

"LeMont, I never figured you for an errand boy." I was genuinely pissed. He'd threatened my friend and now offered a second-hand apology.

"It doesn't matter what you figure me for. What matters is that this ends right here."

"Or what?"

"Ms. Delaney, you came here to look into the murder of an infant. Ellisea Boudet is not within the scope of your interests. You and your friend should let it go."

"Oh, but you're wrong there, Detective. Mr. and Mrs. Clay are very much within the scope of my investigation. Based on the fact that you're sitting here talking to me, I'd say they just moved to first place."

LeMont's face was grim. "The Clays had nothing to do with Doreen Mallory or her baby. It's true the senator contributed some money to Ms. Mallory's ministry. That and a large number of other organizations."

"Money wasn't the only thing the senator gave Doreen." It was time to fish or cut bait. I'd kept Doreen's secret as long as I could. The senator knew he was a suspect. Ellisea probably did, too. Possibly even LeMont. But if he was playing in the dark, I was ready to enlighten him. "The senator might be Rebekah's father."

He was well schooled in showing nothing. I couldn't tell if I'd shocked him or not.

"Ms. Mallory made this accusation? Is that what the DNA test is all about?"

"You got it."

He rose to his feet. "I want to question Ms. Mallory tomorrow morning, at the district, at eight sharp." He turned abruptly and left.

I finished my drink. It was after two o'clock Saturday morning. Hamilton might still welcome me to his bed, but I'd been brought up with better manners, and what little of the DG rules Aunt LouLane had belatedly been able to instill. Going to a man's bed at two A.M. sounded cheap. In fact, it sounded a whole lot like free milk.

Walking through the streets of the Crescent City, I worked hard at convincing myself that I wanted the solitude of my hotel room, where I could anticipate seeing Hamilton at the Black and Orange Ball in only a matter of hours.

22

IT DID ME NO GOOD TO ACCOMPANY DOREEN TO THE POLICE STA-
tion. I'd turned down breakfast with Hamilton for the pleasure
of cooling my heels in a dingy interrogation room. Alone.

I'd warned Doreen that LeMont knew about Clay's possible
paternity. She took it better than I thought. Now that she believed Rebekah was murdered, she wasn't nearly as interested in
protecting the senator. Or Oren Weaver, or anyone else. Doreen
had turned a corner, and to my surprise, I wasn't proud of my
part in making her confront the ugly realities of what had happened to her baby.

These were the things I pondered as I waited for LeMont to finish with her. I kept expecting her lawyer to walk through the door
and considered calling him myself. But I didn't. Doreen was nobody's fool.

After two hours she came out of LeMont's office, looking as

refreshed as if she'd been to a spa. LeMont wore a thundercloud on his forehead.

"I should slap you both in jail for withholding vital evidence," he said angrily. "Obstruction of justice is a serious thing in New Orleans. Maybe that hick-town sheriff looks the other way, but you're on my list, Delaney."

"You weren't interested in evidence," I said, using my best Delta drawl. "You arrested Doreen, and you didn't look any further. As far as you were concerned, Rebekah was hatched. You never even asked about the father."

"Doreen was the logical suspect."

"Anyone but the Clays are logical suspects, aren't they? Tell me, is it Ellisea you're protecting, or the senator?"

LeMont bowed up, his jaw clenching along with his hands. "You're out of line."

"I've told the detective everything," Doreen said. "He's promised me he's going to check out all the suspects."

I had my doubts, but I kept my mouth shut. Further bickering with LeMont would get me nowhere, except maybe a cell.

"I'll be in touch," LeMont said as we started to exit the building. "If you think of anything else vital to the case, do give a ring."

Even though it was Saturday, Doreen had work at the Center. It was a perfect opportunity for me to question her about her investments. We hailed a taxi.

As I suspected, she had no idea how the money was invested. "Michael handles all of that." She dismissed the subject as if we were talking about a choice of motor oil.

"Would you object to owning stock in companies that manufacture munitions?"

"Michael would never invest in such things knowingly." She shifted on the seat so that she could see me better. "Are you saying that I own those kinds of stocks?"

"Yes."

"I'll speak to Michael as soon as we get to the Center. He'll have to sell them." Her mouth was a thin line. "Is it possible he didn't know what he was buying?"

"Tinkie's husband found it immediately. Tinkie didn't know, and neither would I. But Michael is your financial advisor. He should know these things."

"Michael is my right hand even though he's not formally trained in advising. He's self-taught, and I admire that. You have to understand that the things I've accomplished in the last year are because of him. I owe him a lot. But there are times when his concern for money overrides his focus on the things that really matter."

"And what really matters?"

"A sense of peace. Helping others to realize the divinity in themselves. Good friends and a healthy body."

I couldn't argue with her choices. But money made everything on her list a little sweeter. Not even naïveté could totally ignore that fact.

"Doreen, if something untoward should happen to you, who would benefit?"

"I'm perfectly healthy. Nothing's going to happen to me." She smiled at the idea.

"Indulge me."

"The Center. Everything would go to the Center and Michael would oversee it. He knows how important things like the soup kitchen are to me. I think there would be enough money to keep the Center going for a long, long time."

"Then you aren't aware that Michael Anderson is named as your beneficiary on all accounts?" I asked the question calmly.

A frown touched her face. "You know, it seems he mentioned something to me about how it would be best for the money to go into his control. Michael is totally devoted to the goals I'm trying to accomplish."

She paused, seeming to watch the hustle of New Orleans pass by the cab window. "I told him to do whatever he thought best. The most expedient solution. If his name is on the policies, it's because I allowed it. I trust him totally." She looked at me. "Michael may not have the formal training or sophistication of some money managers. He makes mistakes. But he's as devoted to this ministry as I am. Don't ever doubt that."

"Money can be a powerful motivation for a lot of things, good and bad."

The cab pulled up in front of the Center. She opened the door and started to get out. I was riding on to meet Hamilton at an uptown restaurant. "I will speak to him about where the money is invested. I'm sure he'll agree immediately to find other, saner investments."

CHE'S, A SMALL, intimate restaurant with a lovely garden, was the perfect place for a romantic rendezvous. Tables were scattered discreetly amidst bougainvillea, ferns, sawmill palms, and thick banana plants. Unfortunately, Hamilton was at none of the tables.

But he had called in his regrets and his credit card number. He was unavoidably tied up in a business meeting. He would call later in the afternoon.

I had no right to feel irritated. My work had interfered last night. Today he had business. It was part and parcel of who we were. So I ordered a vodka martini and lunch, and enjoyed the dining experience. Maybe it was best that Hamilton didn't see me before the ball. Sort of like bad luck for a groom to see his bride on their wedding day.

That thought conjured up a host of images. Did I even want a wedding day? Had I fallen so far off the normal path of a Daddy's Girl that I no longer cared that my left finger was barren? Not to mention my womb. I glanced furtively around the garden to see if Jitty had somehow slipped behind a potted palm and was practicing mind control.

The waiter brought my espresso and saved me from further ruminations. I was glad to escape confronting the void of my future.

A nap was in order and I caught a cab back to the French Quarter. The Monteleone was beginning to look like home. I undressed and slipped beneath the covers and fell asleep almost instantly, visions of my black-and-orange gown dancing in my head.

THE RAT-A-TAT-TAT OF a tiny fist beating at my door made me think I was at Dahlia House and Tinkie was demanding breakfast. But the room was strange, the smell of the wonderful stargazer lilies almost a drug. I awoke to hear Tinkie's irritated voice on the other side of the hotel door.

"Open up, Sarah Booth. Don't force me to call the manager and tell him that you've stolen the good silver from the dining room."

"Coming!" I jumped out of bed and unlocked the door. Tinkie took one look at me and shook her head.

"You haven't even begun to get ready!"

"It's only"—I checked my watch—"four o'clock. The ball doesn't start until nearly ten."

"That doesn't leave us much time," she said, marching past me and slamming the door. "We have a manicure, a pedicure, pumicing those heels and elbows, waxing the legs." She sighed. "That doesn't even get us above the waist for at least two hours!"

"Tinkie, it's a ball gown, not a bikini."

"Honey, you've just let yourself go to hell in a handbasket."

I was saved from defensive commentary by the ringing of my phone. Hamilton would salve the wounds that Tinkie had opened.

"Hello," I said in a sexy voice.

"I want what's mine. I should inherit whatever Adam's share was. I was his wife. I had his kid."

The voice had the high-pitched drone of a hungry mosquito.

"Who is this?" I asked.

"Kiley. Kiley Crenshaw. And don't play dumb with me. You know who I am, and you tell that Doreen Mallory that whatever money she intended to give to Adam, she owes me. That bastard left me with a kid."

"Adam drowned," I said. The Crenshaws had told Tinkie they didn't believe Kiley's child belonged to Adam.

"What's your point? He got out of it, didn't he? Scot-free, too. He didn't have to change a diaper or do a single damn thing with Joshua."

"He died, Mrs. Crenshaw. It's not like he abandoned you."

"Well, it all amounts to the same thing in my book. I got left with all the responsibility. Now I want my due."

"I'll be sure and tell Doreen," I said. The Crenshaws might not be far off the mark in blaming Kiley for Adam's death. I could see where she might rival the harpies in driving a person to desperate measures.

"Why don't you give me her number and I'll tell her myself."

"I don't think so."

"I can come to New Orleans and find her, you know."

"I advise against it. Doreen has her hands full now. She's not required by law to give any portion to anyone. She was going to share with her brother because she's a generous person. If you try to push her into a corner, she legally doesn't have to give you a dime."

It was the truth and it gave me great satisfaction to tell her.

"How do I know you're not lying?"

"Well, I guess you don't." I hung up and turned to relay Kiley's portion of the conversation to Tinkie. I'd barely let a smile of satisfaction creep over my face when Tinkie tackled me, pushed me back on the bed, grabbed a foot, and set to work on making me beautiful. I was going to look good even if it killed both of us.

Tinkie had pumiced one heel and was tackling the other when a knock on the door gave me hope of rescue. Surely it was Hamilton. He hadn't called all day.

I tried to sit up, but Tinkie slapped a hot bath towel around my face. "We need to open your pores and then shrink them," she said. "Don't move."

Beneath the swaddling of the towel, I recognized Cece's voice. "I brought the Epilady," she said. "If we yank those hairs out by the roots, they won't grow back for the next three weeks."

I sighed. Resistance was useless. I was in the hands of the beauticians from hell. There would be no salvation, only results. I could only hope that Hamilton's first glimpse of me would be worth it.

"Now hold still," Cece said. "This is going to hurt a little."

She wasn't lying. I wouldn't have to shave my legs again. Probably ever. I probably wouldn't be able to use them due to nerve damage.

"I found out something interesting today," Cece said.

I pushed the hot towel off my face. "What?"

"That auto-track I ran on Ellisea?"

"Yeah?"

"I checked out a couple of the addresses I picked up." She grinned. "I canceled her order for shoes at Le Ménage. I hope those were the ones she was planning on wearing to the ball tonight. They were special order. Supposed to be flown in from Dallas today. Too bad, huh?"

"Cece," I said, impressed. She really knew how to hurt a woman.

"But the other discovery was the interesting one. I went to what I thought was another boutique. But it wasn't a boutique at all. It was a tattoo parlor."

"Maybe she had her eyes lined or her lips permanently colored," Tinkie said. "I'd like to do that. Save a lot of time in the morning."

"I don't think so," Cece said.

"What kind was it?"

"Oh, the kind that specializes in things other than tattoos."

"Such as?" I was curious.

"Body piercing. You know, nipple rings, cock studs, that kind of thing."

"Wow," Tinkie and I said in unison.

"I said I was a friend of Ellisea's and mentioned that I'd like to buy her a special...adornment." She crossed one leg over the other. "Dahlings, one would think that the mere mention of Ellisea's name could cause flying monkeys to descend from the sky. They hustled me out the door, closed it, locked it, and pulled the shade."

23

WHEN I'D LIVED IN NEW YORK, I'D SEEN PLENTY OF IMPOSING AR-
chitecture and sophisticated décor. Still, the home of Alexandra
and Christoph Bogata was stunning. The Black and Orange Ball
was a spectacle designed to please all the senses. Tiger lilies were
the only flowers allowed, but they burst from vases and swags and
climbed the legs of tables and staircase railings. In a final touch,
two dozen magnificent blossoms were sewn into the flowing black
taffeta train of the hostess's gown. Her hair, a cascading glory, had
been dyed to match the lilies. A gossamer net of black jet sparkles
held every hair in place.

"Ms. Delaney," she said as she took my hand. "A pleasure to
meet you. I've heard so many interesting things about you."

I couldn't tell if she was being pleasant, catty, or merely gra-
cious. Tinkie and Cece had pulled my hair up into a bun, with
spectacular effect. But their initial, overly zealous efforts had re-

sulted in a sort of temporary paralysis to my facial nerves. I shook Alexandra's hand as I smiled. "Thank you for inviting me. It's an honor to attend."

"Cece has told me that you'll participate in the charity auction tomorrow. I can't thank you enough. It's our biggest fund-raiser, and I've heard that because of Ellisea Clay's participation, we can expect a good bit of attention from the fashion world." She leaned closer. "*Vogue* is sending a reporter!"

I didn't reply. I wanted to wring Cece's neck. I'd told her I didn't want to participate. She was welcome to the gown, though I have to say it was going to be hard to part with Mollie's creation. My entrance had created a small ripple of excited whispers—until it became clear I was a nobody in a somebody's dress. But Mollie would have been proud. My dress was an attention-getter. Even Tinkie had been suitably impressed. In fact, she'd conceded our bet, saying that I'd won hands down.

"Excuse me, Alexandra. I require the attention of your guest."

Hamilton's warm baritone was in my ear and his hand on my elbow. I turned to him with a radiant smile.

"I've been waiting a long time for a moment with Ms. Delaney," Hamilton said.

"Of course," Alexandra replied, though her lips didn't move.

She turned to welcome the next guest. I walked on air beside Hamilton as we made for a quiet corner of the ballroom, where at least five hundred people chatted, talked, drank, ate, and even danced.

Hamilton wore a domino, as did everyone. His was plain black silk. It didn't matter. I could have picked him out of a crowd of fifty thousand.

"I've missed you," he said.

"Likewise."

"Sorry about lunch." He frowned. "Bad situation. Nepal."

"I'm sorry, Hamilton." I could see that he was troubled. "I enjoyed my lunch and took a nap. Then I fell into the hands of the evil stepsisters of fashion."

"Yes, I had clear orders not to call or interfere while you were being prepared."

"Marinated, plucked, pummeled, dressed, and roasted. I'm surprised I can still walk and talk."

He laughed. "You look stunning, Sarah Booth. But then, you always do. No extra preparation was necessary, but I suppose a little pampering is always good for a woman's soul."

If he'd seen the things that had been done to me, he'd never call them pampering. Hair had been ripped from various tender places that were still smarting. Massage, normally a good word, had resulted in my confession to several atrocities I'd never committed.

"You're lucky to have such friends," he said as he waved to Tinkie and Oscar.

Tinkie was beautiful in her black spandex with an overlay of orange net that made her look both ancient and very futuristic. Tinkie could pull off a look.

Cece, her blonde hair coiffed to perfection, wore a slinky black number that was cut so low in the back that no one could help looking for a peek of cheeks. To emphasize the focus, one elegant orange rose was embroidered on her right butt cheek. I had to hand it to her. She had some intriguing butt muscles. She picked up a glass of an orange concoction that a waiter was serving and lifted the glass in our direction.

Hamilton and I waved. That's when I saw Ellisea. She strode across the floor toward Cece, her glare icy and her gaze unwavering.

"You are going to pay big-time," Ellisea said in a voice that halted all conversation in the immediate area. I remembered the last ball I'd seen Cece at. A similar scene had taken place. Was it that Cece loved the limelight or did she just rub arrogant bitches the wrong way?

"Dahling, you look overwrought," Cece said. If she was concerned, she didn't show it. "Try a glass of something. Anything. Before you show your ass completely."

"You canceled my shoes. I know it was you. The saleslady identified a picture of you."

Cece's frown was patently pretend. "Canceled your shoes? Why, dahling, I did you a favor. I knew you were waiting for a house to fall on your sister so you could get your slippers."

Uh-oh. The shit was going to hit the fan. I started forward, but Hamilton's light grasp on my arm held me in check. "If it gets bad, I'll stop it. Look at Cece. She set this up."

He was right. Cece had choreographed this moment in revenge for Ellisea's attempt to blacklist her as emcee of the charity auction. I truly hadn't realized how much that emcee post meant to Cece.

"Tell me, Ms. Cece Dee Falcon, how's the climate in Sweden?"

It was a remark that took my breath away. In fact, those of us who knew Cece's history actually gasped.

When Cece had first come back to Zinnia, we'd shared a bottle of superb port, and Cece had told me of her decision never to hide her sex-change operation. She'd said that trying to hide such a secret would be like trying to bury a dinosaur. Whenever the wind changed, some part of it would be revealed. She said her family hated her for her openness, but that she would never be owned by a secret. I saw how wise her decision had been.

"Ah, Sweden, a land of spectacular views," Cece said, unperturbed. "The midnight sun is something everyone should see."

"How nice can the view be from a hospital window?"

"Depends on the hospital, Ellisea. Of course, there are hospitals and there are clinics. I didn't think Botox required hospital-

ization. Perhaps your treatment went a little deeper than a few in-
jections. Of course, you didn't leave home, did you? The Cos-
grave Clinic?"

"You've been spying on me," Ellisea said.

"Not spying, dahling, digging up dirt. It's what I do for a living. And I'm very, very good."

"The only thing you're good at is pretending to be a woman."

"Dahling, at least my persona attracts men. From the gossip
around town, a man would rather donate an organ than spend an
hour in your company." Cece's eyebrows arched. "Even the old
hippies in the tattoo parlor are terrified of you. What do you do?
Tie them up and beat them?"

Ellisea's face changed. It went from anger to a calculated,
hardened fury. "What are you talking about?"

"Two-three-two-three Chalmette Boulevard," Cece drawled.
"Ring a bell?"

I glanced at Hamilton. His focus was completely on Cece. If he
saw the first sign of distress on her face, he'd stop it. But he was
right. Cece had been itching for this confrontation. It was obviously a public forum by design.

The host and hostess, sensing trouble, began sweeping toward
the two women. I glanced around, wondering where Senator
Clay might be. He was nowhere in sight.

"I'm going to snatch you bald-headed." Ellisea put action into
word. She rushed Cece, slapped her hard on her right cheek, and
grabbed a handful of hair with such force that Cece's head
snapped almost to her shoulder.

Cece had only sipped her drink. With one fluid motion, she
hurled the contents into Ellisea's face. "Oops."

Ellisea stumbled backwards. The orange liquid clung for a moment and then slithered down Ellisea's nose and cheeks and onto
the bodice of her black gown.

Ellisea's mouth opened and shut, opened and shut.

"Dahling, when you threaten someone, you'd better be able to carry it out on the spot. I don't mean calling in some of your daddy's hoodlums, either."

"Aaarrrrgggggghhh!" Ellisea launched herself at Cece. It was almost as if she flew the five feet between them. In a split second she had Cece by the front of her gown. She was wrenching and tearing with harsh, grunting noises.

Cece tossed her empty glass to a passing waiter and then grabbed two handfuls of Ellisea's hair. With a hefty twist of her wrist, she pulled with enough force to make Ellisea howl.

"Christoph, stop it!" Alexandra commanded. "Those two are ruining my ball. If Ellisea is injured, she won't come to the auction. The press coverage will be ruined!"

"On the contrary," Tinkie said, stepping in to block any intervention from either of the hosts. "I think the floor show is fabulous, and once the media hears about this, they'll be at the auction in droves, hoping for a repeat performance."

By this time Cece had swung her leg behind Ellisea and thrown her to the floor. A tuft of dark hair drifted to the floor beside her.

In the most unladylike gesture I'd ever seen Cece perform, she straddled Ellisea and pinned her wrists to the floor. "Apologize," Cece demanded.

To my utter amazement, Ellisea bucked with such strength that Cece was thrown off balance and flung over Ellisea's head. Ellisea rolled, sprang to her feet, and delivered a whopping kick to Cece's ribs.

She drew back her leg for another vicious kick but Hamilton stepped forward and caught the ex-model with one arm around her waist and another at her throat.

"It's gone far enough," he said.

"Not until she's dead," Ellisea panted.

Tinkie and I scrambled to help Cece to her feet. It took her a moment to regain her breath, but she turned to Ellisea. Her eyes sparked with fury. "This isn't over," she said.

"Not by a long shot," Ellisea snarled.

The crowd that had gathered around the two women parted as if Charlton Heston had commanded the Red Sea to move aside. Senator Thaddeus Clay stepped into the breach. He took one look at his struggling wife in Hamilton's arms and let his gaze rove over Cece.

"If you'd escort my wife to the car," he said to Hamilton, "I'd be in your debt."

"If he turns me loose, I'll tear your head off," Ellisea said to her husband. "You craven bastard. You could at least stand up for me."

Clay looked only at Hamilton. "I'll get the chauffeur to bring the car around." He walked over to the Bogatas. "I can only apologize. I'll send a check for ten thousand for your charity function in the morning. If none of this makes the paper, I'll double it to twenty."

"You're only worried about your stupid reputation." A dribble of saliva stretched from Ellisea's mouth almost to the floor. She struggled in Hamilton's strong arms. "You don't care what she did to me. You never care."

Clay turned to look at his wife. His face was completely devoid of expression. "I suspect whatever it was, you deserved it, Ellisea. Now clean up your act before word of this gets back to your father. He would be very displeased." He looked at Hamilton. "Would you escort my wife to the car? I'll get our coats."

He walked away, and Hamilton had no recourse but to lift the struggling Ellisea and carry her in the wake of her husband.

"Cece, are you okay?" Tinkie and I rushed to her. We pulled her dress back on her shoulder, patted her hair back into place, and found the shoe she'd lost in the melee. The crowd around us began to break up and drift apart. The amazing thing was that not a single photograph had been taken. Was it the power of our hosts, the senator, or the Boudet family?

"Cece, Ellisea is a dangerous woman," Tinkie said. Her face was marred with genuine worry. "Her daddy's a mobster."

"So I've been told," Cece said, grabbing another glass of orange liquor from a passing waiter. "This is very good. Grand Marnier and . . . something." She took another sip. "I can't quite discern it, but it has just the perfect bite."

"We all know your taste in clothes, liquor, and all matters of sophistication are impeccable," I said. "What we're worried about is your judgment when it comes to self-preservation. Tinkie's right. Ellisea has a powerful family, and it would appear she has at least part of the NOPD in her pocket."

"Oh, dear. I suppose I'll get a parking ticket wherever I go."

Tinkie and I exchanged glances. Nothing we said was going to shake Cece. She was huffing victory, and it was as potent as glue. And about as deadly.

I felt a light touch on my arm. "It would be best if Cece left town in the morning," Hamilton said. "Ellisea said she was going to get even, and she meant it."

"Did you hear that?" I asked Cece.

"Dahling, threats are a dime a dozen. I'm going to emcee that charity auction tomorrow, and I'll go home to Zinnia when I damn well please. The likes of an over-the-hill fashion model won't run me out of town." One eyebrow arched. "And, dahlings, aren't you even a little curious as to why she got so upset about a tattoo parlor? One would think you're both losing your touch as investigators."

Tinkie sighed. "Everyone has dirty little secrets, Cece. Not all of them are worth pursuing. Now let's do what we came to do and dance."

The rest of the night was truly a fairy tale. In Hamilton's arms,

I felt like Cinderella. Tinkie and Oscar danced by on several occasions, and Cece found a six-six linebacker from the New Orleans Saints who knew how to salsa. Fairy dust had touched us all.

It was well into the wee hours when Hamilton squeezed my hand and asked if I'd had enough dancing. I didn't need a second invitation. We slipped out unnoticed and made our way to his apartment.

They say a girl shouldn't kiss and tell. Sometimes *they* are right. I went to sleep whispering one word. "Enchanted."

When I woke the next morning, Hamilton was gone. There was a knock on the door and I had to jump back into my ball gown to answer it. A young boy from the French market had a basket of fresh strawberries, a bowl of just-whipped cream, and a pot of strong, black coffee.

"Mr. Garrett asked me to tell you something," the young boy said, his gaze firmly on the floor. He was old enough to understand the implications of a woman in ruined makeup and a ball gown at ten in the morning. "He said to tell you that he'd never found it harder to leave, and that he would call you as soon as he could."

I tipped him with the fifty-dollar bill I'd stuck in my shoe for emergencies the night before, fell back in the bed with my breakfast, and savored my memories.

THE SOUND OF an old-fashioned calliope awoke me. I went to the penthouse window and listened to the tune that reminded me of carousel horses, cotton candy, and the county fair. New Orleans was a city of magic. The unexpected could happen at any moment.

It was nearly eleven, and Hamilton hadn't called. I took a shower, borrowed one of his shirts and a pair of sweatpants, and caught a cab back to the Monteleone with my ball gown over my arm. Cece could have it, but I'd be damned if I was going to walk down a runway wearing it or anything else.

Cece was waiting for me in the lobby. She took my arm, led me to the elevator, and escorted me to my room. Once inside she turned on the shower, shoved me into the bathroom, and told me I had five minutes. The charity auction began at noon. We'd miss the luncheon, but that didn't matter. I was going to be ready for the runway at one.

Perhaps it was the lingering influence of Hamilton's gentle caring, but I gave in. It meant a lot to Cece for me to do this. It would only be a few painful hours and then it would be over.

I reapplied my makeup, tried to re-create my hair with about a forty percent effect, put on some sweats, and grabbed the dress. Within twenty minutes, Cece and I were in a cab and headed uptown.

"Have you heard from Ellisea?" I asked.

"Are you kidding? Just watch for an ambush when we get to the restaurant."

"Do you really have the goods on her?"

Cece kept looking out the window. "No."

"Empty threats are the most dangerous?"

"And sometimes the most delicious."

"Are you okay?"

"No," she said, and looked at me. "Sometimes I wonder if I ever will be."

Post-traumatic fight disorder, I thought, but kept it to myself. I understood. After the anger cooled and the temper fled, there was often depression and self-doubt. I covered her hand with mine on the taxi seat. "The bitch deserved everything you gave her," I said. "If anyone dares to say a word to you, I'll deck 'em."

Her smile was worth a million dollars. "Thanks, Sarah Booth. I needed that."

We were late for lunch, but a waiter brought us something to nibble and a glass of wine as we got back into our dresses. Cece was first on the runway and then she took over the microphone as emcee.

Tinkie was radiant, and I made it without tripping. For Mollie's sake I erased my scowl and tried to look as if I were having a good time.

Ellisea was last in the lineup and her walk triggered what seemed to be thousands of flash units. She did look stunning, though I thought I detected a bald spot on one side where Cece had pulled her hair out. Maybe it was just wishful thinking. As soon as she made her walk, Ellisea shed her dress and left the party.

All told, over three hundred thousand dollars was raised for charity. Cece, Tinkie, and I rode back to the Monteleone in a taxi together. None of us was talkative. We were bushed.

"Back on the case tomorrow," Tinkie said as we parted company in the hallway of the hotel.

"Tomorrow," I promised, thrilled with the prospect of another evening alone with Hamilton. I rushed into my room, closed the door, and found the red light of my phone blinking. Almost trembling with anticipation, I retrieved my messages. I was totally unprepared for Lee's terse voice.

"Sarah Booth, you didn't answer your cell phone. Sweetie Pie has been arrested. She was going through garbage and when the owner tried to stop her, she bit the woman. You'd better call home as soon as you can. I'm afraid they want to give her the needle."

24

HAMILTON WASN'T BACK AT HIS APARTMENT AND I DIDN'T HAVE time to find him. It was already four on a Sunday afternoon, and I was determined to have Sweetie out of the pound and home before morning. I left a message for Hamilton, another for Doreen at the Center, and a brief message for Tinkie in her room. Then I headed out across Lake Pontchartrain and northeast toward home. I hadn't told Doreen about Kiley, and I didn't want to do that in a phone message. My life was gradually slipping out of my control.

My first priority, though, was Sweetie Pie. Maybe she was being held at Dr. Matthews's, the veterinarian. She'd had her shots and she wore her tags. Maybe she was there, instead of the pound. My foot pushed harder on the gas. Not the pound! Even the best-run pounds were holding centers for creatures awaiting death. A million unwanted dogs and cats around the nation waited there for adoption, but the truth was, not very many would ever be rescued. I had to get to Sweetie Pie before she confronted the reality of just exactly how precarious a dog's life could be.

There was one person who could help me, and I called him. To my surprise, Rinda answered the phone, but she didn't give me any guff. She put me straight through.

"Coleman, Sweetie Pie's been charged with biting." I tried hard not to cry, but I blinked the tears out of my eyes as I drove.

"I know. She's right here."

"What do you mean?"

"She's here."

"Where, here?"

"She's being held in Sunflower County Jail."

"Not the pound?"

"Sarah Booth, I hope you know me better than that. She has her own cell, and the last time I checked, she was playing cards with a check forger."

The relief and happiness that rose up in my chest almost choked me. "God, Coleman, you are the best." I felt as if the sun had risen on a world expecting only darkness.

"I'm fairly selective in the people I prove that to. Of course, I'd die before I disappointed Sweetie Pie."

"I'm on my way home."

"We'll be here."

I drove straight through to the jail, stopping only once for coffee and a bathroom break. It was nearly eleven o'clock, and Coleman's pickup was still at the courthouse. He'd waited for me. I'd never doubted he would.

He was grinning when he opened the door to the jail. We looked at each other for a long moment. My heart and stomach did a jittery little dance before he stepped aside and cleared the aisle. I ran to my dog. Sweetie's metronome tail beat against the bars of her cell and she bayed a loud greeting. The inmates applauded.

"Sweetie," I said, kneeling down and grasping her ears through the bars. "What have you done?"

"She bit Mrs. Hedgepeth," Coleman said from about three feet behind me.

"Mrs. Hedgepeth?" She was a crotchety old busybody of a woman who used to try to get me sent to a juvenile detention center for eating sand pears that fell off her tree and into the ditch. "Mrs. Hedgepeth lives in town. Sweetie Pie must have done some traveling to get all the way to her yard."

"Mrs. Hedgepeth filed the complaint. She identified Sweetie for the dogcatcher."

"Where did they pick Sweetie up?"

"At Dahlia House, the best I can tell."

I was really confused. Sweetie wouldn't have rushed several miles into town to bite Mrs. Hedgepeth and then go home. It didn't make a lick of sense. Unless... "It's a lie."

There was a chorus of hoots from the jail cells. "The dog is innocent!" They picked up the chant and ran with it.

"Mrs. Hedgepeth had it in for me, and now she's after my dog," I said. But not even that made sense. Mrs. Hedgepeth had had it in for every child in the county. She hated children, cats, and dogs. But nearly three decades had passed since I'd walked by her house on my way to the courthouse after school.

Coleman tried hard not to grin. "I don't believe she was bitten, either, though she had her hand wrapped in about ten miles of gauze. She didn't go to the hospital or the doctor's office. I checked both."

"She's lying. Sweetie doesn't bite!"

"I suspect she's lying. Nonetheless, Reg had to pick Sweetie up and bring her in. He was taking her to the pound when I heard about it and got her brought here. She's perfectly fine, Sarah Booth. She has to be quarantined for ten days, though."

"And if Mrs. Hedgepeth develops rabies? She's mad anyway. There's no telling how far she'll take this."

"She's a mean woman, no doubt about that," Coleman agreed. "But I don't think she'll go through a series of abdominal shots just to spite a dog. And I told Doc Sawyer, if she showed up in the emergency room, to paint a really gruesome picture of the treatment she'll have to receive. Somehow, I think she'll back off this one."

"I could bite her myself," I said.

"The quarantine for you would be a lot longer."

His smile was infectious and I returned it. "Thanks for getting her, Coleman. I didn't want her in the pound."

"Nor I. Reg tries hard. They're swamped, and folks around here are just too ignorant to spay and neuter their pets."

"Is that a legal opinion?"

"Legal and personal. It doesn't take a rocket scientist to see what happens to an unneutered pet." He sighed and helped me to my feet. "Sweetie is fine. I bought her a plate lunch from Millie's, and Lee's been by with chicken and rice." He closed the door to the jail and we were alone in his office. "You look tired and hungry. Want a cheeseburger?"

"Millie's is closed," I said. "So is Burger Haven."

"Coleman's grill is still open. I rented a small house on Grisham Road. A cottage, you might say. But it has a gas barbecue grill, and I happen to have some burgers ready for the flames."

I tried to absorb what he was telling me. He'd moved out on Connie. He must have seen the look on my face.

"It wasn't my choice. She threw me out. I went home day before yesterday and the locks had been changed. She was inside and threatened to hurt herself if I broke the door in. She threw my clothes out the window and told me if I came back she'd kill the baby."

"What are you going to do?"

"My first inclination was to break the door in, handcuff her, and take her to a psychiatrist for treatment. Wisdom prevailed and I simply left."

"Is she safe?"

"Her mother's with her. And her sister. They call me every day and let me know what's going on."

"Are they getting help for her?"

He shook his head. "I don't really know. She's told them so many crazy things, they don't really trust me. They let me know she's eating and okay, but no real details."

"What a mess."

"What about that burger? I've been experimenting and I've developed a Jack Daniel's chocolate malt that goes down smooth and kicks in with a vengeance."

"Sounds like exactly what I need." I cast a lingering look at the door to the jail.

"Sweetie has to stay. Technically, she should be at the pound."

"I know." Still, it was hard to walk away from my loyal canine.

"Sarah Booth, she's fine. Jones is in there and whenever he starts strumming his guitar and singing, Sweetie joins in with that wonderful voice. Those guys love her."

"Okay," I agreed. I was starving, and somewhere during the night I was going to have to tell Coleman about Hamilton. I might have a greedy heart, but it was one that now suffered under the burden of guilty duplicity. It was time to come clean.

I WAS SO full my stomach was a rounded lump beneath my jeans and shirt. I stretched in the hammock and sighed in contentment. Coleman was in a chair beside me. The night was totally dark but not too chilly for the first of November. In the distance, the last of the cicadas and frogs sang about the summer past. Soon their lives would be ending, yet they didn't sound sad. The creatures of nature seemed to have a far superior understanding of the cycle of life. I was the one warring against death.

"Are you going back in the morning?"

I'd filled Coleman in on the case, including the hair-pulling between Cece and Ellisea. He, too, was concerned about the Boudet connection, but he also knew Cece. I hadn't tried to convince him that Doreen was innocent, but as I presented the evidence I'd found, I could see he was being won to her side. He was particularly incensed with Arnold LeMont's connection to Senator Clay and Ellisea, and the possible corruption that it implied.

"I have to," I said, thinking of Kiley Crenshaw and her strident demands. "Chances are I'll have to go to Lafayette and drag that maid back. It's pretty obvious LeMont's not going to do it."

"I'll give him a call in the morning," Coleman offered. "I don't have a lick of authority there, but a little talk, lawman to lawman, might be interesting."

"Thanks, Coleman." It seemed that Coleman had taken on a role in my life—knight in shining armor. I knew enough about fairy tales not to look too deeply beneath the surface, but it was a wonderful thing to have someone who championed my cause every now and again.

We'd deliberately skirted the topics of Connie and Hamilton, but as the night chill touched my body, I knew I couldn't wait much longer. All evening long, Coleman and I might have been good friends and buddies, sharing a burger and a few Jack Daniel's milk shakes. We'd played it by the rules, too. But beneath the surface, a lot more was happening.

"Hamilton was my date for the ball." I just said it. For a long moment my words hung in the November night, and I could imagine what Coleman was imagining.

"He's a wealthy man, Sarah Booth. As I told you once before, he's got the credentials. And he's single." The last was spoken bitterly.

"He's been very good to me, Coleman. And there's more to him than just money and looks. He cares about people. He works for an organization that helps find missing people. People who have been disappeared by political factions."

"You don't have to sing his praises, Sarah Booth. I don't have a leg to stand on. I know that."

I stared up at the stars. There were millions of them, but they had somehow dimmed. "I'm not singing his praises, I just want to be totally honest with you."

"Tell you what. We have right now, just this moment together. Right down the road is Connie and that hornet's nest that has become my life. In the opposite direction is Hamilton and all of the bright and shining things he offers you. We're right here, in this weedy backyard, but we're together. Let's just keep it between the two of us."

The pain in my chest was so intense, I know my heart cracked just a little. Coleman wasn't asking for anything, only a crisp night and some uncomplicated companionship. "You've got it, Coleman," I said, forcing a note of flipness into my voice to hide the pain.

We talked of high school and the way our dreams had shifted and changed, growing smaller and smaller. At one point in time, Coleman had considered professional football. But his father's illness had kept him on a tight leash, binding him to Sunflower County and a job in law enforcement that he'd never considered until he had it.

I was going to be an actress. Not a film star, but an honest-to-God Broadway actress. I was Maggie the Cat and Blanche DuBois. The Big Apple was going to be my snack.

And that city had kicked my ass. I'd come limping home to lick my wounds.

Much the same thing had happened to our classmates and friends. Some had had tremendous success, such as Krystal, the former Daddy's Girl who was now at the top of the country charts. But even with her career success, she'd confronted the narrowing of her dreams. We'd all once thought "happily ever after" was our due.

For all the loss of innocence, though, we'd gained a better understanding of ourselves, and that, Coleman said, was the flip side of our loss.

"So we see ourselves more clearly and accept our limitations?" I asked, a little disappointed in his negative philosophy.

"No," he said, leaning forward to swing the hammock gently with his hands. "We see ourselves clearly and we understand that we have chosen to be where we are."

"You sound like Doreen," I said, surprised.

"Really?"

"You do. With her, it's all about choice."

"When this is all behind her, I'd like to talk to her. In fact, I'd give just about anything if Connie would talk to her."

Against his own rule he'd dragged his wife into the backyard. But he had a valid point. I didn't think Connie's body needed healing; it was her head. Maybe Doreen could help by talking to her. She seemed to have a real way with the folks who gathered in Jackson Square.

"I bet Doreen would come up here to see her, but she can't leave that jurisdiction."

In the dim light that filtered from the kitchen window I could see the hope in Coleman's face. "Maybe Connie would go to New Orleans and talk to her. If she won't go with me, maybe she'll go with her mother and sister."

I watched the play of emotion on his face and wondered at his true agenda. Did he want his wife well? Or did he want her well enough to leave? It wasn't a question I was prepared to ask.

"I'd better get on home," I said, dreading the inevitable confrontation with Jitty.

"By the way, I asked Coot about that tombstone. He said he didn't pay for it. But he said when he saw it, it nearly frightened him to death. It was exactly like he saw Lillith standing there in the flames."

"But she was already dead when the fire started," I said.

"I know," Coleman agreed, "she died of smoke inhalation. But you've got to admit that it makes the hair on the back of your neck stand on end."

He had a point there. He surely did.

I DROVE BACK to Dahlia House with only my thoughts. I won't claim that they were deep, but they were low-down. On so many fronts, my life was terrific and exciting. I had a compelling case to work on, and Hamilton was waiting for me to return to New Orleans so he could sweep me off my feet yet again.

Instead of making me feel wonderful, though, I felt as if I'd lost control. I'd made no real progress on Doreen's case. Sure, Tinkie and I had dug up a lot of leads, but none of them had led to anything concrete. All we could do was throw suspicion on a handful of people. It just wasn't good enough. And emotionally, I wasn't ready to make a commitment to Hamilton—even if he asked, which he hadn't.

I sat in the car outside Dahlia House and stared in at the darkened windows. There was no Sweetie Pie to greet me, and if Reveler knew I'd come home, he wasn't talking. Jitty wasn't even around to accost me as my steps echoed on the porch.

The good thing about coming home is that you don't have to bring a suitcase. I hurried up the steps with one thought in mind, a long hot bath.

"Sarah Booth, girl, water won't wash away what ails you."

Jitty was sitting in the dark. All I could see of her was the light reflected in her eyes.

"I know," I said, unwilling to argue. "I'm tired, Jitty. I don't know what I want. I'm confused. I'm all of the things in life that add up to one big mess."

There was a low chuckle. "Maybe I was bein' a little hard. At least you didn't sleep with the sheriff."

"Coleman's married. How many times do I have to tell you that?"

"How many times do you have to tell yourself?" she asked softly.

For some reason I felt the approach of tears. Anger was my normal reaction, but I had to take a seat on the horsehair sofa to keep from crying.

"Sarah Booth, what do you know about flappers?"

If she was trying to distract me, I could only thank her. "Short skirts, short hair, illegal gin. They were party girls." I thought for a moment. "They were change, I suppose. They were the first modern women."

"You got it. Women began to see themselves in a new way. Some folks thought it was a dangerous way."

"I guess it was the first wave of true independence." I sighed again. I didn't feel very independent or capable. "Sometimes I think all of that is an illusion, Jitty. I'm independent, but I don't want to be. Not all the time."

"For all of the image of gaiety the flapper projected, I think maybe she suffered most of all."

Jitty stepped into the light and I saw her outfit. It was stunning. Crystal beads hung on the sheath dress of aqua shantung. A peacock feather adorned her headdress.

"Who's the most famous flapper?" she asked.

"Zelda Fitzgerald." I'd done a paper on her in college. For the term of the literature course, I was completely absorbed in Zelda.

I admired her courage, her kiss-my-ass attitude toward what others thought of her, her absolute devotion to scenes and pranks. I'd also fallen into the school of thought that her husband stole more from her work than was ethical.

"Zelda Fitzgerald died in an insane asylum."

"I know," I said. "She came to a bad end."

"A very bad end."

I considered a glass of Jack, but didn't have the energy to fix one. "Zelda always sort of reminded me of Mama," I said.

"Lord, Sarah Booth, that's a terrible thing to say."

I looked at Jitty. "Why? Zelda was a remarkable woman."

"Not takin' a thing away from Zelda, but when you make that comparison, you sure do underestimate your mama."

"How so?"

"Your mama didn't give a damn what people thought, that's true. But she didn't flaunt it with pranks and scandal. She fought for causes." Jitty leaned forward. "Your mama was grounded in the importance of life. Seems to me Zelda lived on the edge of the frivolous."

"She might have been a great writer."

"But she chose not to write."

I hated debating with Jitty, especially when I was tired. "I know there's a point here somewhere."

"Illusion-slash-delusion," she said, shrugging her shoulders. The smile that touched her face was beautiful. "Delusion is an art form that brings only disaster. The worst delusion of all is self-delusion."

"And Zelda suffered from self-delusion?"

"I think it became her fortress."

"And Mother?"

"Your mother sometimes created an illusion. For effect. To make a point."

"But she truly didn't care if she aggravated people."

"That's only partially true, Sarah Booth. She cared about agitating you and your father. There were people she cared greatly about. And sometimes, those people needed what she liked to term a wake-up call."

"Grandpa and Grandma Baker?"

"That's right. She felt that they'd fallen victim to their own delusions of wealth and social standing and class. She didn't aim to hurt them."

"But she did."

"All I'm saying is that your mother may have adopted some of the exterior characteristics of the flapper. She was bold and outspoken and her own woman. She drank whiskey and danced with the man she loved in a way that certainly wasn't ladylike."

I couldn't help but smile, remembering Tammy's dream of my parents. They had been a little on the scandalous side when it came to their dancing.

"But beneath all of that was the real thing. She didn't self-destruct, because at her core she was a woman of substance. She didn't suffer from delusions."

"But I do," I said softly. "I'm talking to a ghost."

Jitty chuckled. "Sarah Booth, I'm the least of your troubles, girl. You have some hard choices, but it's our choices that define us. Just remember that."

She was gone.

I went upstairs, took my bath, and set the clock for five A.M. I had to get back to New Orleans and find the evidence that would free Doreen. There was another task that awaited me, too. I could no longer ignore the choices laid before my heart. To continue to do so might be to slip the moorings of happiness forever.

25

"CECE WENT HOME, THANK GOODNESS," TINKIE SAID AS SHE SIPPED her café au lait. "She had to be at work this morning." She bit into a beignet, leaving a fine dusting of powdered sugar beneath her nose. Without thought, she licked her lip in a way that made a waiter collide with a customer. Hot coffee flew, but no one was injured. I could only shake my head and smile.

"I didn't do that deliberately," she said, but there was a glint of pleasure in her eyes. Nondeliberate devastation of the male is one of the highlights of a Daddy's Girl's day. She'd wreaked havoc without intent.

"Coleman's keeping Sweetie in the jail for her term of incarceration."

"That's good for Sweetie, I'm just not sure it's good for you," she said. Her blue eyes probed mine, but I gave nothing away. "What about Coleman, Sarah Booth? What about Hamilton?"

"What about me?" I asked in a monotone.

"Yes. What about you, Sarah Booth? What do you want?"

"I don't have any answers. The best I can do is come up with more questions."

"You're going to have to do a little better than that. I think Hamilton may be falling in love with you."

I sighed.

"I guess I always viewed Hamilton as the unattainable man. He was the brass ring, something to reach for, but forever out of a woman's grasp. But I see him look at you, Sarah Booth, and I know that he can truly be yours. He's a good man. That's a big responsibility."

She gave me a chance to respond, but I remained silent.

"Coleman is a good man, too. I'm not trying to take anything away from him." She started to say something and then stopped. "Be careful. Both of them are vulnerable. They're men." She touched my hand. "You have the power to do a tremendous amount of damage."

"I never asked for that power."

"No. You didn't." She gave a crooked smile. "And that's the end of the lecture. What's on for the case?"

"Can you handle the Kiley matter?" I asked, eager to get off the subject of my love life. I'd told Tinkie about the widow's claim to Adam's share of Doreen's inheritance.

"Sure. I'll check with Doreen and see how she wants to handle it. What are you going to do?"

"Unless LeMont tells me differently, I'm driving to Lafayette." I checked my watch. "And soon. We've waited long enough for Pearline to come home."

Tinkie nodded. "I just have this nagging suspicion that she knows something."

"Maybe we're just desperate." I hadn't been able to shake my depression on the long drive back to New Orleans.

She shrugged. "Desperation is the mother of invention."

"Yes, when all else fails, quote Benjamin Franklin."

"Did he really say that?"

I laughed. "I don't know. Let's just say that neither one of us should ever try to get on a TV quiz show."

"Be careful, Sarah Booth. If Pearline's hiding, it's because she has a reason. Desperate people take desperate measures."

There was that word "desperate" again. Doreen would say the universe was giving me a psychic tap. Though I might be skeptical, I wasn't totally stupid. "I'll look out for 'desperate,'" I promised Tinkie. "If I see it, I'll duck."

She gave me such a dazzling smile that I felt blessed. "I love you, Sarah Booth," she said.

"I love you, too, Tinkie." Funny how easy it was to say to her.

"Girl power!" She held up her knuckles for me in the salute we'd created in second grade when none of the boys wanted to play with us. We bumped knuckles and went our separate ways.

At my car, I used my cell phone to call LeMont. To my surprise he didn't even sound surly.

"Pearline Brewer's giving a statement," he said conversationally.

"She's here, in New Orleans?"

"Yeah, I got a call about five o'clock this morning from another law enforcement . . . agency. It was a good tip. I sent a car to Lafayette with a warrant for Pearline as a material witness."

God bless Coleman. He'd followed through. "Can I talk to Pearline?"

"Sure. As soon as I've finished."

I didn't like the sound of that. Pearline was employed by the Clays. In all probability, so was LeMont. As fond as Tinkie was of old sayings, I had a favorite of my own: A man couldn't serve two masters. I didn't trust LeMont not to coach the witness to protect Ellisea or the senator.

I drove to the Eighth District, figuring I'd have at least a two-hour wait. To my happy surprise, LeMont motioned me back to his office. A petite woman with café-au-lait skin and espresso eyes looked up at me. In that strange, exotic swirling of cultures, Pearline Brewer was an exceptionally lovely woman. I guess I'd expected a maid to be plain or dowdy. Pearline could have been on the cover of any magazine. Her smile was shy.

"I've been waiting to talk to you," I said.

"My mother has been ill, yes," she replied in that strange cadence that was English, but not. I'd heard it along the bayous of Louisiana and sometimes the streets of New Orleans. It was lilting and beautiful and sometimes difficult to decipher.

"You were with Rebekah all evening before she died?" I asked.

I could tell LeMont had been over this ground, but he didn't interfere. Pearline gave a basic rundown of her evening. She'd bathed and fed Rebekah around six, as usual. This was normally the time Doreen came home from either the Center or the Square. But Doreen had called saying she needed to stay later, until eight. Pearline had willingly agreed to stay with the baby.

"She was a pleasure, yes," Pearline said. "Her smile was like being touched by God."

"Pearline, why were Reverend Oren Weaver's fingerprints on Rebekah's baby bottle?" I'd hoped to get her off balance with a sudden shift in direction.

From his desk drawer LeMont removed a plastic evidence bag that contained a baby bottle. It was the kind where fresh sacks of formula could be inserted. He set it on his desk.

Pearline looked down at the floor. "The detective has asked the same question, *chérie.*"

I glanced at LeMont. He shrugged. "I thought you might as well hear the answer with me."

Suddenly he was willing to let me play with his toys. I couldn't help but wonder why.

"So tell us."

"It will break Doreen's heart, yes." She bit her lip and lifted her dark eyes to mine. "Doreen could not help her baby. She prayed for Rebekah. She asked her god to help. But nothing happened, yes. I thought perhaps the true God could help Rebekah. Doreen was working a little late, so I took Rebekah to a revival meeting so that Reverend Weaver could heal her. I took that sweet baby to be healed, and that night she died."

Of all the answers I'd expected, it wasn't this one. So Oren Weaver had held Rebekah, possibly unaware of who she was and that she might be his own daughter. It was a bitter irony.

Pearline's soft sobs filled the office. "It was wrong. Doreen will be so hurt that I didn't trust her to heal her own child, that I took her to Reverend Weaver. But he's healed others on television. I've seen him. I thought it was worth a chance, yes, and I knew my little baby was dying."

"Did Reverend Weaver know this baby was Doreen's?"

Pearline's eyes were horrified at the idea. "Oh, no. I betrayed Doreen by taking her baby to another healer, but I would never have told anyone. I wouldn't tell now except the detective said if I didn't tell the truth I'd go to jail."

I put a hand on Pearline's shoulder and that's all it took. She began to sob in earnest. In a moment I was sitting beside her and she was wetting my chest with her tears.

"Everyone looked at that baby and saw only her deformities, yes. But I looked into her eyes and I saw an angel. She was sent straight from God."

As I patted Pearline's back and did my awkward best to comfort her, I felt a pure and righteous rage building in my own heart. Oren Weaver, the lying bastard, was next on my list for a personal visit.

STORM CLOUDS WERE building to the west as I drove toward Oren Weaver's compound. Doreen had been right about one thing; Pearline hadn't harmed Rebekah. Of all the people walking the planet, Pearline had never even seen Rebekah's medical problems. She'd seen only her spirit and had fallen in love with the infant.

The top on the roadster was down and I liked the cold, rain-promising wind that whipped into my face. The year when I was nine years old, I'd come to New Orleans with my parents. August was never a good month to visit a Southern city below sea level. While it's hot in the Delta, it's suffocating in New Orleans. And it's hurricane season.

A tropical storm that had stalled off the Yucatán Peninsula for a week had suddenly picked up a twenty-mile-an-hour forward speed and roared into the coast of Louisiana as a class three hurricane. It had happened so suddenly that my parents and I hadn't had time to evacuate.

We'd stayed at the Royal Sonasta in the Quarter, and we listened to the howling wind and watched the sheets of rain from the safety of our second-floor room. What I remember most was the flooding. Because portions of New Orleans are below sea level, the storm had drowned the city. Streets were turned into Venetian canals. Things that had long been buried beneath the silty river bottom floated through main intersections. I'd decided never to find myself in New Orleans during another flood.

The rain clouds blowing up from the west were a long shot from hurricane clouds, but I was itchy to leave New Orleans. My skin felt as if it had been peeled back and salted, burning and rubbing in strange places.

The guards at Oren's compound were about as glad to see me as I was to see them. They dicked around with me for ten minutes before they let me through the gate—after a good pat down, of course. It was okay. Just another little score to settle when I finally faced Oren.

True to form, he met me at the front door with no intention of asking me in. I pushed past him and went to the cold den where several young men in suits were sitting in what was obviously a meeting.

"Get lost," I said.

They looked at Weaver, who'd walked in behind me.

"We'll continue this later. Take a fifteen-minute break," he told them. They got up like obedient robots and left the room.

"Ms. Delaney, I'm about ten seconds away from calling the police and having you charged with trespassing."

I handed him my cell phone. "Be my guest. Detective LeMont's probably on his way here now to question you."

He hesitated, reading something dangerous in my face. "What do you want?"

"How did you know that Rebekah Mallory might be your child?"

"Are you completely insane? We've been over this. She isn't my child."

"Reverend, this isn't going to end pretty for you no matter how it goes. I've seen you pay folks to pretend to be healed. The police have your fingerprints on a baby bottle belonging to Rebekah Mallory—the bottle that contained the sedative given to kill her. We have enough circumstantial evidence to tie you to the baby's murder. If the DNA comes back that you're the father, you're going down."

It was a long speech and one I was rather proud of. I detested the man who stood before me. He held out the worst kind of false hope to people who were, in a word, desperate. He stole from them using the cruelest of weapons—their own fear and desperation.

"I'm not Rebekah's father," he said simply. "I'm not. I have no clue how my prints got on any baby bottle, if they're really there. This sounds like a setup."

"Keep hoping," I said, "because it's going to give me intense pleasure to nail you."

He didn't actually take a step back, but I think the hatred in my eyes and voice made him lean away from me. "I offer people hope," he said. "You don't see it, but I do. In a world where most folks know only suffering and pain, I offer the hope of a miracle. That's not a bad thing to do."

"Sure," I said. "You offer as much miracle as they can afford. But the sick thing is, you only offer the illusion of a miracle. If just once you had the real thing, it would be different."

"I did once."

He spoke so softly that I thought I heard him wrong. "What?"

"I've healed people. Truly. Not hundreds of them, but some."

"I don't believe you."

"Ask Doreen."

I remembered what she said about Oren Weaver, that he had the true power to help others if he could just tap into it.

"Who did you heal?"

The strangest look came over his face. "My wife. Myra. She was the first."

"Myra who lives in Baton Rouge and who you have to buy off with hush money for cars?"

He was startled when he realized how much I knew about his life, but instead of getting angry, he smiled. "Myra had something wrong with her leg. She had a lot of pain. Even so, she was a beautiful young woman. I think I fell in love with her the first time I saw her. I never even noticed that she limped."

I fought against the tidal pull of his words. Oren Weaver was a terrific orator. He had the power to lasso me with his words and pull me into his world.

"Myra lived in St. Francisville. She was an only child and over-protected to the point of abuse. She wasn't allowed to go places with her friends. Her parents used her bad leg as an excuse to cripple her even further. I met her by accident. My car broke down and I stopped at her house to use the phone. It was the first time I'd ever been inside one of the planter's homes."

I could see the moss-draped trees of the small town north of New Orleans. Tinkie and I had stopped there for breakfast on our way to New Orleans. It was part of the Episcopalian Louisiana—a rich planter class with treasured Anglo ties. Not for St. Francisville, the evils of Catholicism, and the mixed culture of southern Louisiana. These were purebreds, and as such, their daughters would be guarded against any untoward influences of life.

"They looked on a Baptist revival preacher as akin to Satan himself," Oren said. "I might as well have said the Pope sent me."

"I'll bet Myra now wishes she'd listened to her parents."

"I doubt it," he said. "I should have left her alone, but I couldn't. One day I met her down at the creek behind her house. I told her I wanted to baptize her. What I wanted to do was get her in the water with me. I wanted to see how her dress would cling to her when it was wet. She was so beautiful, and my thoughts weren't on saving her soul."

"You talked her into it?" My estimation of Myra's intelligence dropped.

"I told her I could heal her leg."

"Had you ever healed before?"

"It had never even crossed my mind. But as soon as I said it, I had a clear picture of her leg and what was wrong inside it. There was something growing, something that would move from her leg up to her stomach and kill her. I knew it as surely as I know my name, and I knew that I could stop it. With God's help, my hands could touch her leg and destroy that cancer. And I did." He held my gaze. "Because I loved her so much. God empowered that love."

Goose bumps danced over my skin. Doreen. How much of this had she known?

"Who else have you healed?"

"There was a time when Myra and I first married that I helped people. God gave me visions to see inside their bodies. I knew exactly what to heal and what to destroy." His voice grew tired. "But that was a long time ago. Now I have to pay people to pretend to be healed. But I'm still giving people what they want, what they really need, the hope that miracles still exist."

"You're bilking them out of their money. You're offering false hope."

"False hope is better than no hope at all, Sarah Booth, and if you don't understand that, you've got some hard lessons ahead of you. I'm not cheating these people. They don't really expect me to heal them, but they do expect to leave my revival with the hope that God has the power to somehow touch them. And who am I to say he won't?"

Oren Weaver was a dangerous man, and perhaps a wicked one. I'd lost the ability to tell if he was conning me, conning himself, or if he believed the words he spoke.

"Do you remember the baby with the birth defects?"

"Yes, I do." He locked his hands behind his back. "I didn't want to hold her, but the woman thrust her at me. I had to grab the baby bottle because it slipped from the infant's mouth. She couldn't even try to hold it. Her arms..."

"You didn't know that was Doreen's child?"

"How would I? The woman who brought the baby was Cajun or Creole. I assumed it was her infant."

I didn't believe him. The problem was, I didn't disbelieve him. It was the perfect explanation for the fingerprints on the bottle. And Pearline had confirmed his story.

"You haven't asked the most obvious question," Weaver said, his face tightening, "the one I keep asking myself each day."

"What would that be?"

"How a love like the one I shared with Myra could turn so

twisted and ugly. We despise each other now, you know. She can't abide my touch."

"Let me guess. She caught you sleeping around."

His mouth turned up slightly at the corners. "True, as far as it goes. I've never claimed to be more than a mortal man in the face of temptation. You have no idea how many women throw themselves at me. Not actually me, but who they think I am. I should have resisted, but sometimes the Devil led me to their beds."

"You know what I hate about religion?" I asked.

"I probably couldn't begin to assemble the list."

His words stung me for a moment, but I rallied. "It's how convenient it is to blame everything on the Devil. Oh, just point at Satan and claim a momentary weakness and then ask for forgiveness." My jaw had clenched. "Well, some things can't be forgiven, and I'm willing to bet my family home on the fact that a jury of your peers won't be looking to send Satan to jail. They'll be very happy to see you behind bars if you killed that baby."

SINCE I WAS on a tear of terrorizing potential suspects, I drove to the senator's house. Though I knocked and hammered on the front door, no one answered. I had the sense that someone watched me from inside the house, and that triggered my already hot temper.

Instead of leaving, I cut across the immaculate yard, pushed through some camellia bushes that had to be two hundred years old, and found myself facing a huge gravel car park. A young man in a chauffeur's uniform was scrubbing on a pale blue Jaguar. With the rush of the water hose and the volume of the radio, he didn't hear me. I eased up and stopped. The letters C-H-A-N-D-A-L-A had been spray painted on the car in Day-Glo orange. The chauffeur was doing everything in his power to remove the paint, but it wasn't budging.

I heard someone behind me and turned to find the senator frowning down at me.

"Vandals," he said. "Public figures are always a good target."

"What does it mean?"

He shrugged. "The kids who did it probably have a second-grade education. Who knows what they were trying to write." He motioned the chauffeur forward. "Call the dealer. Tell them to get another car ready, then drive this one over for a trade-in. They can repaint it themselves."

"Sure thing, Senator," the young man said. He hustled to do his employer's bidding.

Senator Clay looked down into my eyes. "I've asked you not to come here," he said. "Ellisea is upset."

"Ellisea seems to stay in a constant state of upset."

"She has medical problems."

I'd be willing to bet they were mental, but I didn't say so. "Senator, has anyone ever mentioned that your wife has become a political liability? That fit she threw Saturday night was a doozy. I'm only wondering how you kept it out of the newspapers."

"Ellisea has problems, but so does every other politician's spouse in D.C., or don't you watch the news?"

He had me there. Politicians were human, and under the microscope of the national press, their flaws were revealed on a daily basis. It was just that I hadn't been to a high-society ball with other political wives and seen them engage in a catfight.

"Why does Ellisea hate Cece so much?" I asked.

"I have no idea."

I saw something in his eyes that quickly vanished. Was it prejudice? I didn't always agree with Clay's politics, but he'd always seemed to uphold the rights of people to practice whatever gender or religion they chose. Like Doreen had pointed out, Clay was in a position to make sweeping changes on issues from the environment to the right to abortion. Was he, at heart, a man who devalued personal freedom?

"You might ask yourself why your friend has it in for my wife," he countered. "There's some jealousy there, I believe. Ellisea was a runway model. Cece may have aspired to that but didn't make it."

"Cece didn't aspire to any such thing, because at the time, a transsexual would never be allowed to become a top fashion model." That was a cold fact. "Does Ellisea frequent the Rainbow Boutique?" I asked. "It's a tattoo parlor on Chalmette Street."

"I have no idea what Ellisea does when I'm out of town. If you're asking if she has tattoos, the answer is no." He took a deep breath. "I have a flight to catch. Please don't come back to this house, Ms. Delaney. I won't be here, and as I told you earlier, it upsets my wife. I think it's best for all accounts if that doesn't happen."

He was asking, not threatening me. "Unless I have specific business with Ellisea, I'll stay away from here—if you'll give me your private phone number in Washington." It was a fair trade in my book.

He pulled a notepad from his pocket, wrote the number, and handed it to me.

"Senator, why don't you and Ellisea have children?" I asked. Most politicians knew the value of the family package when it came to marketing.

"Neither of us ever wanted a child. We were both focused on our careers," he said. He abruptly walked away. I turned to watch him and caught the flutter of a kitchen curtain. It was just a quick glimpse, but it looked like Ellisea. And it looked like someone had beaten the bloody hell out of her.

26

HAMILTON HAD LEFT A MESSAGE FOR ME AT MY HOTEL ROOM, inviting me to dinner. I left him a message accepting with great eagerness. I pondered the cultural implications of dining with a man. Why is it that dating centers around food? Or at least the pretense of food. Hamilton and I might not eat, but food was the offering.

Then again, with Hamilton, food could be a very sensual experience. Was the proffering of food in a dating scene just the teasing of one of the senses—taste? With other senses to be sated soon thereafter? Or was it part of providing by the male? "I be he-man and bring food"?

With a grin I remembered one time Tinkie had dated a man from across the river. He was a bad boy with a cute ass, a wicked grin, and a big motorcycle. It was a brief affair, though, when dinner turned out to be a bag of chips and a six-pack of beer. Tinkie was highly insulted. A man just had to work a little harder than that if he wanted to keep the attention of a Daddy's Girl.

"Heck, I didn't expect caviar," Tinkie had said at the time, "but I thought he might go to the trouble of setting the table or maybe frying up some catfish. It was just that he didn't think enough of me to make any effort at all."

Her point was well taken. Perhaps food was the Daddy's Girl limbo pole—how low would he go? How much effort was he willing to put into the relationship? It wasn't a matter of pocketbook but of preparation. Once again I was forced to admit that DG training might have a grain of merit.

It had been a long day, so I took a shower, changed clothes, and headed for the Center. To my surprise, the place was empty when I got there. Or almost empty. Doreen was alone in her office, looking over what appeared to be a radio script.

"For the new audiotapes," she said, pushing the script aside. "Since I didn't go to Zinnia that day, we started on them. It's going to take several days to finish."

"Did Tinkie talk to Kiley Crenshaw?"

"It's Kiley Welford now. Kiley Rogers-Crenshaw-Grant-McAtie-Welford," Doreen said. "Tinkie did talk to her, and Tinkie advised me against giving her a dime. She said Kiley was white trash."

I couldn't help my smile. Kiley would get on Tinkie's last nerve. "Tinkie's an acute judge of character. Sometimes, Doreen, a sleeping dog is best left alone." What was this? Had I fallen into Aunt LouLane's cedar trunk of old truths and adages? Next I'd be talking about the four-mile trek to school in the snow without shoes.

"I guess I wanted to find my brother. Giving him the money was just an excuse. I wanted *him*." She pushed her dark hair off her forehead. "The money doesn't matter. I'd give it all to Kiley."

"Sometimes giving people money is the worst thing you can do for them."

Doreen looked up and laughed. "The root of all evil."

I shrugged. "Sometimes money allows people to indulge their worst traits."

"Tinkie said something to the same effect, as to how Kiley was the kind of person who would quit her job, buy cigarettes, beer, and sit on the sofa and watch the Jerry Springer show all day long if I gave her the money."

"Well, Tinkie was just more specific than I was."

"You two are quite a team," Doreen said.

We were, and I intended to keep it that way. "Doreen, please don't discourage Tinkie from going to her doctor."

"I wouldn't do that, Sarah Booth."

"Do I have your word?"

She hesitated. "Yes, you do. I would never hurt Tinkie." She started to say something else, but instead she just looked into my eyes. "Tinkie said you went to talk to Oren."

I let the topic of Tinkie go and moved on to the real reason I'd come to see her. "Oren Weaver claims he once healed people."

"He did."

"He lost his power?" I made a hocus-pocus motion with my hands. "Just like that?"

"More like he turned his back on it."

"Do you really believe that?" Now that I'd had time to escape the power of Oren's personality and the persuasion of his words, I'd begun to doubt what he said about Myra. I had to hand it to him, though, he had the power of oration and a great deal of personal charisma.

"Oren did heal his wife. Truly. And some others. Then he got caught up in his own image. He began to believe he was special, and his gift deserted him."

"And you think he can get it back?"

"Spirit is capable of anything, Sarah Booth."

I really wasn't in the mood for a sermon. "I spoke with Pearline." I told her what I'd learned, moving hesitantly around

Pearline's visit to Oren's tent revival, but Doreen wasn't shocked or angry at Pearline's attempts to take Rebekah for healing.

"She loved my baby. She did what she thought was right."

And futile, I could have pointed out, but didn't. "If Oren Weaver's fingerprints are explained away like this, we're back at square one. Yours and Pearline's are the only other prints on the bottle."

DRIVING THROUGH THE crowded streets of the French Quarter like a native—which meant using the sidewalk when necessary— I dialed Tinkie's room. I had thirty minutes to get ready for dinner with Hamilton, and Tinkie wasn't answering in her room or on her cell phone. Which meant she was probably in bed with Oscar. I had to admit that Tinkie managed to keep her priorities in order. She'd never let Oscar feel as if he didn't matter. There was a lesson to be learned there, too.

I parked in the garage and buzzed through the Monteleone lobby. My foot was almost in the elevator when I felt a hand on my shoulder.

"Ms. Delaney?"

I turned to face a young, bleached blonde with a bad perm, angry brown eyes, and a tight, cropped T-shirt that exposed a pierced navel above faded and torn jeans.

"I'm Kiley," she said. "I've come for my money."

Great. Just great. I looked around the lobby and realized that everyone was watching us. I had little choice.

"Come up to my room and we'll talk. I have an engagement in half an hour and I can't be late."

She stepped into the elevator with me. She didn't say a word as we made it to my floor and walked to my room.

"Must be nice to stay in a ritzy hotel," she said, pushing a frizz of hair behind her ear.

I decided that niceties would be wasted. "Doreen doesn't owe you anything, Kiley. She didn't owe Adam. She was going to share with him because she wanted an excuse to get to know her brother."

"She wouldn't have liked him very much," Kiley said, pulling a cigarette from her purse. She lit up. "I figured she'd try to back out. That's why I came here. She owes me. I had Adam's baby. I ought to get something for that." A look of pure distaste passed over her face, and I felt a pang of fear for the child. Kiley was a mother from hell. She didn't even try to pretend that she cared for her child.

"Doreen doesn't owe you a penny." I went into the bathroom and began to draw a bath. I'd give her another five minutes, and then she was going out the door.

"I'll get a lawyer."

"Get a dozen. Lillith, Doreen and Adam's mother, left the money to Doreen. There is no mention of another child. While you may not like this, there isn't a single legal thing you can do about it."

"Doreen's this big healer, talking about spirit and God, but it all just boils down to money." Her smile was knowing and cruel. "It's always just about money. Adam scooted in that church every time the doors opened. He nodded and bowed and scraped to the people he wanted to impress, but it was all just part of his act. You should have seen him when he wasn't with them. He laughed at them. He thought he was smarter than they were." Her eyes were hard as chipped rock. "He hated God."

Kiley was vicious. She wasn't going to get what she wanted, so she was going to try and tarnish Doreen's memory of the brother she'd never even met. It was a pitiful stab at revenge.

"I don't intend on repeating any of this to Doreen."

"You think I'm just trash. Well, let me tell you, when Joshua was born, I took care of him. Adam wouldn't touch him. He wouldn't even look at him. I fed that baby and rocked him and changed him and took him to his doctor appointments. Adam wouldn't even go in his room. If the truth were known, I think Adam killed himself deliberately to get away from me and our baby. So you can wipe that superior look off your face, Ms. Delaney. You don't know a thing about me. Don't judge me until you've walked in my shoes."

She stubbed the cigarette out and walked to the door. "This ain't over. I'll get my share of that money, just you wait and see."

She slammed the door behind her, leaving a lingering trace of smoke.

I'D JUST FINISHED my bath when my phone rang. As tempting as it was not to answer it, I did.

"Dahling," Cece's voice purred over the line, "I wish I were still in New Orleans."

I thought of Ellisea and was glad that Cece had gone home. "What's shaking?" I asked as I dried my toes.

"I need a favor."

"Sure." I was so deep into Cece that it didn't really matter what she asked, I would do it.

"Remember that tattoo parlor I got thrown out of?"

"I remember you talking about the Rainbow Boutique."

"I need you to go there tomorrow and scope it out."

"Is there any particular design you're interested in? Maybe an American flag? Or a heart?"

"So funny I forgot to laugh," Cece said drolly. "I've been thinking. Those guys were terrified. Why? So what if Ellisea has the lower half of her body covered in dragons? Why should they be concerned? Why should they be afraid?"

Cece had a legitimate point, I just didn't know where it might lead, or why. "The best thing would be for you to let this Ellisea thing go," I said. "You got to emcee the charity auction. You won. Let it go."

There was a long pause. "I didn't ask you for advice," Cece said, and I could tell I'd stung her feelings. "I just needed you to do something for me. Forget it."

"Wait a minute. I'll go over there and check it out," I said. "It's no trouble."

"My gut tells me something is very wrong here," Cece said. "I'd do it myself, but I have to go to Memphis in the morning for the Harvest Hunt Ball. The Vice President will be the special guest."

"Goody, goody," I said. I wasn't impressed with the politician or the event.

"Just go there and check it out. And call me."

"Will do," I said, checking the time. I could see the black jeans and red-and-black silk jacket I intended to wear, but the phone cord wasn't long enough to let me touch them.

"Tell Hamilton I said hello," she said with a smug tone in her voice.

"Good-bye, Cece," I said, hanging up and dashing for my clothes.

I was standing outside the hotel when Hamilton drove up in the vintage Caddy convertible he'd rented. It was black with a dove-gray interior, and it looked bad. Behind the wheel, he looked like some kind of modern-day European count.

"I thought we might hit some of the New Orleans nightlife," he said as I got in the front seat. "Maybe find some little club for dinner and dancing, and then see who's playing at Tippatino's."

"I hope it's the blues," I said, feeling a rush of anticipation at the thought of dancing down and dirty with Hamilton. In his black T-shirt and jacket, with his black hair pulled back in a queue, he was the epitome of dark and seductive.

The night was brisk, and Hamilton handed me his leather

jacket out of the backseat of the car. I held my hair to keep it
from whipping in my face as we headed out of the city, across
Lake Pontchartrain, and toward the bayous and marshes that
made up the fringes of New Orleans. These were small pockets of
old neighborhoods where subdivisions hadn't totally eradicated
all of the ethnic roots.

"We're going to Mai's," he said. "Cajun cooking and a house
band."

"Perfect." And it was. It was a small shack set up on pilings on
the lake. We went inside and ordered dirty martinis and found a
small table in a dark bar while we waited for a seat in the dining
room. The band was loud, sweaty, and zydeco. I could feel the
beat of the music getting into my blood. I was ready to party, and
the Devil could take care of tomorrow.

We ate grouper topped with a crawfish sauce that was the best
I'd ever tasted. Blooming onions, fried dill pickles, hot peppers
stuffed with cheese, and martinis. Hamilton's eyes were on me,
sometimes with a look I didn't understand, but always with
pleasure.

When we left Mai's, I was feeling no pain. We drove back across
the lake to Tippatino's, just in time to make it in the front door
before Marva White walked out onstage. My God, the place was
rocking.

Hamilton and I took to the dance floor and joined the throng
of dancers. It took me a moment to realize that I knew the man
dancing beside me. Aaron Neville gave me a smile. It was a night
to remember, in more ways than one.

It was nearly three in the morning when Hamilton swept me
into the car and back to his apartment. For all the liquor we'd
both drunk, we were remarkably sober. He pulled me against his
body as we drove, and I found it natural and right. In the long
night of drinking and dancing, the edges had been worn off
Hamilton. Not edges that he projected, but those that I had per-

ceived. He was no longer a distant fantasy who marched through my dreams and lived in Europe. He was a man, and he was beside me, and he felt good.

Inside his apartment, I turned into his arms and offered my lips for the kiss I'd waited for all evening. He kissed me, but it was slow and tender.

That strange look was in his eyes again when I looked up at him.

"Sarah Booth, will you come back to Paris with me? Just for a visit. You can stay a weekend or a week, as long or as short as you'd like."

I would have followed him into Hades at that moment. "I'd love to visit Paris. To be with you."

"Say you'll come."

"When I finish my case."

He smiled. "I never doubted otherwise. But after that, you'll at least visit me? I'll arrange the ticket whenever you say so."

"Why?" I asked.

"I want you to see what my life is. I want you to have a real chance to know who I am as a person. Tonight I realized something. I want you in my life."

My heart began to flutter. "I am in your life."

"As a fantasy, as the woman who lives across an ocean, a private investigator with green eyes and lacy black underwear."

So I was a fantasy for him also. It was maybe the best compliment I'd ever been paid.

"I want you to know where I live and the people I work with. The streets I walk and where I have coffee. I want you to know me in the way that a woman knows her man."

Hamilton knew many of those things about me. I was living a lifestyle he'd left behind, but it was one he knew. I truthfully had no clue what his life in Paris might be like. In my imagination I saw the Eiffel Tower, small cafés, petite women with poodles. It would be fun to see what it was really like. And it would be a big step to see who Hamilton was in the world he'd chosen to live in.

"I'd love to," I said, meaning it. "Paris in December. It sounds romantic."

"It will be," he said, gathering me in his arms. "I promise." He began to kiss me, and images of Paris fled before the sensations he aroused in me. It was, indeed, a night to remember.

27

HAMILTON HAD BUSINESS IN BATON ROUGE FOR THE DAY, AND
though he left me with the tenderest of kisses, I could tell something was up with his work. There were the finest worry lines
around his eyes. I held his strong shoulders and kissed his face,
wishing to make the worry go away. If only we could stay within
the walls of his apartment for two or three days, without interruption. We'd moved to a plane where there were real possibilities for us, not just midnight fantasies. We needed time together,
but we didn't have that luxury. Lives hung in the balance for him,
and Doreen's future hung in mine. His last look was one of long-
ing as he closed the door.

Tinkie answered her phone in a lazy purr. Oscar was having
room service send up breakfast. Though Tinkie volunteered to do
whatever I needed, I urged her to relax, sample the pleasures of

breakfast in bed, and wait until noon before worrying about anything.

I had two choices before me on this Tuesday morning: LeMont
or taking care of Cece's errand. I chose the latter. I still wasn't certain what game LeMont was playing with me, but my intuition
told me to avoid him.

The tattoo shop was exactly where Cece said it would be, and
it looked just as she'd described it. It was a shotgun-style struc-
ture that used to be someone's home. Now, like the houses
around it, it was zoned commercial.

The front door opened on a living room that fed into what had
once been a dining room that led to one or two bedrooms and
then on to the kitchen. The bathroom would be an add-on, the
caboose of indoor plumbing.

The bell jangled over the door as I walked in, aware immediately that the first two rooms were empty. I kept walking, but I
had the feeling that someone was waiting to pounce on me.

The tattoos were colorful, and I remembered my high school
desire for one. I was glad Aunt LouLane had forbidden it. I'd
wanted a butterfly on my shoulder. Chances are, it would still
look good enough—my skin wasn't sagging yet—but it would
certainly detract from such a dress as the one Mollie had created
for me. Tattoos, after the age of thirty, become a symbol of foolish youth rather than cool.

Beyond the tattoos was a room full of selections for body
piercing. Kiley's navel came to mind, and I wondered why she'd
done it. Lots of kids in the French Quarter, with their multihued
hair, had pierced eyebrows, cheeks, nostrils, chins, belly buttons,
and tongues. I didn't care to take an inventory of what lower ex-
tremities sported gold studs or chains. It was all just a little too
sadomasochistic for me.

"Ah, a virgin," a big, bald man said as he walked through the door. His smile revealed striking white teeth and intelligent eyes in a face crinkled with laugh lines. "Let me see. You've never had anything except your ears pierced, but you have a new lover who's a little more adventurous." His brow furrowed. "Hmmm. You look like the type who wants a nipple ring."

He laughed aloud at my expression.

"How about an eyebrow? Not quite as sensitive as a nipple, but a bit daring."

"Actually, I'm not in the mood for piercing anything, but I do have some questions."

He immediately grew wary. "Are you a cop?"

I shook my head. "But what would it matter? What you do is legal."

"Legal don't mean squat if the NOPD is breathing down my neck. Now, who are you and why are you asking questions?"

With his corded arms and strong chest, he could have worked as a bouncer in a tough bar. No point in pissing him off. "I'm a private investigator from Zinnia, Mississippi. I'm here in town on a case where an infant was killed. I'm helping the accused murderer. She didn't do it." All of this pointed in exactly the opposite direction that Cece was interested in. Maybe he would relax and talk.

His eyebrows rose, and I counted seven studs in the right one. "So what is it you want to know?"

"Is there any symbolism attached to body piercings?"

He thought a moment. "Body piercing is a sort of language. Piercings talk about lifestyle choices, and what a person may do in the pursuit of pleasure." He raised one eyebrow. "The line between pain and pleasure is a thin one."

So I'd been told. Maybe I just didn't want to take a walk on that dark side. I preferred my pleasure to be totally pleasurable. "Do you have to have any medical training to be a body piercer?"

"Not by law. I mean, they've been piercing ears in hair salons for years. Every beautician in New Orleans has a gun to do ears."

"An ear is a little different than a tongue."

"Yeah, an ear's tougher. You really have to punch it through. A tongue, now, that's easy work."

He was jacking with me, but not in an unfriendly way. Just teasing.

"It would seem, though, that some state laws would dictate a certain degree of medical knowledge. You know, what if a person was on a blood thinner or what if you hit an artery?" In some of the places people got pierced there was a tremendous blood flow.

"I can't speak for the other shops, but I've had training. I was a surgical nurse. Trust me, I ask about medications and things like that *before* I even consider a client. There's a lot of bad stuff out there. Hepatitis C or HIV. Man, I don't need that shit in my life."

"You left the paycheck a surgical nurse makes for a tattoo parlor?"

"I make a lot more here, plus I work for myself. I don't have to take orders from some jerk-off doctor who makes bad decisions and then blames the nursing staff."

I could understand that. I'd been around enough doctors with a God complex to understand how wearing such an attitude could be on a nurse. Of course, there was no telling what one of his current clients might do if they didn't care for his handiwork.

"May I look around your shop?"

"Everything except where I do the work," he said. "You've seen most of it. There's one more room with some leather and stuff. Knock yourself out." He left the room and disappeared into the back portion of the house, the area he'd told me not to go into.

I wandered around, checking out the tattoo and piercing selections, which did make me wince. I'd hoped to find some reason that this guy would have been uncomfortable around Cece. But I didn't see anything that I hadn't seen in other tattoo shops in the French Quarter.

"See anything you like?" he asked when he returned.

"Do you ever do things like permanent eyeliner or lipstick?" I wondered if that was what Ellisea Clay had come to this shop for.

"Sure. That's very popular with some of the local entertainers. We do some nipple enhancement, too. You know, so the rosy areolas show up through a gauzy outfit. It's hot down here. Makeup tends to sweat off, but what I put on stays. Forever."

I was getting nowhere fast. We could swap fashion tips all day, and I'd be no closer to finding out what I'd come for. "Has Ellisea Clay had that kind of work done here?" I asked.

That was all it took. He was on me like white on rice, and I was sitting in the dirt in front of the tattoo parlor before I knew what hit me.

"Stay out of here," he said. Like Cece had pointed out, he seemed more afraid than angry. "Don't ever come back here if you know what's good for you."

"When you talk to Ellisea, tell her Sarah Booth Delaney was asking after her," I said as I dusted off my bottom and started toward my car.

As I DROVE back to the Quarter, I dialed Tinkie again. She was eager for me to meet her at Madame Rochelle's Tearoom. She wanted her future read. I found my resistance interesting. In Zinnia, Tammy Odom was often a great help to me. She saw things in the future, and I had no doubt of her psychic gift. Here in New Orleans, I was suspicious of everyone. My first reaction was that such people were charlatans with some angle to play.

I reluctantly agreed to meet Tinkie, hung up, and called Cece to report my trip to the tattoo parlor. She was disappointed that I hadn't found out anything else.

"That man knows Ellisea and he's afraid of something," I said. "Other than that, I can't tell you anything."

"Beans," Cece said. "I'm sure there's something there. Maybe you could follow that guy."

"I seriously doubt he has a lot of personal contact with Ellisea. I'm sure he called her, but I doubt I could convince the NOPD of my need for a wiretap, and that's the only way I'm going to get anything from that guy unless it's at gunpoint."

"Maybe she'll show up there?"

"Doubtful. Especially not if she knows I know about the place. She'll make a point of staying away. And what would I do if she walked up? Demand to know what's going on? Like she'd just tell me."

"Too bad kidnapping and torture are punishable offenses."

I told her about my visit to the Clay house and the vandalization of Ellisea's car.

"They wrote something?" she asked, interested.

"They *tried* to write some word. I don't think they could spell." I gave her the letters the best I could remember.

Cece was quiet. "Something just doesn't ring true here."

"Can you say the word *obsessed*? Cece, you're taking this just a little too far."

"Dahling, obsession is one of the elements of genius, or haven't you heard. And if you want to play tit for tat"—she laughed softly—"I heard you were fairly obsessed with Hamilton."

Obsessed was the wrong word. In the past, I'd been obsessed by the fantasy of him. But now that he was a real person to me, I wasn't obsessed. I was delighted. "He's invited me to Paris."

"When?" Cece squealed.

"When my case is over."

"And you're going?"

I only hesitated a split second, but it was enough.

"You are going, aren't you?" There was a warning in her tone.

"I told him yes. Please don't talk about this to Coleman." I didn't want to ask that, but I had to. If anyone was going to tell Coleman, it should be me.

"What is it you owe Coleman?" she asked.

"Only the same treatment I'd expect from him if the shoe were on the other foot."

"I don't recall that he told you last summer when he and Connie took that cruise."

There was truth in Cece's statement, but issues around Coleman weren't black and white. I had the power to hurt him, and I didn't want to do it.

"Cece, I know you understand this. If I tell him, then I treat him with the respect he deserves because of our long-standing friendship."

"Don't screw this thing with Hamilton up," she cautioned.

"What? Are you and Tinkie double-teaming me?"

"Dahling, we're on your team and we just passed you the touchdown opportunity of the century. Now we intend to do a little blocking for you. All you have to do is run, baby, run."

DOREEN WAS LEADING a class on meditation at the Center when I got there. I had a little while before I was due to meet Tinkie, so I found a space on the floor at the back of the room. Golden sunlight filtered in through the large windows of the room. Outside, the patio bloomed with exotics. It was a lovely space, and many of the people in the class were focusing out the window as they sat cross-legged and listened to Celtic harp music.

I found myself adrift in my own thoughts, even as Doreen's melodic voice urged her class to let go of thought, to move toward an image of white light entering their bodies as they breathed in, of all negative energy departing as they exhaled.

She began a soft chant that was the most peaceful sound in the world. It wrapped itself around me and held me safely.

When Doreen spoke again, I was floating in a pool of golden light. I opened my eyes and looked at the people in the class. They were all ages, all types. Yet it seemed the sunshine outside the window had penetrated them. For that one moment, they looked blissful.

Doreen thanked the class and dismissed them. I waited for her at the back door. "Did you meditate?" she asked.

"I did. It was strangely . . . peaceful."

"I could recommend some books."

"Yours?"

"No, actually there are plenty of people who've done a lot of research into meditation and the connection between mind, body, and spirit. That isn't my field. I just like to meditate."

"It's a little passive."

She laughed out loud. "Sarah Booth, you have the most peculiar ideas sometimes."

"Doreen, have you talked with your lawyer lately?"

She looked up at the skylight as we walked through the Center. "He says he's won cases with less to work with."

He probably had, but he wasn't telling her about the ones he'd lost. "I haven't found anything really helpful to you."

"You have to keep looking, Sarah Booth. You and Tinkie. No one else really cares whether I'm innocent or not. No one else cares who killed my baby."

"I really had my hopes pinned on Pearline, but she didn't kill Rebekah."

"No, she didn't."

"Is it possible the medication could have been put in the formula accidentally?"

"No, I was careful about Rebekah's medications. So was Pearline. Besides, we didn't have any barbiturates in the apartment. I don't use prescription drugs."

I nodded. "You told me that none of the men suspected they could be the father."

"That's right. I never let on to any of them when I got pregnant. And I made it clear to all that I was sleeping with other people."

"And none of the three had access to your apartment?"

"I never gave anyone a key."

I nodded. "We're going to have to narrow this field. We need that DNA test and we need it now."

"I'll call LeMont and see what he says," she volunteered.

"It's a start."

"What's a start?" Michael asked, coming around a corner. He wore a dove-gray suit with a black tie and white shirt. He managed to look both conservative and individual. It was a neat trick.

"The work on the archetype tapes," Doreen answered smoothly. "I was telling Sarah Booth that I had another taping session this afternoon."

"Is there a conflict?" Michael asked.

Doreen had always been so open with Michael, I couldn't help but wonder why she'd chosen not to discuss the DNA with him. But I was glad. It was awkward for a suspect to know every move we made.

"No conflict," I said, smiling. "Tinkie and I are having our tea leaves read."

Michael laughed. "You want to dabble but you're afraid of the real thing, right?"

"What do you mean?"

"Why not just ask Doreen to read your tarot cards?" he suggested.

Doreen shook her head. "Don't push so hard, Michael. The tearoom is perfect for what Tinkie needs." She walked away.

"I'm concerned," Michael said when she was out of earshot. "Have you found anything to help her case?"

"As a matter of fact, we have," I said, deciding on the big bluff. It was sometimes effective in poker. "I'm just not at liberty to discuss it with you now."

I turned and began to walk away when I felt his hand on my shoulder.

"Doreen is the heart of this operation. Can you clear her?" There was something close to anger in his eyes.

"I can't make any promises. I can only tell you that Tinkie and I are on top of things."

28

MADAME ROCHELLE'S TEAROOM WAS A QUAINT LITTLE PLACE WITH half a dozen dainty tables and a warren of back rooms where various psychics foretold the future with cards, palm reading, and patterns of tea leaves.

Tinkie and I ordered some green tea and sipped while we waited our turn.

"I don't think this is a good idea," I said for the third time. "When we get home, we can go see Tammy." I pressed a little harder. "Remember, we have to be home Thursday for your doctor's appointment."

"I haven't forgotten," Tinkie said, her smile patient. "Dr. Graham is far too handsome to disappoint."

I could only admire her courage. I knew how upset and frightened she'd been only a few days before. Now she was able to kid around about her fetish for handsome doctors.

"You promised me," I reminded her.

"I'll make my appointment," she said. She touched my hand on the table. "Only good friends care enough to bully like you do, Sarah Booth."

"I don't care if you call it manipulation, bullying, or mothering, as long as you make that appointment." I sipped the hot tea, knowing exactly why coffee had become the traditional drink in my household. I didn't know anyone who drank tea on a daily basis, and couldn't imagine why anyone would.

A slender woman with dark eyes came over to our table. "Gwendolyn will see you," she said to Tinkie. Tinkie had picked her because the name had appealed to her love of Arthurian legend.

"Come on, Sarah Booth," she said. "You have to go with me." We followed our guide back through several narrow hallways to a curtained cubicle. She drew aside the orange cloth and ushered us in.

My first glimpse of Gwendolyn made me stop in my tracks. She had hair that must have been five feet long. It hung in a braid that fell over one shoulder and swept the floor by her feet. She wore purple, layers of fabric that held no discernible shape, but beneath it all she was slender. Her blue eyes were oddly shaped, almost like teardrops, and she didn't blink as she waited for us to sit.

"What is it you wish to know?" she asked with a hint of an accent.

"Are you from Germany?" I asked.

"You can remain with your friend but you must be quiet," she said firmly.

Tinkie put a finger to her lips and winked at me. "I want to know about my future," she said. "Am I going to have a child?"

Gwendolyn assessed Tinkie's slim figure, her perfect hair and makeup. She reached across her small table and picked up Tinkie's hand. Instead of reading it, she held it.

"I see a girl," she said. "Blonde, with a big smile."

"A girl," Tinkie said with such a rush of emotion that I felt a stab of pain. I hadn't realized how much Tinkie wanted a child.

"She's swinging . . . in a garden."

"I have a garden with a swing," Tinkie said. "Is she alone? Are there other children?"

Gwendolyn's face had gone strangely slack. She squeezed Tinkie's hand and released it. "There is only the one child." She hesitated. "Sometimes decisions can't be undone," she said gently.

"What?" Tinkie said, paling. "What are you saying?"

"Only that we all make choices and take certain paths. Sometimes we can't go back and take a different path."

I looked from one to the other. I had no clue what Gwendolyn was talking about, but whatever it was, she was upsetting Tinkie. My friend dashed tears from her face with angry fists.

"Why are you saying this?"

"I can only tell you what I see," Gwendolyn said. "Your child is alone, but she isn't unhappy. She says to tell you that she understands."

Tinkie stood up so fast that she knocked the psychic's small table over. "I don't know who you are, but you're a very cruel woman."

"No, I'm not," Gwendolyn said. "Think back on this and remember. She understood."

Tinkie slammed out of the small room, with me hot on her heels. I caught up with her on the street and withdrew the hand I'd lifted to grasp her shoulder. One look at her face told me to stow my questions.

It took her eight blocks in high heels before she'd slow enough for me to catch my breath. "You were right, Sarah Booth. We shouldn't have gone there," she said. "Don't ever mention it to me again. I'm going back to the hotel to take a nap unless you need me to do something."

———

HAMILTON WASN'T AT his apartment or answering his cell phone, and I was left with the ugly reality that LeMont had to be dealt with. It was time to fish or cut bait. As soon as I thought the phrase, I cringed. I was becoming some kind of adage addict. I couldn't go half an hour without spouting—or thinking—some old truism.

LeMont answered my call on the second ring.

"I'll meet you at Napoleon's, as long as you're buying," he said.

"Whatever." I still wasn't certain how to play LeMont. He was the joker in the deck. Was he a legitimate police detective or a henchman for the Clays? I didn't know what to make of him, and he wasn't an easy man to read.

The restaurant he'd chosen was as old as anything in the city; Napoleon Bonaparte had once dined there, or at least ordered out. Since I arrived first, I chose the darkest corner and waited. LeMont breezed through the door and I caught a glimpse of how handsome he could be if he allowed it.

I motioned him back to the corner. "We need to talk," he said as he waved the waiter over and gave his drink order.

I wasn't going to argue with that.

"I'm a good detective. I do my job and I do it properly."

Now that was a debatable point, but I didn't say anything.

"My father worked for Henri Boudet. They grew up in the swamps together. Dad was killed when I was fourteen. Mr. Boudet sent money to my mother every week so my family could survive. There were ten of us kids. He put six of us through college, including me."

I hadn't known for certain what the connection between LeMont and Ellisea was, but I hadn't expected this heart-tugging confession of the good deeds of Henri Boudet. "I have to tell you, LeMont, that may be the only good thing I've ever heard about Boudet."

He took the drink the waiter deposited in front of him and swallowed half of it. "He's a bad man. And a powerful one. When he whispers, every politician in this town bends down to listen. But he isn't totally evil. He was good to me and my family."

"So you owe Henri Boudet?"

LeMont shook his head. "I don't owe Henri anything. I don't. And I made that clear to him. But he asked me to look out for Ellisea, as a favor. That I do. I try to keep her safe and out of trouble."

"Sounds like a full-time job."

"It can be. Ellisea is self-destructive. She's...dangerous, but mostly to herself."

"Tell that to Cece."

"Your friend provoked her. Once provoked, Ellisea is like a snake. She doesn't care who she bites, she just strikes."

"How far would you go to protect Ellisea?"

The question pissed him off, but he checked his temper. "Not far enough to jeopardize a case, if that's what you're thinking. I try to keep Ellisea's name out of the paper when she gets in scrapes. When the senator's out of town, I sometimes tail her to make sure she's safe. That's as far as it goes."

He sounded so sincere. But Ted Bundy must have seemed like a nice guy to the girls he picked up—until he killed them.

"Is Ellisea capable of killing a baby if she thought it might jeopardize her husband's career?"

He finished his drink. "Yes, she's capable of that. But she didn't do it. The senator isn't the father. The DNA tests came back. None of those men are the father."

29

DOREEN WASN'T AT THE CENTER AND SHE WASN'T AT HER HOME. But Starla was there, and I accepted the cup of hot tea she offered as I sat shivering in the failing light of the courtyard. I had time to kill until I could find Doreen and wring her neck.

"I've gone over and over this whole thing," Starla said. "I just can't make sense of any of it."

She didn't know the half of it. "I wish I could say that I had some solid leads." With paternity ruled out as a motive, I didn't even have a suspect.

"If Doreen had wanted to kill Rebekah, she could have skipped some of her medication, or simply suffocated her. Why would she put medicine in a bottle that would show up in a blood test? They do tests in every autopsy now. Everyone knows that."

I put down my cup of tea. Starla had hit on something important. "Whoever killed Rebekah knew the murder would be detected," I said.

"The one thing that's bothered me the most is how Doreen could sleep through someone getting into her apartment and drugging her baby," Starla said.

"Not if someone had drugged her, too." Damn! I was a day late and a dollar short. I should have thought of this in the beginning. Doreen's blood had never been tested and now it was too late. If there were any barbiturates in her system from the night Rebekah was murdered, they were long gone.

Starla's eyes widened. "Now that makes sense." She leaned forward and lowered her voice. "If I were you, I'd be looking for someone who meant to hurt Doreen. I don't think someone killed Rebekah to get her out of the way, I think they meant to make Doreen suffer."

ALL THE WAY to the Monteleone, I thought about Starla's words. I'd never viewed the murder as a weapon meant to harpoon Doreen's heart. It put a different slant on everything.

I hurried up to my floor, eager to discuss the possibilities with Tinkie. My hand was lifted to knock on her door when I heard Oscar's voice.

"You're being ridiculous, Tinkie."

"You're being selfish." Tinkie was just as angry as her husband.

"We had an agreement. You knew the terms when we married. Now you want to renegotiate. That's not how it works."

"This isn't a business deal, Oscar. This is our marriage. I'm not renegotiating, I'm trying to tell you how I feel. I want a child. I'm headed toward thirty-five. If I'm going to do this, it should be soon."

"My mother warned me that you'd hit this phase. The biological clock is ticking and you're going into a panic. It's a natural reaction for a primitive animal, but we aren't primates, Tinkie. You knew when we married that I didn't want children."

"Why not, Oscar?"

"I don't want the focus of my life to shift. I don't want to make every decision based on a kid."

"It doesn't have to be like that. We can afford a nanny. We can have help. A child would add to our lives, not diminish them."

Even though I knew I should walk away, I was riveted to the floor. It was as if I were arguing with myself.

"No, Tinkie. We had an agreement. You'll have to honor it."

"That's where you're wrong, Oscar. I *don't* have to honor it." There was a naked threat in her voice. "My father wants a grandchild."

Man, the gloves were coming off fast. Oscar worked for Tinkie's dad at the bank.

"Well, he picked the wrong husband for you, Tinkie. He knows how I stand on the issue."

"He thought you'd change your mind. He told me you'd mellow and want a child as you got older."

"He seriously misjudged me."

"Well, I want one, and what I want should count for something."

"Not in this instance."

Something crashed against the door. I ducked instinctively, even though I was well protected.

"Stop it, Tinkie."

Her answer was another crash. "I won't stop it! I'm furious. I've been angry about this for years. Ever since you made me"— there was another crash and the sound of sobbing—"I shouldn't have listened to you. I should have had the baby then."

"Tinkie," Oscar's voice had gentled. "I love you. Please, don't do this to yourself."

Something really big crashed. Television probably. I cringed.

"This lump in my breast is your fault, Oscar. It's all the anger I've suppressed because you won't let me be a mother."

"Tinkie, you're talking like a madwoman."

"I am mad. I'm furious! And I'm going to show you exactly how mad I am."

The loud crash of glass had to be the ornate mirror over the bed. Tinkie was trashing the room. I backed away from the door and hesitated. Part of me wanted to rush in and grab Tinkie, to hold her until she quit. But a wiser part of me held out. This wasn't my business. No matter how much I cared about my partner, I had no say-so in her marriage.

I went to my room and closed the door. There was another muffled crash from Tinkie's room and I closed my eyes. I'd ended up as a private investigator because of Tinkie. She'd once toyed with the idea of pursuing a fling with Hamilton. Even at the time I'd thought it was odd. Tinkie was a one-man woman, and she seemed to adore Oscar. But there were depths to every relationship that swirled and eddied below the surface. I'd just learned one of Tinkie's bitterest secrets, and I was sorry that I knew.

My phone rang and I went to answer it, hoping the storm in the room next door was over.

"I got some information you might want."

The voice was Kiley Crenshaw-whoever-whoever. I'd forgotten her string of names. "Kiley, I seriously doubt you have anything that would interest me."

"No, I do. Adam knew who his sister was."

She had my attention. "What are you saying?"

"He knew about Doreen Mallory. I've got proof. I got his computer out of the U-Store-It where I took it right after he drowned. He was always hovering over the computer, but he never wanted me to fool with it. So I started thinking there might be something his sister would be interested in seeing. I guess he thought he'd wiped the memory clean before he left, but I'm smarter than he thought. I found a big file about Doreen. He knew a lot about her. He musta known she was his sister."

"How would he know that?" I asked.

"Adam was smart. So am I. You think we're just ignorant rednecks, but we're not. I got an associate's degree in computer science. I've worked at a hospital. In fact, I made more money than Adam. He was too busy at the church and researching his religious saints to be worried about doctor bills and baby formula. He had a real thing for healers like Doreen. He looked 'em up on the Internet and the newspapers. He followed what they were doing, but he was mostly interested in Doreen."

I remembered my visit to his home. "His mother said he was very religious. I'm sure that's why he kept up with Doreen. He couldn't have known she was his sister."

"Then why is her file six times bigger than anyone else's? You'd better take a look at this."

Nothing was easy with Kiley, and I knew where this was headed. "How much will it cost me to look at this stuff?"

"Half the money Doreen got from her mama."

"Bribery is illegal."

Kiley laughed. "This isn't bribery, Ms. Delaney. This is commerce. I got something you want and you're gonna have to pay to get it."

"How do I know any of it's worth looking at? I'm not going to buy a pig in a poke."

"I could e-mail you one of the files," Kiley suggested. "Sort of like a sample."

I didn't have my computer, but Oscar never traveled without a laptop. I could access my e-mail from his computer. If he survived the fight. "Okay, that's a deal," I said, giving her my e-mail address.

"You'll be in touch," she said with growing confidence. "This stuff is gonna make you beg for more."

I hung up, unable to imagine anything that would make me beg Kiley.

Both my cell phone and the hotel phone began to ring at once. I answered the hotel phone and knew I'd made the right choice when I heard Hamilton's voice on the line. Still, I couldn't help but check the number showing on the cell. It was Coleman calling. I tucked the phone under a pillow to muffle the ringing and turned my attention to Hamilton.

"I'm sorry, Sarah Booth, but I'm tied up here in Baton Rouge."

"What's wrong?" I could hear disappointment in his voice, and it gave me a small thrill to realize I knew him that well.

"Julio Martinez has disappeared in Peru. He was a political figure who was gaining power with his campaign to protect the native people and their land. There was a raid on his home. He was taken by a right-wing faction."

"You mean kidnapped."

"He's probably dead."

"Goodness, Hamilton." I didn't know what to say. He sounded upset, as if he'd known Mr. Martinez for a long time. "I'm sorry."

"That's not the worst. They have his family: a wife and three children all under the age of seven. Masked men broke into their home, put burlap sacks over their heads, and took them."

"Did anyone see this?"

"They left Polaroid photographs. They want us to know."

"Will they hurt them?"

"Yes, to make a point. They want everyone to know that those who dare defy them will suffer. They'll kill the Martinezes and their children, and they'll laugh while they're doing it."

"What can I do?" I asked.

"Just understand that I want to be with you, even though I can't. I've booked a flight for Washington, D.C. I should be back tomorrow. Will you wait for me?"

"I'll be here," I said. It was a simple exchange of basic information, but it was so much more than that.

He asked about Tinkie and made me promise to help Cece as long as she stayed out of New Orleans.

"Henri Boudet isn't a man to fool around with," he told me. "He's done some terrible things to people who cross him. Keep telling Cece that until she hears it."

"Gotcha," I said, wondering why I was about to cry. He was leaving for one night. I acted like he was going to serve a thirty-year prison term.

"Be careful, Sarah Booth," he said. "This case may be a lot more volatile than you ever imagined."

I hung up the phone and sat still for a moment. In knowing Hamilton, my world had expanded with a mind-boggling speed. Along with my case, I was now worrying about a family in Peru.

And a sheriff in Sunflower County.

I hesitated before I dialed Coleman back. I remembered what Tammy had said. The lion and the wolf. I'd denied that I was caught between them, but it was a lie. And I'd just begun to feel the first nibbling of their teeth. Neither of them meant to harm me. Neither could fully understand the choice I would soon be forced to make.

I almost hung up when Coleman answered, but I didn't. Sweetie Pie was serving time in his jail. I had to make sure she was okay. "How's my girl?" I asked in the perky voice Aunt LouLane had schooled me in when she still thought it was possible I'd turn out all right. Perky is a DG prerequisite. It covers a multitude of conflicting emotions.

There was raw desperation in Coleman's voice. "Sweetie is fine. It's Connie. She's locked her mother and sister out of the house. She has a gun and she says she's going to kill herself."

My body went cold. I held the phone and said nothing.

"Her mother says she hasn't eaten in two days. Sarah Booth, if I force my way into the house, she may kill herself. If I don't, she may do damage to the baby."

"Coleman, I'm so sorry." I had no advice to offer. As with Tinkie's marriage, this was a decision I had no right to interfere in.

"I don't know what to do," Coleman said, and there was anguish in his tone. "All of my life, I've always had a gut instinct of what to do in times of crisis. Now, when I need it most, it's gone. Good God, Connie is capable of anything."

"Has Doc Sawyer tried to talk to her?" Connie, like me, had grown up with Doc as our family practitioner. He had a way of soothing folks even in the worst of times. My Aunt LouLane had often said he could talk sense into a cow-kicked cur.

"Dewayne's bringing him out to the house now."

"Doc may be able to reason with her." I'd seen the man work miracles before.

"Sarah Booth, whatever happens, this has nothing to do with you. Connie would have done this regardless. Our marriage was dead. She knew that and she tricked me into staying the only way she knew how—with a pregnancy. She knew I'd stay for a baby, and she manipulated events to suit herself. She knew that I'd given you up. You played no part in this."

His words were small stones dropping into water. I felt the ripples but I knew it didn't matter. If something tragic happened to Connie or the baby, that would always be between Coleman and me.

"Here's Doc," Coleman said. "I'll keep you posted."

The line went dead and I was left sitting on the edge of my hotel bed as cold as the marble headstone that marked Lillith Lucas's grave.

30

TINKIE PUT A TENTATIVE HAND ON MY SHOULDER AND GAVE IT A shake. "Sarah Booth?" she whispered. "Are you okay? I knocked and knocked but you didn't answer. The door was open so I just came in."

"I'm fine," I said, though I was far from it. I had no idea how much time had passed since I put the telephone back in its cradle. My mind had simply ceased to process information once the first onslaught of images of Connie and a gun had run through my head.

"Are *you* okay?" I asked. She'd been crying, but her tears were dried, her makeup fresh, and she was dressed to kill.

"Yes. Oscar and I had a fight." She frowned at me. "What's wrong with you?"

"Connie's locked herself in the house with a gun. She says she's going to kill herself."

Tinkie started to say something, thought better of it, and sat down on the bed beside me. "That woman is a lunatic. She's endangering her baby. That's criminal conduct."

"I don't think she's rational, Tinkie. She isn't really thinking this through."

"In any case, there's nothing you can do. You don't have a role to play in this, Sarah Booth. It's just as well you're here. When the ca-ca hits the fan, at least you won't be there to get spattered."

"Right."

"Connie was always unbalanced. The rush of all those pregnancy hormones just pushed her over the edge. Did they send for Doc Sawyer?"

"Yes. He'd just gotten there."

"I could break Coleman's neck for calling and telling you this." She got up and paced the room. "Where's Hamilton?"

"On his way to D.C. He had an emergency. A Peruvian family was kidnapped and likely assassinated."

"Good Lord. You'd think people could behave for a few days and give you and Hamilton a chance." She tapped her foot with exasperation. "Well, you can't just sit there and mope. What are we doing next?"

I went over to the minibar and fixed us both a Jack and water. Tinkie was right. I couldn't just sit on my hands. I had a case to solve. "I need to use Oscar's computer, if he doesn't mind."

"Too bad if he does. I'll be right back." She whisked out of the room and was back in record time. She plugged in the laptop and motioned for me to take it over. In a moment, I had my e-mail pulled up and Kiley's message on the screen. The file she'd attached was easy to open.

In my duty as God's watcher, I have kept close tabs on Doreen Mallory.

She is a vile and contemptible woman. She flaunts herself, using her beauty as a lure. Men watch her with lust in their hearts. She talks of God's healing love, but it is wantonness she worships. Even as I watch, she is leaving the Square with a man. She will take him to her bed and corrupt him. She will ride him until he moans and sends his seed into her.

Others see only her dark curls and flashing eyes, the perfection of her ripe body. But I see the truth. I see Satan unbound. She is unclean of spirit, corrupt of the flesh. She is a sign of the Antichrist. Hail, the Harlot has come unto the City, and the Battle of Armageddon will soon be fought, unless I take the necessary steps.

It is easy to see that Doreen Mallory is following in the footsteps of the mother. She can't deny her blood. She is accursed, branded with the blasphemy of her flesh. She is truly the spawn of Satan and must be destroyed.

"Tinkie!" She was reading over my shoulder and I turned and grabbed her hand. "Kiley wasn't lying. Adam did know that Doreen was his sister. On top of that, I think he may have killed Lillith." I reminded her of my visit with Coot Henderson and the phrase he'd overheard when he'd awakened to find Lillith's house burning.

"I don't know," Tinkie said. "Maybe it's a common phrase among that type of religious person. How old would Adam have been when his mother died?"

I did the math in my head. "In his mid-twenties."

She frowned. "It's strange that Adam knew about Lillith and Doreen. I give you that. But it's a long jump from strange to murder."

She was right; I was jumping to conclusions. But my gut told me I was onto something. The problem was that, though I may have solved Lillith's murder, it was no help in figuring out who'd killed Rebekah. Adam Crenshaw had been dead for four years.

"Kiley says there are other files. She wants to sell them to us."

"If you asked her to, Doreen would buy them. I just don't see the relevance. Adam Crenshaw's been dead for four years. He doesn't figure into Rebekah's murder, and that's what we need to focus on right now."

Tinkie was correct. I'd mention the files to Doreen and she could buy them or not. My big concern at the present was trying to find another suspect in Rebekah's death.

"As fascinating as Kiley's stash of trivia might be, we have real problems," I said. "Doreen lied about the baby's father. It's not the senator or Oren Weaver or Michael." I told her what LeMont had discovered about the DNA tests.

"Damn Doreen!" Tinkie was hot. "She needs to tell us the truth and she needs to do it right now. Grab a jacket. We're going to find her."

I did as Tinkie directed, and I followed her out of the hotel and into the streets of the French Quarter.

There was once a time when the tourist season meant June through September. These days New Orleans showed her stuff all year long. Music poured from the open doorways of bars, where kids churned in and out. It was one big party in a different location on each street corner.

Neon rippled down the streets as Tinkie and I dodged clusters of people. I was reminded of a New York City traffic jam, except there were no cars, only human bodies. We found a current of movement and followed through the worst of the logjam on Bourbon Street until we broke free.

"This has been great, but I'm about ready for Zinnia," Tinkie said.

I wanted to say something about her doctor's appointment, but I shut my mouth. Sometimes the best thing a friend can do is just zip it.

"Do you know where Doreen is?" I asked Tinkie, since she seemed to have a destination in mind.

"There was a meeting of the Jackson Square tarot readers. She mentioned it to me. It's in a restaurant just a few blocks from here."

I knew the Quarter well enough to get around, but Tinkie really *knew* it. I was happy to let her steer, but my mind kept slipping back to images of Connie in her house, holding a gun, blood splatter on a wall.

I was glad to leave those thoughts as Tinkie indicated a dark doorway with gold lettering that read Déjà Vue Restaurant. It was the perfect place for fortune-tellers, I supposed.

It wasn't hard to find the gathering. I recognized several of the people from the Square, but as I searched over the faces, I didn't see Doreen. Starla waved to us, and Tinkie went to talk to her.

The place was loud, so I leaned against a wall and waited. I had no idea what Starla was telling Tinkie, but they both appeared to be upset. Tinkie had just started back toward me when the meeting was called to order.

"There's a move afoot to try and regulate the readers around the Square," a tall man in a black robe began. "We are gathered here tonight to discuss what our options are."

So it wasn't a social event but a movement. I liked the idea of an army of fortune-tellers picketing city hall. It was perfect for New Orleans. Instead of trouble, it would bring the tourists swarming.

"Doreen's in the Desire Projects. She called Starla just after you left," Tinkie said.

Desire was one of the toughest of New Orleans' inner-city projects. It was full of drugs and guns and anger. "What's she doing there?"

"Some kid. A gangbanger, from what Starla says. He's having migraines so severe that he's beating his head against the wall. Doreen's gone to see if she can help him."

"It would seem that Doreen has a death wish," I said, aggravated by her lack of common sense. Desire was a place where even the innocents got injured. The one thing I knew was that Tinkie and I weren't going there to look for her.

"Doreen believes people come into your life for a reason." She shrugged. "I don't think she looks at people or places as dangerous or safe."

"There's nothing else we can do tonight. We'll track her down first thing in the morning," I said.

"I guess we're at a dead end." Tinkie looked as glum as I felt.

The one thing I didn't want was to go back to my hotel room and wait. I dreaded the ringing of the phone, yet it was exactly what I was waiting to hear. We'd just started down the street when I heard the cell phone in my purse ring. I'd forgotten that I was carrying the darn thing.

"Aren't you going to answer it?" Tinkie asked.

Against my better judgment, I answered without even checking caller ID.

"Dahling, you'll never guess what I've discovered," Cece said.

"I hope it pertains to solving this case, because we're going nowhere," I said.

"That word written on Ellisea's Jaguar, well, it does have a meaning."

I frowned at Tinkie. "It's Cece. She's still on that Ellisea tear."

Tinkie took the phone. "Cece, it's time you just got over Ellisea. This is getting— What? Okay, but this better be good." She held the phone so we both could hear.

"'Chandala' is an archaic word that means 'outcast.' Like someone outside of society."

There was a long pause. "So," Tinkie finally said.

"'Outcast,'" Cece repeated. "Don't you get it?"

"No, we don't," I said, not even trying to keep the annoyance out of my voice. "Cece, there are serious things happening in Sunflower County and all over the world. Why are you so obsessed with Ellisea?"

"You shouldn't be so quick to make snap judgments," Cece said in her best take-me-to-task tone. "This is important, Sarah Booth. It bears indirectly on your case. But if you don't want to know, I'll just hang up."

"No!" Tinkie and I both shouted.

"I'm sorry," I said. "I didn't mean to hurt your feelings. It's just that Con—"

"Connie Peters is holed up with a gun, making everyone in Sunflower County turn somersaults to placate her whims. Yes, I know. Dahling, don't be a fool. She's not going to hurt herself. She's crazy like a fox."

"You really think so?" I grabbed on to the thread of hope Cece cast my way.

"I'm positive about it. Think back to high school, Sarah Booth. Was Connie ever at the top of the pyramid? Did she ever do the really dangerous tumbling stunts? The answer is no. Connie always played it safe."

"But she's nuts."

"Not nuts enough to harm herself. This is all payment due from Coleman. She's just getting back at him, and she knows this is the most effective way to do it. It's public, it puts him in a place where he can't take action, and it lets everyone in the county know that he's . . . under her thumb."

"But is he?" I asked, thinking about his rental house and the fact that he had moved out.

"As long as she can injure that baby, he has no recourse but to dance to her tune. If it means sitting all day in his own front yard with medics and Doc Sawyer and everybody driving by and gawking, then that's what he's got to do."

"Enough about Connie, tell us what you found," Tinkie said with some impatience in her voice.

"It's simple," Cece said. "Ellisea Clay is a transsexual."

31

ONCE TINKIE AND I HAD FOUND A BAR, ORDERED DRINKS, AND HAD a sip or two, we called Cece back and pelted her with questions. She'd done her homework and she had all the bases covered. The clincher was the birth records she'd dug up—for a six-pound eight-ounce baby boy, born July 12, 1966, to Henri and Callie Boudet and filed in St. Martin Parish. Another birth, for a daughter, was recorded for the Boudet family on that same day in Tangipahoa Parish. Cece believed the second record was false—that Henri Boudet had used his influence to attempt to change history.

Cece had also put together the pieces of the tattoo parlor. The former nurse who ran it was dispensing hormone shots for needy "ladies." "You were a little bit of help, there, Sarah Booth."

"Glad to be of service."

"Before I break the story, I need to talk to Ellisea. I'll be in New Orleans tomorrow by lunch," Cece said.

"You'd better be careful," I said. "Even Hamilton was concerned for you. This sounds like a story the Boudet family has worked long and hard to keep hidden." That was a major understatement. I wondered how many bodies were in the Louisiana swamps because of Ellisea.

"Don't worry about me. I left a file of all my facts. If anything happens to me, the story will get even bigger play. It's in the Boudets' best interest to make sure nothing unpleasant happens to me."

It was pointless to argue with Cece. She had her teeth sunk in a story that would generate international attention. El, the face that launched the eighties and the fashion icon who had become a powerful senator's wife, was a deception. The public's insatiable lust for scandal would demand every gritty detail.

I didn't see the big deal. High fashion and politics were built on deception and illusion. I thought of Jitty and her constant lectures on the subject. What Cece needed was a good dose of Jitty.

"We'll see you tomorrow," I told Cece before I hung up.

Sitting across the small bar table from me, Tinkie looked depleted. Normally, she was a petite tornado of energy, and it hurt me to see her so down.

"Right now I can't bear to think about the trouble Cece's going to get in," she said with a sigh. "And we're at a total dead end on our case."

I had to agree. "We lost motive on our three prime suspects with the DNA tests. Other than that, Michael made some inappropriate investments. Oren Weaver is a fake, and the senator is married to a former man. Nothing really links back to Rebekah."

"Pretty dismal." Tinkie propped her elbows on the table and her chin sank into her hands.

My own spirits dropped a notch or two, but I had another angle. "Maybe we've been going at this all wrong," I said, remembering what Starla had said. "Maybe someone killed Rebekah to hurt Doreen, not to protect themselves."

Tinkie's eyebrows lifted. "Interesting." Even her posture improved. "Doreen's bound to have enemies."

"Maybe jealous competitors."

"Yes, and possibly local religious groups who find her untraditional teachings to be suspect."

"The problem is opportunity."

Tinkie's eyebrows dropped. "That's a good point. We settled on our original suspects because they had motive. If we change the motive, we have to rethink the whole suspect angle."

"Once we find Doreen, I'm going to wring her neck," I said.

"I'll help."

We finished our drinks and walked back through the crowds toward the Monteleone. Tinkie was lost in her own thoughts, and from the look on her face, they weren't pleasant. When we got to the hotel, she lingered at my door.

"Do you want to spend the night here?" I asked.

"You heard the fight, didn't you?"

"Yes." There was no point lying.

"I'll never love anyone more than Oscar, but I don't know if I can stay with him." She walked into my room and took a seat on the double bed I didn't use. "What am I going to do?"

I sat down beside her and put my arm around her. "I'm all out of answers for either one of us."

"I want a child, Sarah Booth. You know I love Chablis, but that isn't enough anymore. I want a baby. And Oscar says we can't have one."

"You'll work it out. You love each other too much not to."

"I was foolish to listen to my father. He said that Oscar would change his mind. I can't blame Oscar for this. Not really. He said all along he didn't want children. I have only myself to blame. And Daddy."

"Tinkie, you still have plenty of time to have a baby." The clock was ticking, though. I heard each tock inside my own womb.

"I don't want to be sixty when my kid graduates from college." She pushed a strand of hair back from her face. "It just galls me to think of Connie risking her baby to make Coleman pay. I'd like to slap her into next Sunday."

"Not a bad game plan," I said, and we both grinned.

FROM THE DEPTHS of sleep I picked up the ringing telephone. In the other bed, Tinkie sat up and snapped on the light. The bedside clock showed six in the morning.

"Sarah Booth?" Coleman's voice was tired, but the desperation was gone. In fact, so was all emotion.

"How's Connie?" I asked. Out of the corner of my eye I watched Tinkie slide back beneath the covers. She put a pillow over her head to give me some privacy.

"Doc finally got her to open the door and give up the gun. She rode with him to the hospital. They've got her on some IVs to get some nutrition in her."

"And the baby?"

"She won't have a sonogram or any of the tests Doc recommended. She says if we keep pushing, she'll leave the hospital."

"But at least it's a step in the right direction."

"Do you think Doreen could call her?" Coleman asked. "Maybe if she'd talk to her over the phone. It might make a difference. Doc did great, but he's at the end of his rope with her. He says she needs professional help, but she won't go. Doc's afraid to suggest any psychiatric medications because of the baby."

"I have to find Doreen this morning. I'll ask her."

"Connie's in room 208." There was a pause. "Thank you, Sarah Booth."

"I wish I could do more." I hung up the phone with an empty feeling. Coleman wasn't desperate, but he also wasn't there. I had the feeling I'd talked with a stranger.

"I gather Connie's in the hospital," Tinkie said.

I passed along what I'd learned, then ordered coffee from room service. I was too awake to consider going back to bed, and I had work to do. I was so angry with Doreen that the thought of waking her up didn't bother me in the least. After a cup of coffee I started getting dressed.

"I'm coming, too," Tinkie said as she headed to the closet to raid my wardrobe. "Your clothes will be a little big, but they'll do." She looked at the phone. "Oscar didn't even call."

DOREEN WAS ON her patio drinking coffee when we arrived. The smile that originally lit her face faded as she saw our expressions.

"Bad news?"

"Doreen, who is Rebekah's father?" Tinkie said. "The DNA tests came back. There wasn't a match with any of the three."

A confused look touched Doreen's face. "That's impossible. It had to be one of the three."

"Not according to the tests."

"Then there was a mistake. It was either Michael, Oren, or Thad."

She spoke with such conviction that I felt my righteous anger waver. "Are you sure?" Doreen had never made a secret of her sexual activities. Maybe she'd just gotten confused.

"Look, Sarah Booth, I believe in miracles, but this wasn't an immaculate conception. I know who I slept with and I know when I got pregnant."

"Could you have confused the dates?"

"The only men I've slept with in the last two years are those three. I don't think there's a margin there for error."

"Get dressed," I said. "We're going to the Eighth District. We'll be there when LeMont arrives. There's something funny going on here and we need to find out what it is."

While Doreen dressed, we filled her in on her dead brother's obsession with her, and Kiley's attempt to barter information for money.

"Give it to her," Doreen said. "But I want to meet my nephew."

We took a taxi to the police station, and on the way, Tinkie told Doreen about Ellisea.

Instead of commenting, Doreen watched the now familiar Vieux Carré pass by the window. At last she spoke. "Thad never said a word. What a burden that secret must have been." She shook her head. "Thad will be destroyed when it gets out."

"I know," I said.

"He isn't a bad man." She turned back to the window and fell silent for the remainder of the ride. Tinkie and I shared a glance, but we, too, had our own thoughts to pursue. We still weren't talking when we pulled up at the station house and got out.

We were seated on the felon's bench when LeMont walked in promptly at eight. He only shook his head when he saw the three of us. Without wasting a word, he motioned us into his office. "What now?"

"How did you get the samples for the DNA tests?" Tinkie asked.

"The men voluntarily gave us a swab."

"The technician personally took the evidence?" I asked.

"Look, I wasn't in the room watching. The men came in at different times. They volunteered to do this. I didn't think it required a watchdog."

"Can you check with the technician?" I asked. "Something's wrong here."

LeMont picked up a file folder, his face growing red. "I've about had it with you," he said. "We're professional investigators. Just because the test didn't show what you wanted it to show doesn't mean it was a bad test."

"It has to be one of the three men," I said softly. "There are no other candidates."

My tone must have surprised him. He put the folder down. "Ms. Mallory?" he said.

"One of those three men is the father," Doreen said. "There's no doubt. I have no reason to lie about it."

LeMont shook his head slightly and sighed. "All right. I must be losing my mind. I'll ask the technicians. Wait here."

He was gone for almost half an hour, but when he returned, his face was glum. "The technician said he took the swabs personally, but he did leave the room briefly when one of the men was there. He had a call of nature."

"Which man did he leave?" I asked.

LeMont sighed. "He doesn't remember. He's going back through his records to figure it out. If he's successful, he may keep his job. Now beat it. I have work to do."

I gave Tinkie and Doreen a look, and they stepped out of the room.

LeMont gave me an irritated scowl. "What now?"

"Cece knows about Ellisea."

"Knows what?"

He was going to try and bluff it out. "That she was once a man."

His face seemed to relax. "So, it's happened at last. Over the years, Ellisea has made a lot of enemies. When Henri told me about her car, I knew some creep had dug up the truth. I figured they'd try to blackmail her." He leaned back in his chair a little. "It's a relief, you know. I told her a long time ago to tell the truth. But you have to understand her family. Her father wanted to kill her. Callie defended Ellisea." He shrugged. "When Eli decided to have the operation and become a woman, Henri made it very clear that she'd be the best woman in the world. An international beauty. Or else. He really put the screws to Ellisea, and when she doesn't live up to his standards, he sends one of his boys to beat her up a little."

I remembered the glimpse of her in the window. So she had been beaten, but not by her husband, as I'd assumed. "I can almost feel sorry for her," I said.

"You should. She's spent her entire life trying to live up to Henri's expectations, and you know what? She'll never be good enough. Eli was a gentle kid. Always wanting so desperately for his father to love him. But Henri was never much of a father, not even at first. Henri left Callie with Eli back in the swamps while he went to New Orleans to build his empire. That's how we grew up together. My family looked out for Callie because she was alone. Henri hardly saw Eli through the first thirteen years, and then when he finally spent some time with Eli, Henri realized that he would never have the son he wanted. He was repulsed by his own child. And he's made her suffer every day of her life." He stood up. "I guess I'm the only friend Ellisea has."

DOREEN AND TINKIE were waiting for me on the street. After a brief discussion, Doreen went to the Center to call Connie, per Coleman's request. With the paternity issue back in play, Tinkie and I decided to get busy checking deep background on our three primary suspects.

Tinkie chose to talk with Michael, and I went to the local newspaper office to dig up anything I could on the senator and Oren Weaver. If hurting Doreen was the motive for killing Rebekah, I figured there had to be some past connection between one of the men and Doreen Mallory. Doreen insisted there was no prior contact, but memory could be deceptive. The public record was easy enough to check.

I spent the next three hours poring over files at the *Times-Picayune*. Thaddeus Clay had been born in Slidell, just across the lake from New Orleans. His father had been a lawyer with big ambitions. By the time Thad was seven, they were living in the Garden District of New Orleans, on the top rung of the upper middle class.

Like his father, Thad went into law, became a public defender, and was hired as an assistant district attorney. Ellisea was a top runway model at the time, and she swept Thad into the world of glamour, power, and fame.

I couldn't help but wonder if Thad had known about Ellisea's sex change from the start. How much of himself had he traded for what his wife's family could buy him?

I returned to my reading. Clay's rise was meteoric. First it was attorney general, lieutenant governor, governor, and U.S. senator, in which position he'd accrued a tremendous amount of power. But Doreen appeared to be correct. There didn't seem to be any common ground between the senator and Doreen until he became her lover.

The clippings on Oren Weaver were much thinner. Weaver burst onto the Louisiana scene in 1974 with a tent revival outside New Orleans. There were a few articles quoting local clergy who were offended by Weaver's claims of healing, but no real scandal. And no mention of any incident that might have provoked Oren's desire to punish Doreen. All in all, it was a disappointing effort.

I hurried to the luncheon date with Cece and Tinkie. Luck was in my favor and I snagged a parking place just as my phone began to ring. Caller ID showed Kiley. "What do you want now?" I asked.

"Do we have a deal?"

"Since you're so proficient on the Internet, why don't you

e-mail Doreen some pictures. Doreen wants to see her nephew before she gives you anything."

"What are you talking about?"

"Adam's baby. Doreen wants to see him."

"Joshua's dead."

I felt a weight on my chest. "How did he die?" Shaken-baby syndrome, neglect—I prepared myself for anything.

"It was SIDS. He just stopped breathing."

"When did this happen?" I asked. The information was so unexpected that I had trouble grasping it.

"Joshua was about four months old. It was just after Adam died." She took a breath. "He was so beautiful. I just went in to get him up and he was cold."

"Was there an autopsy?" I asked.

"There wasn't any need. The coroner ruled it was Sudden Infant Death Syndrome right away. They didn't need to cut my baby up. He just stopped breathing."

"I'm sorry, Kiley." I couldn't help a pang of sympathy for her. She'd lost her husband and her baby one right after the other. "Adam was already dead when Joshua died?"

"Yeah, he was dead. But don't feel sorry for me about Adam. I was gonna divorce him anyway. He didn't care about me and Joshua. The truth is, he acted like there was something wrong with Joshua."

"Wrong?"

"I think he blamed the baby because we had to get married. I was pregnant." She gave a short, bitter laugh. "It was a helluva price to pay for a few minutes of thrashing around on a blanket. Adam was an awful lover. It was like he was afraid to let it feel good. We only did it once and after it was over he made me get on my knees and pray for forgiveness. He'd said I was dirty and had to be cleansed. I should have realized then that he was totally fucked up. But I was inexperienced. I didn't really know better."

"When he found out you were pregnant, he asked you to marry him?"

"Only because those church folks would have died if they thought their precious Adam had gotten me pregnant. That's all he cared about. What they thought. And he knew I'd go tell them."

"And what did they think?"

"That Adam was the perfect husband and father." She made a disgusted sound. "What a lie. I can't remember a time he ever held Joshua or touched him. Or me either, for that matter. If Adam hadn't drowned, Joshua and I would have left him anyway."

"Kiley, tell me again how Adam died." My words were choppy because my breath was suddenly short. Religious fanaticism had run through Lillith Lucas's family as if it were a genetic disorder.

"He drowned. I told you."

"Tell me the whole story. Where were you? Who was there? Where did they find his body?"

"We were swimming in the Pearl River. There are sandbars up around Sandy Point, and we were just having some fun."

"Who was there?" I wondered if it was members of Adam's church.

"Mostly guys he worked with for the power company. Them and their girlfriends. We were sipping a few beers and maybe toking a joint when Adam wasn't looking. He didn't like liquor or dope. Everything fun had something to do with Satan."

"Where was Joshua?"

"My mother said she'd keep him for the day. I was working two jobs. I needed a day off."

"So what happened?"

"Me and the other girls were on the sandbar. The men had waded out into the river. They were going to see how deep it was, to see if they could jump out of a tree without breaking their necks. Anyway, Adam went down to try to find the bottom and he never came back up."

"He just disappeared?"

"There are some bad currents in the Pearl. Sinkholes and things like that. If one of them gets hold of you, it can pull you down and keep you for days before it turns you loose."

"How long did it keep Adam?"

"For all I know, he's still down there," she said.

"The body wasn't recovered?" I had a bad, bad feeling.

"No. They hunted but he never came up. That's one reason the Crenshaws can't let Adam go."

"Kiley, where are you?"

"I'm at home. Why? What's wrong? You sound scared."

I didn't want her to know how upset I really was. "E-mail me those files now. Doreen will pay for them. Just do it now. And a picture of Adam."

"I don't know if I have one. He was funny about having his picture taken."

"Look for one. It's important. And then it might not be a bad idea for you to take a little vacation."

"I'm not a fool. I want half the money up front. Once you get the files, you won't pay me."

Despite my desire to kill her, I kept my voice level. "E-mail those files now. You'll get your money. You have my word on it. E-mail them and then come down to New Orleans. Check into the Hilton. They have a great spa. Treat yourself. It's on me. In fact, I'll have a room reserved in your name."

"What's going on?"

Lord, you could hand this woman a fistful of money and she'd ask why. "I'll tell you when you get here. Give me a call. And don't call anyone else."

"Okay, Miss Cloak-and-Dagger. But you'd better have my money when I get there."

I sat in the car for a long time, matching and rematching the bits of information Tinkie and I had gathered. There was only one conclusion that made sense. Adam Crenshaw was alive. He hadn't drowned. He was alive, and he was somewhere in New Orleans.

I had no proof, but as I walked into the restaurant, I knew I'd finally figured out who had killed Rebekah Mallory.

32

WITH THEIR HEADS BENT TOGETHER AND WICKED GRINS ON THEIR faces, Cece and Tinkie looked like a couple of co-conspirators in a case of espionage. I took a seat at the table.

"I'm meeting Ellisea tonight," Cece said. She smiled and I thought her incisors had grown at least half an inch. She looked practically wolfish.

"At Commander's Palace," Tinkie said. "I wish I could be a fly on the wall."

They both frowned when I didn't say anything.

Cece tapped her perfect fingernails on the table in Mango Spice staccato. "By the way, Connie's throwing another fit."

"About what?" I asked. As focused as I was on the case, I wanted to hear about Coleman.

Cece rolled her eyes. "One doesn't need a reason when one is Connie Peters. She's making Coleman pay, plain and simple. Doc even said so. He said she needed a good spanking and someone to force her to act her age."

I didn't say anything. Connie was risking the only thing that kept Coleman bound to her: the baby. I doubted she was that stupid. "Coleman asked Doreen to talk to Connie."

"It won't do any good. Connie's in hog heaven. She's not about to change—not when she's got the upper hand." The waiter placed fresh bread and butter on the table and Cece popped a bite into her mouth. "This is divine. What's wrong with you, Sarah Booth?"

"I need to know how a death certificate is issued in Mississippi if a body isn't found."

"Whose body is missing?" Cece asked, signaling the waiter for another drink.

"Adam Crenshaw."

"Doreen's dead brother?" Tinkie's eyebrows rose. "Why would that matter?"

I sipped my iced tea, waiting for the perfect moment. "Because Adam isn't dead."

"Dahling, do you realize how Boris Karloff that sounds?" Cece asked.

"Boris Karloff, Faulkner, name whatever literary tradition you like. I think Adam Crenshaw killed Lillith and Rebekah."

"A serial killer who targets only his blood kin. Now that makes one glad to be an only child," Cece said.

I told them everything I'd learned from Kiley, and threw in the "spawn of Satan" reference Coot Henderson had heard when Lillith died, as well as the mention in Adam's files. By the time I finished, they were both convinced that it was possible Adam Crenshaw wasn't in a watery grave. In fact, it was highly probable that he was walking the streets of the French Quarter—and possibly stalking his sister.

"Think what he might have in store for Doreen, if he burned his own mother to death," Cece said.

I didn't want to think about it. Lillith's tombstone, beautiful though it was, was also symbolic of the torment of her death. She had died in the flames.

Tinkie's depression was gone. She leaned forward and lowered her voice. "Let's say Adam is alive and that he did kill Lillith. Why would he kill Rebekah? To punish his sister for having an illegitimate baby?" she asked.

Motive was the element that was deviling me. Adam might be a religious kook, but why target an innocent infant? I had a theory, but I wasn't certain about it. "I think Rebekah was living proof of Doreen's sin."

"What sin?" Cece asked.

"The sin of lust. Fornication. Adultery. The same sin that Lillith was guilty of."

"This guy is really whacked," Cece said. "But why kill a baby? Why not kill Doreen?"

"I think he wants to punish first. To destroy her."

Tinkie nodded. "If Doreen is convicted of Rebekah's murder, her entire ministry will be destroyed. If she's a murderess, especially a woman who killed her own infant, her message is compromised."

I put my hands on the table, unable to contain my growing excitement. "We've been on the wrong track the entire time," I said.

"This guy shouldn't be hard to spot," Cece said. "He probably has a suitcase with glass eyes and wooden legs. Flannery O'Connor could have written about him."

"Not according to Kiley and his adoptive family. He was a good-looking man. We have to remember that Doreen has thousands of followers. He could be someone she sees on a regular basis, someone who looks as normal as you or me." I was beginning to panic myself.

"He could be anywhere in the city," Cece said. "He could be watching Doreen all the time."

"If we're right about this, I think he's close enough to have slipped something into Doreen's food or drink the night Rebekah was killed," I said. "He planned that murder carefully, down to making sure Doreen was drugged so that she wouldn't wake up."

"But how would he gain access to Doreen's apartment?" Cece asked. "He'd have to have a key to get to the baby's formula."

"We need to talk with Michael. It's possible some of the kids were sent to Doreen's for something. They may have inadvertently allowed someone to copy a key."

"Speaking of Doreen, we've got to tell her," Tinkie said. "She could be in danger."

"Kiley's sending the rest of the files and a picture of Adam, if she can find one. We need Oscar's computer. And I told Kiley to check into the Hilton. Once she gets here, she'll be able to identify Adam."

"Kiley could also be in danger," Cece said. "Someone should stay with her."

"She'll probably get here about five," I said. "We need to read the rest of those files. I can—"

Tinkie frowned. "I'm supposed to see Michael at five. I haven't had a chance to talk to him, but I told him I needed more background information. Sarah Booth, would you mind if I went through the files Kiley sent? You could meet with Michael instead. I have some telephone calls in to his past employers, just a simple background check."

It didn't take a rocket scientist to figure out that Tinkie wanted a reason to talk to Oscar. Their tiff was working on her.

"Sure. Sounds fine. The most important thing is to get a photo, or at least a very good description of Adam. Where are you meeting Michael?"

"Café Du Monde," she said, smiling. "Beignets always pick up my spirits."

"At five?" I checked my watch. I had time to make some phone calls. LeMont was at the top of the list, but I needed to talk to Coleman and I wanted to talk to Hamilton.

"When do you meet Ellisea?" I asked Cece. I wanted to know where my friends were. If Adam Crenshaw was alive and walking the streets of New Orleans, it would be best for all of us to know what the others were doing.

"At six. A little early for dinner, but she insisted."

"Be—"

"Careful," Cece finished. "Dahling, caution is my middle name."

THE HOTEL SEEMED abnormally quiet as I walked through the lobby. A late-afternoon hush had fallen over the city. For one brief instant I wished for magic—something to stop time and motion, except for me and Hamilton. Our hours were running out. Soon he'd return to Paris and I would go home to the Delta. He'd invited me to the City of Light, but I knew myself well enough to know that I wouldn't go unless we established a stronger bond. I could love Hamilton. I could, but I didn't. We hadn't had enough time together to let our feelings grow.

The wonderful scent of the lilies still filled my hotel room. The first thing I did was to book a room for Kiley at the Hilton. The second was to call LeMont.

"My lab tech finally figured out it was Michael Anderson that he left alone. I've already put in a call asking Anderson to come back in for another DNA sample," LeMont said. "I think it's a big waste of time, but we'll do it anyway."

If my current theory was correct, Rebekah's paternity was no longer a real issue. "There's something I have to tell you." I gave him a rundown on what we'd learned about Adam Crenshaw.

"You think he's really alive?" LeMont sounded dubious.

"I think he's alive and I think he killed Rebekah and Lillith. LeMont, he set fire to his mother's house. And I think Doreen may be his next target."

"Because he thinks she's a loose woman?" He was barely able to suppress his amusement. "If that's his criterion for murder, he can have a field day in this town."

"Get in touch with Tinkie. Let her forward some of those files to you. You won't think it's amusing then."

"Sarah Booth, if we arrested everyone who wrote weird things on a computer, there wouldn't be anyone left walking around free."

"Adam's body was never found. His mother burned to death. His niece was murdered. Heck, his son is dead, too. There's a pattern there, LeMont."

"A pattern, but it doesn't prove anything. Adam Crenshaw disappeared in the Pearl River. You think he just held his breath for a few hours and floated downstream?"

"I think he's a very clever man. And I think he's alive. Would you check on him? Maybe he has a record. We need a photo of him. And while you're at it, could you check any records or reports in the death of Joshua Crenshaw? SIDS is beginning to sound mighty convenient."

"I'm not making any promises. I'll do what I can if I have time."

I'd told him; I couldn't make him believe it. "I just thought you should know what we discovered."

"I'll keep it in mind."

"Good-bye, LeMont."

"Sarah Booth, don't hang up. I need to talk to you about Ms. Falcon."

"Don't bother threatening her. Cece's left all the facts on file with her newspaper. If anything happens to her, the story will still get printed." I figured LeMont could pass the word along to the Boudet family since he knew them so well.

"I'd like to talk to Ms. Falcon. Maybe explain a few things. I found Ellisea's so-called friend who vandalized her car. Like I thought, the little pervert thought he could blackmail the Clays. The truth will come out, but an exposé isn't the way to do it. Will you ask Ms. Falcon to talk to me?"

LeMont had the authority to talk to anyone he wanted. All he had to do was flash his badge. "Sure, I'll ask her to talk to you."

"I'll call you when I get the answers on that DNA test."

"Thanks."

I dialed Coleman next. Deputy Dewayne Dattilo answered at the sheriff's office, and I realized I was relieved. Talking to Coleman tore me up.

"How's Connie?" I asked.

"Not good." The Sunflower County deputies had gone to a lot of pains to stay clear of the entanglement of my relationship with Coleman. Dewayne's voice was clipped and I could hear the discomfort in it.

"Is she still in the hospital?"

"Yeah. She's heavily sedated."

"And how's Coleman?"

"He's back in the cell with your dog. I think it's the first time he's slept in a couple of days. Want me to get him?"

"Don't wake him," I said. "I'll call another time. How's Sweetie?"

Dewayne's voice brightened considerably. "I think we need to keep her as the jailhouse mascot. Complaints about food and things have gone down nearly one hundred percent since she arrived."

"Give her a pat for me," I said, mentally blocking the image of Coleman sleeping with my dog beside him. "Dewayne, I need a big favor." I didn't wait for him to evade me. Lillith's tombstone still troubled me. If Adam had burned his mother to death and erected the tombstone, perhaps there was a clue I'd missed. "Could you go to Pine Level Cemetery and write down the inscription on Lillith Lucas's tombstone? And call Al Jenkins at the funeral home and see if he has a record of who paid for that tombstone."

"Is this a joke?"

"No. It's important." I gave him the numbers for the hotel room and my cell phone. He promised to call Al immediately and check the tombstone on his way home from work and give me a call.

I'd cleared the deck to call Hamilton, and my finger trembled as I punched in his number. He answered on the second ring.

"Sarah Booth," he said, relief evident in his voice. "I've left two messages for you."

Indeed, the little red light on my phone was blinking. I'd been so intent on making my calls that I hadn't noticed. "Are they good messages?" I asked, desire making my voice deeper.

"Good in the sense that I'll be back in New Orleans tomorrow for certain. Sarah Booth, if your case is concluded, let's take a few days and go somewhere."

"Where?"

"I don't care. Someplace where there are no phones or fax machines. Someplace where we can talk without interruption. Bring your clothes. We'll pick a destination at the airport and just get on a plane." He sounded exhausted.

"Did you find the Martinez family?"

He hesitated, and in the silence I knew what had happened.

"They're dead, aren't they?"

"Yes."

"And the people who killed them?"

"Will go unpunished. I did everything I could, but Washington is a city of delay and prevarication. No one in power wanted to get involved. Peruvian politics are volatile, and this country relies on their oil. The lives of one good man and his family were of no importance here."

As much as I admired Hamilton and his work, I wondered if I could bear such disappointment, and I knew it must come on a regular basis.

"I'm sorry. I wish I could change things."

"You have, simply by caring. That's the only way to change the world."

He sounded a bit like Doreen. "I'll be at the airport," I said. "I can't wait."

"Wear something easy to remove," he said, and there was the hint of mischief in his voice.

Even though Tinkie had stopped by the Center to talk to Doreen, I decided to call her, too, just to double-check the payment to Kiley. I'd changed my mind about needing the files.

"Is it true? Is Adam alive?" Doreen asked.

"I think there's a strong possibility."

"And you think he wants to kill me." She didn't sound convinced.

"If he's alive, I'd say there's a good chance he's the person responsible for Rebekah's death. And your mother's, too."

"To punish me?"

"He isn't mentally balanced. You can't try and figure out what he's thinking. If he did kill Lillith and Rebekah, he's acting with purpose and deliberation. We may not be able to understand why he's doing what he's doing, but it makes sense that you're the next victim in the pattern he's creating."

"I never even saw him. I never knew he existed. Why would he hate me so?"

"I can't answer that. Doreen, what I need is for you to contact Kiley." I gave her the room number at the Hilton. "Get her to describe Adam. See if he sounds like anyone you know. Maybe someone who's come to you for healing, someone who's a regular client."

"I'll speak with her."

I glanced at my watch. The afternoon was fast getting away from me. "What are you doing this evening?"

"I'm introducing Teko to the other kids at the Center."

"Teko?"

"He's from the projects. He had migraines."

Great, so Doreen was now embracing a gangbanger. "And after that?"

"I have a candlelight vigil on the Square. We do this every November. We have a short ritual and we pray for peace. A lot of people find comfort in the ceremony."

"Doreen, you should cancel—"

"No, Sarah Booth. I won't cancel it. I can't allow someone else control over my life."

It was pointless to try and talk her out of it, even though she'd be a perfect target for a sniper. Of course, the person killing Doreen's family didn't use a gun. He brought death more intimately.

33

THE CROWD AT THE CAFÉ DU MONDE HAD THINNED CONSIDERABLY by five-fifteen. Michael was uncharacteristically late. I finished my coffee and was about to order another when my cell phone rang.

I checked caller ID and answered, eager to hear what Dewayne Dattilo had discovered in the cemetery. The deputy was as good as his word, and incredibly efficient.

"That's a mighty fine headstone," Dewayne said. "I don't think I've ever seen anything quite like it."

"What did the inscription say?" I asked.

"It's a favorite quote of my granny's."

I wanted to jump down the phone and choke Dewayne. Of all times for him to be chatty. I saw Michael headed my way. He strolled through the café, easily threading between the tables.

"What did it say?" I pressed.

"It said, 'Born of fire, she perished in flame.' And then there was the biblical inscription. 'The Lord is slow to anger and rich in unfailing love.' "

"That's it?" I had somehow hoped for more. In thinking through the case, I'd somehow convinced myself that the answer would be found at Lillith's grave.

"That's it. Just the dates of her birth and death."

"Thanks, Dewayne."

"I don't personally believe that the sins of the father are visited on the children, but my granny sure does. She—"

"Sins of the father? What are you talking about?"

"The Scripture. The rest of that line goes, 'The Lord is slow to anger and rich in unfailing love, forgiving every kind of sin and rebellion. Even so, he does not leave sin unpunished, but he punishes the children for the sins of their parents to the third and fourth generations.' "

"Oh, shit." I finally understood. My gaze was riveted on Michael as he drew closer and closer. I realized it was the first time I'd seen him in jeans. The oxblood turtleneck was a perfect compliment to the leather jacket and his complexion. He was a handsome man. Four women at a table in front of me simply stopped talking to watch him pass. He was oblivious to his effect on them.

"Sarah Booth?" Dewayne's voice was tinny and distant in my ear. He was too far away to offer help. I slowly closed the cell phone and put it on the table. Michael was staring at me. How had I missed it? The sins of the father. I'd come so close to figuring out the killer's motive, but I'd missed it by a hair.

Michael had been the only person with access to Doreen's apartment, via Trina Zebrowski, who managed the apartments for Doreen. Michael had appeared in Doreen's life shortly after Adam had disappeared. As her financial advisor, he knew every move Doreen made. Michael had been the only one of the three potential fathers to try and thwart the DNA test, because he knew he was Rebekah's father. I'd been dead wrong when I'd told LeMont that the DNA didn't matter.

I took a deep breath and met his gaze as he made it to the table. Michael, who was both Rebekah's father and Doreen's brother. The sins of the parents.

I couldn't afford to let him know that I knew. "Have a seat," I said as he came up to the table.

"Café au lait," Michael told a passing waitress without even bothering to look at her. He took a seat. "I thought I was meeting Tinkie."

"She got tied up." I forced a smile at the pretty Vietnamese girl as she put his coffee in front of him. She might have been a post for all the notice he took.

"Have you heard any results from the DNA test?" he asked, spooning sugar into his coffee.

"LeMont ran into some problem." My mouth was so dry I could hardly speak. Somehow, I had to stay calm.

"What did you want to ask me?" He settled back in his chair to a comfortable position, as if he had the rest of the day to chat. His dark gaze was devoid of emotion.

"Did any of the kids at the Center have access to Doreen's apartment?" I had to make him believe I didn't suspect him. "Maybe they delivered something."

He shrugged. "Possibly." His gaze locked with mine, and the tiniest smile touched the corners of his mouth. "I thought you wanted to ask me about Adam Crenshaw."

"Doreen's brother?" I fumbled. "He's dead."

"Is he?" Michael sipped his coffee, but his gaze never left mine. "Would it be a miracle if Adam had survived the cold waters of the Pearl River?"

He knew.

He still held his coffee cup. "I got LeMont's call. He wants an-other DNA sample. My time has run out. By the way, where is Tinkie? Is she joining us?"

"Tinkie's busy. You paid for Lillith's tombstone, didn't you?"

"With Doreen's money. Ironic, isn't it?" It was as if a mask had dropped from his face. His dark eyes held a tremendous passion, but his passion was hatred. The buzz and clatter of the people around me faded and there was only him, his voice. "Doreen is a slut and a whore, just like my mother was."

"Rebekah was your daughter," I said.

"Doreen tricked me. She touched me and whispered soft words. She made me believe that she loved me." He was completely emo-tionless. "I tracked her for years, knowing what I had to do. But then I wavered. I listened to her siren song. And I almost lost sight of what I had to do. But then Rebekah was born and I saw her. She was an abomination. God showed me my sin."

Twilight had fallen, and the blue edge of night crept over the eastern horizon. Michael's eyes were dark pools, unreadable.

"Doreen does love you, Michael. Nothing she did was meant to harm another person. She loves you and she loved Rebekah."

Night was almost upon us, and the other patrons of the open-air café were leaving. In a few minutes we'd be alone. Michael leaned forward. He was so close that his breath was warm on my face.

"Are you religious, Sarah Booth?"

The wrong answer could push him over the edge. "In my own way."

"Let me ask you something. Why do you think God punished Doreen by sending her Rebekah?"

"Doreen never considered Rebekah a punishment."

Michael's expression shifted. "You don't think so? Not even deep in her heart when she was alone? You don't think she got down on her knees and begged God for a reason?"

"No, I don't." If I had no faith in the Divine, I had come to believe in Doreen.

"You didn't see that baby. Every breath was a struggle. Doreen talks of a God of love, but God is also wrathful. He metes out punishment for those who deserve it. Rebekah was Doreen's penance, and she knew that. Deep in her heart, she knew. Her penance and Lillith's."

Michael's words echoed in the chill night. Traffic streamed by on Decatur, but the pedestrians were gone. There was only one lone pair of footsteps echoing on the pavement. They softened and finally disappeared.

My gut instinct was to get away from him. Fast.

"Thanks for your time, Michael. I have to meet LeMont." My cell phone rang and I answered it, my gaze still linked with Michael's.

Tinkie was breathless. "Sarah Booth, I'm with Kiley. She brought some pictures of the baby, and one of Adam. He's Michael. Sarah Booth, can you hear me? Michael Anderson *is* Adam Crenshaw."

"I hear you loud and clear," I said. "I'll be right there. Tell LeMont not to do anything rash."

"What?" Tinkie inhaled sharply. "You're still with Michael, aren't you?"

"Yes. We're just leaving the Café Du Monde. Why don't you pick up some candles and meet me at Jackson Square?"

"I'll call LeMont right away. Oh my God, Sarah Booth, just don't let on that you know."

I turned my phone off and held it in my hand. "Sorry. Tinkie had to tell me something."

"She's with Kiley, isn't she?" He brought the gun out of the back of his waistband with practiced ease. "I should have killed Kiley when I killed my son."

I'd suspected that he had killed Joshua, but to hear him confirm it so casually made my heart pound even harder. "Why did you kill Joshua?"

"He was evil. His mother was a whore." He lifted one shoulder in a casual shrug. "God laid a curse on him, just as he did on me and Doreen and all of our offspring."

"Michael, Doreen loves you." It was difficult to speak with the gun pointed right at my heart.

"Love? There is only God's love, but it comes with a heavy price. I've had to work hard to earn his love, but I've almost accomplished my mission. Isn't that interesting, Sarah Booth? Brother and sister both on missions. Doreen, misguided though she is, believes God sent her to heal." His smile unveiled the extent of his madness. "And he sent me to destroy the spawn of Satan."

HIS GRIP ON my elbow was firm but not cruel as we walked across Decatur Street and down one side of the Square. Darkness had fallen and it was early yet, but some fifty people had already gathered for the candlelight ceremony. Among them were some of the young people I'd grown accustomed to seeing at the Center. One of the girls I'd first met saw us, waved, and ran over. Melissa was her name. She had a tall black youth in tow.

"Michael, Ms. Delaney, this is Teko." She tugged the young man forward. "Doreen healed his migraines last night. He's going to help us at the Center now." She turned to the boy. "Teko gave up his gang to help Doreen."

Teko was a tough-looking kid with an insolent stare. My gaze dropped down to his side, where I expected to see a switchblade or a gun. I was hoping, anyway. Michael still had the barrel of his pistol against my spine, hidden by his arm and jacket.

"Where's Doreen?" Michael asked.

"On the cathedral steps," Melissa said. "She wanted to start there because she wants everyone to understand that her beliefs aren't in conflict with Christianity."

"Melissa, would you tell Doreen we need to talk with her? It's urgent."

The girl frowned. "She's getting ready to start the ceremony."

"Just tell her," Michael said. "Now! I don't need your excuses."

Melissa backed up a step, looking at Michael as if she didn't know him. She turned abruptly. Teko fell in behind her. He glanced back over his shoulder once. "Who's that man to be talking to you like that?" he asked Melissa. "Man needs to learn some manners. Got a bad attitude."

They disappeared in the rapidly growing crowd. Now some two hundred people were gathered. I glanced around, hoping to see Tinkie, or better yet, LeMont—with a SWAT team.

"Walk over to the side of the cathedral," Michael said, the gun letting me know that it wasn't a request.

I started out and Michael pulled me to the right, dodging another group of teens who recognized him and waved. "Little vermin," he said. "I'd like to crush them all. I'll have to settle for killing their queen."

34

WE MADE IT THROUGH THE CROWDS AND FOUND A PLACE WHERE WE had a clear view of Doreen. She waved at us but turned back to a cluster of women who thronged around her.

"How did you find out Lillith was your mother?" If I could keep him talking, maybe Tinkie and LeMont would show up before he assassinated Doreen.

"The Crenshaws weren't my first adoptive family. There was another one. They told me how my mother drank and slept with men. They told me how she ranted and preached when Satan took hold of her. They took me one night to hear her. She terrified me. I knew then that she was evil. Once I got old enough to drive, it wasn't difficult to learn a lot about her."

Doreen moved to the top of the third step, the eager crowd spreading across the pavement and into the park. Close to five hundred candles burned. Plaintive Celtic music played.

"Thank you all for coming," Doreen said. "It's wonderful to see so many people gathered here to pool our energy for a healthier planet."

Doreen stood in the golden light of a gas lamp. Only slightly elevated from the crowd, she was still a singular figure. I started to say something and felt Michael's fingers dig into my shoulder.

"Move!" Michael pushed me forward.

I stumbled forward. "Don't do this," I whispered. "Michael, look at Doreen. She's special." The faces turned toward Doreen were filled with a soft happiness. "Look at them, Michael."

"That's the horror if it. Doreen deceives. She has to die."

I recognized a tall blonde woman headed toward me and I tried to dodge to the left, but Michael's grip stopped me. I almost cried out in pain.

"Sarah Booth, dahling," Cece said, coming out of the crowd. She carried a golden candle with intricate designs spiraling up from the base. "I brought a candle for you."

I was afraid that Michael would shoot her if I yelled. "Cece, get out of here!" I spoke softly but with urgency.

Michael moved the barrel of the gun from my back. He eased it past my side so that he had a clear shot at Cece. In the press of people, I didn't think Cece could see the gun.

"Sarah Booth, dahling, don't run away from me." Cece kept coming. Behind her was Teko, his gaze riveted on Michael.

"Cece, run!" I yelled as I pushed backwards, hoping to throw Michael off balance. He stumbled, but quickly regained his footing. "Cece!" I slammed into Michael's arm, pushing the gun to the side. A wild shot rang out and people began to scream and panic.

To my utter amazement, Cece dove at my knees, bringing me down hard. It was a tackle that would have earned her respect on any professional team. We both hit the pavement and rolled. I heard Michael's howl of pain, and the gun skittered toward me. I was about to grab it when a petite, manicured hand picked it up.

I looked up from the pavement to see Tinkie aiming the weapon at Michael.

"Don't even breathe," she said, her voice and hand steady.

Michael was holding his left forearm in his right hand just above the handle of a large knife. Only a few feet away, Teko stood with his feet spread, ready to pounce.

"Come on, man," Teko said, crouching a little lower. "I'll take you down!"

"Not necessary," LeMont said, stepping out of the crowd and grabbing Michael. "I'll take it from here." He called a uniformed officer over. "Get an ambulance," he said. "Get his arm stitched and then take him to the station."

TINKIE HANDED DOREEN a glass of bourbon as she huddled on her patio. LeMont sat just beyond the reach of the soft lighting, his face in shadows. We'd left Cece to handle the crowd at Jackson Square. She said she knew all the words to "Kumbaya."

"Drink a little," Tinkie urged Doreen. "You're shaking." She glanced at me. "You aren't shaking, Sarah Booth, but I don't have to urge you to drink."

"Tell me everything you know," Doreen said, taking the glass and straightening her posture. "I have to understand why my brother hated me so much." Her voice had begun to break, but she kept talking. "My brother and the father of my child."

"Oh, Doreen," Tinkie said, rubbing her shoulders. "You didn't know. You couldn't have known."

"But he did," Doreen said. When she lifted her face, she looked puzzled. "Why did he hate me so much?"

"He hated Lillith and everyone related to her, including himself," Tinkie said gently. "He didn't really know you."

"But Michael had an alibi for that night," Doreen said. "He was with Trina."

"We believe both you and Ms. Zebrowski were drugged," LeMont said.

"Why didn't he just kill me when he killed Rebekah?" Doreen asked.

I did know the answer to that. "Because he wanted to destroy your ministry. By killing Rebekah, and having you convicted of her murder, he thought he could show your followers that you were a false prophet. He wanted to destroy your ministry before he killed you."

"So much hatred," Doreen said, her voice still shaking.

"It's a good thing that Teko kid was there," Tinkie said. "I've never seen someone throw a knife like that."

"It wasn't just coincidence," Doreen said softly. "All things happen for a reason."

The sound of the patio door creaking open made all of us freeze. I half-expected to see Cece arrive, but it wasn't my tall, elegant friend. The latest arrival was short and wearing a nun's habit.

"Sister Mary Magdalen," Doreen said, rising. She went to the nun and hugged her.

"I came as soon as I heard," the sister said. "I'm so sorry, Doreen."

As if on cue, Tinkie, LeMont, and I rose. It was time to go. Sister Mary Magdalen might be able to offer the comfort we didn't know how to give.

"I HAVE TO patch things up with Oscar," Tinkie said as the elevator stopped on our floor. "I can't go on like this."

"Good luck," I said, hugging her. "I'm going to bed. I'm so tired I can hardly stand up."

Tinkie grasped my hand. "Did you ever think it was Michael?" she asked.

I thought about it. "I should have, I guess. But I never would have thought Rebekah's father and Doreen's brother were one and the same."

"Me, neither," she said. "When are you going home?"

"I'm picking Hamilton up at the airport at ten." I couldn't suppress my smile. "Then we're going away for a few days."

"And Cece said you were going to screw this up," Tinkie said, squeezing my hand. "I never lost faith in you."

35

BY EIGHT O'CLOCK THE NEXT MORNING, I'D DETERMINED THAT I needed to go shopping. Everything I'd brought from home was dirty. I'd been forced to wear an incredibly risqué thong and matching push-up bra under my black jeans and a green sweater.

I was short on clean clothes, but I'd awakened refreshed and eager for the day. Hamilton was coming back. In fact, he should already be on his plane, taking off from Dulles.

I repacked all of my things, which consisted of throwing them helter-skelter into the suitcase, settled my bill via the television checkout, and then scratched a hurried note asking Tinkie to make sure Kiley checked out of the Hilton, since she was living the good life on my credit card.

At eight-thirty, I placed a call to Doreen. Sister Mary Magdalen answered. Doreen was asleep.

"Doreen and I will be in Zinnia in a few days," the nun said. "I need to settle the bill, and Doreen wants to visit her mother's grave."

"Is Doreen really okay?" I asked.

"She is," Sister Mary Magdalen said. "As hard as it is to see sometimes, we both know that all things happen for a reason."

"Does she really believe that?" I asked.

"She does," the sister said. "And so do I."

I was thinking about faith—Doreen's in a Divine plan and Tinkie's in me—when the telephone rang.

"Hello," I said, eager to hear Hamilton's voice.

"Ms. Delaney?"

The male caller's voice was somewhat familiar, but I couldn't place it. "Yes?"

"It's Dewayne Dattilo."

"Has something happened to Sweetie Pie?" She had only a few more days in detention.

"The hound is perfectly fine," Dewayne said. "It's ... well, the sheriff said I shouldn't call you, but I felt like I had to do it."

"What's wrong?"

"Mrs. Peters is asking to talk to you."

"Connie wants to talk to me?" I sat down on the bed. "Why?"

"She said she'd go into psychiatric treatment if you'd talk to her. Sheriff Peters said no one was to call you, but I just thought if you could really talk her into getting some help, we could put an end to all of this. It's taking a heavy toll on the sheriff."

I closed my eyes. "Where is Coleman?"

"He's at the hospital with her." There was a pause. "He said he'd skin anybody who called you. I was hoping you wouldn't have to tell him it was me."

"Thanks, Dewayne. You did the right thing." The hand holding the phone had begun to sweat.

"Are you coming?"

I straightened my back. "Yes. I'm on the way right now."

After replacing the phone, I tore up the note I'd written Tinkie and wrote a new one, asking her to meet Hamilton's plane and explain that I'd gone home to Zinnia. If Tinkie retrieved him from the airport she would still have time to make her doctor's appointment. As I slipped out of my room with my bags, I slid the note under Tinkie's door. I'd call her from the car when I was out of town.

Sure, it was cowardly. So much for her faith in me. Besides, I didn't need Tinkie to tell me what I was leaving behind. I'd have a nice, long drive to think of Hamilton and what I was walking away from. In going to Zinnia, I had made my choice. I would never be able to convince Hamilton or myself otherwise.

Did I love Coleman more? I couldn't answer that. But I'd known him longer. He was part of my life. Maybe I didn't have the courage to live a fantasy. Maybe it was just that fantasies should never have a chance to become reality. I didn't have any answers. I only had regret for what couldn't be.

THE BLINDS WERE drawn in Connie's room and I stepped into the semi-dusk, giving my eyes time to adjust. Two vases of flowers brightened the otherwise bleak room.

"So you came."

I stepped closer to the bed, trying not to show the shock I felt. Connie was thin, but she had on make-up and her hair had been washed and styled. I'd expected Olivia de Havilland in *The Snake Pit* and I'd gotten Farrah Fawcett in a hospital bed.

"I hear you want to talk." I wanted this conversation over with. I had the distinct feeling I'd been played.

"Does Coleman know you're here?" she asked.

"No. One of the deputies called me."

Her top lip curled. "I knew he wouldn't ask you to get involved in this. He wants to act like you're not to blame for what's happened to us."

It would do no good to deny it. "The deputy said you'd agree to psychiatric treatment if I came to talk to you."

"And you trusted the word of a crazy woman?"

I'd just seen crazy down in New Orleans. Connie wasn't even a pale shade of the real thing. "Look, Connie, I walked out on a lot of important things. Are you going to honor your word?"

"I just wanted to see if you'd come. That tells me plenty about how deep you're in this with my husband." Bright spots of anger burned on her cheeks. "That woman in New Orleans said that your relationship with my husband wasn't the issue. She said that I had to learn to love and value myself. I figured you paid her to tell me all that happy horseshit."

"I came because Coleman is my friend. You're destroying him, Connie. You know that."

"Yes," she said. "I do. And I don't think it's punishment enough for a lying cheater. And don't hand me any of that karma crap, either."

"Coleman has never cheated on you," I said, even though I knew I was wasting my breath.

"You mean he's never physically committed adultery."

"That's right. You know that, too. You're falsely accusing Coleman."

"Oh, I don't think so. There are all kinds of ways to cheat. Coleman thinks about you all the time. He daydreams the things he'd like to do to you." She raised up on her elbows and I could see the bony points of her shoulders. I'd never really believed that a person could be too thin, but Connie was living proof that it could happen.

"Coleman is maried to you. He made a decision to stay with

you, if you'd let him. You're pushing him away, Connie, and you're destroying yourself in the bargain."

"As if you cared what happened to me," she said.

"I don't care what happens to you. It would suit me just fine if you evaporated. But Coleman cares about his baby." I looked at her body and wondered how much damage she'd already done to the fetus. Malnutrition could have severe consequences.

"Yes, Coleman cares about the baby. To him, I'm an expendable host." Her eyes narrowed. "I hate this baby."

"Connie, are you going to talk to a psychiatrist?" I kept my voice level, but her potential for self-destruction was scaring me.

"On one condition."

"What's that?"

"You give me your word that you won't see Coleman."

"You have my word. I haven't been seeing him."

"Liar! I know about the cozy cookout you two had."

She was well informed for a woman who'd barricaded herself in a house. Then again, it was Zinnia. The grapevine was always in full bloom when it came to gossip.

"We had burgers. We talked. There's no harm in what we did."

"I want your word it won't happen again."

The fact that Connie was trying to blackmail me irked me to the max. "You have my word that Coleman and I won't carry on a romantic relationship. That's as good as it gets."

She leaned back in the bed. "That's not good enough." She pressed the call button and a nurse entered the room almost immediately.

"I'm checking out," Connie said. "Bring me whatever papers I need to sign." The nurse hustled out of the room, making a beeline for a telephone, no doubt.

"Good luck, Connie," I said. "I hope you wake up before you destroy everything you claim you care about." I stepped out of the room and into Coleman's arms.

He pulled me against his chest and held me so tightly I almost couldn't breathe. "I didn't want you involved in this," he said into my hair.

I didn't answer. The feel of his arms was too safe, too necessary. I simply closed my eyes and let myself have him for a few seconds.

There was the sound of a clearing throat and I opened my eyes to see Doc Sawyer standing beside us. Coleman and I stepped apart.

"What are you going to do?" Doc asked. He studiously avoided meeting my gaze.

"Bring me the papers. I'll have her institutionalized," Coleman said.

"Coleman," I touched his arm. "She isn't crazy."

"I don't care to put a label on what she is, Sarah Booth. All I know is that she's endangering herself and my baby. I can't let it go on. If they have to put her in a straitjacket and force-feed her, then that's how it's going to be. Once the baby is born, she can kill herself, if that's her choice."

Doc sighed. "I'll get the papers," he said, "but you realize this is only temporary. She can fight this if she chooses."

"Doc, do you think this is the right thing to do?" I asked.

He looked from Coleman back to me. "I don't have a clue what's right or fair in this world, Sarah Booth. I do know that Connie's a danger to herself and her baby. Does she have that right? Maybe. Maybe not. I do know this has to end. I'll get the paperwork." He walked down the hospital corridor, his shoes soundless.

Coleman and I were left facing each other. All I wanted was to walk back into his arms, to have him hold me. But I couldn't. There was something in his eyes that warned me to keep my distance. I was about to be hurt.

"I'm taking Connie to a private clinic in Arizona. I think it would be best to get her away from here completely. I'm stepping down as sheriff so I can spend the next five months with her, until the baby comes."

"And after that?" I asked, my chest hurting so badly I could hardly breathe.

"I don't know."

I nodded.

He touched my cheek, then turned and followed Doc down the corridor.

36

A COLD FRONT WAS MOVING IN OUT OF LOUISIANA, AND I SAT ON the front porch steps with Sweetie Pie between my feet and a tall Jack at my side. I'd gotten my dog out of hock after a personal visit to Mrs. Hedgepeth. After our brief conversation, she'd decided that maybe it wasn't Sweetie Pie who'd bitten her.

Now I leaned forward and stroked Sweetie's long, silky ears. The bitter wind scattered the leaves on the sycamore trees and traced icy fingers down my face and neck. I liked the cold. It numbed me.

Coleman was gone. Gordon Walters had taken over the sheriff's office on an appointed basis. The county was ablaze with gossip.

A lot of folks were talking *about* me, but neither Tinkie nor Cece were speaking *to* me. My last conversation with Tinkie had been when she'd called me from the New Orleans airport to tell me about the look on Hamilton's face when I'd failed to meet him. Since then, both Tinkie and Cece had studiously ignored me. I'd heard rumors, via Millie, that something big was in the works with Cece. But I'd spent the last three days basically alone. Except for my most reliable friend, Jack Daniel's.

"You know what followed the days of the flapper, don't you?"

I looked over my shoulder to see Jitty dressed in shapeless, somber, knee-length black. A cloche hat was pulled tight on her head, shadowing her eyes.

"Let's see, after the flapper came the Great Depression," I said without enthusiasm.

"That's right, Sarah Booth. I'd say that's exactly where you are."

She was right. Yeah! All of my friends and my ghost were right and I was wrong. I'd lost on all fronts. Hamilton had never even left the New Orleans airport when I didn't show up. He'd booked a flight for Paris and flew out two hours later.

I'd tried six times to call him, but he wasn't taking my calls. I didn't blame him. In fact, I admired him. He made a decision and stuck with it, unlike me.

Jitty took a seat beside me. "You can get him back, you know."

"Which one?"

She shook her head. "That's the problem, Sarah Booth. That's why you're sittin' here all alone. You hadn't really made up your mind. That's the worst insult you can hand a person."

"Let me ask you something, Jitty. What would you have done if I'd gone to Paris and married Hamilton?"

She gazed out at the beautiful white trunks of the sycamores. "I don't know," she said. "I've spent my entire existence here at Dahlia House. This is home to me."

"And to me, too," I said. "Paris was a dream, a fantasy. This is real. This house, the people around me. My dog and my horse."

"Sarah Booth, you know as well as I do that you can build a reality wherever you go."

She spoke with kindness, and I smiled at her. "New York was a dream. I had a fantasy of working on Broadway. The reality was something very different."

"You can build whatever reality you want, anywhere you choose," she said. "Never doubt that. You just have to have faith."

Faith. It was a word that had begun to constantly recur in my life. I thought of Doreen. All charges against her had been dropped. Adam Crenshaw, alias Michael Anderson, was in jail on one count of murder, and the police were investigating the deaths of Joshua Crenshaw and Lillith Lucas.

"How do you tell the difference between illusion and delusion, between faith and fantasy?" I asked. Certainly the line had blurred for Adam. Blurred so badly that he'd killed his own children and his mother.

"That's a tricky one, Sarah Booth." She leaned over to whisper in my ear. "You shouldn't ask an illusion such things."

"I need a better answer than that."

"You don't need me to tell you," she said. "You already know."

"Cop-out," I accused.

"You have to trust yourself to know the difference." Jitty started to shimmer, a sure sign that she was making one of her famous getaways.

"Don't go! Which was the illusion, Hamilton or Coleman?"

The shimmer swept through her, highlighting her chocolate eyes. "Whichever one you had chosen," she said. "That would have been your reality."

She was gone. I sipped my drink and felt Sweetie Pie begin to wiggle. She was doing her company's-a-comin' hound-dog dance. Looking down the drive, I didn't recognize the car that came toward me at breakneck speed, scattering dead leaves behind it like a small tornado. It was silver, sleek, and expensive-looking. For a moment my heart flipped. It was exactly the kind of car Hamilton might drive.

I stood up as the car pulled near the steps. The tinted glass shielded the occupants, but when the driver's door swung open and a long leg encased in black leather stepped out, I knew it wasn't Hamilton.

Cece was behind the wheel and Tinkie got out on the passenger side, Chablis in her arms. She put the little fluff of fur down so that Chablis could properly greet Sweetie, who slurped her once, picked her up in her mouth, and trotted off with her.

"We decided that it was pointless to stay mad with you," Tinkie said. "Besides, I wanted to show Cece the terrific office you set up for us."

"Yes, dahling, if you choose to trash your life over and over again, we aren't going to punish you." Cece took my drink from my hand, sniffed it, and made a face.

"Tinkie, what did the doctor say?" I'd been on pins and needles for days, wondering how her appointment had gone.

"I didn't go," Tinkie said. Her blue gaze was serene. "There was no need. I'm perfectly fine."

"You promised," I said, a flush of anger rising in my face. Deep down I'd been afraid something like this would happen.

"The lump is gone," Tinkie said. "I'm positive of it. There's no need for a biopsy."

Cece put her hand on my shoulder and squeezed lightly. "It's her decision to make," she said softly. "Just like we had to let you make your own decision about Hamilton." She turned me slightly so that I was looking at her car.

"How do you like it, dahling?"

"It's a Jaguar. A new one." Not the most brilliant deduction, but I was still trying to get over being angry at Tinkie.

Cece preened. "Yes, I bought it today."

I arched an eyebrow. "You got an advance for your big story on Ellisea?"

"I decided not to do the story on Ellisea."

I took the glass from her hand and took a long swallow. "Say that again," I requested.

"I'm not doing the story."

I looked at Tinkie, who nodded. "Why not?" I asked.

Cece cocked one hip and rolled her eyes. "I suppose it's because—"

"She thought what it would be like if someone wrote that kind of story about her," Tinkie said.

"But Cece was wise enough not to hide her past," I said.

"LeMont told me a little about Ellisea's family," Cece said. "I decided not to write it. It's not a story that helps anyone or illuminates anything. It would only bring heartache."

"So how can you afford a Jag?" I asked.

"I have a job offer from the *Times-Picayune*." Cece ran her hand over the car's fender. "It's about the largest newspaper in the South, and they want me to be society editor! Can you imagine? After all those years when no one would give me a job! Do you know how long I wanted to work at that paper and live in New Orleans? It's going to be a big pay raise, too."

"That's great, Cece." I forced a big smile. Damn! Cece wasn't afraid to grasp a fantasy and make it real.

"I've dreamed about this for half my life," Cece said. "I just never believed I'd have the chance."

"I don't like it one bit," Tinkie said. "What will we do without Cece?"

Now that was a good question. What would we do?

"Dahling, New Orleans isn't that far away." She lightly gripped my elbow. "Aren't you going to invite us in for a drink? I feel like celebrating."

"Absolutely," I said, leading the way to the front parlor, where I poured generous amounts of liquor into my mother's beautiful highball glasses. "Let me get some ice. Tinkie, why don't you show Cece the office?"

"I heard from Hamilton," Tinkie said.

That stopped me in my tracks. I turned back to face her. "What did he say?"

"You broke his heart, Sarah Booth."

I couldn't tell if she was teasing me or not. "Really, Tinkie, what did he say?"

"He said that if he ever doubted that a fantasy could be real, he'd think of you."

"Did you tell him about . . . Coleman?"

"Yes. I told him that Coleman had taken his wife to Arizona."

I waited, wondering what it was that I hoped to hear.

"He said he hoped Connie got well and that Coleman left her."

"Did you tell him it wouldn't matter to me?" I held her gaze. In the past couple of days, I'd given it a lot of thought. It was true that I'd made a decision when I left Hamilton at the airport and came home to Zinnia. It was just as true that Coleman had made his choice, too.

"I won't lie to him, Sarah Booth. Besides, he wouldn't believe me. You made a choice."

"So did Coleman. So did Hamilton when he didn't come after me. We've all made choices in our lives, but that doesn't mean we don't regret some of them."

Tinkie walked over to me, her five-inch heels tap-tapping on the hardwood floor. "I know that better than most," she said, taking my hand. "Hamilton is hurt now. Badly hurt. Give him time."

I wanted to tell her that I was hurt, too. But instead I gave her a quick hug and stepped through the door into the dining room. I picked up the ice bucket and went into the kitchen. I heard them both heading toward the new office. In a moment I heard Cece's squeal of approval.

I glanced out the kitchen window and saw Sweetie Pie and Chablis running through the pasture where Reveler grazed.

Sweetie was loping, but Chablis was giving it everything she had to keep up. They ran past the horse and into the small family cemetery where everyone I'd ever loved was buried.

Coleman and Hamilton were gone. My reality was the view from my kitchen window and the sounds of my friends in the office, probably talking about me.

"Time is the biggest illusion of all, Sarah Booth."

I saw Jitty's wavering reflection in the sheen of the refrigerator door and turned around to face her. "Time heals all wounds," I said, remembering Aunt LouLane's favorite, and most foolish, adage. "I wish that were true."

Jitty's laugh was soft and easy. "You suffer from the biggest delusion of all, Sarah Booth. You think things come to an end." She stepped closer to me. "There is no end. Not to what you feel for people, or what they feel for you. Have faith, Sarah Booth."

"Sarah Booth, are you going to talk to yourself or bring us some ice?" Tinkie called. I heard her footsteps fast approaching.

"Faith in what?" I asked Jitty, reaching out to hold her before she vanished. I grasped only air.

Her smile was enigmatic. "In your own ability to love," she said just before she disappeared.

"Who in the world are you talking to?" Tinkie said as she pushed through the swinging door. She glanced around the kitchen.

"Do you believe I'll ever find real love?" I asked Tinkie.

She didn't hesitate. She put her arm around me and gave a squeeze. "You already have, Sarah Booth. You have me. And all the rest of your friends."

About the Author

A native of Mississippi, CAROLYN HAINES lives in southern Alabama on a farm with her husband, horses, dogs, and cats. She has been honored with an Alabama State Council on the Arts literary fellowship for her writing, a family with enough idiosyncracies to give her material for the rest of her life, and a bevy of terrific friends. She is a former photojournalist.

M   Haines, Carolyn
HAI   Hallowed bones

DATE DUE

MAY 21 '04			
JUN 16 '04			
JUN 25 '04			
JUL 14 '04			
JUL 24 '04			
JUL 31 '04			
AUG 14 '04			
AUG 26 '04			
SEP 02 '04			
SEP 15 '04			
SEP 29 '04			